ALICE AND THE ASSASSIN

Center Point
Large Print

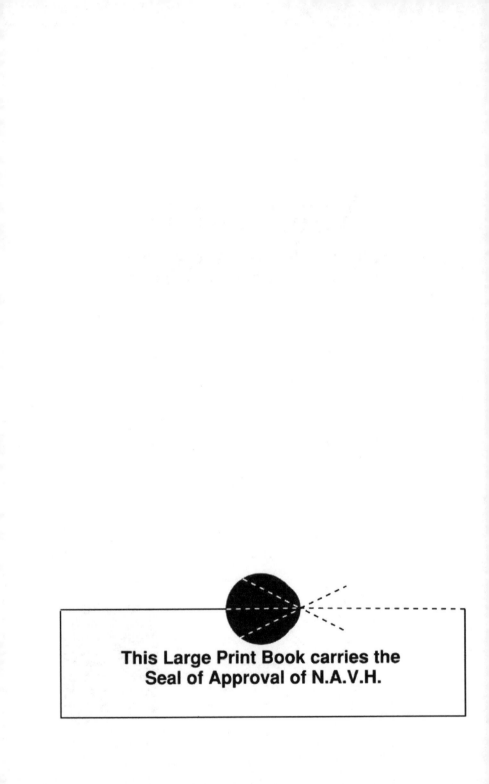

**This Large Print Book carries the
Seal of Approval of N.A.V.H.**

ALICE AND THE ASSASSIN

An Alice Roosevelt Mystery

R. J. Koreto

CENTER POINT LARGE PRINT
THORNDIKE, MAINE

This Center Point Large Print edition is published in the year 2017 by arrangement with Crooked Lane Books, an imprint of The Quick Brown Fox and Company, LLC.

The text of this Large Print edition is unabridged.
In other aspects, this book may vary
from the original edition.
Printed in the United States of America
on permanent paper.
Set in 16-point Times New Roman type.

ISBN: 978-1-68324-370-0

Library of Congress Cataloging-in-Publication Data

Names: Koreto, R. J.
Title: Alice and the assassin : an Alice Roosevelt mystery / R. J. Koreto.
Description: Center Point Large Print edition. | Thorndike, Maine : Center Point Large Print, 2017.
Identifiers: LCCN 2017004023 | ISBN 9781683243700 (hardcover : alk. paper)
Subjects: LCSH: Longworth, Alice Roosevelt, 1884-1980—Fiction. | McKinley, William, 1843–1901—Assassination—Fiction. | Large type books. | GSAFD: Mystery fiction.
Classification: LCC PS3611.O739 A78 2017 | DDC 813/.6—dc23
LC record available at https://lccn.loc.gov/2017004023

For my parents,
Paul and Vivienne Feldman Koreto,
and for my grandfather, Robert Feldman,
who told me about these times

ALICE AND THE ASSASSIN

I valued my independence from an early age and was always something of an individualist . . . Well, a show-off anyway.

—Alice Roosevelt

Chapter 1

Mariah always said that I'd do anything for a pretty face, and she might be right, but I guess I'm not that different from most other men. And I'd like to meet the one who could refuse Alice when she challenged you. In all fairness, though, it wasn't just because she was pretty—Alice may have had her mother's face and figure, but she was her father's daughter through and through. And in the end, I don't care what Mariah says—I don't have a single regret.

It all began that late afternoon downtown, in February 1902, in the New York headquarters of the US Secret Service. Alice had a deck of playing cards and a steely-eyed look that even her father, one of the bravest men I knew, had learned to fear.

"Mr. St. Clair, I haven't forgotten you said you could shoot a hole through all the aces in five seconds. Prove it."

"Right here?"

"Unless you're afraid."

I grinned. "I don't know what Mr. Harris would say."

"I don't know either. And I don't care." She marched to the end of the conference room and removed the four presidential portraits from the wall—Washington, Adams, Jefferson, and

Madison. It took her only a few moments to pull the aces out of the box and fasten them to the wall with straight pins.

"Just get back here behind me." I then took off my jacket and pulled out my Colt New Service revolver. "Here we go."

It's a powerful pistol, and I've hardly ever fired it indoors, so even I was startled by the noise in the room. Alice didn't look shaken at all, however, and ran to the end of the room. I hadn't lost my touch—I could see neat dead-center holes in each card.

"You really did it. Son of a *bitch*." She fetched a quarter out of her purse and flipped it to me. "You won the bet, but it was worth it to see shooting like that."

Naturally, Mr. Harris entered his room at that moment. He was agent in charge of the New York office and technically my supervisor. His eyes went to the holes in the wall, then Alice—who looked right back at him without flinching—and then me.

"What are you doing, Mr. St. Clair?" he said wearily. "This is a government building."

"Oh, nevermind. It'll be hidden by the portraits, and it's a double-thick wall there," Alice said, but Mr. Harris just sighed again. If it had been anyone else but me and Alice, Mr. Harris would've been surprised and angry, but he's learned to cut us some slack.

"What bothers you so much?" asked Alice. "That a young woman spent an afternoon in your office?

Or are you annoyed because of who my father is? Or that I have my bodyguard shoot holes in your walls?"

"All of the above, Miss Roosevelt. Anyway, you're only *here* because of who your father is. And don't the two of you need to be on your way?"

"Yes. As soon as Mr. St. Clair rolls me a cigarette."

It wasn't in the job description, so to speak, but there had been no time to ease into this assignment and make it formal. President McKinley was killed back in September, and Mr. Roosevelt found himself trying to manage Alice and the country at the same time. A few weeks of that, and it became clear it wasn't going to work. So he had called me into his office in early November and said, "St. Clair, I've got a new job for you. You're going to be Alice's minder. Can you do it?"

"Whatever you want, Mr. President," I'd responded.

He laughed and clapped me on the shoulder, like in the old days. "You used to call me 'Colonel.' And before that, 'Mr. Theodore.' "

Life changes, and you roll with it. I used to be Sergeant St. Clair of the First Volunteer Cavalry, the Rough Riders, and now I'm Special Agent St. Clair of the Secret Service. Babysitting Alice seemed like a cushy job, and I told the president it beat charging up San Juan Hill.

"You say that now. But I promise you, you'll wish you were back in Cuba before the year is out."

Now it was already into the new year, and I had come to realize that the president had a point, but again, I don't have any regrets.

"I'm not your maid, Miss Alice. This is the last time. Now pay attention while I show you, and next time you buy your own tobacco and roll your own damn cigarette."

"Watch your mouth," she said.

"That's funny coming from you, Princess."

"And don't call me 'Princess.'"

Mr. Harris just shook his head and left while I got out my tobacco and Alice followed along. Her long fingers were deft with the paper, and she waited with a raised eyebrow for me to strike a match on a boot nail and light her up.

"We ought to go now," I said. I reloaded my Colt and got my long Western riding coat out of the closet. It gets more than a few looks on the streets of Manhattan, but I'm used to it, and it's got plenty of pockets. Alice had this elegant fur coat with a hood, which suited her well, and we headed out. We made quite a couple—the cowboy and the president's daughter.

I had a nice little runabout parked around the corner, and Alice certainly enjoyed it. It belonged to the Roosevelt family, but I was the only one who drove it. Still, the thing about driving a car is that you can't easily get to your gun, and I didn't like the look of the downtown crowds, so I removed it from its holster and placed it on the seat between us.

"Don't touch it," I said.

"I wasn't going to."

"Yes, you were."

I had learned something the first time I had met her. I was sent to meet Mr. Wilkie, the Secret Service director, in the White House, and we met on the top floor. He was there, shaking his head and cleaning his glasses with his handkerchief. "Mr. St. Clair, welcome to Washington. Your charge is on the roof smoking a cigarette. The staircase is right behind me. Best of luck." He put his glasses back on, shook my hand, and left.

It had taken me about five minutes to pluck the badly rolled cigarette out of her mouth, flick it over the edge of the building, and then talk her down.

"Any chance we could come to some sort of a working relationship?" I had asked. She had looked me up and down.

"A small one," she had said. "If you can show me how to properly roll a cigarette. Cowboys know these things, I've heard."

"Maybe I can help—if you can learn when and where to smoke them," I had responded.

So things had rolled along like that for a while, and then one day in New York, some man who looked a little odd wanted—rather forcefully—to make Alice's acquaintance on Fifth Avenue, and it took me all of three seconds to tie him into a knot on the sidewalk while we waited for the police.

"That was very impressive, Mr. St. Clair," she had

said, and I don't think her eyes could've gotten any bigger. "I believe that was the most exciting thing I've ever seen." She looked at me differently from then on, and things went a little more smoothly after that. Not perfect, but better.

Anyway, that afternoon I pulled into traffic. It was one of those damp winter days, not too cold. Workingmen were heading home, and women were still making a few last purchases from peddlers before everyone packed up for the day.

"Can we stop at a little barbershop off of Houston?" she asked.

I ran my hand over my chin. "Is that a hint I need a shave?" I'm used to doing it myself.

"Don't be an idiot. He's my bookie."

"So that's why you had the office boy bring you back the *Racing Form* when he went out for lunch." Alice had enjoyed herself with a hot dog and a bottle of beer. "By the way, what was that potato thing you were eating?"

"A knish. I can't get enough of them, but just try to get them uptown."

I'll admit New York took a little getting used to, but you never run out of new things to eat here.

Alice directed me to a little side street and a barbershop that looked none too clean.

"Don't bother parking. I'll be right out," she said.

"I'm not supposed to leave you alone outside."

"Oh, for God's sake," she said, and we went inside together. Barbers were cutting and shaving

16

men, and they looked at Alice as she strode in past waiting patrons reading the latest issue of the *Police Gazette*. A quick-eyed man sat at a table in the back, briskly taking bets and money, and when it was Alice's turn, she looked as happy as a child with a kitten, practically jumping with excitement.

"A good week, miss," said the bookie, paying out. He looked up at me. "Hey, sport, you want to give the lady some room? You'll get your turn."

"Don't mind him," said Alice. "He's with me."

"Sorry, didn't realize. Mister—did you know how good your girl is at picking the ponies?"

Alice laughed and looked me up and down. "I'm not his girl. He's my bodyguard."

"What?" said the bookie, wondering if there was a joke he was missing. He clearly had no idea who his customer was.

"My bodyguard. You think I'm going to come into a dump like this alone?" She carefully counted her money and placed another bet with some of her winnings, and we got back into the car.

"He thought you were my 'young man,'" she said. "Dear God."

"The man must've been blind," I said, glancing at her. "It should've been obvious you're too young for me."

"What the hell is that supposed to mean?" she said.

I shrugged. "You're seventeen. I'm thirty."

"That's just thirteen years, not so much."

"Glad you think so."

"If you weren't driving, I'd hit you." And she waved her hand, a sign that this particular conversation was over and she was changing the subject. "So what was going on in the meeting this morning? You must've had every field agent in New York jammed into that conference room."

"There's a reason they call it the *Secret* Service."

"You work for my father. Of course you can tell me." It was halfway between a wheedle and an order. I might as well; she'd find out soon enough.

"The word came from Washington. It was officially determined that Leon Czolgosz acted alone in killing President McKinley—there were no additional conspirators and no further danger to the presidential family."

She gave me a cool look. "So that means I'm no longer stuck with you every minute?"

"Nope. You're still stuck with me. It just means I might let you get out a little more."

"Oh, you'll let me? How kind of you." She snuggled down into her furs and lost herself in thought. We continued farther uptown, and soon we were alongside Central Park, where I go when I want a little room. They even have sheep there, and every now and then I visit the shepherds and share a drink and a smoke, and we talk about livestock—there aren't many in New York who can do that.

"Additional conspirators," said Alice suddenly.

18

"What made them think Czolgosz had any associates?"

"Hmm? Oh, yeah, there was this one gal in particular, Emma Goldman. Apparently she had met Czolgosz some weeks before he shot McKinley. A bit of a rabble rouser with a history of violence. She supposedly helped the guy who tried to shoot What's-his-name, the steel magnate—"

"Henry Clay Frick. He's a bully and boor. If she tried to kill him, I'm predisposed to like her. So what did they do to her?"

I didn't know the details, just what had been mentioned in the meeting. "Let her go, I think, after holding her for a while. I guess she didn't really have anything to do with McKinley after all. So what's on for tonight?"

"Tonight? Aunt Anna has some people coming over. I have to be nice to them." Aunt Anna is President Roosevelt's older sister. She practically raised Alice after Alice's mother died in child-birth, and she is the only one who can control her. So, as Alice would say, I'm predisposed to like her, although I'm not sure it's a two-way street.

"The usual crowd—men looking for positions in Washington, women looking for dinner invitations to the White House, the old families, the newly rich, local politicians. I'll have to put on a smart dress and be polite and hope some of them are interesting." She didn't sound hopeful. "How about you?"

"I might scrounge a dinner from your cook, Dulcie; find a card game; maybe visit Mariah later, after she gets back from work."

Alice's eyes narrowed; she gave me that look whenever I mentioned Mariah. She hated few things more than being made a fool of, and she suspected I wasn't telling her the truth about Mariah.

"She's your sister, right?"

"Half sister, technically."

"So you have the same mother but different fathers?"

"Other way around. Same father but different mothers."

"Ha!" she said in triumph. "You said her last name was Flores. Why isn't she St. Clair if you have the same father?"

"Flores is her married name."

"You said she lived alone. You never mentioned a husband."

"She was married, but it didn't take. But she kept the name anyway."

"Does she look like you? I mean, can you tell that you're brother and sister?" She was trying to catch me out. Actually, we look nothing alike. I take after our father, but Mariah looks more like her mother. She's a good head shorter than I am, with black hair and a darker complexion, while I'm fair with blond hair.

"Not at all," I said cheerfully. And Alice lapsed into silence for another mile.

"I want to meet her," said Alice eventually.

"Mariah? Sure. One night when she's not working, I'll have her cook us dinner. She's a great cook."

"No, not her," she said, irritated. "I mean, I would like to meet her, but I was talking about Emma Goldman."

"Why?"

"I'm curious."

I laughed but realized I had walked into this. The worst thing you could do is excite Alice's curiosity. She got bored very easily, and giving her anything new, no matter how inappropriate, could be dangerous. "That's a hell of a reason, Princess. I happen to know she's in New York, but I don't know where."

"I bet Mr. Harris knows," she said.

"I bet he won't tell you," I responded. "And I have no reason to ask him."

"Very well. You won a quarter from me today. I want it back. I'll bet you I get Emma Goldman's address by the end of the evening."

I took Alice's gloved hand in mine. "Done." And with that, we pulled up to the Caledonia, where Alice's aunt, Anna Roosevelt Cowles, had taken an apartment while her husband, an admiral, was away at sea.

The Caledonia takes up a square block on the West Side and rents apartments to the best people who want more room and a better view than you get from the townhouses farther downtown. She

21

set up house there after Mr. Roosevelt became vice president and moved to Washington, and she helped out as his unofficial New York hostess. Washington may be the capital, but from what I could tell, lots of important things still happened only in New York.

With the assignment, I got a small room in the building's half basement. It's warm and has a window, so I'm fine with it. The building almost looks like a castle, with fancy stonework and statues of imaginary animals on the corners. Alice says they're called gargoyles, and one day I'm going to climb out a window to have a closer look.

I parked the car in the Caledonia garage and walked Alice through the front entrance, where the doorman greeted one of the building's most famous residents. I took off my Stetson and gave the doorman a salute. He nodded back. I think he feels a little sorry for me.

The elevator took us up to the apartment, where a maid, alerted by the doorman, was already opening the door for us.

"Miss Alice, your aunt was asking for you. Your dress is laid out."

"Very good," said Alice. She handed the maid her coat and gloves and turned back to me. "I'll see you later," she said, disappearing down the hall. I like the entranceway to the apartment. It's probably bigger than my room downstairs, with a chandelier like something out of a hotel. One of the pictures on the wall is of Mr. Roosevelt's ranch back in the

Dakotas, and I never tire of looking at it, the plains and the sky going on forever.

The maid seemed a little unclear about what I was to do next. They still haven't learned where I fit in socially.

"If it's all right with you, I'll just make myself at home in the kitchen," I said. And she watched me to make sure I went where I was supposed to go and not where the guests were gathering.

"You again," said Dulcie.

"Good to see you, too," I said. I hung up my coat, hat, and pistol in the service entrance hall and loosened my jacket. That was the worst part of the job. Mr. Harris says all agents have to wear a proper suit—something I didn't even own before I started—and Mr. Roosevelt kindly advanced me the money to buy one.

"Any chance for some food?" I asked, going for charm, but Dulcie wasn't having any of it. She turned. Her round face was red and sweaty, and there was a knife in her hand. I had no doubt she had the strength and will to gut me like a salmon.

"You know the rules. You leave your tobacco and your flask in your coat. No smoking or drinking. And I'll see what I can do."

"Even the president smokes and drinks," I said.

"He ain't president here. I'm president of this kitchen. You have a problem with that?"

"No, ma'am." I sat down at the kitchen table, and it didn't take long for her to drop a plate in front of me with some chicken, cabbage, and potatoes. Dulcie isn't as good a cook as Mariah, but I doubt the Roosevelts' guests would be interested in what Mariah cooks, so maybe I'm being unfair.

"Very good, ma'am. Much appreciated." She grunted and went back to her stove and cutting board. When I was done, I found yesterday's newspaper in the trash and figured that would keep me busy until the evening was over. I looked at the kitchen clock and wondered if Alice would be able to win back her quarter by getting Emma Goldman's address—and what I was going to do if Alice wanted to visit her.

I'd gotten comfortable and even managed to coax a slice of apple pie and a cup of very good coffee from Dulcie when Alice burst into the kitchen. She had cleaned up nicely for sure, looking a lot more like a young lady of fashion than the naughty schoolgirl who was reading a beer-stained *Racing Form* in the office earlier.

"Miss Alice, what are you doing here?" asked Dulcie. She glared at me as if this was somehow my fault. "This is my kitchen, not a reception area."

"I'm just fetching Mr. St. Clair, and then we'll both be out of your hair." She grabbed my hand and started dragging me out.

"Miss Alice, I can't go out there."

"Oh, don't be difficult. There are lots of people I want you to introduce you to and who will love to meet you. And I want you to see me win my quarter back. I'm sure we can find someone. And if you help me, I may call it even."

More than a few people looked up as Alice led me into what was called "the game room." It had a pool table, comfortable chairs, and a small bar. I had never been in it, but Alice had mentioned it as the place where the younger set gathered during parties. We found it well populated with men in evening suits and ladies in fine dresses, and everybody seemed in good spirits.

"Everyone! This is Mr. St. Clair, who's in charge of making sure nothing horrible happens to me." I was then introduced to the sons and daughters of the best families in New York. Everyone was nice enough, but for the most part, the names went in one ear and out the other.

I found myself standing with a young woman called Clemmie who had a pair of lovely china-blue eyes and a magnificent mane of chestnut hair. She gave me a knowing look.

"We haven't met before, Mr. St. Clair, but I've heard all about you. Alice talks about you all the time."

"Does she really?" I asked, amused to discover that while I'm sitting in some mansion's kitchen, Alice is in the ballroom talking about me.

"Oh, yes, she told us you were a deputy sheriff and a cowboy working for her father and then a hero on San Juan Hill with the Rough Riders." Then she looked a little sly. "She told us how handsome you were, but now I can see that for myself." I didn't know how to respond to that, but Clemmie kept rolling along, now glancing at my feet.

"Are those real cowboy boots? Where are your spurs?"

"They tear the carpet up something awful," I said, and that gave her a moment's pause before she laughed. Then she lowered her voice to a whisper.

"Did you fight Indians out West?" she asked. "But actually, Alice said your grandmother was a full-blooded Cheyenne." And there was quite a sparkle in those eyes.

Meanwhile, Alice was jumping from man to man like a bee among flowers in the field, talking and smiling, gently touching arms with her long, white fingers.

Clemmie now leaned over close to me. "Can I trust you with a secret, Mr. St. Clair?"

"Unless you're trying to kidnap Miss Alice, yes."

She giggled. "No. It's something else. I think you have a rival for Alice's affections."

"I don't have any rival regarding Miss Alice, unless he wants my job," I said, and I was serious, but Clemmie seemed to find that funny.

"Preston van Schuyler is coming. He practically lived at Sagamore Hill last summer." That was before my time, so this was news to me.

"So something like a romance?"

"Something like—on his side, anyway," said

Clemmie. "He's very charming and amusing, and the Van Schuylers have piles of money. She'll pretend it's nothing, but she can't help but be aware of his attentions." But then again, Alice expected everyone to pay attention to her, so that was nothing new.

"You're a pretty sharp young lady, Miss Clemmie," I said. "Would you like to join the Secret Service yourself?"

"Oh, Mr. St. Clair," she said and laughed loudly. She placed a glove-clad hand on my arm.

At that point, Alice's darting eyes landed on me and Clemmie. She frowned and made her way to us. "And what are the pair of you discussing?" she asked a little sharply.

"Oh, Alice, your Mr. St. Clair is just as you described him."

Alice just gave me a hard look. "Well, aren't you chatty this evening? We're supposed to be trying to find someone who can help us with some inquires. Clemmie—what does your father do again? Something in banking, isn't it?"

"He's a director of the Chase National Bank," said Clemmie, full of pride. "He's been to London and Geneva and lots of other places."

"I'm sure he's a marvelous banker, but we need someone in law. Is your father a lawyer? Does he know any lawyers?"

"Of course he knows lawyers. My cousin Norris is a lawyer, too."

"Where does he work?" asked Alice, seeing a promising lead.

"He's at one of the best law firms in New York."

"But does he know any criminals?" persisted Alice.

"He's not *that* kind of lawyer," she said, a little hurt. Alice just shook her head.

A young man stepped over and linked his arm into Clemmie's. "Come on, we need a fourth for bridge." He led her away, but not before I had a chance to wink at her and watch her blush. Alice saw the whole thing and gave me a dirty look.

"But nevermind. This is a waste of time. We need someone with a connection to Buffalo. That's where Czolgosz killed McKinley, so I'd imagine authorities in Buffalo are more likely to have a record of Emma Goldman than New York authorities, even if she does live here. Now who do I know who's familiar with Buffalo?" She looked around the room, frowning, but then her eyes landed on a slim young man talking with a group of other boys who had just entered. They were laughing about something. He stepped over to us.

"Alice! I'm so glad to see you." He greeted her warmly and gave her a kiss on her cheek. He was almost as tall as I was, but of a lighter build and closer to Alice's age than mine. He wore his suit like he was used to it.

"So glad you made it, Preston. It's been too long."

"And such a dull winter so far. But when the Roosevelts throw a party, I know a good time will be had by all."

"With everything, of course, I don't think we've seen each other since you came out to Sagamore Hill for the end-of-season house party and we went bathing in the ocean."

"I know. My father has kept me busy. We must do it again, unless . . . you'll be in Washington soon?" And he raised an eyebrow.

"Perhaps," she said, and then she suddenly seemed to remember I was there. "Preston, this is Mr. St. Clair of the Secret Service."

He looked me up and down. "Is that a uniform?" he asked.

"That would sort of defeat the purpose of being secret," I said. It got a smile out of Alice.

"Of course," said Preston, and he reached out his hand. I took it and squeezed it harder than necessary. "Preston van Schuyler. We're old friends of the Roosevelts."

"Do you also live in New York?" I asked. In that set, there were two kinds of people: those who lived in New York and the rest of the world.

"Yes, I do, not very far from here. I take it that you are not a native of the city?"

"Just beyond the river," I said.

"The Hudson?"

"The Mississippi."

"Ah. Well, we've been here for some generations.

29

Although we have properties in Buffalo as well, where we have extensive interests."

"Oh, yes, Buffalo. I forgot about Buffalo. And all the connections your family has. You know everyone," said Alice. "Mr. St. Clair and I are in the middle of an investigation, and no one seems to be able to help."

"An investigation?"

"Oh, absolutely. I've become very curious about some of the loose ends left after President McKinley's assassination and am trying to find certain people who can help us."

Preston looked back and forth between us and then settled on me. "Isn't this more in your line, Mr. St. Clair?"

"Miss Alice is taking her own path in this. I'm just along for the ride."

"Exactly," said Alice. "We're looking for a woman named Emma Goldman, and—"

Preston looked shocked. "Emma Goldman? Alice—she's an anarchist, a known troublemaker who narrowly escaped a murder conviction. You can't possibly want to see her."

"She won't be boring, I'm sure." Alice looked over her shoulder. A couple of the young men were shooting pool and doing a pretty bad job of it. The bridge game seemed lively. "So what do you expect me to do?" she continued. "Attend party after party like this? Where's your spirit of adventure? But what can I expect from a boy who graduated from

Yale?" Mr. Roosevelt had gone to Harvard, and apparently there's this big rivalry.

"What makes you think I can help?"

"The Van Schuylers have almost as many connections as the Roosevelts and are even better known in Buffalo. Can you call someone there? There must be an office of the attorney general in Buffalo, and they'd do a favor for the Van Schuylers."

"For God's sake, Alice, I can't just call up and ask something like that out of the blue."

"Oh, where's your sense of adventure? You were so much fun last summer."

He smiled and shook his head. "Alice, you don't know what you're asking. What are you going to do? You can't mean to visit her?"

"Why not? I'm curious. Everyone tells me that it was an anarchist who killed McKinley, and I had to be kept on a short leash while they made sure they weren't going to kill me, too, so of course I want to meet one."

Preston looked a little stupefied at that and then appealed to me again. The fun was over. "Mr. St. Clair, this is your doing. I've known Alice for years, and this is nothing a Roosevelt would do."

"Maybe you don't know her as well as you think," I said. Alice smiled slyly at that and gave me a sidelong glance.

"I've known her since she was six," he said. And I thought, *Maybe you never really listened to her.*

31

"If you two silly men would stop arguing, we have things to do. Preston, can you make a telephone call tonight? I'm sure they'll have records of her in Buffalo, since that's where McKinley was killed."

He sighed. "First thing in the morning."

"Surely you can do it tonight. I remember Father always said that there was a night clerk at major state offices in case of emergencies, and you can call tonight so I can take care of this tomorrow morning. Come—both of you. There's a telephone in Aunt Anna's parlor."

And without waiting to see if we were following, she took off. Preston and I both shrugged and headed after her. Aunt Anna's parlor was another room I had heard about but never seen. It was an odd little room, actually. The furniture was something you'd expect from any well-born lady's room, but the desk contained neatly stacked account books, a collection of pens, and the telephone. Mrs. Cowles worked here.

Van Schuyler looked at the telephone and seemed to be weighing something in his mind, but I couldn't figure out what. "It'll be a few moments, Alice. I have to call a friend of mine who will know the right supervisor for this case, and hopefully he has what you want and can put me in touch with the night clerk." And then, with little enthusiasm, he picked up the phone and started dialing.

We didn't want to breathe down his neck, so we stepped to the other side of the room by a small bookcase, and Alice pushed the volumes to one side to make a space.

"While we're waiting, you can roll me a cigarette," she said.

"I thought the agreement was you'd take care of your own smoking needs."

"Look at how I'm dressed. Do you think I carry around tobacco and rolling paper in an outfit like this?"

I fished out the tobacco and began rolling her one. We heard Preston murmuring into the phone.

"You don't like him, do you?" she said.

"What makes you say that?"

"That's a nasty trick, answering a question with a question. You're jealous, I think."

"Because he grew up in a fine house and went to Yale, and I left school when I was fourteen? He ain't the first rich person I met, Miss Alice."

"No, not that kind of jealous. I mean jealous because you think that I like him more than I like you."

"I get a nice salary for being with you. What Preston gets out of it is beyond me," I said.

Alice did not like that answer, and I got the icy glare for it. "Once again, I have a good mind to strike you," she said.

"Assault on a federal officer is a felony."

"Aren't you being amusing tonight?" she said and then thanked me for the cigarette and paused so I could light it for her.

33

She puffed away in contented silence for a few minutes, and I reviewed the novels on Mrs. Cowles's shelf until Preston hung up the phone. We watched him write something on a piece of notepaper and fold it in half before standing up and coming over to us. He wore a satisfied smile. He began to hand it to Alice but snatched it away. She pouted. "It isn't free," he said. "Cal Atherton did you a favor, and he wants it repaid. He'd like a job in Washington. Can you talk with your father?"

"I'll write him tomorrow," she said as she snatched the paper. Van Schuyler laughed. "Oh, good, right here in Manhattan. Easy for a visit. Meanwhile, what do you get out of this?" she said.

"Helping you," he said. Alice rolled her eyes.

"You flatter me, but it's because now he owes you a favor for giving him a chance to do me a favor, which means I have to get my father to introduce him to someone in Washington."

"You're your father's daughter," said Van Schuyler, laughing again. "But do be careful, Alice. Emma Goldman is known to be vicious. And she has vicious friends."

"Oh, don't worry. Mr. St. Clair will be protecting me. He carries a revolver, you know, and he's terribly good with it."

"Are you, indeed?" said Preston dryly. But he put on a brave face. He gave Alice a quick kiss on her cheek, nodded to me, and left. I reached for the same quarter she'd given me earlier and flipped it back to her.

"So you bartered for it. Nicely done," I said.

"You don't have to sound so sullen about it. Anyway, I'll buy you some more tobacco to make up for it. The thing is, I have the address, and that's what's important. You can take me there tomorrow."

"But I thought it was just to win the bet."

"Don't be silly. Of course we're going."

"I don't think so," I said. And for that, I once again got the steely-eyed look.

"What do you mean that you won't take me? You're my bodyguard, not my nanny."

"I can't guard you properly with those people in the neighborhoods they live in."

"How dare you tell me where I can and can't go!" She was gripping the back of the chair so tightly, I thought she'd break it.

"Listen, I'm just a workingman. I have to get up early tomorrow. I'm going back to my room downstairs before your aunt catches me and wonders what I'm up to. Good night, Princess," I said.

"I hate you calling me that. I *hate* it."

I saw myself out. Deciding it was too late to bother Mariah, especially as I had already eaten, I just went back to my room. I gave myself a final cigarette and shot of bourbon and went to sleep. Alice and I both knew it wasn't over and that she'd eventually get her way.

But it would do her good to make her work for it.

Chapter 2

I got up the next morning and decided not to press my luck and cadge a free breakfast from Dulcie. I was in no rush for another encounter with Alice anyway. I ordered bacon and eggs at a little place under the el before heading back to the Caledonia to see what the program was for the day.

A maid let me in. "Miss Alice isn't ready yet, but Mrs. Cowles would like to see you," she said, and that was a jolt. She's not someone you want to cross, and this was the first time we'd be having a conversation. Of course, we knew each other and had exchanged polite greetings. I never failed to take my Stetson off indoors and say, "Yes, ma'am," but I always felt I was a bit of an intruder.

I was led into the same parlor as last night. Mrs. Cowles was sitting at the desk. She smiled.

"Thank you, Mr. St. Clair, for joining me this morning. Please take a seat." I focused my attention on her. She was not beautiful and probably never had been, but you could see real intelligence and strength in that face. It wasn't obvious that she was Alice's aunt, but I sure could tell she was Mr. Roosevelt's sister.

"You have a rather interesting job, guarding my niece," she started. "I'd be curious to know what kind of background you have that prepared you for it."

"When I was fifteen, I began working on various ranches, including Mr. Roosevelt's. I wore a badge in Laramie for a while, which is a tough town, until Mr. Roosevelt sent for me to join him in the Rough Riders. Then he was kind enough to get me a place in the Secret Service, and as you know, Mrs. Cowles, I became Miss Alice's bodyguard after he moved into the White House."

She nodded. "It seems you have a history of getting into danger. Not of protecting people from it."

I grinned. "That may be, ma'am, but I'm still here. I must be doing something right."

She just stared at me for a few moments, then matched me with a grin of her own. "You're good for Alice in one respect. You can think on your feet. My brother may have chosen well. But I will remind you you're no longer taking chances with your own safety but with the safety of my niece. And don't be fooled—she really is quite young."

"I'll keep that in mind, ma'am, I promise. No man is dearer to me than Mr. Roosevelt, and his daughter's welfare is of the greatest importance to me."

I thought that would settle it, but I saw a shadow pass over her face. "My brother and I may differ on what is appropriate in raising a child—but nevermind. You seem to take your job seriously.

I'm glad we had a chance to talk." She looked me straight in the eye. "And I'm sure we will talk further."

And I knew she was serious about that. Theodore Roosevelt may have hired me, but Anna Roosevelt Cowles was my new boss.

I didn't get a chance to say any more because Alice stormed into the room. "Mr. St. Clair, they said you were here. I'm almost ready to go. Aunt Anna—I thought we'd see a museum or two and maybe get some shopping done."

"Very good. I have some meetings myself. Don't be late tonight."

"Why?" asked Alice.

"Because I said so," said Mrs. Cowles, and with that, she swept out of the room.

"First I have you telling me what I can't do and now my aunt telling me what I must do. This will have to change," said Alice. "Oh, very well, let's go." I knew we'd come back to the Emma Goldman visit. It was just a matter of when and how. It turned out to be pretty quickly.

"I don't see why visiting one single woman is such a problem," she said as we walked along Central Park West, next to the park.

"Neither do I. And that's why we're not going. Now, where are we headed today?"

"You heard me tell my aunt we were going to the museum."

"Miss Alice, by now I know there's a big difference

between what you tell your aunt and what we're going to do."

She gave me her sly smile. "Very good, Mr. St. Clair. We're going to the Central Park Zoo."

"I don't see what's wrong with that."

"It's what we're going to do there. Professor Aspinall is a director at the zoo, and he has a collection of snakes. He's an old friend of Father's. And he once told me to come by anytime and he'd show them to me and advise me on what kind to get as a pet. He might even have one he could give me."

"A pet? You want a pet snake?"

"I love snakes," she said. "Don't you?"

"We had rattlers in Wyoming," I said. "Once or twice, I shot and ate them."

"You ate snakes?" she said with that look she had when she suspected I was lying but wasn't sure.

"You have to cook them a long time," I said.

"Well, I haven't had that pleasure. Anyway, Dr. Aspinall says there are some pythons that make good pets."

It wasn't too crowded in the park that day: some young men having a good time and passing around a bottle, a few workingmen using the park to travel between the East Side and West Side, and a handful of couples enjoying the relative privacy of the park in winter. But by then, I knew someone was following us and had been almost since we left the Caledonia.

We passed under one of the bridges, and as we

emerged, I leaned down to Alice. "Just keep going," I said. She can be stubborn, but she keeps a cool head, and she did as I asked. I stepped to one side, out of sight, and Alice kept walking. A moment later, the man who was following us emerged from the dim light of the tunnel. He saw Alice alone, frowned, and turned, but he was too late. I grabbed his jacket lapels, slammed him against the bridge wall, and then searched him, turning up nothing more dangerous than a little pen knife.

"Agent St. Clair, US Secret Service. Why are you following us?"

"I can walk where I want to," he protested. "That's not a crime."

Alice quickly came back and looked at the man with great curiosity. He was dressed in shabby clothes, not like a laborer, but in something a sales clerk in a low-end store might wear.

"You've been following us ever since we left the Caledonia. I was onto you after the first block. Now, why were you following us?" Sure, we were used to a certain amount of attention. Alice was already becoming famous. But young men of fashion or ladies hoping to scrape an acquaintanceship were one thing; there was no reason for a man like this to follow us.

"I don't know what you're talking about," he whined. "Now let go of me."

"I have an idea," said Alice. "Let's take him to the Tombs. I haven't been since I was a little girl." The

Tombs was the nickname for police headquarters, and it contained probably the worst prison this side of the Mississippi. Alice had no doubt seen some of it, anyway, when Mr. Roosevelt was a city police commissioner.

"Oh, God, no," he said, terror crossing his face.

"Do you know who I am?" asked Alice. "I'm Alice Roosevelt, daughter of the president. My father still has friends downtown, and they will be very displeased to find out that you were threatening me."

That was entirely unnecessary, of course. I was sure he knew who he was following.

"Now be fair, miss. I didn't threaten anyone here. I don't even have a weapon. I was just reporting, like I was told to do."

"Reporting? You mean you're a journalist? For a newspaper? I've met a lot of them, but none who looks like you."

"Not exactly, miss. You see, I work for a private investigator."

"Ooh? Really?" That seemed to excite her, and I watched her eyes shine. This was proving to be even more fun than the possibility of getting a pet snake. "You mean like the Pinkertons?"

"Well, sort of. We're a smaller outfit. It's called Barnaby & Associates. Midtown." He produced a business card from his jacket. "That's me, Jonas Griffith."

"Most interesting," said Alice, and she pocketed

the card. "Now, who's paying you to follow me?"

Griffith seemed a little more relaxed, as we seemed to accept his story and the prospect of a stretch in the Tombs was receding. "I would tell you if I knew. Mr. Barnaby just gives us our jobs, and that's it."

"And when did he give you this one?" asked Alice.

"Early this morning," said Griffith. "Listen, that's all I know. Can I go now? I didn't really do anything." He looked back and forth between us.

I looked at Alice, and she just shrugged. "You're the lawman here, Mr. St. Clair."

"I'll tell you what. I'm going to let you go. But I don't want to see you again, is that clear?"

Griffith smiled in an attempt at comradeship, one professional to another. "I know, or it's the Tombs."

"No, it's New York Hospital," I said. He paled at that. I let Griffith go and watched him walk quickly back to Central Park West.

"See? The day is turning out to be fun after all," I said. "I let you question a suspect, and we still have time to get you a snake."

"That was rather entertaining," she said. "What happens next? Do we go visit Mr. Barnaby?"

"We? We don't do anything. I'll leave a message later with Mr. Harris. I doubt if it's anything serious. Maybe a newspaper has taken to hiring private investigators to help them track down stories. And while we're on the subject, can we work on a lower profile? There's no need for loudly voiced public announcements that you're the president's daughter."

"Oh, very well," she said. "But don't change the subject. Why can't we go now? You can't say it's dangerous. It's a private agency with midtown offices. After all, it was me he was tailing. I think I have a right to know why."

She looked determined, and she did have a point. It might even distract her from asking me again to take her to see Emma Goldman—or having to explain to Mrs. Cowles why we were returning to the Caledonia with a python.

And I was a little curious myself.

"Oh, all right," I said. She clapped her hands. We walked out of the park and caught one of those new electric cabs downtown. They give a smooth and quiet ride, and it didn't take long to get there. Alice looked very pleased with herself.

Barnaby & Associates had offices in a small building on a narrow but busy street. The sidewalk was full of office boys, secretaries, and men of business who gave us a few glances but were generally in a rush to get somewhere else. The place card downstairs listed a few businesses—a coffee and tea importer, a dealer in commercial stationery, a firm of surveyors, and on the third floor, Barnaby & Associates, Private Investigators.

Nothing seemed dangerous, so we walked up to the third floor and entered through a wooden door with the firm's name written in gold letters on frosted glass. A young woman sat at a desk pecking away at a typewriter, and there was a private office just beyond. The place was neat but not fancy, not like some of the places I had taken Alice to. Some battered cabinets and shelves but no pictures on the walls, which weren't cracked but could've used a painting.

I thought of flashing my Secret Service badge and just walking in, but Alice looked like she wanted to take it in hand herself. Her talk with Griffith had seemed to make her happy, so I thought I'd let her have her way.

"We'd like to see Mr. Barnaby as soon as possible."

"I'll see if he's available," she said, looking curiously at both us. "May I have your name?"

"Alice—" She gave me a sidelong glance. "Just tell him Miss Alice," she said.

"Very well," she said, and she got up and went into the private office, closing the door behind her. I hid my grin behind my Stetson, and Alice looked immensely proud of herself.

The door opened a moment later, and we were ushered in to see Mr. Barnaby. He was a prosperous-looking man in his midfifties, wearing a good suit and a gold watch chain across his waist. He stood, greeted both of us, and invited us to take seats.

"Miss Alice? Say, wait a minute . . . you're Alice Roosevelt, aren't you?"

"Yes, but we're trying to keep a low profile, as

they say, so please be discreet about our visit. And this is my assistant, Mr. St. Clair."

I gave a quick salute.

"I'll get right to the point," said Alice. "We intercepted one of your operatives this morning—a Mr. Griffith. We were very displeased at being followed like that and would like to know who commissioned you and why."

He seemed a little stunned, and I didn't blame him. Alice had put him in a tight place.

Mr. Barnaby started by smiling. "I understand your predicament. However, the actions of my firm are legal, and I'm afraid our client list is confidential."

"Is it really?" she asked. "Honest citizens are subject to—?" Her eyes darted around and landed on a file cabinet against the wall. She pushed her chair back, got up, and opened the first drawer.

"See here! You can't do that!" Mr. Barnaby stood up and began moving around his desk.

"I wouldn't do that. I'm not just Miss Roosevelt's assistant; I'm also Secret Service." I showed him my badge. "I'm afraid I can't let you lay a hand on her."

"Those are my files. I can't just let her go through them. You're a lawman. Stop her." He looked desperately at Alice, who was frowning as she attempted to make sense of his files.

"I wish I could. You know, her father is one of the smartest and bravest men I ever met, and even he

45

can't manage her. What chance do you or I have? Better just let her have her way."

Barnaby looked for something to say, but meanwhile, Alice wasn't making much progress. "Mr. Barnaby, I can't make heads or tails out of this. Now, I can spread this out and spend an hour or so looking for what I want. Or you can tell me, and we'll be done soon. If it helps, I promise not to let anyone know where the information came from."

Barnaby sighed and gently closed the file drawer.

"Very well. Stay away from my files, and I'll tell you."

Alice and Barnaby sat back down. "I was hired by the Great Erie & Albany Boat Company," he said.

"That's a company. Do you have a person's name?"

"No. I just got a request from the corporate secretary."

"And his name?"

She folded her arms across her chest, and I saw her foot tapping. She was getting annoyed.

"The secretary is just some expensive lawyer in a fine office downtown, a name not in these files, and even if I gave it to you, it wouldn't do you any good. He'd tell you nothing and wouldn't even admit to knowing about the Great Erie. But I feel bad for upsetting you, and I will be honest, because I don't want any trouble with the Roosevelt family or"— he spared a glance for me—"the Secret Service.

So I'll be as open as I can. The Great Erie doesn't really exist. It's a financial fiction—just a name on some documents in a bank vault somewhere, a list of directors and shareholders that own other companies. That's all. And the secretary, this lawyer, sent me a private messenger requesting I have an operative follow you, and if you attempted to visit a Miss Emma Goldman, we were to report back—how long you were there, even if we could figure out what you were talking about."

"Why did they want you to do that?"

Barnaby shrugged. "I don't ask why. It doesn't matter. We just do what we're paid for."

Alice leaned back and frowned. The only sound was the clock ticking on the wall, and I let my eyes flash back and forth between the two of them. I didn't think Barnaby had any more to say, and apparently neither did Alice, because she got up so quickly she startled both of us.

"Thank you, Mr. Barnaby. We'll be going now." And she headed out without even checking if I was following.

Barnaby rose. "Mr. St. Clair, may I ask what happened to the man I sent to follow you?"

"I made him in one block. He's probably in some bar drinking and hoping you won't fire him."

Barnaby smiled at that. "If you ever get tired of your job, I could use someone like you," he said.

"Thanks, but I don't really blend in, and I'd hate to give up my riding coat, boots, and Stetson." I gave him a quick salute and followed Alice downstairs to the entranceway. She was waiting for me with an impatient look on her face.

"First of all, you don't leave a room without me like that. That's the way we do it." She sighed and rolled her eyes. "Second, what the hell was that bit about me being your assistant?"

"I'm questioning. You're assisting. I didn't realize you were such a stickler for formality, Special Agent St. Clair of the US Secret Service. Anyway, we don't have time to discuss this. Now we really do have to visit Emma Goldman. She's only just downtown off Bowery."

"What do you mean by 'have to'?"

She seemed genuinely confused at my question. "Someone cares very much about my visiting Emma Goldman. Why? How can you not want to know why?"

"Miss Alice, like I said, this is something we need to pass on to Mr. Harris back at the office—"

"And he'll ignore you because they already closed the case. You told me that yesterday. This is important—someone is interested because we're still looking into a close connection to the McKinley assassination. You're Secret Service. You can't ignore this."

I sighed. "I'm not saying yes. But let's stop and think. Are you sure you've never heard of that company, the Great Erie? All kinds of business-people are in and out of your house."

"No, it was completely new. And you heard what he said—it's not even a real company. But think on this, Mr. St. Clair—I didn't even know who Miss Goldman was until last night. So someone discovered my interest in her very quickly."

"Perhaps the same man who was able to do you a favor precisely because he has a Buffalo and Great Lakes connection—Preston van Schuyler?" I said.

Alice made a face. "You really don't like him, do you? Why not? Are you still being jealous?"

I shrugged. It was hard to put into words. "Nah. He just seems a little too cocksure."

"That's very funny coming from you, Cowboy. But it could've been anyone. There were lots of people around when I was asking Preston about Miss Goldman—and I mentioned her name to lots of other people that evening, even before I dragged you along. Most of Aunt Anna's friends were appalled I even knew who she was. Also, Preston's friend could've gossiped about it. If Preston really wanted to keep me away from Emma Goldman, he wouldn't have helped me find her. It's ridiculous. But we're wasting time. We have to see what Miss Goldman has to say."

I paused. I could say no. I could insist we go back to the zoo and pick up her damn snake. About half of me just wanted to indulge Alice, and half of me actually wanted to know the answers to Alice's questions. And what could one lady do to us, after all?

"All right, here's the deal. We go downtown and check it out. If I think everything looks all right, we'll visit. Fair enough?" And it was a pleasure to see her face light up.

"You're a good man, Mr. St. Clair." She linked her arm into mine and dragged me outside onto the sidewalk.

I hailed a cab. The driver looked a little skeptical but seemed to think we were all right and agreed to take us. I had him let us off a block away from Emma Goldman's address, just off the Bowery, so I could look around. A few bums were passed out in doorways, and I saw a couple of petty criminals who might pick a pocket or grab a bag, but no one appeared outwardly violent.

We found the house easily enough. I'd like to say it had seen better days, but it had probably always looked as bad as it did now. The information we had said she was on the top floor, and as we walked up, I kept a close eye on the other doors. There were cooking smells, and I heard a baby crying, but I couldn't see much because the walls were dark and there was little light.

We finally reached Miss Goldman's apartment, and Alice knocked. We didn't hear anyone say anything, but a few moments later, the door was opened by a scary-looking woman. She looked to be in her thirties but had one of the hardest faces I had seen on a female, and I'm guessing a frown was her normal expression. She might not have been bad-looking if she had cared, which she obviously didn't.

"Well?" She looked Alice up and down and didn't seem to like what she saw. "Who are you, and what do you want?" Her English had a Russian-sounding accent but was clear.

"My name is Alice Roosevelt. And I want to discuss items of mutual interest."

"Alice Roosevelt?"

"Yes. And keep your voice down. We don't need the whole building knowing our business. And this is my Secret Service bodyguard, Mr. St. Clair."

"A pleasure, ma'am," I said. But it obviously wasn't a pleasure on her side. She just kept looking back and forth between us.

"I want to talk about Leon Czolgosz. Do you think we could come in? It's most awkward talking in the hallway like this."

She didn't say anything but opened the door wider, and we walked in. It wasn't much of a place, but I'm guessing there's not a lot of money in being an anarchist. There were a few mismatched chairs around a painted wooden table piled with books and papers. We took seats without being invited, and by then, Miss Goldman seemed to have found herself.

"I'm honored that the government sees fit to send the president's daughter to threaten me," she said, giving me a look. "Accompanied by a hired thug."

51

Alice laughed. "A thug? Mr. St. Clair is an honest workingman and a war hero."

"The Spanish-American War? So you helped build an American empire over the slaughter of innocents?"

"Oh, don't be silly, Miss Goldman," Alice said with a wave of her hand. "Mr. St. Clair was a sergeant. But nevermind. Neither of us is here to threaten you. We have some questions about Leon Czolgosz's role in President McKinley's assassination."

Miss Goldman just stared at Alice stupidly for a few moments. "Why are you here, Miss Roosevelt? Your colleagues in the police were persuasive enough during my stay with them. You think you'll get more out of me?"

Alice sighed. "For God's sake, I'm not here to interrogate you. I will be honest with you. I will tell you I was going to come out of—"

"The idle rich and their idle curiosity," said Miss Goldman, and her mouth twisted into a bitter smile.

"I'm not idle. We are rich, but Roosevelts are never idle. My father wouldn't hear of it. Now, I'm talking, so please don't interrupt until I'm done. I was going to say, 'Out of concern for my family.' And on my way here, Mr. St. Clair and I were accosted by a private investigator hired by an unknown person who was concerned about my visiting you. I now wonder if you and I have a common enemy. Why is someone concerned about our meeting? I would like to know what you know about Leon Czolgosz. Whatever you told the police."

"This is true?" asked Miss Goldman, seeming a little uncertain now.

"Why would I lie about it? I am here about my family."

Miss Goldman considered her for a moment. "I will tell you, then. He visited me twice briefly. I recommended some books and we spoke for a few minutes." She paused. "You will probably hear, if you haven't already, that I have written articles defending him." She gave Alice a challenging look, daring her to disagree. But Alice didn't explode; she just looked at Miss Goldman curiously, as if she were some rare bird in a zoo.

"Really? How perfectly horrible of you. But you didn't assist him?"

"As I told the police, no, I didn't. I had no knowledge of his intentions beforehand. But I applauded his actions. Is that horrible enough for you, Miss Roosevelt?"

Alice nodded absently. "If I accept that Mr. Czolgosz didn't have your help, will you tell me whether you know if he had anyone else's?"

Miss Goldman pursed her lips. "Do you know what I like about you, Miss Roosevelt?"

Alice laughed fully and openly, like a child. "I didn't think there was anything you liked about me," she replied. And at that, even Miss Goldman relaxed her face enough to smile.

"You pronounced his name correctly, Leon Czolgosz. It's more than the police did. That showed a certain care. It made me curious. And that's the reason I let you in."

"I move in political circles. One has to pronounce everyone's names correctly. And I see that you possess curiosity. That means there's something I like about you too, Miss Goldman."

"I'm glad to hear it. But you asked whether Leon Czolgosz had any help. That's the first time anyone has asked me that question. The men who detained me only asked if *I* had helped. They didn't ask if others did. So I will give you my opinion as a reward for your open-mindedness. In our brief meetings, it was clear to me that however strong his heart, he lacked the intelligence and sense of purpose to do something like that of his own volition."

"So he was being used by someone else?"

"Very good, Miss Roosevelt."

"One of your anarchist friends?" Alice raised an eyebrow. "Or am I pushing you too far?"

"Not an anarchist. Indeed, you will find I am alone among my colleagues in supporting him. Someone from your circle, Miss Roosevelt. Someone who used Czolgosz to kill the president for his own ends. Look to your own. Among your own class, you'll find the common enemy to both of us."

She had a point there. We had learned there were

divisions among the anarchists, and even though all of them wanted to see the government go, most of them stopped short of political murder. In the wake of the killing, some of them condemned Czolgosz as bringing down the government's wrath on the movement.

In fact, Czolgosz wasn't even part of any of the anarchist groups being tracked, and before he killed McKinley, some anarchists thought he was a government spy. Goldman, who was on the edge even by anarchist standards, seemed to be hanging on to that fact. Alice wasn't having it, though. She just glared. "You're stupid and ignorant if you think that's the way men in power get things done."

"And you're stupid and naïve if you think they don't." She stood. "This has been interesting, but I think we're done here, Miss Roosevelt. Still, if you think anarchists are behind this, take yourself to the Freethinker Club, just a few blocks down on the Bowery. Ask about Czolgosz, and you'll see how wrong you are. It's time for you to leave. Believe yourself fortunate I spoke with you at all, considering who your father is."

That was the wrong thing to say, I could've told Miss Goldman. I sat up straight and prepared to prevent a fistfight between a pair of women, which is a much harder task than it sounds.

Alice stood as well. "My father has devoted his life to building this country. All I can see is you and your kind working to destroy it. But you've been helpful, and for that, I thank you." Alice then leaned over the table. "However, I will leave you with some advice. Don't ever criticize my father to my face again. Ever." Then and there, it was easy to forget she was only seventeen.

I tipped my hat to Miss Goldman. "Ma'am," I said, and I felt her hate-filled eyes on our backs as we left the apartment.

Outside, it took Alice a few moments in silence to gather herself.

"What a ghastly person," she finally said. "How could she think that of my father? She was just so . . . twisted. But for all that, she seemed truthful. I'm not saying she was right, but I think she was telling us the truth as she saw it."

"I agree. And I have to say, I know I wasn't keen on bringing you here and didn't think there was much point. But I'm not too proud to admit I was wrong. You pulled off a neat trick. The questions you asked and the way you asked them—you got something out of her. Nicely done."

She looked at me sharply, as if she thought I was making fun of her or patronizing her. And when she realized I wasn't, she looked suddenly shy.

"Thank you, Mr. St. Clair. You know, it's not all that different from talking to people at some political soiree. People ask each other things and lie when you talk to them, all the while wanting something from you, so you lie right back."

I laughed. "If your father could hear you."

"Nevermind Father. If my Aunt Anna heard me." She giggled and grabbed my hand. "Come. Let's go see that Freethinker Club."

"Miss Alice, be reasonable. It's one thing to pay a visit to Miss Goldman, but we can't very well go into a room full of anarchists. You'd have better luck jumping into a lion's den. At least with lions, it wouldn't be personal."

"But we have to go. You heard what she said. Czolgosz may have had someone pulling his strings. And it sounds like he was not truly supported by the anarchists. We have to talk to more of them. It can't hurt to have a look. And I bet they're mostly just big talk. Anyway, it's your duty to make sure there are no more anarchists plotting against us."

She half dragged me along the street to a tavern about as broken-looking as I've ever seen. It was several steps down under another tenement, and it was easy to miss because the wooden sign with the name was cracked and weathered. I could hardly see through the window.

I looked up and down the street. No one was around. I figured I could leave her alone for half a minute.

"Wait here. I'm going to have a quick look. Don't move, and don't follow me until I call for you."

I pushed through the door. It was dark and smoky inside, and the place looked as if it had been furnished by the same firm that fixed up

57

Miss Goldman's apartment. It was crowded, and I saw equal numbers of men and women, which was odd for a bar. They were plainly dressed, but not in rags. Everyone here worked. The city clothes were the only thing that separated this tavern from some bars I knew back home. I had handled things there, and I could handle them here.

I got some looks, but I was used to that. Still, there was no open hostility. You can usually tell when someone is carrying a pistol, and it didn't seem anyone was.

I stuck my head out and watched Alice grin as I waved her in.

Chapter 3

I took her by the hand and led her to an empty table close to the door, seating both of us with our backs against the wall, and made sure my Colt was in easy reach.

A waitress came over, not looking too well trained for her job. She looked us up and down.

"Can I get you folks some lunch? We've got a chicken stew."

"Yes, please. And a couple of beers," said Alice. The waitress stepped away, and Alice's eyes darted around. "So how do we meet these people?"

"I have a feeling they'll want to meet us." Me in my riding coat and Alice in her furs—we were probably the most unusual thing that had happened to that place in a while. We saw the waitress speak to a few other people, and then she came back with our food and drinks. I've had worse beer, although I can't remember when, and the chicken in that stew must've died of old age.

But we didn't have too long to contemplate our disappointment alone. A man in his thirties, also holding a beer, pulled up a chair and sat down without being invited. His suit was no better than mine and a little older.

"There's a meeting here at four o'clock. Are you

here for that?" he asked. His smile indicated he knew the answer already.

"We're not here for the food," I said, and he laughed.

"I don't know about you," and then he pointed a thumb at Alice, "but she's certainly used to better. Anyway, they call me Nicky."

"I'm Alice. And this is St. Clair," said Alice.

"Alice, we are honored," and he gave her a mocking bow. She had become famous, indeed, in recent months. "So I take it you're slumming, Miss Roo—"

"Alice. Call me Alice. If you won't share your surname, why should I share mine? And no, I'm not slumming. I want some information. Now, are you the man in charge of this place?"

He laughed again, and there was definite good humor there, not the bitterness we had heard from Miss Goldman. This Nicky had a friendly, open face—but his eyes were sharp. "In charge? Of this crew? You have a pretty high opinion of me if you think I could be 'in charge' here. Let's say I have a certain organizing role. Like this afternoon's meeting. So what are you here for? To warn me off violence? But you, St. Clair, you're the one who came in here armed."

"Just for self-protection," I said.

"If you had any sense of self-protection, you might've avoided this place altogether."

"That sounds a lot like a threat," said Alice. "We're

60

here for a talk, and I hardly think our behavior merits a threat."

"Your behavior, Alice? How about the behavior of you and your class over the last one hundred years—"

"Oh, for God's sake, Nicky, spare me a speech. I've been lectured enough for one day. I'm stuck with this damn slop and watered-down beer, and the chair is sticky. You and I have reasons to share information. I'll even go first to show my good faith. What do you say?"

Nicky looked like he had been slapped. He shook his head and drained his glass.

"If you want me to talk, I'll need more beer. On your tab." He waved to the waitress, and she came back with another glass. He took a deep drink. "Now, what have you to say?"

"We have reasons to look into the behavior of Leon Czolgosz. It was our understanding he had been affiliated with the anarchist movement—"

"A damned lie!" shouted Nicky. He stood up so fast, he spilled some of his beer.

"Sit down," said Alice coldly. Under the table, I put my hand on my gun. "And be quiet until I'm done speaking. I'm not buying you another drink." People were looking at us, and I started to hope Alice would finish this up quickly.

Reluctantly, Nicky sat down.

"As I was saying, we were beginning to realize that Czolgosz was not acting with your movement but perhaps was the tool of other people. We spoke with Emma Goldman, and she seemed to think Czolgosz didn't have the personality or passion to assassinate a man. And St. Clair and I were accosted by a private investigator with an unknown client who was concerned about our questions. There. I've been open and honest with you. Now tell me—can you confirm Czolgosz was not acting with your association? Give me a reason to think he wasn't, and we'll leave you in peace. Better yet, tell me someone else was controlling him."

Nicky leaned back and pondered that. "Czolgosz is dead and buried. Why do you care?"

"If someone was using him, he may use someone else to commit more political killings. The fact that a private investigator expressed interest in my visiting Emma Goldman's house shows that there are people out there who care what I learn. Czolgosz isn't as dead and buried as we'd all like to think." She crossed her arms across her chest and looked angry but also a little proud of herself.

"There's something in that. But as the saying goes, 'If you dine with the devil, you'd better have a long spoon.' I'm not sure I can trust you, Alice. Thanks for the beer. Enjoy the rest of your lunch." He stood again, and I glanced sideways at Alice. Nicky was a damned fool if he thought that was the end of the conversation.

"Don't you walk away from me," she said, rising

up. "I was open and honest with you, and I expect you to be the same with me."

"Complaints about fairness coming from the ruling class? That's a funny one." He grinned and turned to go.

"I'll be back," said Alice, and her voice rose. "This is the best chicken stew I've ever had. The best beer I've ever drunk. I'll be back tomorrow and the next day. With more bodyguards. And police officers outside. Day after day. This establishment will be very popular."

That certainly got Nicky's attention. It also got everyone else's attention, and curious glances became outright stares. A little crowd began to gather. Alice either didn't notice or didn't care, but I did.

Nicky reluctantly sat back down. "You won," he said with bad grace. "Let's make this quick. I don't hold with Emma Goldman. I don't hold with Leon Czolgosz. He wasn't one of us. Have you heard the phrase 'propaganda of the deed'?" It was new to both of us.

"It refers to an action, an important action, that not only accomplishes something itself but serves as a statement and beacon to others. A political assassination is an example. But not all of us believe in this method. Emma Goldman often does, but she does not speak for all of us. Or even most of us."

Alice quietly absorbed his explanation. "Do you think Czolgosz worked alone? Or did he have help? Miss Goldman said someone was pulling his strings."

"Perhaps," said Nicky cautiously. "But no one here. To show my good faith in return, I will tell you one more thing. And then you will leave. Czolgosz was from an immigrant family, and you may not see it from where you live, but this city is more and more a city of immigrants. If you are interested in what has happened, I would think about that. I would talk to some immigrants."

The conversation was over, but we were now surrounded. Alice and I stood. A woman in the crowd fixed a look on me.

"You. You work for a living. You should be joining us."

"I'm not an educated man. I had to look up 'anarchy' in the dictionary right after President McKinley was shot. It sounded a lot like Laramie on a Saturday night, so I think I'll give it a miss. Now, can you all please move and let us out?"

"And if we don't? You're going to shoot us?" taunted someone.

"No. I can move you without shooting you. But my mother raised me to be polite. I said, 'please.' " That got a laugh, and the crowd stepped back. Alice dropped some money on the table for our lunches, and a few moments later, we were back on the street.

"That's it," I said. "We're done with anarchists."

"But look what we found. Czolgosz was a man

of mystery. He's been disowned by the anarchists even though he said he was one and was clearly known to them."

"That doesn't take us any farther forward. Dozens of investigators couldn't find any important connection between Czolgosz's actions and the anarchist movement. They held Emma Goldman for a few weeks but then let her go. He was a lone wolf. We knew that."

"Yes, but you're forgetting two things," said Alice, talking to me like I was an especially slow schoolboy. "Emma Goldman, although she defended him, still said he was incapable of acting alone. That must be her true opinion—why lie? So even his only public defender felt he was part of a larger conspiracy. And let's not forget what got us here in the first place—someone is nervous about our interest."

"All right, that makes a certain amount of sense."

"It makes perfect sense. And finally, there's Nicky's comment about the immigrants. That's where we have to look next."

"Immigrants? That's one thing Nicky got right. This town is full of them. From every part of the world. They speak a dozen languages, and they're organized into hundreds of groups. How are you going to look into all of them?"

"Don't worry. I'll figure it out."

"But another day. We have to get all the way uptown, and your Aunt Anna warned you not to be late. So I guess we'll take the el." The elevated train was a pretty quick way of getting around Manhattan. Normally, I didn't take Alice on it because the enclosed space and crowds made trying to protect her a difficult proposition. But after what we had done today, it seemed silly to think of the el as dangerous, and there were no cabs to be found in that neighborhood anyway.

Alice practically jumped with delight at the novelty, and except for a few knowing glances from people who recognized her, we made it uptown without incident. Alice loved it, looking out the windows as the neighborhoods passed by us.

She grinned at me. "You know how to show a girl a good time, Mr. St. Clair," she said.

We had reached our station and were heading down the stairs and toward the Caledonia before we knew it.

When we reached her block, Alice raised an eyebrow at the sight of half a dozen police cars on the street. The Caledonia has service entrances at the back and side, and by each one was a pair of cops holding shotguns.

"What's going on?" asked Alice. I shrugged. There were more heavily armed cops by the front entrance as well as a pair of guys in suits. I recognized them from my time in Washington, and they gave me a quick smile and nod.

Alice turned on me sharply when we entered the lobby. "You know them—more Secret Service?

Did they decide I need more protection from anarchists?"

"From your behavior today, I think the anarchists need protection from you."

"Very funny."

We made it up to the apartment, and the maid let us in.

"There's a visitor in the parlor, miss," she said, but Alice still didn't get it. She handed her coat to the maid and walked quickly to the parlor with me on her heels. An unmistakable figure was waiting in the room reading a newspaper.

Alice shrieked and ran to him. Nothing filled her with more joy than seeing her father, and if she looked like an adult giving Emma Goldman a dressing down, here she looked like she was six. She threw her arms around him as she closed her eyes, and he picked her up with that hearty laugh I knew so well.

"It's wonderful to see you, Baby Lee," he said, using his special pet name for her.

"I'm so glad to see you again, too," she said. Then he noticed me.

"Sergeant St. Clair, come over and say hello," he boomed.

"It would be my pleasure, Mr. President," I said.

Chapter 4

Mr. Roosevelt slapped me on the back and pumped my hand, and everyone was all smiles. But after her initial joy, Alice expressed her dissatisfaction with me.

"You knew he was coming," she said. "You knew and you didn't tell me."

"As I've said before, Miss Alice, they call it the *Secret* Service."

"Don't blame him," said President Roosevelt. "No one was to be told, not even Anna, although I imagine she guessed. I'm only here tonight, meeting with a few influential men, then I'm off to Chicago. Washington may be this nation's political capital, but great men are all over, and I want to meet them."

I spoke up before Alice could continue any argument. "You're looking well, Mr. President. But I'm not Sergeant St. Clair anymore. I'm Special Agent St. Clair."

"Of course, of course. And I'm not Colonel Roosevelt anymore, either. We haven't done too badly for ourselves, have we?" He laughed again. "My girl hasn't been giving you too much trouble, has she?" We both gave Alice a look, and I had to admire the utter coolness with which she met our glances.

"Not at all, sir," I said.

"Glad to hear it. You're a good man, St. Clair."

"Thank you, sir. And now, with your permission, Mr. President, I'll let you and Miss Alice get reacquainted." I was planning to see if Dulcie had any more of her great coffee to wash out the taste of that stew, but Alice had something else on her mind.

"If you don't mind, Father, I have something to discuss with you, and I'd like Mr. St. Clair to stay while I do." I don't know if the president noticed, but her eyes slid up to me for a moment.

"Indeed. What are you up to that requires Mr. St. Clair here before you tell me?" He seemed amused, and I just sat down on a chair, wondering which direction Alice was going with this.

"I've found myself increasingly interested in politics. And although I do want to join you in Washington, I am finding a great deal of interest right here in New York. More than a third of this city is foreign-born. Did you know that? They're quite a political force to be reckoned with, don't you agree, Father?"

Nicely done, Alice. The only question was how much Mr. Roosevelt would swallow.

He nodded and considered that for a while before turning to me. "St. Clair—just what kind of background do you have, anyway?"

"Well, sir, there's some Cajun, German, Swedish, and my grandmother was a full-blooded Cheyenne."

"There you are," said Mr. Roosevelt. "Mr. St. Clair is the face of America. A bit of everything." Alice seemed a little dubious about my recitation. "Wave after wave came here—look how entrenched the Irish are, with that magnificent cathedral of theirs on Fifth Avenue. But all who arrive have to become Americans, speak our language, and give loyalty to our government and no other. Is that what you're concerned about?"

"Yes, I am," she said, sitting tall on the couch. "It's a place where I think I can help. We Roosevelts have always been New Yorkers, but you're in Washington now. I'd like to continue the family political tradition here. Perhaps start conversations with leaders in the immigrant community, help them become good Americans." She smiled. "And good Republicans."

And the president laughed at that. "Glad to hear it, and I couldn't be more pleased that you're giving yourself something good to do. Go forth, and keep me posted on what you're doing. But—"

Here it came. Mr. Roosevelt knew his daughter. "You will do this under the protection of Mr. St. Clair. You won't go anywhere without him, and if he feels something is too dangerous, his authority is absolute. Is that understood?"

Alice looked like she was going to argue the point but thought better of it. She glanced back and forth between me and her father, then decided she had won enough of a victory and should stand pat.

"Yes, Father," she said.

"You can rely on me, Mr. President," I said.

"Very good, then. My brave girl is going out in the world. Keep your Aunt Anna informed, since she's here on the ground, so to speak. Now, where were you going to start?"

"You know New York better than Mr. St. Clair or I. You were police commissioner. Can you think of anyone in the police force who could point us in the right direction?"

The president thought. "Yes—try Captain Michael O'Hara. He was invaluable to me when I was commissioner. He's the man who knows what's really happening in the city and can make some introductions."

"This is very exciting," said Alice, and she gave her father a kiss on the cheek.

"I'm looking forward to your reports. Now, St. Clair, what are you carrying nowadays?"

I pulled out my revolver and handed it over. "The Colt New Service, sir. Takes a .45 caliber cartridge, and it's a darn sight more powerful than the M1892 you had in Cuba."

"Mr. St. Clair won't let me touch it," complained Alice.

"A soldier doesn't let others handle his weapon," said the president.

"He's letting you."

"Ah, my dear, but I'm the commander in chief."

Mr. Roosevelt snapped it open, looked it over,

and then closed it and aimed it at the far wall, and I wondered if he'd try to do what I'd done in the office the day before. I didn't see his sister being too pleased with that. And just as I thought about Mrs. Cowles, in she walked.

"How delightful, to come home to see my brother the president brandishing firearms in front of his daughter. I figured you had arrived, from the army downstairs, but I didn't think you needed your own weapon."

Mr. Roosevelt just grinned as we both stood, and he handed me back my revolver. Mrs. Cowles let her brother give her a dutiful kiss. "Just armory talk with Mr. St. Clair. Good to see you, Anna. You're looking well. Keeping busy as always, I assume? I'm only staying overnight, gone in the early morning. We can have a quiet family dinner and talk over some new projects Alice has thought up."

Mrs. Cowles gave Alice a look. "Really?" she said dryly, but the girl didn't blush a bit. Then Mrs. Cowles gave me a look as if this were somehow my fault, and I thought it was time to make an exit.

"Seeing as it's a family evening, I'll take myself off, with your permission, Mr. President."

"Yes, of course. We'll be staying in this evening anyway. Thanks again for all your work."

I made my good-byes and was almost out the front door when I heard Alice say, "I didn't tell Mr. St. Clair when we'll need to leave tomorrow morning," and she came running up. Her eyes were as bright as the crystals in the chandelier over our heads, and her father's visit had put some color into her cheeks.

"What do you think? Father is supporting our investigations. Isn't this exciting? We'll visit Captain O'Hara first thing tomorrow."

"I'll be here bright and early, Miss Alice, and ready to go with the motorcar."

She took my hand. "Tell me you're as excited as I am. Tell me that."

"Oh, I am. This is going to be a thrill and a half, Miss Alice. As long as your father doesn't find out what you're really up to and your aunt doesn't find out where we'll be going, we'll be just fine."

But Alice was undaunted. "Father has often praised your bravery to me. You can't possibly be worried. And a man like you must find this a lot more exciting than taking me from store to store."

"I have to admit you're right about that. We'll drive down to the Tombs right after breakfast, I promise, and take it from there after we talk with Captain O'Hara."

"That's the spirit!" She practically jumped as if she were a little girl again. Then I saw a crafty look. Alice's intentions can change quickly, and you have to watch out. "Anyway, if you're worried, you can get me my own Colt New Service Revolver."

"It's not something typically carried by seventeen-year-old girls," I said. "But if anyone

73

can talk me into getting her one, it would be you."

"Mr. St. Clair, I think that's the nicest thing you've ever said to me." With that, she turned and headed back to the parlor but paused to look over her shoulder and give me a parting shot: "Are you visiting your sister, Mariah? Say hello. And I really want to meet her." She made that last line sound like a royal command, and with that, I beat a retreat.

I had some thoughts to order, so I walked through Central Park. Mariah had a nice little apartment in Yorkville, on the East Side, not far from the East River. I picked up a bottle of wine just across the street from where she lives. Mariah found a place in a building that's better cared for than Emma Goldman's. Her apartment is larger too, and Mariah is a good housekeeper, so the place has always felt comfortable to me.

Mariah greeted me as she always does, with a kiss on the cheek and a light slap to my face. She was looking good. She had let her curly black hair down after work, tying it back simply so that it framed her olive-complexioned face.

"Wine." She looked at the bottle and shook her head. "Will you look at us? We didn't even know what wine was when we were kids. Thanks—we'll have it tonight. Now, set the table. I'm frying up some chicken. And collard greens. They're not easy to find in this town."

"God bless you." I poured us some wine. Mariah

doesn't have any stemware, but it tastes just as good in mugs. "As the family cook, have you ever heard of something called a 'knish'?"

"Can't say I have. If it's food, I haven't heard of half the things people eat in this city. What's it like?"

"It's a potato thing. Alice seems to like them a lot."

"She does, does she? How's work with her?"

"Taking a turn. She's on some new venture, and we'll be mixing with some different crowds, solving some damn mystery that's in her own mind."

Mariah gave me a shrewd look, drank some more wine, and said, "You're getting fat, lazy, and comfortable. You used to drive cattle, settle gunfights, and go to war, and now you're whining about having to drive some girl around New York. Your biggest worry has become who you're going to wheedle a free meal out of. So Alice Roosevelt wants an adventure? When you were her age, you used to want them, too."

"Maybe I'm done with adventure," I said.

"That's great. You could live another fifty years. How do you plan on spending them? Playing poker and telling the same damn stories about Saturday nights in Laramie and charging up San Juan Hill? It's going to be a long, long fifty years. Especially for those of us who have to listen."

We didn't talk for a while as she cut up the chicken and I brooded into my wine.

"I think Alice is going to be good for you if you let her. She'll help you find your way back."

"Alice doesn't even know where she's going. How is she going to help me?"

"You'll help each other. You followed her pa up San Juan Hill. Maybe you need to see where the daughter leads you, and you'll find yourself where you need to be."

I nodded. "Perhaps. Or maybe it's time for me to take my savings and head back home. Buy some stock, get married, have children." I looked up at Mariah, but she just shook her head.

"Honey, you're not ready for that final adventure yet, I can tell you that much. Anyway, Special Agent St. Clair of the Secret Service, you have to get yourself something to do besides trying to impress young women with your shooting skills. That's just sad."

"Who told you I did that?" I asked like an idiot.

"You did. Just now. For God's sake, I know you. Now I want to meet this Alice of yours."

"She's not my Alice. She's a kid, and I'm her armed nanny."

"If you say so. I'm off again tomorrow evening. Bring her around for dinner."

"She'd like that. She keeps asking after you and doesn't believe you're my sister."

"I know the feeling. Sometimes I'm like your mother. Now, don't talk to me, I'm going to get busy frying."

We didn't talk more about Alice that evening, but Mariah had given me a lot to think about. When it got late, I decided I didn't want to head all the way back to the Caledonia, so Mariah gave me a blanket, and I fell asleep on the kitchen floor.

Chapter 5

I woke up early by habit. I let Mariah sleep and grabbed a couple of pieces of chicken to take with me. It was keen and cold and felt better than the damp weather that had been hanging over the city. The frost crackled under my boots as I walked through the park, and for a few moments, I forgot I was in New York.

At the Caledonia, the maid said Miss Alice was still having breakfast, and I showed myself into the kitchen. Dulcie gave me some coffee and cream with bad grace.

"Miss Alice won't be home for dinner tonight," I said.

"Taking her to Delmonico's?" she asked.

"Too much money for food that isn't half as good as yours," I said. She looked at me hard to see if I was making fun of her, but my face was straight.

Alice found me in the kitchen when I was on my second cup. She wore a simple warm dress, and her hair was done up neatly.

"You're up early, Mr. St. Clair."

"I work with Roosevelts. They're always up early. Did your father get off all right?"

"Yes, he did. He told me he wanted me to make him proud."

I drained my coffee. "Then we'd better get going."

A few minutes later, we were in the motorcar and heading down to the Tombs. It's been in lower Manhattan since before I was born. Its nickname comes from the decoration, which makes it look like where they buried kings in Egypt, or so they say. But it might as well come from the feeling you get being there. It scares the hell out of me, I don't mind saying, and maybe that's the idea. I'd like to think there was more than one would-be criminal who stayed on the straight and narrow from fear they'd end up there. It's a heavy, squat building. Just look at it once, and you'll think once inside, you're never going to leave. Maybe that was the idea.

"Tell me why we're doing this again, Miss Alice?"

"It's about the assassination, what no one else looked at before. Something happened in the immigrant community, which triggered Czolgosz's actions. That's where the anarchists are pointing us, and we know someone's worried, because he took pains to have me followed when I expressed interest in the whole business."

We parked the car, and Alice wasted no time heading up the stairs in her purposeful tread. Some knew who she was, others didn't, but all paid attention to her, which she loved, even if she pretended she didn't notice.

"Good morning," she said to the desk sergeant, who looked too young to remember when Mr. Roosevelt had been commissioner. "I'm Alice

Roosevelt. And this is Mr. St. Clair of the Secret Service. We're here to see Captain Michael O'Hara."

The sergeant gave her a startled look and then turned to me. "What does the Secret Service want here?"

"Talk to the lady, pal," I said.

"Captain O'Hara," repeated Alice in a tone that said she wasn't going to say it again.

"You said 'Roosevelt'?" he asked. "Very well." He looked like he was going to ask another question, but he stopped and gave us directions to Captain O'Hara's office.

"I used to be allowed to visit my father here sometimes," she said as she looked around. "He did so much here but was never fully appreciated. Let's hope this Captain O'Hara Father recommends does more than just humor us."

She knocked on an office door, and we heard a "Come in!" I've worked with a lot of Irish cops in New York, and he didn't seem at first glance different from any of them: on the large side with a red face and white hair. I've nothing against Catholics, but I knew enough about New York to know there were still places people with names like "O'Hara" would never be admitted. Still, they've done all right for themselves, especially in the police department.

O'Hara looked a little surprised for a moment as Alice just stood there with a raised eyebrow.

"My gosh—it's you, isn't it, Miss Roosevelt? I

haven't seen you since you visited as a little girl. Make yourself at home, and tell me what I can do for you."

"My father said you could help me with some political . . . investigations. Oh, and this is Mr. St. Clair, of the Secret Service." O'Hara eyed me warily before giving me a meaty hand to shake. New York cops don't always appreciate federal lawmen on their turf.

We sat down in hard wooden chairs, and I looked around. You had to be higher up than a captain to get an office more suitable for guests. The walls were covered with bulletins and wanted posters, many stained with weeks and months of cigar smoke. The captain had a wire box on his desk overflowing with official papers, and I was sure he hadn't read any of them.

"You say something 'political,' Miss Roosevelt. Are you here with a message or request from the president? I owe him a lot, and I pay my debts."

"I appreciate that, Captain. And I know my father would too. It's a small favor, really. I've developed an interest in the immigrant population in this city. I thought you might be able to give me the names of some leaders among immigrant communities. I'd like to meet them."

Captain O'Hara twirled a pen on his fingers for a few moments. "Just between us, can I ask what the president's interest is?"

"I hope I didn't give you the impression I was a

messenger from my father in this instance. I'm here on my own account."

"I see. And can I ask what you hope to get out of this?" He was still smiling. Alice smiled right back.

"I don't want to trouble you with that, Captain. It's political." And that wiped the smile off his face. You don't get to be a New York police captain without some sense of politics, and he clearly wanted to know what was going on.

"Very well. It's your affair, Miss Roosevelt. It's just that some of these are dangerous—"

"I'll take care of that, Captain," I said. Alice seemed to like that—she turned away and gave me a quick smile.

"I'm sure you will," said O'Hara, and he gave me a hard look. "I'll tell you what. Let's start with two names. Two men I know—men I can trust to behave themselves when a Roosevelt comes calling." He opened a notebook, and the only sound for a few moments was the scratching of his pen. Then O'Hara tore out the page, folded it in half, and handed it to Alice.

"Here are the two names. And where you can find them."

"You knew where they lived," said Alice. "You didn't have to look them up. I find that interesting."

Captain O'Hara leaned back in his chair and gave some thought to what he was planning to say. "They're known to us, Miss Roosevelt."

Alice looked at the paper. "One appears to be

Chinese. The other is Italian. I'm sure they'll be helpful. I don't suppose you know anyone of Polish extraction?"

O'Hara nodded at that and then looked at Alice with a new understanding. "Leon Czolgosz. That's what this is about. Now I understand. Mr. St. Clair, I don't know why the Secret Service is still involved in this, and I don't want to know. But why the hell are you involving the president's daughter?"

"It's not my show, Captain. And I don't know how your mother raised you, but mine would've slapped me for using language like that in front of a lady."

Alice got that superior, amused look and glanced back and forth between us. "Nevermind the language, Captain. I was wondering about Leon Czolgosz, among other things. He seems to be a bit of a cipher. He's dead, of course, so there's no talking to him. But I'd like to talk to someone who did know him. I thought you might know"—Alice glanced again at the paper—"someone who's 'known to the police,' in your parlance."

"Miss Roosevelt, is this something you should really be asking about? Does your father know what you're doing?"

"You could call him," said Alice. "But he's traveling and very busy, so I don't think you'll want to do that. And you don't want to upset Mr. St. Clair here, because he's just a crazy cowboy, and he's going to be very unhappy if we don't get everything we want."

It was the perfect chance to shut this whole thing down then and there. Weeks and months later, I asked myself why I hadn't. Sometimes I told myself it was because I knew we were onto something big—that it was our duty to follow this to the end. But in the middle of the night, when there is nothing around to keep you from being honest with yourself, I had to admit I missed the old days, and Mariah's words echoed. I was simply bored.

So I just smiled and shrugged—*what can you do?*

O'Hara looked a little dumbfounded for a few moments, then reached into his desk drawer and produced a bottle and a glass. He poured himself a shot and offered me one.

"It's a little early for me. But you go ahead," I said. "Miss Alice?"

"What is it?" she asked.

"Whisky," said O'Hara. "Scotch whisky."

"No, thank you. I might've said yes to brandy, but not scotch whisky."

So O'Hara drank alone and then gave me a sour look, still thinking this was some sort of Secret Service plot and wondering just how crazy I might be. By this point, I think he just wanted to get us out of his office. "The New York Police Department was asked to look into anarchist connections in the city. We detained Emma Goldman—but you no doubt knew that.

Czolgosz's connections with others were very slim—nothing much there. But we found one other person of interest. His family is all out in the Midwest, but he had one cousin who had come east looking for work. His name was Stanislaw Dunilsky. He had no apparent connections to the anarchists and didn't give us much useful info, but you're welcome to try to talk to him. Anyway, he had no police record and had a clear work history with no complaints from his employers. That's all I can tell you."

O'Hara didn't know Dunilsky's address by heart, but he dug a record book from his desk drawer and wrote out another note for Alice.

"You have been very helpful, Captain O'Hara." She stood, and I followed suit. "Thank you. Now come on, Mr. St. Clair. I'm sure Captain O'Hara is very busy, and we don't want to take up more of his valuable time."

"Good day," he said. "I hope you know what you're doing."

At that, Alice turned back. "Was that directed at me or Mr. St. Clair?"

"Since you ask, miss, it was directed at Mr. St. Clair."

"Very interesting," she said as she headed out again, without even checking to see if I was following her. But I stayed long enough to shake O'Hara's hand again and thank him for his time and trouble. As I said, my mother raised me right.

At least Alice had waited for me before running out the front door this time.

"I suppose that went about as well as could be expected," she said, brandishing the papers like trophies. "He didn't like giving us those names, but he did anyway. Come, let's go visit this Czolgosz cousin, Dunilsky. The immigrant leaders will always be around, but I want to get to this cousin before he leaves town."

As we walked back to the motorcar, I looked at the address. Another low-end street, not far from Emma Goldman's and probably not more pleasant.

"When we get there, I'm going to have a look first, like before," I said. "You know the deal."

"You heard Captain O'Hara. He's not an anarchist and has no criminal record."

"Maybe not. But you heard your father: I'm in charge of safety. If everything looks all right, we can go up, but only if I'm sure."

"Oh, very well," she said. "But I think you're making a fuss over nothing. I have full confidence in your abilities."

"Thanks for the compliment," I said.

"You don't have to say it like that. I meant it. I really did."

I parked in front of the house and gave it a look-over. It seemed quiet and reasonably well kept. I guessed everyone who worked here probably had a job, including Dunilsky, so unless he had a night shift, we probably wouldn't even find him.

"Why are you nervous here?" asked Alice.

"I'm not nervous, Miss Alice. I'm never nervous. I'm cautious."

"Well you weren't this cautious around Emma Goldman."

"She wasn't known to be violent herself. But I don't know about this Dunilsky. He was cousin to a killer. So I'm being cautious."

I saw no one in the entryway, so we headed to the third floor, with me leading.

"Do you think—"

But I cut her off and took her hand as we went up the stairs so she wouldn't get any ideas and charge right in. It was quiet in that building, and I didn't like it. Even with people at work, there should've been something happening—a mother with children, an old lady peering through a crack.

We made it to the third-floor landing, and I saw the door at the end of the hall. I held my breath and, still leading Alice, walked slowly down the hall. I spared a glance for her, and her eyes were big and her jaw set. The floor creaked under my heavy boots.

I was right. There was something wrong, and it was a good thing I had taken it slow: I heard the click. With my left arm, I slammed Alice against the wall, and with my right, I drew my Colt. Then the door exploded as a bullet came whizzing by us in the dim hallway.

Chapter 6

I shot a second later, and it should've gone right between his eyes if he was standing.

But I didn't hear a fall or anything else for a moment.

"You all right?" I asked Alice.

"Yes, I'm fine." No whimper there, and I admired her for it.

There were no more shots, so I said, "We're the police. There are several of us here. Open the door slowly and throw out the gun, butt first."

"Don't hurt me. I'll do what you say," said a voice, and I heard a tremble. I kept my finger on the trigger and my arm against Alice as the door opened a crack. I saw the gun handed backward, like I asked, and then dropped on the landing. It was an old Colt Peacemaker; I hadn't seen one in years.

"Now open the door slowly. I want to see one hand on the door and one over your head."

Again, he did as I asked. The ruined door creaked open slowly, and I saw a short, pale man wearing a laborer's pants, a white shirt that was not too clean, and a pair of suspenders. He hadn't shaved in several days, and the stubble showed starkly. His eyes were red, and I could smell the drink halfway down the hall. He put both his hands up and just stood there, shaking.

I picked up the pistol. Then I headed into the apartment and gave Dunilsky a quick pat down, but he seemed harmless by this point. He was lucky he hadn't shot his own foot off. There was a chair just behind the door; he had clearly been sitting in it when he shot at us, which is why my shot went over his head. He probably couldn't trust himself to stand up.

I pushed him back into the chair and gave the apartment a quick look. He was alone there, with only empty bottles and dirty dishes. I waved Alice to come in, and she looked around, wide-eyed. The windows were closed and the shades pulled down, so I opened them to let some air and light in. Even with the cold, it was an improvement.

While I did that, Alice had stopped looking and started doing.

"Are you Mr. Dunilsky—Stanislaw Dunilsky?" The man slowly nodded. "My name is Alice. This is my friend, Mr. St. Clair. Please take that chair and move it to this table, and we'll sit together." She said it as if she meant to be obeyed, but also with a certain kindness, like a mother to a difficult child. Dunilsky nodded again and brought the chair to the wooden table. He reached for a bottle at his feet, but Alice immediately snatched it from him.

"You've had enough. Wait here." She walked to the little kitchen. "Do you have any coffee? Nevermind, I found a bit." I didn't know Alice knew how to do anything in a kitchen, but in short order, she had made a pot and served a cup to Dunilsky. "You have no cream or sugar, but it should do you some good as is." He mechanically started to drink it.

"Why did you shoot at us?" she asked.

"You're not the police," he finally said in a flat midwestern accent. He sounded resigned. "You're going to kill me."

"I am the police, and we aren't going to kill you." I showed him my badge—no need to try to explain what the Secret Service was. He looked at it and nodded.

"So why did you shoot at us?" Alice asked again.

"I thought you came from the Archangel," he said.

"Who?"

"The Archangel," he said, laughing a little hysterically. By this point, I was all for grabbing him and taking him down to the Tombs, but Alice just looked up at me and shook her head. Her eyes darted to an old coat hanging on a peg by the door, and she pointed. I took it down and gave it to her and watched while she draped it over Dunilsky's shoulders. He glanced up at her with gratitude.

I'd never seen Alice as having a lot of patience, but she surprised me that day. She laid a hand on his arm as he drank more coffee and said, "Start from the beginning. Tell me about your cousin, about Leon Czolgosz." He nodded and started to talk slowly, looking into his cup.

"Leon and I grew up together and came to New York looking for work. We found jobs by the docks. The pay was good enough, and we were getting by, but Leon..." he grasped for the words. "Leon wanted something else. He always had ideas . . . he was angry a lot. Me, I just wanted to work, put a few dollars away, and get on—not make any trouble. But he was talking to other people . . . trouble-makers. Then last spring he heard there were jobs up in Buffalo and decided to go up to see about it. He was restless like that."

"Did you like him?" asked Alice.

He looked up and blinked. "Yes. I mean, we knew each other all our lives. We were family. But he was always saying things, and he'd get us into trouble. He wanted me to go with him to Buffalo, but I didn't. I was glad he wasn't around me making enemies, and I was glad to see him go."

"Enemies?"

Dunilsky smiled at that, a little shyly, and risked a glance at Alice. "Who are you again?"

"Alice. You can just call me Alice. Mr. St. Clair and I are here to help. Now tell me about these enemies."

"Like I said, Leon got mixed up with some . . . they called themselves 'anarchists.' But you must know this. Everyone knows what he did and why."

"I can hear what you're saying—that he got mixed up with the anarchists."

"He talked like that. Went to some bars, meetings

in the park. But it was all talk. I don't think he really believed all that stuff. He wasn't really part of a group."

"So he really wasn't one of them? That's what you're saying, isn't it?"

Dunilsky sighed, and Alice poured him more coffee. I found a third chair, turned it around, and sat, leaning on the chair back in complete fascination. Alice was certainly enjoying herself—that much was clear.

"Leon wasn't . . . he didn't think of things for himself, you know? He was always easy to talk into something. But I'll tell you, I don't think that anyone . . . I mean, no one could believe it when he killed the president. I know he did it, but anyone who knew him thought he was all talk."

Alice cocked her head at him. "Rather like, you tell someone you're so angry you could kill them, but you don't really mean it. You calm down the next day."

"Yes, you're right," he said, pleased Alice understood him.

"Very well. Now, tell me about this Archangel. Let's get to why you're shooting at people through doors."

Dunilsky had been looking a little better, but now the haunted look returned.

"Leon came back. About a month before he killed the president. He was staying with me and told me that he had met some men in Buffalo—more anarchists, I guess—and one who was powerful, a man he only called the Archangel."

"Was this man the leader of the anarchist group—this Archangel?"

Dunilsky shook his head. "I don't know. But he was a man of great power, and Leon didn't seem to know who he really was. Leon was terrified of him, and I couldn't get any sense out of him. I'll tell you, Alice, that it put the fear of God into me. I thought it all over . . . afterward. They executed Leon, and few people knew we were related, so I thought I could just move on. But that's when things got really bad."

"You started getting threats?" I asked. It must've taken some threats to reduce this man to such a wreck.

"Yes, Mr. St. Clair. All kinds of things at the docks: accidents that almost killed me, derricks that dropped boxes just a few feet from where I stood, carts that suddenly came loose and almost ran me over. I began to be seen as a sort of bad luck charm. So I quit my job and began working nights at odd jobs, where they couldn't get to me, but I made less, and my few savings were getting used up. Twice I was attacked walking home and only got away because I was looking around carefully and could always run fast. I haven't left this apartment in more than a week now, waiting for them to come at me."

"Why didn't you call the police?" Alice asked.

He laughed with no amusement. "The police? In this city? Getting them to pay attention to a common workman, a son of immigrants?" He looked at her as if for the first time, taking in her expensive clothes and uptown accent. "Who are you?"

"I said, a friend. And we might be able to help."

"Tell me where you got that gun of yours," I asked.

"It was my father's. He left it to me. He worked out West at one point and picked it up there."

"Well, there's not much we can do to help you if you're going to keep firing pistols through doors."

At that, Alice stood. "Mr. St. Clair, join me in the kitchen." We left Dunilsky for the relative privacy of the apartment's only other room.

"We have to do something," she said. "Dunilsky's a connection to someone who was pulling the strings—this Archangel. He might be able to lead us to the person who's actually responsible for McKinley's death. We don't really know why Czolgosz did it—maybe someone was pulling his strings."

"I don't know, Miss Alice. I've never heard a story like that before. It's like something out of a child's fairy tale. Some figure named the Archangel? I think drink has turned his head, or he's gone mad. We can't just accept his word as true."

"I know. But what if this is part of a bigger plot?

What if this Archangel is real and is planning something else. Wait—" She stepped back into the room. "Mr. Dunilsky, we need something. We want to help, but is there anything you can tell me about the Archangel? We need more details."

He looked into the empty coffee cup, then up at Alice. "You took away my last bottle, but do you have some tobacco? I haven't smoked in four days. It's the longest I've gone since I was fifteen."

Alice just turned to me, and with a sigh, I got out my wrapping paper and tobacco. Dunilsky looked in no fit state to roll his own, so I did it for him and then struck a match. He inhaled with complete delight.

"The Archangel, Mr. Dunilsky? We've made you coffee and given you a cigarette, and you can be very grateful Mr. St. Clair didn't put a bullet between your eyes. I need a little more than a story." At that, Dunilsky got a crafty look on his face and looked back and forth between us.

"Would you like a picture?" he said in a whisper. "Because I have a picture. He doesn't know I have it—not yet—but he knows Leon got one, and I think he's now figured out Leon left it with me. A picture of the Archangel . . ." Dunilsky got up and looked around the small apartment, as if someone else besides me and Alice were there. He knelt by the bed, and his fingers slipped along the edge until he found a small tear. Then he reached in. Carefully, he pulled out a piece of paper and handed it to Alice like a cat showing off a mouse he'd killed.

She unfolded it and showed it to me. Yeah, it was an Archangel. It was a picture of some sort of heavenly being, a little too handsome to be real, with rays of light shooting from his head and wings visible over his shoulder. I don't know much about art, but you could tell this wasn't too fancy—more like something one the church-going types hand out outside of saloons. There was more than one of them in Laramie.

"Leon gave this to you?" asked Alice. He nodded. "Where did Leon get it from?"

"He stole it from the Archangel. It took him a while to figure that out," he said with a sly smile.

We had both hoped it would be something a little more useful, but Dunilsky—and apparently Czolgosz, too—had thought it was important, so I folded it again and stuck it in my pocket. Dunilsky suddenly remembered something as he continued to stand by his bed, like how he probably hadn't slept in days, and he crawled in and closed his eyes.

"Well, they say craziness goes through families, and this proves it, Miss Alice. God knows what's going on or what that picture means, but we'll get nothing more from him."

"There is something in what he says. Even crazy people talk about things that really happen. There is something there—that picture means something.

But again, what can we do with him? We can't just leave him here."

"I don't see what else we can do," I said.

And then I heard footsteps outside. The door slowly opened, and in walked a cop.

"Who are you? I've heard reports of shots here." He looked at the door. "Coming and going, as I see."

I identified myself and watched his eyes narrow. "What's the Secret Service doing here? And who's she?"

Alice started to talk, but I motioned for her to be silent. She glared but did as I asked. "She's with me. And my business here is my own."

The cop considered that for a moment and saw there was nothing more to be said on that score. "This guy has been giving us trouble for some weeks. The building is empty during the day because no one wants to be around the lunatic with the gun. He works nights, so at least he's gone while everyone is sleeping." He looked over my shoulder to the bed. "Did you kill him?"

"He's sleeping. Why didn't you do something about him?"

The cop shrugged. "He hadn't actually broken the law, at least not seriously. Apparently just spent his time complaining that someone was coming to kill him."

"You failed to intervene when he complained and failed again when the residents complained. What exactly do you do to earn your keep, Officer?" said Alice. The cop looked a little astonished. And then Alice really put her foot into it. "You're just lucky that my father isn't still in charge . . ." Then the light of understanding came into the cop's eyes.

"Say, you're his daughter—you're Miss Roosevelt. What are—"

"Nevermind," I said. I gave Alice a dirty look, but she didn't bat an eyelash. "Listen, I've got a job for you, son, and if you know what's good for you, you'll do it and keep your mouth shut."

I roused Dunilsky. "Come on, my friend. Time to get moving."

"What . . . ?"

"This nice officer is going to take you to a safe place where the Archangel can't get at you and you won't blow anyone's head off."

He was so dazed at that point, he would've gone anywhere with anyone who wasn't actively trying to kill him. I produced my card and a pencil from my pocket and wrote on the back, "O'Hara—keep him safe. We'll speak later." I gave it to the cop. Maybe after Dunilsky calmed down and sobered up, we could get more sense out of him.

"Take him to Captain O'Hara down at the Tombs, and only O'Hara. No one else. Got it? If he's not in, you wait, and don't let him out of your sight."

"Yes, sir," he said, and then he nodded to Alice.

"And good day to you, too, miss." Exhausted and half drunk, Dunilsky went along with no protest, leaving me and Alice alone in the apartment.

"There's nothing more to see here. I think it's time to visit our immigrant contacts."

"Wait," I said. "People are shooting at us, and Dunilsky wasn't even supposed to be dangerous."

She raised an eyebrow. "But he only tried to kill us because someone was trying to kill him. Now that person—this Archangel—is the one who's really dangerous. Is he the person behind the Great Erie & Albany Boat Company, who hires a private detective the moment we show an interest in Emma Goldman?"

"She was a connection to a Czolgosz, the man who killed the president. But that's over."

"Maybe it's not," said Alice. "Maybe we walked into something that's still going on. Like I said, maybe Czolgosz wasn't working alone anyway. Dunilsky knows more than he's saying. Someone called the Archangel is after him. And the anarchists tell us to look toward the immigrants—Dunilsky and Czolgosz are from immigrant families. There's something there, I know it." You only have that kind of confidence when you're that young.

"I don't know," I said. "It all could just be a string of coincidences."

"But what if it's not? What if there are still people out there who already engineered the death of one president? You're in the Secret Service and you're supposed to protect the presidential family. You can't tell me that we haven't stumbled onto something that could still be a threat to my family, to my father."

"I don't know, Miss Alice . . ."

"You know I'm right, and this is more fun than drinking coffee in a kitchen somewhere while I make nice with good Republican ladies. Let's at least visit those men whose names Captain O'Hara gave us. If nothing else turns up, I'll admit we're on the wrong track."

Heck, I'll admit I was still curious, too. And Captain O'Hara was sure these guys were safe. At least no one would be shooting at us. I hoped.

Chapter 7

We locked the door behind us, although there didn't seem much point, considering how little he had inside worth stealing. I checked the first address on the paper Captain O'Hara had given us. "We're supposed to look up Mr. Zhao of the Hip Leong tong," I said as we headed into the street.

"A tong. It's a sort of a club, isn't it? I remember Father mentioned them when I was a little girl and he was commissioner."

"Yes, they call themselves clubs or societies. If you were less charitable, you might call them a gang. And when it comes to the Chinese, most here aren't too charitable toward them."

"Why not? I don't think I've ever met, really spoken with, anyone from China."

"I met a few out West, when I had a job guarding supplies by a railroad. Good hard workers, didn't drink, did what they were told without a fuss."

"So why don't people like them?"

"They don't look like us, I guess. At least the Irish are white."

"But the Irish pray in the wrong churches," said Alice. "My God, how horrible we are."

It was a short drive to Chinatown and the headquarters of the Hip Leong tong. Chinatown was crowded and poor but orderly as those neighborhoods go. It's the markets there that catch your eye, with kinds of food you don't see anywhere else in the city, maybe in the entire country—especially the seafood. And your ear, meanwhile, takes in the chatter of the wives arguing with the shopkeepers. Most of the signs were in Chinese, and it became easy to imagine we were in China.

The tong occupied a solid, well-kept building—not fancy, but in good repair. We might've walked right by it, but signs in English and Chinese announced what it was. I parked the car, and we stepped into a small but nicely appointed lobby. The interior also made it look like we were in China, with painted scenes of mountains and wooden screens with Chinese characters.

We hardly noticed a man sitting behind a black polished desk by a door. He wore a Chinese outfit, a silk jacket. He stood, smiled, and bowed.

"May I help you?" he asked.

"My name is Alice Roosevelt. My . . . companion and I would like to speak with Mr. Zhao about a matter of importance. Captain O'Hara of the police said Mr. Zhao could be helpful."

"If you will wait here, I will see if Mr. Zhao is available." He bowed again and disappeared through the door. I heard it lock behind him.

"I don't think he knew who I was," said Alice, a little nettled. I laughed.

"He may have. The Chinese don't choose to show

a lot of emotion, especially to outsiders. I sure bet this Mr. Zhao will know who you are."

The doorman came back. "Mr. Zhao would be pleased if you would join him for lunch."

"We accept," said Alice, and we followed the doorman through the door, along a short hallway, and up a narrow staircase. I felt all right about this place, and the doorman didn't seem to be armed, which was a relief.

On the second floor, we were shown into a nice-sized dining room with a round table already set for three. Mr. Zhao was seated, but he stood and bowed. "Miss Roosevelt. I am honored. If you and your companion would like to take a seat, we will dine shortly."

"Thank you. This is Mr. St. Clair."

"Mr. St. Clair. You are . . . the term is 'bodyguard'?"

"Something like that," I said. I was getting a little confused with the bowing, so I stuck my hand out, and with only a slight hesitation, Mr. Zhao reached out and took it. He was dressed like a New York businessman, in a simple but well-fitted suit. I guessed he was around fifty, and he looked open and honest, with a welcoming smile.

A waiter came in and poured tea from a pot that I knew Mariah would just love. I'm more of a coffee man myself, but the tea was good, and Alice raised an eyebrow after a sip.

"It is very good," she said, and Mr. Zhao seemed pleased.

"High praise from the daughter of the American president," he said. "This tea is not widely available outside of our community. I will give you some to take to your esteemed father. Does he drink tea?"

"He might if he had this," said Alice, and Mr. Zhao laughed.

A waiter came in with a tray and started to serve. I didn't know much about Chinese food, but I could see lots of vegetables and meat that looked like chicken or pork. As I told Alice, I've eaten a rattlesnake, so this didn't seem like it was going to be a challenge. But I was wrong. No fork, just a pair of little sticks.

Alice picked them up right away. I don't know where she learned, but she and Mr. Zhao used them as if they were extra fingers. It was Alice who first saw me staring stupidly at them. She sighed and turned to our host.

"Mr. Zhao, I'm afraid Mr. St. Clair is having a little trouble. His knowledge of Oriental practices is somewhat limited." She glared at me for embarrassing her. Mr. Zhao laughed, but not unkindly. He rang for the waiter, spoke to him in Chinese, and a minute later I had a fork. Anyway, the food was surprisingly good, with seasonings I couldn't place. I made my mind up to return to Chinatown and bring my own fork.

Alice liked the food as much as I did, and Mr. Zhao watched her speculatively. It was a toss-up to see who would speak first, but eventually Alice did.

"My friend Captain O'Hara of the police recommended I speak with you, because I have an interest in immigrants."

"Indeed. May I ask if it is simple curiosity or something deeper?" I saw Mr. Zhao's face change. The cheerful mask fell, and I saw a shrewdness there. He knew the president's daughter didn't come downtown just to amuse herself, and Alice was aware of it too.

"Let's say it's family interest," she said. "The previous president was killed by someone from the immigrant community. It's true I was curious about the assassination. But someone, I found, had a great interest in whom I was talking with."

"And that only increased your curiosity," said Mr. Zhao. "But you come here. The man who killed President McKinley was from East Europe, I believe. Poland, I think. Not Chinese."

"So you have no disagreement with the government?" asked Alice.

"That is a different question, Miss Roosevelt. Are you asking if my countrymen are members of the anarchist movement? It is true that among the anarchists are the very few white men who believe the strict laws limiting Chinese immigration are unfair. There is a sympathy for us among the anarchists, even if few Chinese themselves actually belong to that group. Are you here to investigate the anarchist murder of President McKinley, along with your companion from the US Secret Service?"

"So what gave me away?" I asked.

"To what other august body would Mr. Roosevelt entrust his daughter?"

"Fair enough," I said. "By the way, these dumplings are great."

"I'm glad you like them. They're steamed. That's what gives them their particular texture."

"If we can get back to our subject," said Alice, giving me yet another glare.

"What was your subject?" asked Mr. Zhao, and he said it politely enough, but Alice was taken aback. It looked like she was going to snap at him but kept herself under control—just.

"Very well. I will be open with you. Someone with money—someone we don't know—is concerned with my interest in Emma Goldman, a figure in the anarchist movement. I don't know who cares or why, but Miss Goldman was a strong supporter of Leon Czolgosz, who killed McKinley. The anarchists think this may have to do with immigrants. I was wondering if you, a leader in the immigrant community, knew of any recent interest in your neighborhood, an interest from someone unusual."

"So you want a favor?" asked Mr. Zhao.

"I suppose that's one way to put it," said Alice.

"Is there something you could do for me?"

"Like get my father to change government policy? You overestimate my influence, sir."

"Perhaps I overestimate your father," Mr. Zhao said.

"No one has ever overestimated my father," Alice spat out as the color rose in her face.

But Mr. Zhao decided to be genial about it. "Forgive me. No offense was intended. The father occupies an esteemed position in our culture, and it speaks well of you that you hold your father in such high regard. No, I was thinking of something smaller. I remember when your father held the position of police commissioner. Perhaps you, your family, still have friends in the department. A waiter in my employ was arrested for something . . . small. A misunderstanding. If I write his name down and give it to you, perhaps you can explain."

"Oh, very well. But I hope you have something interesting to tell me in return."

"Perhaps. You wanted something unusual. In April of last year, I had a visit from a lawyer. He had a request for me."

"What kind of lawyer?" I asked. I had been in this town long enough to know about lawyers. "One of the shysters who hangs around the Tombs or an uptown lawyer in a good suit?"

"A nice distinction, Mr. St. Clair. It was the second kind, a man from a noble firm. He said he had a client who needed workers, many workers, for jobs in Buffalo on the port. He wanted help with finding such workers in my community. And I did help him. I have never seen anything like that before—so many workers needed upstate. But I was happy to help out my countrymen, many of whom needed the work. What that has to do with Miss Goldman or Mr. Czolgosz, I have no idea. But that was the only unusual incident I can recall."

"And the company he worked for—the Great Erie & Albany Boat Company?" asked Alice, hoping to build a connection.

Mr. Zhao was confused at that. "No. That name is new to me. The lawyer didn't mention that. He said he represented a family-owned company. The family was named Van Schuyler."

That surprised Alice, and she leaned back and pursed her lips. And then she shot me a look: *Don't you dare tease me about this later.*

"Did he tell you why he suddenly needed so many workers?" asked Alice.

Mr. Zhao paused and smiled. "Would you be offended if I gave you some advice? I don't ask questions I don't need the answer to. It has made my life much simpler."

I thought that would upset Alice, but she just nodded, and I could see her filing the advice away for later.

"I want to thank you for the information, Mr. Zhao," said Alice. "One more question. Does the name 'Archangel' mean anything to you?"

"As in the heavenly being? No, that name is also unfamiliar to me."

"Thank you. You have been most helpful, and I promise to speak with the right people about your waiter."

Mr. Zhao nodded in acknowledgment. "So tell me, Miss Roosevelt, will the information I gave you help reveal who is tracking you? Is it someone from this Van Schuyler family?"

Alice smiled brilliantly at that. "But Mr. Zhao, didn't you just tell me there's nothing to be gained by asking questions you don't need the answer to?"

I admired him for laughing at that. Heck, I admired them both. And with good wishes and thanks on both sides, we made our way back to the street.

Alice was in a funny mood after the meeting. She was proud she had uncovered a useful link to some powerful people, those who had the money to pay for a private detective to follow us. She just stood on the street for a few minutes looking regal, and the cold wind put some color in her cheeks.

"Disappointed to find your sweetheart was having us followed?" I finally asked.

"How witty of you, Mr. St. Clair," she said. "I knew I could count on you for a childish comment. Preston was a friend, a congenial companion who made a few trips to Sagamore Hill during a hot summer. That's all. Is that understood?"

I bowed. "Message received, Miss Alice. But to the matter at hand, what do you make of that— the Van Schuylers recruiting large numbers of immigrant workers for their upstate facilities? The anarchists at the Freethinker Club told us to look toward the immigrants. They may have even meant the Van Schuylers in particular—word spreads."

"Yes, I can see that too," she said. "I suppose that's something, although I can't immediately see what. Anyway, we have no idea if Preston van Schuyler was behind this. If it is the family, it's more likely his father or someone else, not someone junior like Preston. It's just a coincidence—I asked Preston to help us because his family has interests in Buffalo, so of course they're hiring people to work on the Great Lakes. There were probably half a dozen other people at that party with investments upstate who were hiring."

"If you say so," I said.

"And why should they want to follow me any-way? Also, there's nothing to connect the Van Schuylers with the Great Erie. Or to Leon Czolgosz, for that matter. And since the Van Schuylers have extensive shipping interests in the Great Lakes, why shouldn't they seek employees in Chinatown? So can you make something out of that?" We just stood there, watching the frost from our breath.

I grinned. "The Secret Service doesn't believe in coincidences. But speaking as a man, I know

Preston would really appreciate your spirited defense."

"God, you're an idiot. But you are right that there may be something there, more than a coincidence. Anarchists are always trying to stir up the workers, so they'd follow them upstate. That doesn't mean the Van Schuylers are involved, but it does mean we need to think more about that connection. The sudden appearance of all those workers may have led to anarchist activity and thus to the assassination. There's a lot we don't know about that, but we do have another appointment."

So we got into the car and drove to the second name Captain O'Hara had given us.

Chapter 8

D on Abruzzo," Alice read from the paper. "He's Italian, but I never heard the name 'Don.'"

"It's not a name. It's a title, like some people get to be 'sir' in England."

"You're joking. Some Little Italy immigrant was knighted by King Victor Emmanuel?"

"Not exactly. It's sort of a mark of respect the leaders insist on—we got a little update on the various groups when I joined the New York office. Anyway, 'Don' is a big deal there. In fact, you should know these guys are a little touchy. You might want to watch how you talk to them."

"What's that supposed to mean?"

"You can come off a little strong," I said.

"I should hope so. My father would be proud to see how strong I am."

"I'm sure, but these folks are a little proud, too, all right?"

I knew the Italians. The city was full of them, a lot of them in poor neighborhoods, and they usually had big families. Some were good, some were bad, and most of them were just trying to earn a living and go to Mass on Sundays. I hadn't really thought about it, but as we walked along the streets of Little Italy, I realized it wasn't that different from Chinatown, or half a dozen other neighborhoods where all the immigrants lived. Here, women in shawls looked over chickens and argued loudly in Italian.

The address Captain O'Hara had given us was for a restaurant called Mezzaluna. There were apartments upstairs, and the shades were lowered on most of them, although I could see at least one face looking down at us.

Alice and I walked in together. The place had been done up nice—a lot of pillars like I hear they have in those old buildings in Rome and paintings of Italy on the wall that made me hope I couldvisit someday. It wasn't crowded that time of day. A few men were drinking, and all of them turned around to have a look at us.

"We should come here for dinner sometime," said Alice.

"All right. We'll bring your Aunt Anna down here, too. If they have a table for eight, we can get your father and the rest of your family here as well."

"And they'd thank me for it," she said.

A waiter scurried up to us and asked if we wanted a table.

"We'd like to see a Mr. Abruzzo. I'm sorry, *Don* Abruzzo," said Alice, and I thought, *What a place and time to show off how clever she was.*

"Oh," he said, seeming at a loss. "May I ask your names?"

"Miss Roosevelt. And Mr. St. Clair," she said. "We are here at the recommendation of Captain O'Hara."

That seemed to worry him. He paused and then left, disappearing into a back room.

"If we keep on like this, you're going to become famous," I said. Alice gave me a smug smile.

"*More* famous," she said.

The waiter came back, still looking a little unsure of himself. "Follow me, please," he said. We followed him past the bar into a little room in the back. There was a comfortable round table and another bar. Three men sat at the table with their backs to the wall, and another man stood by the bar.

The waiter made quick introductions, nodding to the man in the middle, before leaving with equal speed. "Don Abruzzo, this is Miss Roosevelt and Mr. St. Clair."

"Please, take a seat," said Don Abruzzo, who waved a hand but didn't bother standing. I took in everyone. Abruzzo himself was a well-groomed man in his forties, wearing as good a suit as any Fifth Avenue banker might own, and a barber who knew his business had shaved him that morning. The two men flanking him were also well dressed.

It was the guy by the bar I didn't like so much. Guns are heavy, and it's hard to hide it when you're carrying one. This man's suit was probably even cheaper than mine, making him a worker, not a manager. I didn't care that Captain O'Hara had said these guys were all right; I don't like to have someone I don't know carrying a gun near me or

Miss Alice, especially when he's out of my direct sight.

"It's getting a little crowded here," I said, and I pointed back with my thumb at the bar guy.

"You are nervous, Mr. St. Clair?" Don Abruzzo asked in a light accent.

"Mr. St. Clair is never nervous. He is cautious," said Alice. "He's a Secret Service agent and is here to protect me. He's been a cowboy and war hero and is the best of men. So can we make this a private party?"

Don Abruzzo raised an eyebrow at that. "So just you and me?" he asked.

"No, Mr. St. Clair remains. That's part of the deal, Don Abruzzo. You, me, and Mr. St. Clair. You must know that I wouldn't come here if it wasn't important. And private."

"My associates stay," he said.

"Oh, for God's sake, aren't you listening? Are you a coward or just stupid?"

I sighed, and for a minute, Don Abruzzo looked angry, while the bar guy suddenly shifted. I didn't want to start anything by reaching for my Colt, but I knew I could outdraw him.

"I wonder, when you marry, if your husband will be able to properly control you?" he asked.

"I'd hate to think so," I said before Alice could get a word in. Don Abruzzo didn't say anything for a moment, and then he laughed. He said something quickly in Italian to the other men. The bar guy reached for a bottle of red wine and put it down on the table with three glasses. Then he left and the other two men did, too, closing the door behind them.

Don Abruzzo poured the wine. "I don't know if you've had this wine. It's one of the oldest wines in Italy, perhaps in the world. It comes from Naples. In English, it's called 'The Tears of Christ,' and it's grown on the slopes of Mt. Vesuvius. *Cento di questi giorni.* That means, 'I wish you one hundred of these days.' " And we drank. It was better than the bottle I had bought for Mariah the other night, so I was fine.

"So tell me, Miss Roosevelt, what kind of service I may provide to President Roosevelt, who has sent his daughter and trusted friend to me as emissaries?"

I thought she'd start the same way she had with Mr. Zhao, but she got right to the point, probably because I had teased her about Preston earlier, and she was all worked up about the Van Schuylers possibly being involved.

"I have found that a family named Van Schuyler has been hiring a lot of workers for a project upstate, on the Great Lakes. We want to know why. Perhaps the Van Schuyler family has sought out your help in finding workers and you have some information."

"I would think that you would have official ways of finding that out," he said, looking closely at Alice.

"Maybe I want an unofficial way."

"Ah. So this is not about the president investigating a problem. It's about Roosevelts and Van Schuylers. I see." Don Abruzzo drank some more wine. "My sister's son has a position in the Street Department. He would like to be a supervisor, but they don't give jobs like that to Italians. Perhaps you could speak with someone? You come from a well-known family."

Alice rolled her eyes. "Oh, God. More horse trading. So you want me to see your nephew gets the job? Oh, very well. Write out his name, and I'll call the commissioner tomorrow."

"Thank you very much. But you were asking about the Van Schuylers? Yes, an associate of theirs, a lawyer, came to me looking for workers. I was able to help him. It seemed they needed a lot of men to work on the Great Lake ports."

"Did he mention the name of the company? The Great Erie & Albany Boat Company?"

Abruzzo shook his head. "He just said it was for the family company. He didn't mention that name. And it's not familiar to me from anywhere else."

"What about Archangel? Is that name familiar to you?"

He gave himself a few moments on that. "There are three with that title in the Bible—Michael, Gabriel, and Raphael."

"But here—do you know anyone with that name

here? Yes, I see it in your face. I think you do."

He topped off our glasses, which pleased me, because I liked this wine, and Mr. Zhao hadn't offered any beer. Then he reached into his jacket pocket and produced a couple of cigars.

"Do you smoke, Mr. St. Clair?"

"Cigarettes mostly. But I won't say no to a good cigar." He snipped them, gave me one, and lit both of them for us. Alice looked on, a little stupefied, while I puffed. I hadn't had such a good smoke in years, and between this cigar and the wine, I was feeling very good about our host.

"What in God's name is going on here?" she asked.

"I think Don Abruzzo is giving us—well, giving you—a lesson in patience. Some things have to be considered deeply. Do I have that right, Don Abruzzo?"

"Well spoken, Mr. St. Clair."

"Well, you could at least have the decency to offer me a cigar, too," said Alice.

"I did not mean to give any offense," he said, and he produced a third cigar, which Alice began puffing away at with great pleasure.

"So about this Archangel," she said after a few moments of companionable silence.

"If I tell you, I need to know that you will think about it carefully and not do anything to make problems for me."

"I know how to behave," she said. *Sure,* I thought.

Drinking wine and smoking cigars with strange men in Little Italy.

"You're doing me a favor, Miss Roosevelt, so I will do you one. There is a man I know. He doesn't work for me. He is not a member of my family. But we know each other. His name is Cesare. Men with serious problems hire Cesare to fix them."

"Fix them?" asked Alice.

"Kill people. This Cesare is an assassin. Do I have that right?" I asked.

"Your words, Mr. St. Clair, not mine. But some weeks ago, this Cesare, who talks too much, spoke about someone who had offered him money, a lot of money, to work for him. I didn't want to know any names. But he said it anyway. He told me the Archangel was going to pay him. I thought he was drunk, but now you say you know of a man named Archangel."

Alice's eyes lit up, and she leaned over the table. "Did he say anything else? Anything that would let us know who this Archangel is or where he comes from?"

"Are you wondering if the Van Schuylers hired Cesare?"

"I've known the Van Schuylers all my life. I hardly think they'd hire assassins."

Don Abruzzo pointed his cigar at Alice. "There were great men in Naples. And they hired men as they needed. I don't see great men in New York doing anything different. But I think I've told you all I know. If you seek out this Archangel, I wish you success. If you want to see this Cesare, I will tell you where he lives."

He stood. The meeting was over. He stepped over to the bar and wrote out the name of his nephew and the address for Cesare, which he handed to Alice.

"I thank you for your help and time, Don Abruzzo," she said with a great solemnity that seemed to impress him. Then she grinned. "And your wine and your cigar."

"My pleasure. And if your father visits, I will make him as welcome." We shook hands and then saw our way out through the restaurant and back onto the street, with everyone watching us again.

"We have something," said Alice with a hint of triumph in her voice. "We know the Archangel is a real person, not a product of Dunilsky's ravings. He connects us to the immigrants, who connect us to the anarchists."

"And don't forget that the Van Schuylers were hiring immigrants for the Great Lakes. If they wanted to stay secret, why not create a fake name to hide themselves? And who better than Preston to know we were looking into Emma Goldman?"

"I haven't forgotten that," snapped Alice. "We have no proof that the Great Erie is connected to the Van Schuylers. But very well—you are right, I suppose, about their suspicious behavior. No matter how you look at it, there's something worth investigating. And yes, we know Czolgosz was working in the Great Lakes region, where he may have met this Archangel. And that proves what I said earlier: I think we're still on the right path. There are too many connections for there to be a coincidence."

"Speaking of the Van Schuylers, Miss Alice, why didn't your boy Preston mention all the work his family is doing?"

"His uncle runs the company, not him. They're expanding their business ventures, clearly."

"I'll give you that. But where to next?"

"We have to visit Cesare."

"Yes. Let's make a nice visit to a hired killer."

"But—"

I held up my hand. "Enough. I'm too tired to argue this. Even if I was going to take you there, it's too late. And we have dinner plans."

"But I told Dulcie yesterday I'd be home for dinner."

"And I told her this morning you wouldn't. You had an interesting lunch and now you're having an interesting dinner. We're going to Mariah's."

"Really? I wanted to—but . . ."

"But what?"

"If I had known we were visiting, I would've worn something nicer."

"I think that's fine," I said.

"From an expert in ladies' clothing. But nevermind. I've wanted to meet her very much."

"And Mariah wants to meet you as well."

We got into the car and headed uptown.

"Did you mean that? When Don Abruzzo said he hoped I'd have a husband someday who would control me, and you said you hoped not?"

I gave her a glance. After what we had done that day, I had forgotten how young Alice was, but now, seeing the hint of shyness and uncertainty on her face, she didn't look a day older than her seventeen years.

"Yes. I just think it would be a shame if someone tried to snuff out that spirit of yours. Not that I'd give good odds of any man being able to do that." She smiled at that and looked a little proud of herself. Then she gave another one of her sidelong glances.

"Mr. St. Clair, how come you're not married yet?" She was a little hesitant asking that, which was unusual for her.

I shrugged. "I don't really know. I've been pretty busy. And Mariah says I'm not ready yet."

"I think you would be if you met the right woman," she said with absolute sureness.

I laughed. "You're so smart, Miss Alice. You tell me what the right woman looks like."

She looked closely at me again to make sure I wasn't teasing her. "Very well. Although you are hardworking, you need a push. You need a strong woman to give you purpose and move you along."

"Oh, I do, do I?" I said. "I thought I was doing all right."

"Just all right. You could do better. So who do you think is your ideal wife?"

"Never gave it much thought," I said. "Maybe a nice quiet girl who does what she's told."

She didn't like that. Crossed her arms and didn't saying anything for a while. I thought she was angry, but looking back on it later, she was hurt.

After a few minutes, I tried to get her to talk again. "When we were with Don Abruzzo, you called me 'the best of men.' Did you mean that?"

"That? Merely a rhetorical phrase to show you occupied a position of trust," she said, and no actress ever delivered her lines with such loftiness. I bit my lip to keep from laughing and watched her blush before putting my eyes back on the road.

"Mr. St. Clair, do we have time to stop by my bookie off of Houston?"

"Miss Alice, I believe we do."

Chapter 9

I could smell Mariah's cooking down the hall. I had a couple of bottles of beer stuck in my coat pocket, and Alice held a bouquet of flowers that she had insisted on buying for her hostess. We knocked and Mariah let us in.

The two women gave each other a quick look up and down. "Mariah, this is Miss Alice Roosevelt. Miss Alice, my sister, Mrs. Mariah Flores."

"Flowers? Aren't you sweet. Joey, be a dear and find a glass to put them in. I'm almost done in the kitchen. You two make yourselves comfortable, and I'll join you in a moment."

I set up the flowers and grabbed a couple of glasses for the beer as we stepped into the parlor and sat on the couch.

"You didn't tell me how beautiful she was," said Alice, like she was accusing me of hiding something.

"Boys were always hanging around the house, from when she was younger than you." She wore her hair loose more often than not, and with those black ringlets falling across her pretty face, she led the young men of the county on a merry dance.

"Do you think she'll like me?" asked Alice.

"Why shouldn't she?" I asked. "And since when

have you ever worried about what anyone thought about you?"

"But she's *your* sister," said Alice, as if that explained everything, and then Mariah joined us. She had shed her apron and adjusted her hair, and she sat down next to me. I poured her a glass of beer and watched while she gazed at Alice.

"You are every bit as lovely as your pictures," she said. "You're still very young, though. You'll grow into yourself in the next couple of years."

"Thank you," said Alice, a little nonplussed.

"Is Joey behaving himself?" she asked.

"Yes. Your brother—Mr. St. Clair—is being a perfect gentleman."

Mariah laughed at that, and I started getting a little nervous, seeing where this conversation was going. "He's done some growing up, then. You should've known him back in the day."

Alice gave me a sidelong glance. "Did your brother leave a trail of broken hearts?" she asked.

"More like a trail of angry fathers with shotguns," said Mariah.

"Oh, be fair," I said.

Mariah laughed, but Alice didn't join her. She just looked at me solemnly. "I would've thought you'd be a little more constant," she said.

"Well, we can't all find our true love right off the bat, like you did with Preston van Schuyler," I said.

Alice glared and Mariah said, "No gentleman

teases a lady like that. Hon, you can hit Joey if you want, and I won't blame you."

"I think I'll just ignore him," said Alice, turning away from me, and Mariah nodded in agreement.

"Come to the table. It's dinnertime."

I handed forks to Alice, who looked a little confused at first. Roosevelts don't set their own tables. But it only took a few moments for her to realize what she needed to do, and with a small look of amusement, she carefully set them on the table. Meanwhile, Mariah dished out dinner from the pots.

"It smells delicious, Mrs. Flores," she said.

"Thanks, hon. And call me Mariah."

"Then call me Alice," she said.

We sat at the table, and Alice looked curiously at the bowls.

"It's called chili con carne. It's not fancy, but Joey has liked it since he was a little boy, and he says I make the best. It's meat and beans and a whole lot of spices, and it's pretty hot, so be careful."

The chili was a little bit of back home, and Alice liked it fine, eating it eagerly and washing it down with beer.

"What a day. Chinese food, Italian wine, and now chili con carne in Yorkville."

"You need to get out more," said Mariah, and Alice met her eye and said, "Yes. Yes I do. You're a talented cook. Where did you learn?"

"Here and there, out West with Joey here, and

126

I spent some time in Texas and Louisiana. If you ever want to eat well, hon, go to New Orleans."

"I will. I want to go everywhere. Oh, but there's something I wanted to ask you. Your brother said you had been married, but it 'didn't take.' I was wondering why he didn't take."

I slammed my fork on the edge of my bowl. "Oh, for God's sake, Miss Alice!"

"What? If she doesn't want to talk about it, I'm not going to make her, but no one in society discusses marriage, so I was curious."

Mariah pursed her lips and eyed Alice. "You're something, hon. I bet you get bored easily."

"There's nothing worse than being bored." And then her mischievous smile appeared. "Except being boring."

"I'll drink to that," Mariah said, downing her beer. "But about me and Carlos Flores. I wasn't much older than you. You never know what some-one is like until you try to build your lives together, and then maybe you think you have the same plans, but you don't. That's what's important— where you're going. Think on that."

Alice nodded solemnly. "I'll think on that. Mean-while, your brother and I are hunting assassins."

"Joey told me you two were up to something. How's the detective work going?"

I started to talk, but Mariah cut me off. She wanted to hear from Alice.

"Well enough. But I can't see the 'why.' I can't

imagine why someone cares that we were looking into anarchists. Someone spent money and time to follow us and effort to keep me from finding out who they are. Why does anyone care?"

"Doesn't Joey have any ideas? He's the lawman in the family."

"Oh, he's very smart. But he's playing his cards close to his chest. He teases me and says he thinks it's the Van Schuyler family, but I think there's something else on his mind."

"Well, we all have our blind spots, hon. But have you thought about what motivates people?"

"It must be power," Alice said. "Isn't that what everyone wants? Power?"

I laughed, and Alice looked offended. "Sorry, Miss Alice. I'm not poking fun at you. Where Mariah and I come from, no one has power. No one gets power. You hope for a few extra coins so you can buy a shot of whisky after a week of backbreaking work. In Laramie, I broke up fights over two bits."

That seemed to really affect her. "I suppose my background has been a little . . . narrow," she said. "But this is good. We have money and power. What else?"

"Desire," said Mariah. "Just wanting something because you want it."

"Ooh, I like that one," said Alice. "Whatever it is, someone wants it badly, because they hired an assassin, and we're going to visit him tomorrow."

Mariah gave me a dubious look at that. I just shrugged. We were getting into dangerous territory, so I changed the subject. "Mariah, tell Miss Alice about the French Quarter." She's a good storyteller, and soon she had Alice entranced.

"You ought to visit sometime, Alice. I think you'd like it. But while you're here in New York, you two be careful, all right?"

Alice slipped her arm into mine and looked me in the eye. "I have no fear. Your brother may be silly and childish sometimes, but he's an excellent bodyguard, and you should be very proud of him. I'm pleased to have him at my side."

Mariah raised an eyebrow.

After dinner, we started to clean up, and Mariah told Alice she was a guest and should just sit in the parlor. But Alice said Roosevelts didn't just sit around, and she helped. Then she sat on the couch while Mariah made some coffee, but by the time it was ready, the girl was asleep.

"It was a busy, exciting day, and between the wine earlier and the beer tonight, it's no wonder. She's pretty young. I forget that sometimes."

Mariah gave me another one of her slight slaps. "Well don't. She's a firecracker, all right, and pretty sharp, but never forget how young she is."

"For God's sake, what kind of guy do you think I am?"

"You don't want me to answer that. Anyway, it's not you I'm worried about. It's her. She's taken a fancy to you, Joey. Young girls are jealous and possessive, and when you come from a background like that, you expect to get what you want."

"What are you talking about? She's just a kid who enjoys having her own private cowboy." Alice wasn't the only one who had had a long day, so it didn't sink in for a while.

"Yes, right. I'm talking about a cowboy and war hero who's fast on the draw, and for all her sophistication, she's very impressionable."

"You're the one who told me to follow her, to not get so fat and comfortable."

"And that's fine, but tone down the charm a bit."

"I can't help it," I said, grinning.

Mariah just rolled her eyes. "You're drunk. Have some coffee."

So I had two cups, and then I thought it was time we headed home. "Hey, Sleeping Beauty, time to get up." I touched her gently on her shoulder. Alice roused herself, looking surprised and then embarrassed.

"I am so sorry. How rude of me."

"It's been a long day," said Mariah. "And it was a compliment to my cooking. Joey always fills up and then goes to sleep, too. I really enjoyed having you over, Alice."

"And I'd like to thank you for having me over. I've wanted to meet you, and I'm glad I did."

I fetched our coats, and as Mariah watched me

strap on my Colt, she said again, "You two be careful."

"Mr. St. Clair takes good care of me," said Alice, nestling into her fur coat.

"I can believe that, Alice. And you take care of my baby brother."

We drove back to the Caledonia, and Alice, who was usually chatty, kept silent, even though she stayed wide awake in the cold. We had almost reached home when she said, "What did Mariah mean when she said I should take care of you?"

"Just big sister talk. She thinks I need looking after."

"You always seemed like a man who could take care of himself." I shrugged. "But I consider Mariah my friend now, so if she asks me to look after you, I will." She was very serious about it; there was no coy smile. And so I said thank you, and that's all we spoke that evening until we said good-night at her apartment door.

After I got into my bed, I kept turning over Mariah's words. I had always thought Alice just found me a little more entertaining than her New York friends because she had never met anyone like me before, but maybe it had gone a little beyond that. It would be something to watch out for, especially from a girl who didn't like to be thwarted.

Chapter 10

Dulcie was making griddle cakes and sausage the next morning, which I consumed with delight, along with more of her great coffee.

"When are you going to get married so I don't have to feed you?" she said.

"Why should I saddle myself with a wife if you're going to cook for me?" I replied, and that got no better reply than any other joke I made.

Alice came to get me as I was wiping my hands. She had gotten a full night's sleep and was looking as keen as a coonhound.

"Dulcie, that blueberry preserve was divine."

"Glad you liked it, Miss Alice," she said with barely more civility than I received.

"If you're ready, Mr. St. Clair, we have work to do," she said, and a moment later we were out the door and on our way to the car.

"Where are we going?"

"Don't be silly. We're going to visit Cesare and find out if he can tell us anything about the Archangel."

"You don't see any flaw in this plan? Trying to get information out of a hired killer?"

"Ah, but he's a *hired* killer. And no one has hired him to kill us. I see no reason for him to be uncivil."

"I'm so glad you see it that way."

Alice sighed theatrically. "Things were going

so well, and I thought we had reached a modus operandi. And now you're being so difficult."

"How about a compromise? We grab a few cops and they arrest this Cesare for something— anything—say, keeping a canary without a license." New York City cops didn't need much of an excuse to haul someone like Cesare down to the Tombs. "Once he's safely there, you can talk to him as long as you want."

She thought that over. "That shows some imagination. I agree."

We headed down to Little Italy again. I wanted to drive by the place to see what we were up against before we brought in the cavalry, but there was already a squad of cops out front. It was one of the darker streets in the neighborhood, and what little light there was was blocked by hanging laundry. Unlike the busy main streets, here no one stopped. Wives carried their bags quickly to their homes, looking down and not showing any curiosity. A few men in scruffy suits briefly gazed at us, but when the cops gave them some hard looks, they moved on quickly.

I parked the car and we approached one of the boys in blue.

"What's going on?" I asked.

"Who wants to know?" he snapped back.

It's not fun walking a beat in this weather, I admit. I flashed my badge. "Now who's in charge here?"

"Lieutenant Breen. He's upstairs. Some Italian

got blown away. You know what they're like, always killing each other."

Alice sighed and turned away, glancing around the street, as if the answer were out there. A beggar, seeing a rare crowd on this street, sidled up to me and Alice. It was morning, but he was already halfway drunk. Alice absently gave him a coin before one of the cops prodded him with a billy club and told him to move on.

I turned to Alice. "Stay down here with the police. I'll be back in a moment."

"You're joking, right?" she said as she pushed past me.

"Hey, who the hell is the lady?" said the cop we were talking to.

"She's the new assistant commissioner. Watch your mouth," I said, and I followed Alice up the stairs.

"This isn't going to be pretty," I said, but she ignored me. Upstairs, we saw more cops by an open door.

"Who the hell are you two?" asked the guy who was clearly the lieutenant, and I told him.

"What's the Secret Service's interest here?"

"They call it the *Secret* Service," I said. I never get tired of that, but Breen rolled his eyes.

"Who's the lady?" Alice was looking over the apartment, hoping for something interesting, but the corpse was already covered with a sheet. It was another low-end apartment badly cleaned and smelling of death and booze. There was a crucifix on the wall.

"I'm Alice Roosevelt," she said. "We were hoping to have a few words with that man, Cesare. But I guess that's not going to happen now." She seemed disappointed. "How did he die, lieutenant? And when?"

"Roosevelt, eh? The president's daughter? I knew your father back in the day, miss. Following in his footsteps?" He found that funny. "But what brings you here? The guy was as crooked as you'll find and no doubt killed by someone equally as bad."

Alice just gave him a quick smile. "I'm sure. So you don't know when he died?"

The lieutenant just looked at me, and I shrugged. "I don't know what's going on here, but he was killed probably yesterday, by a gunshot. No one saw anything; no one heard anything. No one ever does in this neighborhood. Two criminals falling out. We'll take away the body, mark it as unsolved, and that'll be the end of it."

"Surely you will investigate?" asked Alice.

The lieutenant didn't answer that; he just gave me a "better you than me" look and shook his head. "Listen, I have places to go. The men will stay here until the wagon comes to take the body away. Until then, you're welcome to stay here and enjoy yourselves."

Alice just crossed her arms and disappeared into

her thoughts for a while. "It's a hell of a coincidence," she said.

"The lieutenant is right. These people are always killing each other."

"Perhaps," she said. Then she turned to one of the cops guarding the body and waiting for the city wagon to take it away—probably to Hart Island, where everyone in the city who hasn't made other arrangements gets buried.

"How did he die?" she asked. "I know it was a gun, but can you tell how closely it happened?"

The cop shrugged. "I can't say for sure, but there were powder burns on his shirt. From the mess, I'd say it was something like a .44 caliber."

"Did you find another gun here?"

"Yeah. A revolver under the mattress. The lieutenant took it."

Alice turned to me. "So Cesare let someone get close to him. Look at the door—it's not broken down. So he opened it for someone, and it was someone he trusted, because he didn't have his gun with him."

"Could be," I said. "Where do we go from here?"

"I want to know who killed him. I want to know why he died as soon as I wanted to talk to him." She practically stamped her foot, then glared at me as I laughed. "What's so funny?"

"Your belief that this whole thing is all about you. Someone shot Cesare just to frustrate Alice Roosevelt."

Her eyes narrowed. "Someone did. And we're going to talk to the neighbors."

"Miss Alice, it's one criminal killing another. No one will admit to seeing anything. No one wants any trouble from the gangs. Which one of us is less likely to get some cooperation—a girl in a mink coat or a cowboy with a badge?"

Another sigh. And then she gave me a slow smile. "I know who might've seen something," she said. "Come on." We headed downstairs and out the building, and she looked left and right before seeing a figure shuffling along the sidewalk: the drunk who got money out of her a few minutes ago. Alice practically raced after him.

"You! Stop! I want to talk to you." He looked a little fearful, and I think he thought about running, but seeing me coming along too changed his mind.

"I didn't do anything," he said. "I moved on when they told me to."

"I know. You're not in trouble. Here—I have some more money." She produced a silver dollar in her gloved hand. The beggar reached for it, but Alice nimbly stepped away.

"First, you have to answer some questions. And I'll know if you're lying, so tell the truth. Now, you probably live around here—I doubt if you just wandered into this neighborhood. So you know a man was killed there. Did you see anything? Did anyone odd-looking go in and out of this building? I won't tell anyone you told me." The silver coin caught the sun, and the beggar couldn't take his eyes off it.

"There was a man. I don't know if he was the killer. I don't even know for sure if he visited the dead man. You see, I'm being honest with you, miss. But he was an odd one, and everyone knew you stayed away from Cesare, and if there was anything bad going on, it was with him, and I swear to God that was the truth."

"Tell me about him—this visitor," said Alice. She looked skeptical.

"He was dressed fancy—a real gent. He came at nights. I'd take a walk around at nights, 'cause there are card games in the bars, and the winners might be willing to share a few pennies with me. And so, maybe three times I saw this man get out of a carriage, a nice carriage, wearing nice clothes."

"A suit? Like mine?" I asked, opening my coat. I wanted to see if he was really thinking or just spinning a tale to earn the dollar.

He frowned. "No. Like a real gent—no offense, sir. You know what I mean: a fine coat and black jacket, like you see on Fifth Avenue." This guy had clearly given it some thought. He knew what he saw, and I wondered where he'd been in life before he started to drink.

"What did he look like? Would you recognize him again?" asked Alice.

He shook his head. "It was dark, and he tucked his face under his hat brim. But he gave me money.

Not as much as you, miss," he said, bringing the subject back to the silver dollar. "And he said something funny the last time I saw him. I said, 'Thank you, sir; you're a saint,' and he laughed in a funny way and said, 'I'm no saint. I'm an Archangel.'"

Alice's eyes got big. "Are you sure? He said, 'Archangel'?"

"Yes, miss. I know the word. From better days."

"Thank you. You've earned your dollar." She handed him the coin. His eyes lit up, but then he frowned.

"This is something bad, isn't it?"

"You might want to find another neighborhood for a while," I said, and he nodded and walked away.

Chapter 11

Alice looked like the cat who got the cream. "So we're getting closer to the Archangel. We know more about him. He's a wealthy man. A dangerous man. And if there is a conspiracy, what better suspect than a man of wealth who hides himself with a name like 'the Archangel'?"

"All right, Miss Alice. I admit this is something pretty important."

"And it shows there's an ongoing conspiracy. We could all be in danger here—my father could be in danger. Czolgosz was executed, but there are still killings related to him going on."

"I'll admit there's something there. But let's not draw conclusions too quickly; there's a lot we don't know."

But nothing would dampen her enthusiasm. "Oh, but this shows we're on the right track. Everything is connected. I bet Mr. Dunilsky, now that he's had some time to collect himself, will remember more details. No—let's give him another day. You'll be glad to hear, Mr. St. Clair, that we're done with these neighborhoods. There's nothing more for us to uncover here. But let's get the car—we're going uptown."

"Where?"

She gave me a look full of mischief. "You'll be

delighted to hear that we'll be talking with Preston van Schuyler. You can stop your teasing. I'm going to ask him about his family's business." We got into the car. "Uptown, to West Fifty-Fourth Street."

"What are you going to talk to him about?" I asked.

"As I said, the Archangel is a man of wealth. The mysterious Great Erie, considering its name, is probably connected with Great Lakes shipping—like the Van Schuylers. Men of wealth and power in this state all know each other. Meanwhile, huge numbers of immigrants are being moved upstate, including Czolgosz, who killed McKinley in Buffalo. There's money at work here, Mr. St. Clair—big money."

This was taking us to a different place, with people you had to speak with very carefully and couldn't just drag downtown for questioning. It some ways, this was going to be even more dangerous. Not that I could scare off Alice.

"So is West Fifty-Fourth where the Van Schuylers live?"

"Oh, they're somewhere up there. But Preston spends most of his time at the University Club. It's a splendid new building, and that's where we're going."

"So what kind of club is this? I mean, what do people do there?"

"It's one of the finest clubs in New York, where some of the best people go. They drink, they dine, and I think there's a gymnasium there."

"Do you belong?" I asked.

"Oh, no. Women can't belong. Men only. Rather unsporting of them, I think, although we can visit."

"We're far more broad-minded in Wyoming," I said. "We gave women the vote years ago, and the Laramie Friendship Society admits everyone."

"The 'Laramie Friendship Society'—it was a local club?" She got that suspicious look.

"Oh, yes. Day and resident visitors, men and women, and a bar that the manageress was proud to say made up for in quantity what it lacked in quality."

Alice just stared at me for a while before speaking. "It was a bordello, wasn't it? You're appalling, Mr. St. Clair. But someday you and I will visit Laramie. I'm very curious."

"Happy to be your tour guide, Miss Alice. But for now, I don't think that the University Club is going to be as entertaining as the Laramie Friendship Society."

"I'm sure you're right," she said.

The West Fifties were only a few miles from where we had spent the last few days in lower Manhattan, but it might as well have been another country: men in fine suits, motorcars with chauffeurs, well-polished carriages, and ladies in their furs. On the Lower East Side, I stood out as a little different. But here, I felt everyone's eyes were on me. As I parked, one of the chauffeurs gave me a look, and I like to think he was a little jealous that I didn't have to wear my Sunday best.

With Alice, I had been in some of the best places in the city, but nothing was as fine as the lobby of that club, from the polished wood floor to the chandeliers to the heavy curtains around the windows. Alice took it all in with a little amusement, and as if she could read my mind, she said, "I agree, Mr. St. Clair. Whoever is running this place did a very thorough job of reaching into the pockets of the very best people in this town."

A porter stepped over to us.

"My name is Alice Roosevelt. I'm looking for one of your members, Preston van Schuyler."

"Of course, Miss Roosevelt." He practically bowed. Then he took in my coat, suit, and side-arm. He didn't like any of it. "Please wait here one moment. I will see if Mr. Van Schuyler is in residence."

He left us cooling our heels in the entranceway while he consulted a book in a little alcove. I watched him frown. And then he came back.

"I beg your pardon, but although Mr. Van Schuyler is in residence, he has left word that he does not want to be disturbed. You may leave a message, if you wish, and it will be delivered to him later."

"I am sure he will see me. If you tell me where we may likely find him this time of day . . ."

"I'm afraid club rules preclude that," he said.

"You can't be serious," she said. Alice crossed

her arms across her chest. "You can't really mean to keep me out of here, can you?"

The porter was not happy. "Please understand, miss. I am an employee of the club and must follow the rules of the club secretary and the board."

"We'll see about that," she said, turning on her heels. I gave the porter a look of sympathy and fancied I got one in return. I followed Alice out the door and back onto the sidewalk.

She peered up at the building, which now seemed as forbidding as a castle.

"Preston is avoiding us," said Alice. "I cornered him at the party the other night, and now he's embarrassed. Or worried. Or angry. Perhaps our activities got back to him and he doesn't want to be blamed by his uncle for our curiosity about the family company." She grinned.

"I don't know if you can draw those conclusions. He may just want to be left alone. Maybe he's busy."

Alice gave me a pitying look. "I doubt if he's doing any real work. He's not the type. And he's the most sociable of men. Also, I know in clubs like this you have to go out of your way to stop visitors. He wants to avoid me."

She frowned and continued to look up at the building. "Let me think . . . there must be a service entrance around the back. Come."

Alice took off along the block and I followed. We

saw a small alley just wide enough for deliveries, and by an unmarked door a couple of kitchen workers were braving the cold to smoke.

"So this opens to the kitchen." She gave me a sly look, and I was quickly on my guard. "Kitchen staff aren't used to working with members of New York society the way club porters are."

"Miss Alice—" But I was too late. She took off down the alley, and I scrambled to follow her. She brushed by the workers, and soon we found ourselves in the University Club kitchen. Maybe she thought we could just slip through the kitchen and up the back stairs, but it wasn't to be. A chef stopped us, and I guess those who work in kitchens have bad tempers as a rule, because he looked as angry as Dulcie did when I was in her kitchen, and like Dulcie, he had a big knife in his hand.

"Who are you? This is my kitchen. No visitors. Now out, or I'll call the police!"

"Don't you talk that way to me," said Alice. "We're from the city Health Department."

"What?" said the chef.

I figured I might as well be hung for a sheep as a lamb. I pulled out my badge. "Inspector Dawson. This is my secretary, Miss Allendale. We have to look at all facilities in this club."

The poor man was too stunned to speak. Alice and I walked around the kitchen as the kitchen workers looked at us curiously. We pretended to know what we were doing. The smells were pretty good, and I hoped to eat there someday, though it was unlikely I ever would.

"It looks good enough, I suppose. But we do have to discuss our preliminary findings with the club secretary. The stairs are this way? Thank you." And before the chef could say anything, we were up the back stairs. We were barely out of earshot when Alice started laughing.

"Mr. St. Clair—you were brilliant. I didn't think you had it in you. Nicely done!" She gave my arm a squeeze.

"Well, what could I do, with you starting like that? For God's sake, Miss Alice."

"Oh, don't pretend you didn't find that fun." And I shut up, because she was right, and I didn't want to admit it.

At the top of the stairs was a door. Alice opened it slightly and took a look, then opened it a little farther and motioned for me to follow. We found ourselves in a little hallway. We closed the door behind us, and a few steps took us into the main corridor. A few gentlemen looked at us a little oddly, but Alice was well dressed and walked like she knew where she was going, so no one questioned us.

We passed by a waiter, and Alice stopped him. "Excuse me, we seem to have gotten lost. Do you know Mr. Van Schuyler? We're trying to find him."

"Oh, ah, yes, miss. He's usually in the reading

room during the day, just down that way and then a left. But miss—"

"Thank you!" she said with a wave of her hand, and we were off.

We headed down the hall, and I looked around. Whoever had decorated the place hadn't stopped at the lobby but kept it up through the hallways and into the reading room. It was furnished with tall leather chairs that were probably more comfortable than my bed, plenty of leather-bound books, pretty much every newspaper in New York, and illustrated magazines. A cheery fire completed the picture.

We found Preston writing at a small desk. He never heard us coming, as the carpet was thick enough to muffle an approaching bull elephant.

"Are we interrupting, Preston?" Alice asked when she was practically on top of him.

"Oh! Alice! But how . . . what are you doing here?"

"How did I get in here? Oh, you know me better than that. Why were you trying to avoid me? The porter downstairs said you were not to be disturbed by anyone."

He sighed. "Alice, I'm sorry. It's just that . . ." he struggled to find the words.

"It came out you helped me find Emma Goldman, and it's caused you some difficulties?"

"Something like that," he said a little sheepishly.

"Anyway, we're not interrupting anything important, are we?"

"Just a few things . . ." He gestured to the papers. "Family business. My uncle gives me bits and pieces, and you have no idea how dull it is. I've been out of school over a year now working on our operations in Buffalo, but it's getting rather tedious. Anyway, the family's been talking about sending me on a grand tour."

"Well, I think you deserve it as a belated present for your degree from the second-best school in the country." More Harvard–Yale rivalry.

Preston glanced at me quickly. "So how can I be of service? Is this just a friendly visit? Or do you need more introductions to anarchists?" He forced a smile at the last one.

"Actually, you can help us," she said. "Is there a place we can talk?"

"Yes, there is. Technically, nonmembers are not allowed in this room, but I'd be happy to give you a drink at the bar, if it's not too early for you. A glass of sweet sherry, perhaps?" Alice wrinkled her nose. A brandy and soda was more in her line, but it wasn't something a young lady could order in the guest bar of the University Club.

"Mr. St. Clair, you look like a scotch whisky man."

"If you're buying, Mr. Van Schuyler, I'll take a bourbon."

"Bourbon? Never developed a taste for it myself, but to each his own." He led us down the hall, and my boots seemed to thunder on the heavily polished

148

wood. Preston linked his arm with Alice's, and I followed closely behind.

"You said at the party you spend a lot of time here," she said. "That's why I looked for you here rather than your uncle's place."

"I wasn't entirely honest with you, I'm afraid. I actually spend all my time here. I have a room here, when I'm in town, rather than at home."

"Not your uncle's townhouse?"

I heard the hesitation in his voice. "It's just a little more congenial here. Other young men to socialize with and all that."

The bar wasn't too crowded, and in short order, a waiter in a white jacket took our orders and returned with drinks.

"So did you meet with Emma Goldman? Mrs. Cowles would hand my head to me if she knew I helped you two," he said.

"Yes, but it was hardly dangerous. She's exceedingly unpleasant, however. Do you know, even many of the other anarchists don't like her? Imagine that, being so unpopular even anarchists won't have you. But we've had a couple of lively days, haven't we, Mr. St. Clair?"

" 'Lively' is as good a word as any," I said.

"And she was just the first person we spoke with. We've met lots of immigrants and learned something about your family, Preston. Apparently, you Van Schuylers have been hiring a great many workers for your Great Lakes facilities in recent months. I'm rather curious about that."

"Are you?" he asked. He drank more scotch to give himself time to think. "How does this fit in with your investigations into anarchists?"

"We found out that your family has been hiring huge numbers of immigrants for its facilities upstate. And that Leon Czolgosz worked upstate. I'll just bet he worked for your family's company. You're the biggest employer upstate, I'm sure. Also, we ran into a cousin of his, a man named Dunilsky, who was almost driven to insanity by a feeling he was being persecuted—because of something Czolgosz heard or saw, something that may have happened in your neck of the woods."

Preston closed his eyes and looked pained for a moment.

"Alice. Be reasonable. Do you know how many people my family employs, both permanent staff and casual laborers? We didn't even know we employed Czolgosz until after it all happened— imagine the embarrassment to my family if this got out. And to yours, too. I've been a guest at your home. The papers would make something out of that."

"You must know something. Even if you're not running the show, it can't have escaped your notice that Van Schuyler shipping agents have been hiring immigrant laborers en masse for projects upstate. I want to know why."

"Why do you want to know?"

"Let's just say that some person—or people—with a strong connection to the Great Lakes has been very curious about my interest in Emma Goldman and the anarchists. Your family is heavily involved in the Great Lakes. McKinley was killed in Buffalo by an anarchist. Czolgosz was an anarchist and an employee of yours. Lots of connections, Preston. I'm by no means suggesting that the Van Schuylers are guilty of anything, but I need to know what your family knows. Why all the new employees?"

Having delivered her speech, Alice just leaned back and glared at Preston. He sighed and turned to me.

"This must be very boring for you, Mr. St. Clair. I'm sure I could get them to give you some beer and food in the staff dining room."

"I love learning new things," I said. "Don't mind me." Alice patted my hand.

"Very well, then. A little background. Do you know how trade works on the Great Lakes? The traffic goes both ways: food from the west and supplies back on the return trip."

Even I knew that. I had driven enough cattle over the years and knew how cows raised on the range ended up as roasts in New York kitchens.

"So what you're really saying is that there's a lot of money to be made in trade," said Alice. "And your family wants to make more of it."

He sighed again, and I rarely saw anyone look as

unhappy as Preston did at that moment. "Alice, my uncle doesn't want to make more of it. He wants to make all of it. He's been trying to create a monopoly on the Great Lakes. That's why he was bringing so many workers up there, to offer more services and more facilities. To put everyone else out of business, or at least under his thumb." He finished his drink and waved to the waiter for another. Alice just stared at him as he took some more Dutch courage.

"My father would hate that. You know how he feels about fair business dealings. He's talked about it enough. Preston—how could you let this happen? How could you?"

Now, almost any man can take it if his woman is angry at him. But when she's disappointed in him—that's the worst. So my heart went out to him. I didn't like the man, but he was obviously out of his depth here.

"Miss Alice, be fair. He wasn't running this. And he's come clean. Mostly," I said.

Preston gave me a look of absolute gratitude, but Alice, as I knew she would, jumped at the last part.

"What do you mean 'mostly'?"

Where I came from, fights over "monopolies" turned into range wars. Preston took my meaning.

"Things may have gotten . . . a little rough. My cousin, Shaw Brantley, who helps run the company, doesn't have a lot of restraint. But that's just the impression I got. I can't say for sure, I swear." He pleaded with his eyes.

Alice pursed her lips. She was already moving to the next step. "Have you heard of the Great Erie & Albany Boat Company?"

Preston nodded slowly. "Yes. I believe it's a name for a sort of partnership of some of our rivals. They've been quietly banding together to fight us because we've gotten so big."

"Can you give me more details? What exactly is your family up to?"

"Tell me why, again, you want to know this?"

Alice leaned back and crossed her arms. She gestured to me with a toss of her head. "That one does it, too—answers questions with questions. It's very irritating. And we're off the subject. I'm not accusing you of anything. But it seems the Great Erie, in addition to causing trouble for your company, was also paying to have me followed. And I want to know why. The more we ask, the more questions we find. It's just getting messier."

To say nothing of the connection to McKinley's assassination—something I was still hoping might be coincidence.

He sighed. "A fair question. Well, let's start with something you may not know: my Uncle Henry was with McKinley when he was shot. I mean, he was part of the crowd behind the president, but most of the worthies in Buffalo were there, so that's not unusual. I don't want you to think I'm hiding anything, but obviously no one wants to be associated with something like that."

"I can understand that," said Alice. "Anything else?"

He seemed to be ordering his thoughts. "I don't have a great deal to do with the company, you have to understand. It's really my uncle's firm. Well, Father ran it with him when he was alive. I don't do much—I mean, they have me meet people, shake hands, and all that to represent the firm—but day by day it's really Shaw who runs it, like I said. He's married to my cousin Julia—Uncle Henry's daughter. He's Uncle's right-hand man. I knew he was making plans to expand, but that was all."

He seemed apologetic, embarrassed, and afraid all at once. Alice put a hand on his arm.

"But you're the nephew. You're a blood relation, not Mr. Brantley."

Preston seemed grateful for her soft-spoken understanding. "Thank you, Alice. But Shaw is a good ten years older than I am and has been in the business for years, making his mark while I was still a schoolboy. I don't care, really. It's not like I want to run the business."

"What do you want to do?" asked Alice.

"See a bit of the world, I think. Maybe take my inheritance and start something fresh somewhere, maybe in South America or Africa."

"That sounds delightful, and I'm sure it will do you a world of good. But right now we have to figure out what's going on up by the Great Lakes. Could you arrange for me to meet your family? I don't think I've seen your uncle since I was a little girl. Surely it's time for a dinner invitation."

Preston sighed and shook his head. "Alice—they're a little . . . they're not a social bunch. My uncle has become rather moody since my aunt died some years back. They hardly entertain anymore. Just business acquaintances."

"For heaven's sake, our families have known each other for years. It's time we reconnected. Do something. I'm the president's daughter. Out of sheer curiosity, they should want to accept an invitation to meet. And it's rude not to after we've played host to you at Sagamore Hill. Arrange it."

Preston nodded. "I shouldn't have avoided you. If you're going to be looking into this, I should be part of it, too."

Alice stood, and so did he. "Thank you, Preston. We'll talk about this again later. You're doing the right thing. By the way"—and she spared a glance for me—"did you tell anyone else that we got your help in finding Emma Goldman's address so we could visit her?"

He looked embarrassed at that, and I figured that was one of the reasons he was nervous about seeing Alice again.

"I might've let a few people know . . . I called my uncle that night to tell him I had done you a favor, thinking he'd be pleased I was obliging a powerful family like yours, but when he found out exactly what I did . . . he thought it was ridiculous and was furious at me."

So once Uncle Henry knew, there was no telling who set the private detectives onto us.

"Quite all right. It just helps us . . . understand a little more."

He smiled a little shyly at her. She presented her cheek for him to kiss. Then I shook his hand, a little too hard again, and thanked him for the bourbon.

"Oh, just one more thing," asked Alice. "Does the term 'Archangel' mean anything to you?"

He shook his head. "No—not outside of the Bible. Why do you ask?"

"Just a name someone threw out—a nickname, actually, nothing important."

We made our way out of the club and back onto the street. Alice just stood on the steps, frowning, her breath making little clouds.

"I feel rather sorry for him," she said, sounding almost maternal.

"For his birthday, you can buy him a spine," I said.

"Oh, I know you don't really mean that. You were sympathetic. You know what he went through. Not everyone grew up with the advantages you did."

I looked at her closely but couldn't find even a trace of humor in what she said. "Have you gone mad? He was born into a wealthy family, raised by nannies, sent to the best schools—everything handed to him. And I've worked every damn day of my life since I was fifteen. You think *I* was the one with the advantages?"

And Alice just shook her head, amazed at my

stupidity. "But of course, Mr. St. Clair. You had a life that built your character. You were very fortunate. Of course, you don't have to be poor—my father grew up with a strong character despite having financial advantages. But we shouldn't blame Preston because of his poor upbringing."

"Yes. Well, if I had my choice, I'd have been happy to build my character on Fifth Avenue and not on the Great Plains."

She just waved her hand to indicate the conversation had become boring and was now over. "Enough. We have things to do. I have more questions for Mr. Dunilsky now that we've spoken with Preston. I bet he knows more about Czolgosz and what happened with the Van Schuylers than he realized, and I'm guessing he's in a more receptive frame of mind to talk. And I would like another knish—we'll pick some up on our way downtown."

I have to admit the knish was pretty good. Alice wanted a beer too, but I told her we needed clear heads, and she'd already had a sherry, and I didn't care if she hadn't finished it. Alice made a token resistance, but in the end she seemed happy enough with a Coke.

"That was fun, sneaking into the club like that," she said, still glowing from the memory of it.

"Yes. But let's not do that too often."

"Only when we must," she said with a little smirk. "But you thought on your feet. Where did you get the name 'Dawson'?"

"My mother's maiden name."

"Ah. And how did I come to be Miss Allendale?"

"The schoolmistress in Laramie when I was a deputy. Suzanne Allendale."

Maybe it was something in my voice or a look in my eye.

"A friend of yours?" she asked.

I grinned. "You could say that," I said, and Alice blushed and then looked annoyed.

"Why did you give me her name? Was she like me?"

"Yeah, she never did what she was told to do either," I said.

"You're quite a wit, Mr. St. Clair."

Well fortified, we made our way to the Tombs and presented ourselves to the sergeant on duty, who was eating roast beef and mustard.

"We're here to visit Stanislaw Dunilsky."

The officer shrugged. "Sorry, you're too late. He offed himself early this morning. Or late last night. I don't have the paperwork yet." He went back to the roast beef and mustard.

"He killed himself? How? Wasn't anyone watching him?"

"Lady, I just said, I don't have the paperwork. Can you come back later?"

That was the wrong thing to say to Alice. She grabbed his lunch from him. "I need your full attention when I speak with you. Mr. Dunilsky was an important witness. I was counting on speaking with him today. And when I find out whose incompetence led to his death, it's going to be the worst day in that miserable bastard's life. Now find out what happened. Or get Captain O'Hara down here."

It astonished him. Heck, I knew Alice and it astonished me. After the initial shock, I felt bad. We should've seen it coming. Meanwhile, the sergeant had flagged down a passing officer, who led us to O'Hara's office. Alice didn't even knock but pushed past the officer and entered directly. "You're dismissed," she said to the officer and took a seat without being asked. I closed the door behind me and sat down, too.

O'Hara sighed, poured himself a whisky, and said, "I can guess why you're here. I'm sorry. We gave him his own cell, one of the nicer upstairs ones. He seemed exhausted but not especially upset. He tore up the mattress and hanged himself from the window bars. I wouldn't have thought it of him, but you never know. Again, I'm really sorry."

"You seem sure it was a suicide," said Alice.

O'Hara's eyes narrowed. "Well, what else would it be? You think someone killed him? He was alone in there." Alice just glared until O'Hara got the meaning. "For God's sake, Miss Roosevelt, you think one of us killed him? We don't work that way. And even if we did, why would we want to kill some drunk?"

"He wasn't 'some drunk.' He was a witness

159

to some important events, and it may be very convenient for some if he's dead. And don't pretend I don't know what goes on here. My father found this place a cesspool and had to do a lot of cleaning up when he became commissioner, and it's a pity he was called to higher things before he finished the job." She held up a hand to stop O'Hara's protests. "I don't have time to discuss this. Now I want to see his cell."

"There's nothing to see," said O'Hara. "Strips of mattress fabric tied to the bars and turned into a makeshift noose. He stood on the bed frame, and that was that. It's all been cleaned out now anyway. Probably another prisoner in there by now."

"How convenient," said Alice. Now that started to make O'Hara angry.

"Now look here, miss: I understand you're upset, but there's no need—" he cut himself off and appealed to me. "Mr. St. Clair, you're older and you've been around. Please explain the facts of life to your charge here."

"The problem isn't that she doesn't understand them. The problem is that she does," I said. O'Hara just dismissed me with a shake of his head, but Alice looked at me and smiled.

"Thank you, Mr. St. Clair. I did not expect such a philosophical observation from you." She turned back to O'Hara. "Very well, there is nothing to see. Who had access to him?"

"Access? The guard on duty looks in on everyone

160

on his hallway every hour. Food is slipped through a slot. And that's it, really. Oh, and some shyster."

"What?" asked Alice, and that caught my attention, too.

"A shyster. You know, a lawyer. I didn't see him myself, but apparently he was pretty sharp looking. I wouldn't have thought Dunilsky would have someone that good, but you said he wasn't a normal prisoner."

"His name. Did you get a name for this lawyer?"

"Now that's something I can help you with. After his body was found, I pulled the duty log." He shuffled through some papers on his desk. "Late last night, he was visited by some uptown-looking lawyer. Everyone has to sign in. Here we go . . . 'Conrad Urquhart, Esq., of Henshaw, Urquhart and Paulson, attorneys-at-law.' I even have his address if you want it. Not one of the usual crew down here."

"Does the log say how long he was there?"

"I see where you're going with this, and you're wrong. The guard said he was a well-dressed older man, not someone who could forcibly kill a young man like Dunilsky. And anyway, Dunilsky was definitely alive when the guard saw Urquhart out of the cell, and even during the next check. That's for certain. Again, I'm sorry about this, but things happen sometimes. Who knows what was going through his mind?"

"I guess we'll never know," said Alice with a real edge to her voice. "But meanwhile, did it ever occur to you to wonder why an uptown lawyer like this Mr. Urquhart was visiting some drunk workman here?"

But I knew what Captain O'Hara would say before Alice was even done asking the question, and I bet she did, too. As we had already learned, wise men don't ask questions they don't need answers to.

There wasn't much else to say after that, so Alice and I took a quick leave. O'Hara looked relieved and gave me a look of sympathy that was becoming more common.

"What do you think?" I asked when we found ourselves outside. Even in the cold, I was glad to be rid of the stench of that place, which came through even in the offices of police captains.

"That lawyer had something to do with this."

"He didn't kill him."

"Maybe not. But were there threats? Bribes? Did he frighten him so badly he thought there was nothing for it but killing himself? Or maybe . . . I'm being judgmental. Maybe he was really looking out for Mr. Dunilsky, and then someone else killed him before he could talk more." I could see what was coming. "But we won't know unless we ask. Start up the motorcar. There's still time to visit Mr. Urquhart today."

At least his office wouldn't stink, no one would be shooting at us, and there was a chance of a hot cup of coffee.

Chapter 12

As it turned out, I was right on all counts. The offices were about as fine as you could expect from a top law firm, and they had probably bought their carpets and furniture from the same place the University Club did. And why not? I'm sure the partners here were all members as well.

A uniformed office boy ushered us into a handsome reception area presided over by a serious-looking young clerk behind a desk that wouldn't have even fit in my apartment. He stood as we entered.

"Good afternoon. I'm Alice Roosevelt, and this is my"—I saw some amusement in her eyes—"factotum, Mr. St. Clair. I don't have an appointment, but I was hoping to see Mr. Urquhart on urgent business."

"Roosevelt you said? Very well. Please have a seat and I'll see if he's available." The office boy was still standing there, and the clerk sent him out for coffee as we sat on some very comfortable chairs. The coffee was at least as good as the blend Dulcie served, and there was cream, too, so I was in no rush to see Mr. Urquhart.

But it wasn't too long before the clerk showed us into a large, beautiful room with lots of wood and leather and plenty of heat. Mr. Urquhart stood, and he looked every inch the part, from the handsome suit to the silver hair to the manicured hands that waved us in.

"Please have a seat, Miss Roosevelt, and Mr. St. Clair. My clerk said you were Miss Roosevelt's 'factotum'?" He smiled. "Is that the official title of Secret Service agents on family duty?"

"It is for me," I said, and he laughed.

"Very well. I'd invite you to wait outside and enjoy more coffee, but I imagine the rules of your job require you to stay in Miss Roosevelt's presence. Now, Miss Roosevelt, how can my firm be of service to the president's daughter?"

"I was hoping you could help me with a friend of mine who was your client, a Stanislaw Dunilsky. Did you know he died just a few hours after you visited him last night? I wanted to make sure you knew. Were you aware of the peculiar circumstances of his last months?"

I'll give it to Urquhart. The whole thing was probably the nastiest surprise of his life, from the death of his client to the fact that Alice Roosevelt was in his office questioning him about it. And yet he remained remarkably unruffled, although we could see the lines of tension in his forehead.

After a few moments, he said, "Before I continue, may I ask what your interest is in regard to Mr. Dunilsky?"

"Is answering a question with a question the new conversational fashion? I don't much care for it. Let's just say I had a personal interest in Mr. Dunilsky's well-being, and I imagine you and I share that. You were his attorney, it seems. And I wonder how a man who could barely feed himself and pay his rent could afford your services."

He leaned back and steepled his fingers. You could tell he was thinking about what he could say, how much he *could* admit, and how much he *had* to admit.

"How fascinating, Miss Roosevelt. I can't begin to guess how you came by this information. But yes, I represented—briefly represented—Mr. Dunilsky. I had not known he was dead. Since you have the advantage of me in terms of information, could you share with me the cause of his death?"

"It appears to be a suicide."

"He seemed to be despondent, but I wouldn't have thought . . . but I am sorry. I suppose that concludes my business with him."

"But not with me," said Alice. "I was a friend of his. Maybe his only one, I thought. But someone was paying your fees, and I doubt if he had a dime to his name."

He smiled benevolently. "You're a bright young lady, but that's no more than I'd expect from the daughter of such a distinguished family, whose father is one of our greatest men. So you must know that I cannot give you the information you seek. It's confidential, even after the death of my client."

That seemed to end the conversation. I didn't

think that the filing cabinet trick she pulled at the private investigator's office was going to work here.

"Of course," she said, matching him smile for smile. "But can you tell me anything about the Great Erie & Albany Boat Company?"

That hit Urquhart again—and he made a mistake. "Where did you hear the name of that company?"

Alice decided not to answer him and turned to me instead. "Now that's interesting, Mr. St. Clair. He doesn't deny knowing about it; he just wonders where we got the name."

"I didn't say I knew the name. I simply wondered at the context," he said, a trifle annoyed. "I don't want to be rude, Miss Roosevelt, but I don't really see where this is going. If you have some actual business to discuss, let me know; otherwise, I don't think we have much to review."

"Very well. Mr. St. Clair and I found ourselves followed by a private investigator who, after some persuasion, admitted he had been hired by the Great Erie & Albany Boat Company. It seems to be an invisible company. And then our searches led to Mr. Dunilsky, who was the cousin of the infamous Leon Czolgosz, who worked on the Great Lakes. It all seems a bit much to be coincidence."

"I see. You've made a cogent case for your queries, Miss Roosevelt, and I am sorry that you were disturbed by a private investigator. But I can neither confirm nor deny that I have a client by the name of Great Erie or that they had any hand in following you. And in answer to what I'm sure will be your next question, any conversation I had with Mr. Dunilsky is also confidential. Now if that is all . . ." He started to stand, and Alice and I followed suit.

"Oh, very well," she said with a sweet smile that didn't fool me for a minute. I didn't know what was coming, but I did know this wasn't the end of it. "Mr. St. Clair, do you remember when that rather slovenly reporter from the *New York Herald* accosted me on the street last month?" I did, and I had sent him away with a flea in his ear. "Well, I bet the *Herald* would love a story about an uptown lawyer visiting the now-dead cousin of a political assassin and how it fits in with a private investigator following the president's daughter. Let's drive there right now." And with that, she started to leave.

The *Herald* was probably the most sensationalist newspaper in New York. An exclusive interview with Miss Alice Roosevelt in connection with McKinley's death and an uptown law firm? It would be the biggest story of the year. I didn't know what Mr. Roosevelt would say if Alice did something like that, but I knew Mrs. Cowles's wrath would be a sight to behold if Alice gave an interview to a paper like that all on her own.

"Miss Roosevelt, you can't be serious." Urquhart's face was filled with horror, and Alice pivoted back quickly.

"I swear that if you don't help me right now, I will

tell everything I know to the *Herald*. They'll want to take a photograph too, no doubt. Heaven knows what you'll be telling them when their reporters show up on your doorstep. Good day, sir." She only took three more steps before Mr. Urquhart stopped her.

"All right, Miss Roosevelt. You made your point. Please—sit down." We resumed our seats, and I never saw anyone look as pleased with herself as Alice did at that moment. Weeks later, I still got sick at the prospect of sitting in the *Herald* offices watching Alice tell all to those cigar-chewing hacks.

"I can give you some information," said Urquhart, "in exchange for your word that you will not go to the papers."

She just folded her arms. "Very well. Now start talking."

He sighed. "Yes, I represent the Great Erie & Albany Boat Company. I act as its secretary. You are correct that, in a sense, it is an invisible company. It has no real assets. It is merely a convenient name for a consortium of Great Lakes shipping companies with a common goal. I cannot tell you anything about its membership—I would be disbarred. But there are some very sensitive business negotiations going on, and someone at the Great Erie told me you had been thinking for some time about Emma Goldman. It was feared that your questions would lead to Czolgosz, whom Goldman had spoken to, and thus to Buffalo. We didn't want the president's daughter looking into the Great Lakes shipping industry right now. We didn't want the attention." He held up his hand. "It's not that there's anything illegal going on, but it's sensitive, and we were concerned."

Alice nodded. "That makes some sense. But back to how we found you. Why were you visiting Mr. Dunilsky in the jail?"

"The same reason. We've been watching him, worried about what he might say regarding Czolgosz and if he had discussed anything he knew about what was going on upstate."

"Does the name 'Archangel' mean anything to you?"

He laughed and seemed genuinely surprised. "I know what an archangel is, but as a name? No. Why do you ask?"

"I also have my secrets. You've answered my questions, but I still don't know how any of this connects with Czolgosz's assassination of McKinley."

Urquhart shook his head. "It doesn't. It's all a horrible coincidence. But not that surprising. Buffalo is an important city—that's why there is so much business there and likely why Czolgosz was working there. It's why the Pan-American Exposition was held there—which is why the president came. Miss Roosevelt, you just walked into a business deal, and an unfortunate sidebar is that it shed light on some deals businessmen want to remain private for now. That's all. If your interest, along with that of the Secret Service, is in Czolgosz and the assassination, I wish you success. I'm glad we had this talk—it shows we're seeking different things and that I was wrong to have had you followed. I apologize."

There was silence for a few moments, and then Alice slowly nodded. "Thank you for being so frank. I appreciate it. I will keep my word and will refrain from talking to the press. Now, I know how busy you are, and I won't keep you any longer." She briefly held out her hand to Urquhart, and now all smiles, he showed us out the door.

Everything seemed settled, but Alice was as taut as a bowstring. She wrapped herself in her furs, and neither of us said a word until we were in the car.

"Home?" I said.

"Bastard," she said. "No, not you. Him, Urquhart. Liar. All the political meetings I've listened to, men lying so much and so often they even lose track of the difference between lies and the truth. What does he do? Prepares wills and trusts for old families over old scotch. He has no head for political maneuvering. Dear God, did he really think he'd get something by a Roosevelt?"

"Even a seventeen-year-old Roosevelt?" I asked.

That amused her. "Yes, even a seventeen-year-old Roosevelt. All you have to do is be quiet and pay attention and you learn. Urquhart is an imbecile.

He said someone told him I'd been interested in Emma Goldman for some time. But our interest began that same day. Whoever is holding Urquhart's leash told him to get someone on us right away. He talked too much. When you're lying, keep it simple. He shouldn't have assumed I had been interested in Goldman for a long time. So why is he lying? Or is his master lying? Who is really behind the Great Erie? Who's giving him his orders? If he's lying about that, he's probably lying about why he visited Dunilsky. Did he show up to just to find out what Dunilsky knew—before arranging for him to be killed?"

"You know, Miss Alice, I agree with all that. But we're still left with the question of who really put the private investigator on us. Yes, I know someone could've overheard, but our best bet is still Preston."

"Someone was lying somewhere. Starting with that lawyer. I can't tell whose side everyone is on. We only have Preston's word that the Great Erie is his family's opponent."

"Preston's lying? I thought we were assuming he was on our side."

"Don't be funny. Of course he is. But he could've been lied to himself. We don't even know if there's a family schism—maybe they're fighting each other. Or maybe we're all completely wrong about who the Great Erie is. Preston doesn't know what's going on. All I know for sure is that it's time to meet that family. That's the only way we're going to find out what's really going on here. Meanwhile, this wasn't a wasted trip—we know a very expensive and well-connected man like Urquhart is involved and needs to lie about it, and that tells us that we're right about Dunilsky being involved."

"Sounds reasonable to me. But there's something else we know, Miss Alice. I'd stake my monthly salary that Urquhart had no idea who the Archangel was. I don't think that surprise was made up."

"I agree. And that's what's first on our agenda tomorrow morning. We're going to track down the Archangel. Dunilsky and Cesare: people we want to speak with keep dying. Is the Archangel the one killing them? We keep running into more and more angles, lies, and plots the more we look into this. And I'm wondering . . ." She let her voice drift away as if she was afraid of what she was going to say. "I'm wondering if someone isn't done with the assassinations . . . if Czolgosz wasn't the end but the beginning."

The thought had crossed my mind too.

Chapter 13

Alice said we were going to have a busy day the next day, so I needed to be upstairs early. I began to wonder if I was overstaying my welcome in Dulcie's kitchen, but she gave me a funny look when I walked in—almost sly.

"Looks like you've been promoted, Mr. St. Clair. The maid was told to set a place for you in the breakfast room." For the first time, I saw a look of genuine amusement on her face.

The breakfast room was a small, informal room off the kitchen where the family usually ate. Most days that meant Mrs. Cowles and Alice, but it had never meant me. Wondering if Dulcie was just setting me up, I carefully stuck my head into the room, and Alice was drinking coffee and reading the paper. There was a pile of waffles on the table, along with bacon and a jar of what was no doubt real maple syrup, the best thing ever to come out of New England.

Alice put down the *Tribune*. "Good morning, Mr. St. Clair. It seemed silly for you to get under Dulcie's feet, especially when there's so much for us to discuss. Now, here we have the image that we got from Mr. Dunilsky—the Archangel." She produced the paper we had taken from his rooms. "As I noted yesterday, it's been very unfortunate that our two greatest leads are dead by violence—that is, Dunilsky and Cesare, the assassin. But we still have the Archangel. Now, this was printed somewhere. If we can find the printer, maybe we can find the Archangel."

"But what if this was printed in Buffalo? Isn't that where Czolgosz met the Archangel anyway?"

Alice gave me a superior smile. "It's a sunny day. Take the page and hold it up to the light by the window." I reluctantly left the hot waffles and did as Alice asked.

"There's a pattern behind the image." I have a good eye and was able to make it out: a row of buildings and, underneath, the words "New York City Paper Company, Broadway."

"It's called a watermark. Father pointed them out to me when I was a child. It says where the paper was made. And this paper was made in New York City. I bet a New York City printer used New York City paper. Now, here is the *Tribune*, a good Republican newspaper. I telephoned the printing office last night, and it seems that all the printers, at least the good commercial ones, know each other. They gave me a list." She produced another piece of paper, covered with her elegant writing. "We're going to visit them and find out where this illustration came from."

It seemed like pretty tame stuff after what we had been doing, so even if it seemed a little boring, I was fine with it.

"Very clever, Miss Alice. The motorcar is all ready, so just one more waffle, and we're ready to go."

"Yes, they are divine, aren't they?" At that point, Mrs. Cowles entered the room and raised an eyebrow. I stood up.

"Good morning, ma'am."

"And good morning to you, Mr. St. Clair, and to you as well, Alice. You two are up early."

"I will be making many visits today, so we needed to be up with the sun. And it seemed more efficient for Mr. St. Clair to join me for breakfast so we could go over our plans while we ate."

"Ah, efficiency. That was the problem," said Mrs. Cowles, looking a little dubious about the whole arrangement. "I'm just having some coffee. I'm addressing a breakfast meeting of the Women's Improvement Guild and will probably be gone most of the day. What are you doing, Alice?"

"This and that. I need some new gloves, and I heard there are some prints at the New York Historical Society that seem worth a look, and I still haven't forgotten my determination to get a pet snake."

"Delightful," said Mrs. Cowles. "I may be back for lunch, but if not, I'll see you at dinner." She finished her coffee and was out the door a minute later.

"This will catch up with you," I told Alice, but she just waved away my concerns.

A few minutes later, we were out the door ourselves and in the car heading to the first of the printers on Alice's list. The first four didn't get us anywhere—no, they didn't print it, and no, they didn't know who did. But it wasn't a total loss, as they agreed it was New York City paper, and that probably meant a local printer.

With the fifth printer, we finally got somewhere. The place was the same as the rest: hot, with every surface covered in black ink, and filled with the tang of the alcohol used to clean the place. The presses were loud and reminded me of the steamship that took us to Cuba.

After Alice had introduced herself to a worker as the president's daughter for the fifth time that day and as we were waiting for him to fetch the manager, I asked, "Alice, do you have to throw your name around everywhere we go? You know how gossip can spread, even in a big town like this."

"I suppose you have a point, but the Roosevelt name does open a lot of doors."

The manager, a Mr. Peters, seemed tickled to have the president's daughter visit his establishment and took us into his office, where things were a little quieter. He was a tall man in his fifties, lanky but muscled, because as far as I could tell, printing seemed to be a pretty physical business. And although he washed his hands before shaking ours, it looked to me as if the ink had permanently stained his skin.

"Miss Roosevelt and Mr. St. Clair, please take a seat." The chairs were a little rickety, but it seemed they'd last through our visit. "What can I do for the president's daughter?" He had the heavy accent of those who had spent their entire lives on the island of Manhattan. "Did you want some party invitations, perhaps? We really do more commercial work, but we'd be happy to help with whatever you need."

"Thank you. But what I really need is some help finding out who printed something. I wanted to know if it came from your establishment." She gave him the picture of the Archangel.

Mr. Peters looked it over and then handed it back. "Yes, Miss Roosevelt. It was some months back, but it was printed here. I recognize the work. This was definitely ours. Did you want something similar? I can introduce you to some artists we work with if this is the kind of thing you're looking for."

"Excellent," said Alice. "Can you tell me who placed the order? I need to speak with him."

Mr. Peters thought that over for a moment and then got a big ledger from a row of shelves.

"This may take a few minutes," he said.

"Take your time," said Alice, and her eyes were shining. Mr. Peters's fingers turned page after page and slid down one column after another on the lined, green paper.

"Here we are. Artwork provided by the client.

Five hundred copies printed. That's odd—we rarely do such small print runs. And something else—no name here."

"No name?" asked Alice. She stood up and marched right over to the ledger herself, as if she couldn't believe what Peters was saying.

"Wait one moment," he said, frowning, and stepped through a back door. "Mr. Berger? Could you step in here for a moment?"

Berger seemed to be a bookkeeper, not a printer. His hands were clean, and he wore a white shirt with no trace of a stain.

"This is Mr. Berger, our business manager. Berger, there was something odd about this order here. I remember the print job, but not the man."

Berger looked over the ledger and then at Alice's copy of the Archangel. "Yes, Mr. Peters. I remember. Rather odd. I told him we'd have to impose a surcharge because the job was so small, but he accepted that without argument, paid in cash, and walked off with the prints in a box under his arm. If he gave me his name, I don't remember."

"Thanks, Berger. I remember now how it played out. This young lady here is Miss Roosevelt, the president's daughter, and she was trying to find the man who ordered these prints."

"A pleasure to meet you, Miss Roosevelt—a pleasure and an honor. I am so sorry I could not be of more help. If the man comes back to place another order, I will be sure to get his name." He bowed out and returned to his office. Alice turned her attention back to Mr. Peters, folding her arms across her chest. She was practically tapping her foot with impatience, as if to say, *Well, Mr. Peters, I'm still waiting for you to help me with this.*

Mr. Peters, meanwhile, was staring at the picture. "I might be able to give you some help, Miss Roosevelt. I have some interest in prints. Before your time, but in the days of the clipper ships, it was common for shippers to slap fanciful company symbols on their crates. This looks like one of them. We used to do a fair amount of these back in the day, but hardly at all anymore. I'm wondering if a seafaring man could tell you where this came from. And that might lead to the man you seek."

"I suppose we will have to be satisfied with that," said Alice. "Very well. Thank you for your time and help. It was much appreciated. Good day. Mr. St. Clair, we must be off." And she swept out of the room.

Poor Peters seemed a little stunned by the whole thing, including the rapid departure of the First Daughter. At least he'd have an amusing story to tell over beer when they closed up for the day. He and I shook hands, I gave him another thanks, and then I had to hustle to catch up with Alice.

"There you are. Why were you dawdling? We've wasted half the day, and I'd be delighted never to set foot in another printing office again. So now we know this is a nautical theme. We need a sailor."

"Your father was assistant secretary of the navy. He must know plenty of seafaring men."

"Yes, but he'd want to know why I'm asking about them, and I'd rather not go into details yet. Let me think—I must know someone . . ." I watched her mentally go through the list of Roosevelt friends and acquaintances, which must've been pretty long. And then she said, "I have it. But we'll have to drive quickly if we're going to make it to City Island."

"City Island? Why are we going there?" I had heard of it, but I had never been there myself—a little island off of the Bronx known for fishing and shipbuilding.

"Just get into the motorcar and start driving. I'll explain as we go." We got into the car and started driving uptown. "I had a great aunt Myrtle. Well, not really a great aunt—some old friend, a girlhood acquaintance of my grandmother's, who used to come to family events and all that. She horrified everyone by marrying a sea captain who sailed for a shipping company, and eventually he got a piece of the business, and they settled down nicely. His name was Cranshaw, Elias Cranshaw, but everyone just called him 'the Commodore.' Anyway, Aunt Myrtle died some years back, but he washed up in a small house in City Island."

"One of those funny old salts who sits around and tells stories?" I asked.

"Maybe when he's not drinking. It was rather a lost cause. He always drank. I imagine he still does. When Aunt Myrtle married the Commodore, she made it her life's work to get him to stop. It didn't work. Her nagging made him drink more, and so she yelled more and apparently died of apoplexy. They never had children, and now, as I understand, he's all alone on City Island with a live-in cook/housekeeper, and he rarely leaves the house."

"Now that no one's nagging him, why does he still drink?" I asked.

"Force of habit, I'd imagine. Or maybe the housekeeper keeps after him. I haven't seen him since I was a little girl. He's a rather horrible old man from all accounts, but you struck a memory when you brought up my father—the Commodore used to call on him occasionally for informal advice when my father was assistant secretary of the navy. If we catch him when he's sober, he might be able to help us."

"What do you expect to find out?"

"Preston told us that the Great Erie is made up of the Van Schuylers' opponents. So maybe this Archangel works for one of those companies. The Van Schuylers hired Cesare and someone else hired the Archangel, perhaps named for the sign of the company he comes from, if that's indeed what this picture is."

It was a long drive all the way to the end of Manhattan, into the Bronx, and then over a short bridge onto City Island. The place had a real ocean feeling to it, with the smell of fish, the seagulls, and a motley fleet of sailboats on the water.

"Do you know where he lives?"

"Not exactly . . ."

"It's not a big island, but I don't want to drive round and round."

"Don't fuss. He's a prominent man. I'll ask that old sailor over there. I bet he knows." He was a fisherman repairing a net.

I pulled to the side, and the fisherman gave the car a once-over. Maybe there was a truck or two on the island, but not much in the way of personal motorcars.

"We're looking for Commodore Cranshaw. Do you know where he lives?" Alice called out.

The fisherman gave us a hard look, then smiled. "Missionaries, are you? The first ones who've come in a fancy motorcar, anyway."

"We're not missionaries. What made you think that? We're looking for the Commodore."

The man shook his head. "Have it your way. Make a right on the next street and then keep going until you see it: a large white house with the name outside."

We thanked him, and I put the car in gear again.

"What was that about missionaries?" I asked.

"I have no idea," said Alice. "Are people coming

182

to convert him? It seems like a long way to travel to convert one drunken sea captain. Anyway, what missionaries wear mink coats?"

"You think he knows mink from squirrel?" I asked. "This is another part of the world, Miss Alice."

We found the house easily. A solid, well-kept-looking place with a pleasantly weathered look from years of exposure to the salt water. I pulled the motorcar into a little alley along the side, and we rang the front doorbell. It was answered a few moments later by a woman who looked to be in her sixties. I assumed she was the housekeeper we had heard about, and she was as scary an individual as I had met since my days as a Wyoming lawman. She had a face like a Sunday school teacher who had just caught you drinking gin in the churchyard, and her appearance wasn't helped by a severely pulled-back bun of black hair and a matching black dress.

I could see those hard eyes trying to make sense of us. She was smarter than the fisherman and could see Alice was someone with money. But I don't think she figured me out.

"Yes?" she asked.

"I'm Alice Roosevelt. I visited here once with my father when I was a little girl. I'm here to call on Commodore Cranshaw. And this is Mr. St. Clair. As the president's daughter, I get a bodyguard." That cut no ice with the housekeeper, who continued to glare at us. "And as the president's daughter, I'm not usually left on doorsteps."

That seemed to do something, as the housekeeper stepped back without saying a word and let us enter. She took our coats, hung them in a hall closet, and then led us into a simple and neat parlor that hadn't been updated much in half a century.

"Take a seat. I will be back with coffee. It is all we have to drink here," she said, which seemed odd and rather unnecessary. Anyway, most drunks I knew were usually willing to share. Alice and I looked around the room, and a moment later, the Commodore himself arrived. He looked welcoming, at least. My guess was that he was on the far side of eighty, but he walked straight and had a full head of white hair. He had that same ruddy, weather-beaten face you see in old men who have spent most of their lives outdoors. But it was clear he hadn't been drinking, and in fact, I didn't smell any strong drink anywhere.

"Miss Roosevelt? How kind of you to call." Alice made introductions, and the Commodore gave me a firm handshake. "You're with the Secret Service? Very good, sir, very good." He was hearty, even cheerful. I looked at Alice, and she just shrugged. But his earnest tone seemed strange.

The housekeeper came back with coffee—which was hot, if nothing else—and some slightly stale cookies before she bowed out.

"Miss Roosevelt, I can see in your eyes that I'm

not what you expected, and I don't blame you at all. Several years back, I am pleased to say I had a conversion, thanks to the intercession of my housekeeper, Mrs. Ottley, and I am a new man. I have put my trust in Jesus and am a better man for it. I have not had a drop of strong drink in over a year, praise the Lord."

Frankly, I would've rather dealt with a drunk. I looked at Alice, who was infamous in her family for not even making token appearances at church, and she wasn't any happier than I was. At least the missionary comment made sense now—he probably had religious visitors and likely contributed to religious causes.

"I hope, Miss Roosevelt, that you too have found the joys that go along with submitting to the will of the Lord."

"I'm not particularly good at submitting," said Alice, and the Commodore frowned at that. He looked like he was about to say something, but Alice rolled right over him. "I'm sure you have things to do—like go to church. But we need your help here." She produced the picture of the Archangel. "A friend told me that pictures like this were commonly used on cargo carried by the great sailing ships perhaps a half century ago. I was hoping that as a seafaring man you could identify it for me and tell me which shipping company it was associated with." She handed it to the Commodore, who gave her a long look.

"It's the Archangel," he said.

"That's what I was told," said Alice, practically jumping out of her chair. "But which shipping company does it represent?"

The Commodore slowly nodded. "I have some old pictures, and I could look them up, but it so happens I remember this one. I remember it well. It was famous once, back in sailing days."

"Can you tell us?" asked Alice, barely concealing her impatience.

"Let me write it down for you," he said with a strange smile. He got up slowly and stepped over to a small table in the corner. Alice watched while, with great care, he wrote out the name, blotted the paper, and then stuck it in his shirt pocket. I was half afraid Alice would just get up and pull it out of his pocket after he sat down opposite us again.

"Before we can get started, Miss Roosevelt, can you tell me why you want this information?"

"It's a long story. But we're looking for a man, and the only clue we have is that he handed out this paper—the Archangel. I had hoped that finding what shipping company this image represented would ultimately lead us to our man."

"I see. But knowledge is dangerous, Miss Roosevelt, and I confess that I am concerned that with your lack of religious conviction, you will not use this information for a noble purpose. Do you want this for money? For power? All earthly riches are an illusion, and there is no power except the Lord's. This seems like a very unusual situation here—a very odd request for a young girl to make. I need to make sure your motives are completely virtuous."

Alice was not happy with that. "Commodore, I am sorry my religious convictions—or, as I should say, lack of religious convictions—don't meet with your approval. But I assure you my motives are of the highest. I am the president's daughter, I may remind you." She got that steely-eyed look. I was thinking about the Roosevelt name getting thrown around once more. But the Commodore just responded with a benevolent gaze.

"I know all that. Perhaps if you give me a few days to think it over and pray on it before I give you this paper. You could join me, you know, both of you. And perhaps by your actions, I can judge your motives."

I could practically see the steam coming out of Alice's ears, and her mouth was set tight. She was so close, and this man was going to thwart her because he didn't approve of her lack of religion.

"Would it help if I made it official—turned this into a Secret Service matter?" I asked.

He seemed to consider that. "I suppose. But it would have to go through official channels. Because of my sinful past, I've become very concerned with my actions and how they affect other people, and with such an odd request, I want to make sure everyone's motives are sound. You do understand that, don't you? I hope to win your souls for God. I want you to want it so much you will join me in church and pray for guidance."

So that was it: a "conversion" was the price for the information. He was going to use it to bring us to God, and there was no telling how long that would take. There are all kinds of crazies.

Alice sighed dramatically, stood, and walked to the window. The Commodore watched with the same gentle smile, tinged with a little lunacy. The housekeeper came back to pick up the cups and plates on a tray.

"I think Miss Roosevelt and Mr. St. Clair will be joining us for services," he said.

"There's always room for more in the army of the Lord," she said. "I'll be in the kitchen if you need me." She left, and Alice was still staring out the window, but suddenly, she started peering intently, then cried out.

"Mr. St. Clair, there are a couple of men trying to steal the motorcar! Quick!" I had my Colt out in a second, headed for the door, and heard Alice saying, "Commodore, could you go with Mr. St. Clair? If they're local, you may recognize them." For an old man, he moved pretty quickly, and I heard him following me as I ran out the door to the alley.

Maybe they had seen Alice watching them, but when I reached the motorcar, no one was there.

There didn't seem to be any marks on it either. Were they looking for something? We hadn't left anything of value behind.

The Commodore came puffing behind me and looked around. "We don't have much crime here, praise the Lord, but there are always a few around, particularly among the young, who haven't found God and who are steeped in sin."

I sighed and holstered the Colt. Motorcars were unusual here, and I bet it was just a couple of kids—not with any evil intent, but just curiosity. Alice has a pretty sharp eye, and I thought she would've realized that was the case before panicking, but I made allowances because she was upset.

I shrugged, and we went back into the house. Alice had fetched her coat and was holding mine.

"I'm afraid your terms are unsatisfactory," she said to the Commodore, who seemed a little surprised. I think he thought we wanted the name enough to join him at church. And I figured that Alice would've stayed to argue the point more, but she was young and impulsive. "If you won't help us, you won't help us, and I'm sure we can find a seafaring man who is happy to assist a pair of unrepentant sinners. Thank you for your hospitality." We donned our coats and left.

"You look a little disappointed, Mr. St. Clair," she said as we drove away. But she didn't seem too upset. She had a sly look, and I wondered what was up.

"I wish we could've worked it out. Now we have to find someone else," I said.

"No we don't," she said. "While the two of you were chasing car thieves that existed nowhere but in my imagination, I tore the blotting paper off his desk. We have it—in reverse. Find a place where we can look at it inside, safe from wind and damp."

I laughed. "My hat's off to you, Miss Alice."

She looked smug. "It *was* rather clever, wasn't it?" And then came that sidelong glance. "I'm glad I impressed you."

We found a bar that tended to local workers. From the look of the place and the state of the furniture, it had hosted some lively events. Fortunately, we were there between shift changes, so we had the place mostly to ourselves. We took a booth and ordered beer and sandwiches, and Alice produced the paper. She looked at it and frowned, then handed it to me. "It's clear enough, but I don't understand."

It was backward but clear: "Van Schuyler Shipping."

"Well, we thought this was a possibility," I said. "Dunilsky got it from Czolgosz, who was working for the Van Schuylers. We knew that."

"But if the Archangel, whoever he is, is in league with the Van Schuylers, why terrorize his own people? And why kill Cesare? I assumed this picture would lead us back to a shipping company that was part of the Great Erie & Albany Boat Company and Urquhart. But . . ." The beer arrived and she moodily drank it, and we didn't talk again until the food came and we started eating.

"It seems that maybe your boy Preston knew more than he said," I offered. "You know, he denied knowing about the Archangel. You'd think he'd know this illustration if it's related to the family."

"But they may not use it anymore. This goes back a half century or more, when he wasn't involved in the business. My God, you really want to demonize him, don't you? You haven't seen him at his best, I admit. But he is amusing. When we were together at Sagamore Hill, he was never boring."

"And that's enough?"

"It is for me. But let's go home. We have some plans to make, and I have a lot to think about."

I guess it was a combination of our active day, the beer, and Alice's introduction to larceny, but by the time we crossed back into Manhattan, she had fallen asleep against my shoulder. She was just a bump in the road away from tumbling out of the seat, so I put my arm around her, and she leaned against me without opening her eyes. Alice didn't wake until we reached the Caledonia, when she suddenly sat up and rubbed her eyes.

"I fell asleep? I keep doing that with you, now and at your sister's. I used to fall asleep with my father when we drove in a carriage, and he always said it was because of the rocking motion and sound of the hoofbeats, but I think it was because I was so comfortable with him."

I thought on that for a few moments, and then we parked the car and headed upstairs. The maid greeted us as usual—but she looked a little harried, as if something had happened.

"Miss Roosevelt, Mrs. Cowles said she wanted to see you as soon as you were back."

"Probably some event I'll have to make an appearance at. I wonder if anyone fun will be there."

"You too, Mr. St. Clair," said the maid. "Mrs. Cowles said she wanted to see both of you." Alice and I looked at each other. Usually, I wasn't consulted on future events—just told when I had to show up. This didn't sound good.

Chapter 14

M rs. Cowles was in the parlor in a comfortable chair, reading a book.

"Oh, good. Take a seat. Both of you." My heart sank further. Her tone was clipped, and her jaw was set. We sat down on the couch opposite Mrs. Cowles.

"Alice, I don't know what upsets me more: first, that you engaged in appalling behavior—visiting crime scenes and dangerous bars that serve as the haunts of the most vulgar people, bothering senior officers at the Tombs, and harassing leading members of the legal profession in their offices— or second, that you actually thought you could do all these things without my knowing. I, who know everyone in New York and meet with dozens of people each day. Did you think that all, or even some of this, would escape my notice? Are you that unbelievably stupid, Alice? Or did you think I was?" The volume just went up and up as she spoke and practically ended with a shout.

"May I ask what events you object to in particular?" asked Alice. Her voice was soft but not humble. It was a good gambit—find out what the opponent knows before defending yourself. But Mrs. Cowles was way ahead of her.

"I found out enough. One can only assume that

there are a few things you two did I haven't heard about yet. But I will, believe me. This ends now."

"Ma'am, if I may—" I started, and that earned me a cutting glance.

"You may not, Mr. St. Clair. Right now, I'm just assuming that you are merely incompetent and ignorant and not willfully malicious. This is my gift to you. Don't abuse it."

"Yes, ma'am," I said, resolving to ride this one out quietly, as Mrs. Cowles turned back to Alice.

"I take some of the blame for not supervising you enough. There will be some changes here. I will talk with my brother about your going to Washington in the near future and getting used to working with your stepmother in official hosting duties. Is that clear?"

"Yes, Aunt Anna," she said. "In fact, I expect to be going to the Van Schuylers for dinner soon, and perhaps other events, in return for our hosting Preston last summer."

Aunt Anna just looked at her, as if there was some trick. "Very well," she said cautiously. "That sounds appropriate. He seems like a decent young man. But I have just one more thing to discuss with both of you. Mr. St. Clair—"

"Yes, ma'am?"

"You're clearly a man of many talents and skills. However, serving as a nursemaid to a willful young girl isn't one of them. I spoke to your supervisor, Mr. Harris, and apparently the Secret Service has an office in San Francisco. It's a rough-and-tumble town, I understand, and you probably miss the West, so I think it should suit you nicely. You can pack and leave as soon as Mr. Harris has arranged for a replacement."

Before I could even take this in, Alice said, "No."

"I beg your pardon?" asked Mrs. Cowles.

"I said, 'no.' I understand your unhappiness with my recent activities, but I won't hear of Mr. St. Clair being replaced. I won't hear of it."

"I have no interest whatsoever in your opinion here. Mr. St. Clair, we have no need for your services for the rest of the day. You may go back to your room."

But Alice grabbed my arm. "Mr. St. Clair is staying. Now and always. Anything you can say to me you can say to him." I really wished she had let me leave.

"Very well. Mr. St. Clair is a glorified ranch hand, and I don't care if he has a box full of medals. I gave him a chance, but it's been made clear that an ex–army sergeant whose law enforcement experience consists of settling fights in Laramie brothels is not an appropriate companion for a young woman from one of this city's—one of this country's—leading families."

"I swear, Aunt Anna, that if you send Mr. St. Clair away, I will never leave this apartment—not to go to Washington, not to go to any events—and I won't leave my room except for meals. And you know I mean it."

A dead silence settled on the room. Mrs. Cowles broke it first.

"We'll set aside a final decision on your bodyguard until I have had a chance to discuss it with your father. As for you, Mr. St. Clair—you've won a reprieve, it seems. Work to deserve it. Miss Roosevelt will be staying in tonight, so you're off duty until tomorrow morning."

"Yes, ma'am, and thank you." I stood and didn't dare meet Alice's eyes with Mrs. Cowles in the room. Normally, I'd stop and see what Dulcie was planning for dinner, but I headed straight out the door and didn't stop until I was on my bed downstairs with a bottle of bourbon. San Francisco. I'd never been but had heard a lot about it, and maybe Mrs. Cowles had a point. A guy like me could get ahead there, and there were opportunities for Mariah there, too.

I'd been up early, and all that driving was tiring, so I fell asleep quickly, still in my boots. I don't know how long I had been asleep when I was woken up by knocking. I combed my fingers through my hair and opened the door. It was Alice.

"Miss Alice, don't you think you're in enough trouble—don't you think we're *both* in enough trouble—without you coming down here?"

"You never stop fussing, do you? One mild disagreement and you fall to pieces. Anyway,

Aunt Anna had to run out for something, so don't worry. So this is your room? Rather cozy, but you keep it neat."

"Alice, you can't be down here."

"Then you'd better invite me in before someone notices." With a mock flourish, I invited her in and closed the door. She took the only chair, and I sat at the edge of the bed.

"I just wanted to tell you we can get a little later start tomorrow. I'm still making a list of people to talk with. But you can join me for breakfast again, if you want. Aunt Anna gets up very early, and I could use the company."

"My pleasure. And I guess I ought to thank you for your spirited defense. I really appreciate it," I said, then grinned. "I'd like to visit San Francisco someday, but not right now."

"I'm glad. I don't like having to get used to someone new."

"Now I'm hurt. I thought it was because I was so charming."

I saw a little color come to her cheeks. "Don't flatter yourself. Aunt Anna was right. You are just a glorified ranch hand, but I have gotten used to you."

"Your Aunt Anna was right about something else. I do have a box full of medals." I keep my few personal effects under my bed. I rustled around for a minute and came out with a bronze medal on a blue ribbon. I stood up, then pinned it on Alice's dress. "You deserve something for standing up to your aunt like that."

She looked at the medal with wonder. "How did you earn this medal?"

"The governor of Wyoming gave it to me for settling more fights in brothels than any other deputy sheriff in the state."

She laughed. "Thank you, Mr. St. Clair. I'm just . . . well nevermind. Dulcie will have dinner ready soon, and she throws all kinds of fits when I'm late. And we've had enough arguments for one day, don't you think?" She stood, and I opened the door for her. She took three steps, and looked over her shoulder at me.

"Good night, Cowboy."

"Good night, Princess."

Chapter 15

I confess to a little concern the next morning. I didn't know if Alice had had an additional talk with her aunt or what my position was. But I doubted if Dulcie cared one way or another, so I went straight upstairs. After the maid let me in, I slipped into the kitchen, where Dulcie was cracking eggs and frying bacon.

"I guess it's a regular thing now—you're with the family for breakfast. Congratulations," she said with a smirk. So I went through, and Mrs. Cowles and Alice were already having coffee. I said good morning. The maid came around to give me a cup and say that breakfast would be ready in a minute.

"We've reached a truce," said Alice. "You will stay, and I will limit my visits to more appropriate venues. Aunt Anna has realized I can do the most good by cultivating the better families in New York with a view to becoming more useful to my father in Washington."

"Very good, Miss Alice. Ma'am."

"I've been invited to the Van Schuylers for dinner tomorrow," said Alice. At that point, the maid came in with the plates, and Mrs. Cowles was distracted just long enough for Alice to wink at me.

"Aunt Anna, for all the time I spent with Preston this summer, I don't know the family very well.

Preston has been a little . . . shy about discussing them. Maybe because he's an orphan."

Mrs. Cowles thought that over for a moment. "You know what your father would say. He believes that men should make their own way in the world, and you should judge them by their own achievements. Whatever happened among the Van Schuylers isn't relevant to what Preston does."

"So what happened?" asked Alice.

"What happened where?"

"If you won't talk about it, then it must be something horrific."

"You might want to curb these ghoulish interests of yours. Preston had a rather tragic childhood. He lost his mother when she was very young. She was a fragile girl, I remember, both emotionally and physically. His father had a rather strong personality. It perhaps wasn't the best of matches. Fortunately, Preston hasn't seemed to inherit either of his parents' . . . shortcomings."

"How come his uncle never comes to any events?" asked Alice.

"He's not a very social man. He lost his wife young as well, when he had a little daughter."

"Preston's cousin. I met her briefly when I was a little girl."

"I think she is fragile, too. It's a difficult family. And in many ways, an unfortunate one."

"My start in life was hardly auspicious either," said Alice.

"And who knows, Alice. You might even turn out acceptably after all."

I laughed at that, but a glare from Alice silenced me quickly.

"What are your plans today?" asked Mrs. Cowles.

"I thought I'd visit Elfrida Wissington. She seemed to like me as a little girl, but I haven't seen her in years, and I've heard she knows absolutely everyone."

Mrs. Cowles seemed amused at that. "Yes. She found you outrageous when you were a child. But also entertaining, at least in small doses. She must be past ninety by now. She never goes out anymore. I think she's bedridden and doesn't even admit anyone outside of her immediate family—and not even all of them. There was something scandalous years ago—with her daughter, I think, and her grandson."

"I heard something about that," said Alice.

"You hear entirely too much. But anyway, if she decides to see you, you may find her useful in learning more about the families in the city. She could be entertaining, back in her day. And I daresay, Mr. St. Clair, it will be a somewhat less complex assignment than previous tasks."

"Yes, ma'am."

There were a few more pleasantries, and then Mrs. Cowles told us she had appointments to keep and said good-bye. And after a final cup of coffee, Alice said it was time to visit Mrs. Wissington, who lived in a townhouse on the East Side.

"So this is still about the Van Schuylers?" I asked.

"It's about my doing a good deed and visiting an elderly woman who probably has few visitors at this point in her life. And if the Van Schuylers come up—well, all to the good. I think we've hit a dead end with the anarchists and Archangel. We have to approach this case from a different angle. This is ultimately about the Van Schuylers—and whatever unsavory connections they may have. And we need to know more about them, especially if Preston is going to be so shy."

"It's easy for you to be so casual, Miss Alice. Oh, very well. I always did want to see San Francisco." I got my hat and coat, and we were out the door. It was all very well to joke about it, but I knew Mrs. Cowles was serious, and I wasn't going to get another chance. Mariah was right, not that I blame her. I needed another adventure in my life. And I'm not going to blame Alice either, but she was like her father. Once she started leading, it was hard not to follow.

It wasn't much of a drive at all to the East Side and one of the fine New York mansions many of the old families still lived in. It was a great pile—all marble and columns—and I never saw a less-welcoming place. Even the sidewalks were forbidding there; no panhandlers waited with their hands out. And I doubt if this street ever saw women dragging food home from the markets. No, cooks would place orders using the telephone, and delivery vans would come around the back later.

Alice didn't pause at all and rang the bell. A servant in a suit that was a lot nicer than mine opened the door.

"Alice Roosevelt, here to see Mrs. Wissington."

His eyes flickered for a moment. He knew who she was, and there was no need to introduce me, because he knew who I was, too.

"Please come in," he said, and we were shown into a little parlor that was elegant and clean. And why not? It didn't seem as if anyone had used that room in recent memory, and you could've just picked up the whole room and put it in the Metropolitan Museum of Art. I was almost afraid to sit in the chairs, but Alice had no problem, and I joined suit.

The manservant came down a few moments later and said, "I'm afraid that Mrs. Wissington is not able to see you now."

"I am sorry to hear that. But before I leave, could you just tell her that I'll be visiting her grandson, Mr. Quentin Laine, and ask if she has a message she'd like me to pass along?"

That flicker in the eyes again. He was thinking that over. I felt a little bad for him because I saw the size of that staircase, and I doubted if he was looking forward to another round trip.

"Very good, Miss Roosevelt," he said.

"So what was that all about?" I asked when he had left. Alice was looking smug again.

"I don't really know," she said. "All I know is that some years back, he had to leave the city very suddenly. I've heard he was in Boston, Baltimore, Dallas, and half a dozen other towns—maybe all of them. No one told me what he did—got involved with an actress, caught cheating at cards, something like that. But I know she'll be terrified if I'm going to see him, bringing stories and gossip back to New York."

"Threats and blackmail. You're going to get quite a reputation in this town, Miss Alice."

"I should hope so," she said. The manservant came back a few moments later.

"If you would follow me, miss. Your companion is welcome to remain in the kitchen, where the cook will be instructed to give him some refreshment." I bet they had the same good coffee that the Roosevelts had, and I was looking forward to it.

"Mr. St. Clair will remain with me. It's my father's rule." He looked like he was going to argue the point, but a look at Alice's face convinced him of what a waste that would be.

"Very good, miss. Please follow me." We walked up the stairs, and on the landing, I saw a portrait of a woman in clothes from my grandmother's day. I assumed that was Mrs. Wissington, and she certainly was a looker in her day.

"Stop staring," said Alice in a harsh whisper.

"I'm just admiring," I said.

The servant knocked on a door and opened it

without waiting for a reply. It was a sort of sitting room, and there was a very old lady sitting in a comfortable chair. The room was overwarm, but nevertheless, the old lady was well wrapped in a quilted jacket. Her hair had been done up right, and even nestled in that big chair, you could sense the strength of her personality. And right now, she didn't look any happier than Mrs. Cowles had yesterday afternoon.

"Miss Alice Roosevelt . . . and companion," the servant said. We took our seats, and he left.

"Good morning, Mrs. Wissington," said Alice, but we didn't get a greeting back.

"You were a difficult, willful child, and I see little has changed. Why are you planning to visit Quentin?"

"My father thought it would be a good idea for me to see a bit of the country."

Mrs. Wissington didn't say anything right away, and then she said, "You're lying. You have no idea where Quentin is and no intention of seeing him. I can tell that now. But why do you want to see me?"

"Why don't *you* want to see *me?*" Alice responded. Mrs. Wissington didn't say anything immediately but spared a glance at me.

"Who's he?"

"My bodyguard. Mrs. Wissington, this is Mr. St. Clair of the Secret Service."

"A pleasure, ma'am," I said, but I got very little response either.

"I don't envy you your job. But back to you, Alice. I don't suppose that you will understand, but I'm tired of people." She sighed. "But you're here, and it's easier to suffer you than to go through the bother of throwing you out. So suppose you tell me why you went to so much trouble to visit me?"

"You know everything. And everyone. There are some people I want more information about, and I think you can help me. You're a Wissington. You've been a central figure in this city all your life."

"Once I was, Alice. When I was hostess to so many—to you, your father, and his father before him—all the best families. But that was a long time ago. Family problems . . . but you know what happened, or part of it. My grandson Quentin, his mother's marriage . . . but nevermind. After a while, I didn't wish to see anyone. I doubt if I know the people you are interested in."

"Oh, I'd wager you know what is happening in society. Old habits die hard. I'm sure you know more than you pretend. There are others I could've come to, Mrs. Wissington, but I came to you because the family I want to know about has also had problems."

" 'Had problems'—what a way to describe it. You were a terribly behaved child, and you're an impudent young woman."

That didn't affect Alice, who just leaned back in her chair and smiled. "My Aunt Anna says that you found me amusing as a little girl."

"Did she now? How is your aunt? I hear she married, which none of us expected. She also had a difficult childhood—'had problems,' as you'd put it."

"She is well, thank you, and she spends much of her days helping and advising my father. As I will someday. But for now, I want to know about another family. The Van Schuylers. I know there's something scandalous in their family history, but I don't know what. I want you to tell me."

"The Van Schuylers. My goodness. That was a long time ago." She got a shrewd look in her eye. "I heard about the son, Preston . . . oh, dear me!" She started to laugh, and Alice looked surprised and then annoyed. It was not the reaction she expected. "He's courting you, and you're trying to find out about the family. Well, you're a little young to think about marriage, but why not? You could've told me what this was about, and I would've seen you without all this nonsense."

It was all I could do not to laugh myself. Alice gave me a deadly look, but it was her own fault. I could've just as easily been drinking coffee in the kitchen and getting to know a maid or two.

"I assure you, there has been no offer of marriage or even a casual engagement between me and Preston van Schuyler."

But she was still laughing. "It's no concern of mine whom you marry, but I pity your husband, Alice."

Alice was going to come back with something nasty, I could tell, but then remembered why we were there and pulled back at the last minute, for which I was both proud and grateful.

"Let's just say there's a friendship, and before it develops further, I'd like to know a little more about the family. It's something my father might do if he wasn't so busy."

"Very well, let me see what I can tell you. Of all of them, I knew Preston's mother best—her name was Sophronia. He was a little boy when she died. I'd be surprised if he even remembered her. Her people were from Virginia, an old family. The men fought with Robert E. Lee and, before that, in the War of Independence. She was gracious and kind, and why she married John van Schuyler, I'll never know."

"What was wrong with him?" asked Alice.

She considered that for a moment. "It wasn't that there was anything wrong with him. But he was a hard man. The Van Schuylers were always hard. They're Dutch, a mercantile people. Like the Roosevelts. And they meant to succeed. I don't think Sophronia ever adapted to that, accepted that. It was not an entirely happy marriage, I'm afraid. The story was that she wanted to raise Preston as a Southern gentleman, and John wanted a boy who would take over and expand the family empire."

"Well, he took after her anyway," said Alice, a little defensively. "Preston is a gentleman."

The old lady shrugged. "That's welcome news. And surprising, considering that family. I'll take your word for it. The last time I saw him, he was still in short pants and getting bread and jam all over his shirt."

"How did she die?"

"I don't remember the details after all this time. Tuberculosis, I think, but she was so worn out, there was no fighting it."

Alice nodded, and it seemed to affect her. "What about the rest of the family? Do you know them? I know he has a cousin, a little older, but he never talks about her—his Uncle Henry's daughter."

"That would be Julia. I don't know much about her. Her mother was from a good Philadelphia family and also died young. The women in that family don't have much luck. Maybe if either Henry's or John's wife had lived. But Julia, she married a man named Shaw Brantley. I heard he was from Chicago, but I don't know anything about him. They don't mix much in society. They don't have children, and she has some sort of illness like her mother and aunt." She shook her head. "I sometimes thought there was a curse on that house."

"I think we bring curses on ourselves," said Alice.

"That's a very . . . odd thing to say," said Mrs. Wissington. "As I said, you were willful and difficult, but you weren't stupid. But you could break the curse. I bet you could stand up to the Van Schuylers if you married into that family."

The old lady had a malicious gleam in her eye, but Alice didn't give her the satisfaction of a reaction. "You said the Van Schuylers were hard. How so?"

Mrs. Wissington considered that. "Your grandmother, your father's mother, was a Southern girl, a gracious and beautiful lady. Her brothers both fought for the South. But she died when your mother did, so you never knew her. A pity. It was an odd time, those years after the war. We tried to find a sense of balance. But John van Schuyler had nothing but contempt for the old Southern culture. He was heard to publicly tell his wife he wouldn't see his son grow up as a useless Southern aristocrat, a remnant of a beaten and broken society."

"How hard?" persisted Alice. "What were they capable of, the Van Schuylers?"

Mrs. Wissington seemed to be enjoying herself now. There was color in her cheeks and a glint in her eye, and it was clear that, intentionally or not, Alice had done a good deed by bullying her way into the house.

"Oh, there were stories. I could sit all day and tell you the gossip. Did you know how Preston's father died?"

"I heard he drowned in a swimming accident. That's what Preston told me."

"Ha! That's the public story. But the two brothers were terribly competitive with each other. John was going to sail on a newly launched ship, but the captain didn't like the look of the weather, so the story goes, and wanted to delay. John agreed. Henry taunted him, called him a coward, so John ordered the boat to sail. A storm hit, and the ship capsized. Everyone, including John, died. They didn't tell Preston then. I don't know if anyone ever did."

"That's . . . horrible," said Alice. "It's unimaginable. Gambling with lives like that."

"You're young. There's a lot you haven't seen." The old lady turned to me.

"You there—where are you from? You're not from around here. I've never seen a man look as uncomfortable in a suit as you do."

"I'm from Wyoming, ma'am—born and raised. I worked for Mr. Roosevelt on his ranch and fought at his side in Cuba."

"You know what it means to be hard, Mr. St. Clair, I can tell. I'm getting tired. Explain it to the girl sometime. Are you married?"

"No, ma'am. Still haven't gotten around to it."

"There's plenty of time. Meanwhile," her eyes were full of merriment, "Alice, I'm thinking your husband will have to be a man of real strength and spirit." She turned her gaze on me. "In fact, I'm wondering if she'd be better off with you than with Preston van Schuyler." And she laughed long and loud at that.

We got what we came for, so we said our good-byes and were shown out. Mrs. Wissington said she'd always be at home for us, and why not? We had probably given her more entertainment than she'd had all year.

But Alice was still in a snit over the way it had gone with the old lady—the way it had ended. And I was still blushing. The old lady must've been a piece of work back in the day.

"Oh, cheer up. We learned something useful. Even in society, the Van Schuylers are known as hard men. And your Preston isn't. He's more like his mother, apparently."

"Will you please stop making remarks about him?" she said.

"I'm on your side, Princess. So Preston is a nice guy—nothing wrong with that. But did it ever occur to you that he's a threat?"

"To whom?"

"To his family—what's left of it. I'm no lawyer, Miss Alice, but where I come from, there are people who own land and people who don't, and what happens to it when you die is important. Now, Preston's father and mother are dead, so he must own half the business. Even if he has no interest in running it, he still owns it."

Alice stopped in the street at that and cocked her head at me. "That's a very shrewd observation. I never . . . I mean, I didn't ever really stop to think about who owns a business, or how much, or where the money comes from."

We slipped into the car. "You wouldn't," I said.

"That's a nasty remark, Mr. St. Clair. There's no

call to resent me because I was born into a wealthy family."

"I don't resent you. I'm just reminding you that other people think about different things than you do."

"It's also true of you," she retorted. "You have no idea how people of my class think."

"I'm learning that every day I'm with you. Now, where are we going next?"

"We have another appointment today, but for now, head to Park Avenue, and then we can have some lunch."

We drove through the park, and Alice looked thoughtful, as if she was framing how to tell me something.

"Do you know about my late Uncle Elliott, Father's younger brother? He died when I was a little girl."

"He had some health problems, I understand," I said cautiously.

"That's one way to put it. He was a drunk and a philanderer. Aunt Anna would have a fit if she knew how much I heard when no one thought I was around and listening." Someone else might've discussed this as a tragedy or in whispers to avoid a family scandal, but Alice discussed it with the delight of a child doing something she wasn't supposed to do and getting away with it.

"They had to lock him up at one point, and my father had to take over his affairs. Uncle Elliott still managed to find time to father a bastard."

"Are you supposed to be telling me this?" I asked.

"You know I can tell you anything."

"Maybe Mrs. Cowles would disagree. But about your Uncle Elliott—he was Miss Eleanor's father, right?"

"Yes, that's right. Poor Eleanor." And there was a mix of pity and satisfaction there. Sharing isn't one of Alice's strong suits, and she didn't much like her father's attachment to his niece.

"She was at the house last Christmas. Seemed like a good sort. Well-spoken, serious, dutiful."

"Yes, everything I'm not," said Alice with glee. "I suppose she'll do. But we've lost track of what we were talking about—what happens to some men and the way they turn out, why my father has done so much and Uncle Elliott ended up as he did. And you wonder that about the Van Schuylers and Preston. Anyway, we have one more thing to do today, but first, let's have ourselves a nice lunch."

"What's the 'one more thing'?" I asked.

"I'll tell you over lunch. You can leave the car. We're just going a few blocks to dine. It's a present—for you." Her eyes glittered, and I should've been curious, even happy, but this had the sound of a bribe, not a thank-you, and I wondered what for.

214

Chapter 16

Still, I was pleased when we stopped in front of Burton's. I had heard about it, of course, but there was no way I could afford it on my wages. They said it was the best steak in New York, and it wasn't lost on me that with all my years of driving cattle, I had found myself in a city where I couldn't afford to eat beef.

For all the high prices, it wasn't too fancy inside, with brass railings, wooden booths with high backs, and sawdust on the floor. The maître d', as Mariah had told me he was called, was standing behind a tall table. He was dressed in one of those tuxedo suits that were now popular, and his eyes lit up when he saw Alice.

"Miss Roosevelt, a pleasure to see you." She extended her hand, and he actually kissed it.

"Frankie, it has been too long since I was here. I so miss the lunches I had here with my father when he still lived in the city."

"We miss him as well but are pleased that he has risen to such heights. Are you here for lunch today?"

"A table for two, if we may," she said. Frankie's eyes took me in quickly. Even though they served steaks, I don't think he'd had too many cowboy customers. Alice looked amused. "But you seem busy, so if you don't have a table . . ."

"Miss Roosevelt, there is always a table for you," he said. He snapped his fingers, and a waiter came by, also dressed in a tuxedo, but with an apron around his waist instead of a jacket. A few quiet words, and then he led us to a booth.

I looked around. Alice may well have been the only woman in the place. Men came here to talk about business over a big lunch. I imagined Mr. Roosevelt coming here with his daughter, laughing with delight at the place and joking with other patrons and the waiters.

The waiter handed us menus, but Alice just waved them away. "What we always had," said Alice. "And make his the biggest you have. Also, beers for both of us."

"Of course, Miss Roosevelt," he said, and with a nod, he headed off to the kitchen.

"They know me here," she said a little smugly.

"So I gathered," I said.

"You'll love it. Father would take me here every week once upon a time." She had a dreamy look for a few moments. Our beer arrived shortly, in chilled glasses, which was a treat. Alice took a sip, then gave me a look.

"Now, we have one more appointment today, as I said. Tomorrow is the Van Schuyler dinner, and there's a little detail I didn't go over with you. You're invited too, it seems."

"Well, of course I'm going. You know the rules. I accompany you outside the house at all times." I had done it enough times before, eating dinner in the kitchen and, if there was enough staff, maybe getting in a quick card game.

"That's not exactly it," said Alice, looking a little evasive. "You see, you've been invited too—but as a guest. Preston made that clear in his letter, saying you were to come to dinner."

"For God's sake, Miss Alice, you know I can't do that. What was he thinking?"

"Maybe he likes you. It's an offer of friendship. Even if you don't like him."

"I don't really dislike him. But . . . it's a little odd, you have to admit." I figured he was doing it to somehow embarrass me, but there was no point in starting a fight with Alice over it.

"I suppose. But I could use an extra pair of eyes and ears over dinner. Now, at a house like the Van Schuylers', men dress for dinner, as you've no doubt noticed."

I grinned. "Well, I guess I'll have to cancel. I don't own evening clothes."

"I'm ahead of you, Mr. St. Clair. I called your boss, Mr. Harris, right after I got the invitation and told him you needed to be with me at a large event, and with a little persuasion, he agreed to cover the cost. Not a purchase, of course, but there are establishments where you can rent a suit for the evening. We'll go after lunch."

"I can't tell you how little I want to do this," I said.

"You'll love it," said Alice, full of confidence, and I felt a little better when the biggest steak I had seen in years was placed in front of me. With a side of fried potatoes and spinach, it was a real restorative on a cold and busy day, and I was in a better frame of mind when it was time to head to the tailors'.

We drove to a small but clean place, not far from where Mariah lived. The block was host to a number of modest storefronts, a butcher, and a baker—nothing fancy, but all respectable. The clothes shop we entered had a simple sign out front: "S. Lieberman, Tailors and Suits for Hire." Inside, it was clean, with suits hanging on racks and bolts of cloth piled high on work tables.

The tailor had me take off my coat and jacket and proceeded to measure me and write down the notes in a little book.

"You can't wear this," he said, pointing to my Colt. "It'll spoil the line of the jacket."

"I have to keep it with me. But I have a shoulder holster. Just give me some extra room in the shoulder."

He sighed and finished his measurements. "Stay here, miss. You—come to the back with me." He produced a suit and shirt, and in short order, I was dressed to go. He led me up front, where the light was better and he had a mirror. Alice's eyes got big, and she held her hand to her mouth.

"Well, Mr. St. Clair, you do clean up well. My God, you look good."

The tailor gave an appreciative look. "Broad in chest, narrow in waist—a good build for evening wear. I have a few adjustments to make. You need it tomorrow?"

"Yes. Please deliver it to the Caledonia."

I looked in the mirror, but it was like looking at a stranger. It was a pleasure to get back into my own suit and head back to the Caledonia.

"You do know, Mr. St. Clair, you carry off clothes like that as well as any man? No society lady would be ashamed to be in your company."

"If you say so, Miss Alice," and that was pretty much it until we were home.

Only one more thing happened that day. When I saw Alice back into the apartment, Mrs. Cowles was just inside the door, and I thought we were in for it again. But she was smiling, and over her shoulder I could see a man I didn't recognize.

"Alice, I'm so glad you're home. We have an unexpected dinner guest. Mr. Nicholas Longworth is a legislator from Ohio—and a Harvard graduate, like your father, who has given him letters of introduction to some men in Washington."

Longworth stepped forward. Now here was a man who could wear clothes. He was as elegant a dandy as I had ever seen, like someone who had stepped out of a magazine illustration.

"Miss Roosevelt, a pleasure. Your family

has offered me so many kindnesses, and now I look forward to making your acquaintance over dinner." In self-assurance and charm, I'd give him points over Preston van Schuyler any day. I was going to slip away quietly, but Alice decided to introduce me.

"Mr. Longworth, this is Mr. St. Clair, my Secret Service bodyguard and a veteran of the Rough Riders."

He didn't look me up and down, or he did it so quickly, I didn't notice. He stuck out his hand and gave me a firm handshake.

"You must be a remarkable man," he said.

"I appreciate the compliment, sir, but I don't see what I've done to deserve it."

"Mr. Roosevelt entrusted his eldest daughter to your protection, and he wouldn't make such a decision lightly."

"Well then, thank you again, and you have a nice visit in New York City," I said, and as I slipped away, I noticed he had started a conversation with Alice, and she seemed interested.

Chapter 17

We had a late breakfast the next morning, and it seemed as if I'd be getting to eat in the family room every day. It saved me the choice of spending money or having to try to charm Dulcie, but I did have to watch my manners better.

Mrs. Cowles had already eaten and left for the day, so it was just the two of us. Alice was so excited she could hardly eat, which was a shame because we were having waffles again.

"Tonight's very important," she said. "We may not have as good a chance again to question the Van Schuylers. I want to know what they are really up to, and we have to watch their faces when we bring up the Archangel, the Great Erie, Dunilsky—"

"Miss Alice, all you're going to get is both of us thrown out on our ear. You can't just say things like that."

She gave her head a toss. "You underestimate me. I'm not going to question them like some petty thief in the backrooms of the Tombs. You will see how a political discussion proceeds. And they won't expect it from the president's young daughter. Your job is keeping your eyes and ears open. They'll be a little interested in you. You're almost exotic. So draw them out." She paused. "Preston's cousin Julia will no doubt be there. Women seem to find you interesting, so you can talk to her." She said it like she knew it was true but didn't know why.

"All right. I'll follow your lead and make sure I don't forget which is the fish fork."

"Were you this difficult heading up San Juan Hill?"

"When I was running up San Juan Hill, I knew what I was doing. So is there anything else on for today?"

"We could just sit here all day while you eat waffles, but there's a musical program that sounds rather promising, and some Republican ladies Aunt Anna wants me to meet will be there."

"Some Sousa marches? I rather liked those at the concert we went to last month."

"Mozart, I think," she said.

You take the rough with the smooth.

Shortly after we came back that afternoon, a delivery man dropped off my evening suit. I let it hang on the back of my door as I lay in bed and just looked at it. I remembered when I was a boy, we spent the summer barefoot because shoes were a luxury, so we saved them for when there was snow on the ground.

I did what I could to clean up and then went through the complicated process of getting into the evening wear. It took a little while, but the tailor had done a good job, and the shoulder holster fit neatly under the jacket. The shoes felt a little odd—I was used to my cowboy boots. I didn't have a full-length mirror, just a little one for shaving and washing up, but everything seemed to go together all right.

My riding coat clearly wasn't going to go with this, nevermind my Stetson, but we weren't going to be outside long, and I could make do. I gave one more try at smoothing my hair down and went upstairs to pick up Alice. A maid let me in, and she couldn't hide the surprise in her eyes. "Miss Roosevelt will be out in a moment," she said. I watched her head into the kitchen, and a moment later, Dulcie came, drying her hands on a towel. She was smiling and then gave a genuine laugh. "Oh, my," she said. "Well fancy that. I never would've believed it." She laughed again and, shaking her head, went back to the kitchen.

I wasn't left alone long. Alice was as dolled up as I had ever seen her, wearing a really grand dress, and her hair was done up fancy.

"You look lovely, Miss Alice," I said, and she gave a little twirl.

"Thank you. And those clothes really suit you."

We were interrupted by the opening of the door behind me as Mrs. Cowles came striding in. Alice winked at me and then stood right next to me and slipped her arm in mine.

"We're just about to leave for the Van Schuylers. Don't Mr. St. Clair and I make a handsome couple?" she asked.

Mrs. Cowles raised an eyebrow. "Most handsome,"

she said dryly. I wasn't entirely happy with Alice's observation or Mrs. Cowles's response. We might have to talk about this later. I was not a "couple" with Alice Roosevelt.

But Alice didn't see anything wrong. Heck, she doubled down. "Could I have Mr. St. Clair escort me to the Ballentine Ball in the spring? I'd be the envy of all the other girls."

"You'd have to check with Mr. St. Clair's superior. I believe he'd be entitled to hazard pay. I hope you enjoy yourselves this evening."

We'd really have to talk later.

We were out the door and in the car in a few minutes. The Van Schuylers weren't far. If I had been on my own, I probably would've walked.

A serious-looking servant let us in, but the Van Schuylers were not in evidence.

"Miss Alice Roosevelt. Mr. Joseph St. Clair," said Alice. He bowed, and we followed him into a sort of large parlor where everyone was gathering. It was some room, dominated by a marble fireplace. On the mantle, vases of glass and silver shone, and maids had polished all the wood until you could practically use it as a mirror. The furniture was all leather with brass fittings, and I got the sense this was a room designed to impress, not to live in.

The servant announced us, which didn't seem entirely necessary, but things are done a certain way in society.

I was used to sizing everyone up quickly. I saw

Preston, looking as he had at the party at Alice's, and he quickly came over and gave her a kiss on the cheek, which brought color to her face. "St. Clair, glad to see you again," he said, shaking my hand.

Over his shoulder, I saw three more people: two men and a young woman who seemed just a few years older than Alice.

"Please, let me introduce you to my family."

I followed along, curious not only to meet these people but to see how I was going to be introduced.

First was the older man.

"Uncle Henry—this is Alice Roosevelt and her Secret Service bodyguard, Joseph St. Clair. It seems protocol requires him to be at Alice's side at all times." A bit of a smile there from Alice. "This is my uncle, Henry van Schuyler."

"A pleasure," he said. Even though he was past sixty, his face was strong and unlined. "I haven't seen you since you were a little girl, Alice. Thank you for playing host to Preston for so much of the summer. And Mr. St. Clair, welcome to our home." His handshake was firm.

"And this is my cousin, Julia. I think you two ladies met when we were all children." Now *she* was interesting. Julia was pale and slender—too slender, actually—and her cheeks were a little hollow. She could've been a pretty girl, with a few more pounds on her. I might've thought she had consumption, but she wasn't coughing.

She gave us the ghost of a smile, and her voice

was barely above a whisper. "Delighted to see you again, Alice. We were very young when we met last. Glad to make your acquaintance, Mr. St. Clair."

"And finally, Shaw Brantley, my cousin-in-law, so to speak—Julia's husband. I don't think you've met." Brantley was noticeably shorter than I was, but broad across the chest, and he had a solid look about him. A full black beard completed the look, and I wondered at how opposite he seemed from his wife. "Miss Roosevelt, it's a great pleasure to meet you. Mr. St. Clair—you are here in a protective rather than investigative role?" I couldn't be completely sure, but I thought he smiled.

"Mr. St. Clair is devoted entirely to keeping me safe," Alice replied.

"I wouldn't have thought you'd be in danger here," said Brantley.

"Mr. St. Clair is very cautious," said Alice.

"It's wise. We're unfortunately living in violent times," said Van Schuyler. "You never know where trouble will come from next. I understand from Preston that you are from Wyoming, Mr. St. Clair? You have your share of violence there, I believe?"

"Our share, but no more," I said, and he nodded as if I had said something profound.

"Perhaps being in law enforcement, you are aware of the anarchist problem we have here?"

"You'd be surprised what we know," said Alice. "They're really a fascinating group."

Van Schuyler frowned. " 'Fascinating' isn't the

word I'd use," he said. "I know your father has condemned them strongly, and I approve of his stance."

"We don't tolerate them in our business," said Brantley. "Anyone found to even be associating with known anarchists is immediately dismissed." He had a flat midwestern accent.

"Your business? I understand from Preston that it's largely centered on the Great Lakes these days. I'm rather curious. I haven't been farther upstate than Albany, and I know very little about the Great Lakes. Perhaps, Mr. Brantley, you could educate me?" Alice's eyes were large, and she had as modest a look as she could possibly achieve. Brantley raised an eyebrow.

And then dinner was announced.

The rich used a lot of knives, forks, and spoons, which is not a problem if you have someone else washing them for you. You work from the outside in, so it's pretty easy to figure out, as long as you pay attention.

I was seated next to Julia Brantley, who stared mournfully at her soup, took one spoonful, and then carefully placed her spoon back on the table. I didn't know why, because it was good soup. But if she was ill, that might explain it.

"We were talking about the Great Lakes," said Alice. "It was my understanding that your firm has been greatly expanding its operations."

Brantley and Van Schuyler both looked a little

startled at that, and then Van Schuyler gave a wry look at his nephew. "Have you been talking about the family business with Miss Roosevelt? I wouldn't have thought she'd be interested."

"Alice is interested in a great many things. You'd be surprised," said Preston with a grin.

"I would be," said Van Schuyler. "I know I'm old, but in my day, when we had a few minutes with a young woman, we had better things to discuss than the family business." He gave a smile to Alice, who forced one back.

"Miss Roosevelt, do you realize that Chicago barely existed one hundred years ago?" said Brantley. "Today, it's the fifth-largest city in the world. New York City's population has about doubled in the past decade. We believe Great Lakes transportation will be essential to the growth of this region. There is nothing unusual in that."

She nodded, and then Van Schuyler changed the subject. "I hope your father is adjusting to his new position. It's hard enough to become president when one is elected, but to have the position thrust on one so suddenly, with violence . . ."

"Father has been up to every challenge he's been given," said Alice. "But you mentioned violence. I understand it was your great misfortune to be with McKinley when he was killed."

"Unfortunately, yes. I was standing a little to the back, however, so I didn't see anything."

Alice clearly resented the implication that she

228

was just seeking gruesome details, but she held her tongue. "But I am interested in the Great Lakes trade. It's in my blood, seeing as we're among the oldest families in New York. And I'm sure with all the changes and growth in the area, the Van Schuylers aren't the only ones who see opportunity."

The reactions were different. Preston could barely seem to contain his delight at Alice's questions, but Brantley and Van Schuyler clearly were hoping the subject had been exhausted.

"We're the biggest, but not the only ones," said Van Schuyler. "There's plenty of room in the Great Lakes for all kinds of shipping."

"I'm sure, I'm sure," said Alice. And then she turned to me. "Mr. St. Clair. What was the name of that company we heard? I think it was someone at Aunt Anna's party . . ."

"The Great Erie & Albany Boat Company," I said.

Now that really got Van Schuyler's attention, and Brantley looked a little shaken, too. I thought they'd be angry at Alice's persistence, but for just a moment, I saw fear in their expressions.

Then Van Schuyler leaned back in his chair, looking disgusted.

"That's the name of a group of our competitors," said Brantley patiently. "Jealous of our hard-won success, they have banded together to try to block our plans for expansion—an expansion, I may add, that will benefit everyone. But we need new facilities, new boats, and that requires a great many workers. We hired them quietly so as not to excite attention, but unfortunately, it only bred rumors."

"Of course," said Alice, trying to look sympathetic. "Supervising such a great many workers must be a difficult and complicated task. You must have many projects going on at once."

"You're your father's daughter," said Van Schuyler, who seemed pleased to have someone interested in his plans. "He's always been fascinated by large projects like this. I'm afraid that we've been so busy we haven't been as social as we might've been. But I look forward to meeting your father again. It's been too long. In fact, we're launching a new ship in New York port, near South Street, and have sent an invitation to your father to attend. We well know his interest in maritime affairs, as he was undersecretary of the navy some years back."

"I didn't know we were launching a new ship," said Preston.

"It isn't widely known. It was all being done under the name of a local ship builder in Newport News to keep our plans quiet so our competitors wouldn't quickly move against us. But now that we're almost upon the launch, we're ready to announce it. It's a connection for our cargo for points south. It's been docked in South Street for a few weeks for final outfitting. We're hiring a crew and additional dockworkers. But we're keeping the security high to avoid trouble from competitors and . . . others."

"Such as the Archangel?" asked Alice. And

I thought, *There goes the diplomacy*. But it did have an effect, that's for sure. Brantley and Van Schuyler looked at each other, and this time there wasn't room for doubt. They weren't angry. They were terrified.

Brantley looked like he was going to say something, but Van Schuyler cut him off. Preston was openly smirking at the discomfort Alice was putting his uncle through.

"May I ask where you heard that name, Miss Roosevelt?" asked Van Schuyler.

I thought Alice was going to complain, yet again, about answering questions with questions, but instead she just said, "I find it amusing to visit some of my father's old colleagues in the Tombs, and one of them mentioned an odd case, a figure called the Archangel. We know of at least one worker upstate who was terrified of him."

"St. Clair—you take Miss Roosevelt to the Tombs? I wouldn't have thought that appropriate."

I shrugged. "I'm just her bodyguard, not her nanny." And Brantley barked a laugh.

But Alice was still waiting for an answer to her question, which came from Van Schuyler. "Miss Roosevelt, I wanted to avoid such an unpleasant subject, but it seems that anarchists have been trying to convert our workers to their demented causes, and when our workers proved far too sensible, the anarchists tried to terrorize them. And I want to emphasize that every large shipping company has been hit by the Archangel. The name is used widely for these faceless fearmongers—a sort of blasphemous joke." He smiled to restore good humor. "But I think we're in danger of boring some of our company. Preston here has little interest in company affairs," he added with an indulgent look. "And my daughter is in danger of getting very bored, and that's unfair. Now, Preston is thinking of taking a grand tour. It might be amusing to discuss what cities he should visit."

"But Uncle, I thought you wanted me to become more involved in the family business?" Preston said it deliberately to tweak his Uncle Henry. I could see the older man's jaw set tightly.

"You're taking that trip. We discussed it."

"But maybe I've changed my mind. Maybe I want to take my father's place?" He was clearly entertained at what he was doing.

You could tell the old man wanted to lash out, but he mastered himself. "Miss Roosevelt, perhaps with your charms you might have more influence with my nephew than I do. Perhaps you could convince him to take such a trip, to help mature him before settling into business, and suggest some cities to visit."

And Alice decided she had pushed things far enough. At least for now. "Paris, you must visit Paris. And that's just to start with. After Europe, you must see the Orient. I very much want to see Peking."

I saw Preston give her a quick wink, and they were off and running on a discussion of world cities that didn't particularly interest me.

It didn't seem to interest Julia any more than the business discussion had. It wasn't that the food was taking all her attention, either. There'd been a pretty good fish course, followed by a roast, but Julia didn't seem to touch any of it. She hardly met anyone's eyes, and Brantley didn't seem to spare a lot of attention for his wife.

"Have you lived all your life in New York, Mrs. Brantley?" I asked. It wasn't the most original conversational line, and I already knew the answer was probably "yes," but it might get something going.

She seemed a little startled. "Yes, I have," she said, giving me a shy look. "I've always lived in this house." She paused. "We have a place in Buffalo, too, but we don't go there very often." I think she was considering asking me a question in return but couldn't bring herself to do it.

"I grew up in Wyoming, just outside of Laramie," I said. She gave me the smallest smile.

"I understand it's a very . . . empty state," she said.

"It is, ma'am. It's one of the biggest states, but far fewer people live in that whole state than on this one island. It's a beautiful part of the country, and I often find myself missing it very much."

She got a dreamy look in her eye at that. "It must

be lovely to just be so alone there. To be by yourself for hours and for days without anyone else. I am never alone. I am never by myself. Are you married, Mr. St. Clair?"

"Not yet," I said.

"You have a kind face. I think you would be kind to your wife, wouldn't you?"

From the corner of my eye, I could see Brantley glancing at us with some curiosity.

"I'm sure I would. I have a sister. Her name is Mariah. And I'm sure she would expect me to behave myself."

I wanted to ask her something that would help us, but I doubt she knew anything. She seemed to be in her own little world.

"I would've liked a sister," she said.

"You have your cousin Preston," I said. "A cousin is almost like a brother or sister."

"Preston is a man—and I already know about men," she said in a tone as if I had missed something very obvious, and maybe I had. There weren't any other women in this house, and the Van Schuylers did not seem to be a very social group, which is perhaps why she seemed a little . . . odd.

Eventually, a maid came around and took away our plates. Julia still hadn't eaten anything.

"You know, if you ever wanted to see the West, ma'am, it's easy now with all the railroad lines. I'd be happy to accompany you and Mr. Brantley.

I still have family out there, and we'd be delighted to show you some Western hospitality."

Julia looked at me curiously. "You really are very kind, Mr. St. Clair. I'm sure you mean very well, but Mr. Brantley and I . . . I don't really—" She struggled for words, but never got there, because her husband jumped in.

"Now dear, I think you've been monopolizing Mr. St. Clair's time. He's been very indulgent, but let's not take advantage of his good nature."

The poor woman seemed embarrassed at that and just looked down. In other circumstances, I'd have told Shaw to mind his own damn business, but Alice had already ruffled a few feathers, and I didn't see any point in making things worse for Julia by jumping to her defense. Maybe if the poor girl was being badgered, that would explain the lack of appetite.

But I saw Alice taking it all in, and I realized we'd be coming back to Julia before the evening was over.

For now, Brantley was content to continue the conversation I was having with his wife, but on his own terms.

"I don't think we'll be taking any trips West soon, but if Preston is going to see the Orient, he might want to finish up at California and see a bit of the country by train on his way back east. You wouldn't want to go, Julia," he said with a laugh. "Red Indians on the warpath. Am I right, Mr. St. Clair?"

"I'm a quarter Cheyenne," I said. "But I'll put in a good word for Preston if he'd like."

Brantley and Van Schuyler didn't seem to know what to make of that, but Preston seemed amused, and Alice was trying hard not to laugh.

After dinner, we all went to a lounge with some very comfortable furniture. I made myself at home in a deep chair where I could easily keep an eye on everyone. Then the servant who had let us in came around with glasses and poured us all some of the best brandy I ever had. He didn't offer anything at all to Julia, who took a seat near the hearth and hugged herself as if she was cold.

"I do so like your dress, Mrs. Brantley," said Alice. "I need to increase my wardrobe before I relocate to Washington. Who is your dressmaker? I need some more fashionable dresses."

"Oh, the same woman my late mother used. I . . . I don't use her very often. I have her name somewhere."

"Very good. Perhaps when you find it, you could bring it to me in person at the Caledonia, where I'm currently living with my aunt, and we can have a lady's luncheon. Would you like that, Mrs. Brantley?"

As Alice rolled on, Mrs. Brantley looked more and more stricken, as if she was being told she was being sent to a surgeon instead of being invited for one of Dulcie's lunches. "Thank you, Miss Roosevelt I . . . I . . . will you excuse me?

I'm suddenly feeling a little unwell." And she practically ran out of the room.

I thought Mr. Brantley would follow, and so must Alice have, for she glared at him when no one left. "My wife has a nervous temperament, Miss Roosevelt. Fortunately, her maid is very good at soothing her."

"Maids are very useful for things like that," said Alice brightly. "But perhaps a friend, another lady, would be even more welcome. If you gentlemen will excuse me . . ." and she took off after Julia. Brantley looked like he was going to say something, do something, but realized too late that Alice had gotten a march on him, and there was nothing to be done. He just grimaced and settled back into his chair. Preston continued to look amused, which seemed to have become his standard expression in Alice's presence.

And Van Schuyler? I wouldn't want to play cards with him—he was unreadable. It was quiet for a few moments as we enjoyed our brandy, and then he turned to his nephew.

"Preston, I don't imagine Miss Roosevelt will be long with Julia. She usually wants to go straight to sleep after one of her spells. When Miss Roosevelt leaves her, you two young people will no doubt want to spend time together. Why don't you wait for her in the green parlor? She can find you there when she's done talking with Julia."

Preston was being dismissed. He looked like

he might argue it for a moment, then downed the rest of his brandy and gave in with good grace. Or maybe he just wanted to see Alice.

I briefly wondered if I would be dismissed, too, as Alice's companion, but Van Schuyler quickly ended any confusion.

"Can I offer you a cigar, Mr. St. Clair?" He opened a wooden box by arm.

"Thank you, sir, yes." I lit it up, and it was even better than the one Don Abruzzo had given me. I felt a little bad for Alice, who wasn't there to have one, too. Van Schuyler and Brantley also lit up, and both of them were watching me very closely.

"I understand that you worked with the president when he was ranching in the Dakotas. It must've been very hard work. Especially for someone who was as young as you must've been," said Van Schuyler.

"You grow up fast there. I found myself up in the Dakotas looking for work, and Mr. Roosevelt was hiring."

"What my father-in-law is getting at, is that you know what hard work is. You know what it is to take responsibility. Preston doesn't. And Miss Roosevelt certainly doesn't," said Brantley. "We are responsible for hundreds of workers, for business partners who have entrusted us with their money and their futures. I am sure, as a ranch hand, as a lawman, and as a Secret Service agent, that you have had to make hard decisions, that you have had to . . . be strict. So have we. Alice seems to think something mysterious was happening upstate. But it was just business as usual. Hard business. I don't want you to think our business is any more than that."

I took a couple of puffs on my cigar. Now this was interesting. "Why would I think what Alice was talking about was any more than that?" I asked.

"We've heard rumors. Rumors about rumors, if you will," said Van Schuyler. "That people are saying our work upstate is about more than just being hard. That there is something"—he waved his arm, leaving a curl of smoke—"something sinister. Rumors of this Archangel. And maybe you found out we've been hiring many people in recent months, and that's how rumors get started. But let me set the record straight. We're a large presence in Buffalo and were so busy there around the time of the assassination. And we were plagued by anarchists even before one of the bunch killed McKinley. People do like to gossip. But you are an experienced man, Mr. St. Clair. And I think you understand that what we are doing is business as usual."

They were being vague, but I knew what was going on. Alice's mention of the Archangel had upset them. And they were thinking that if Alice knew about the Archangel, there could be other things she might know.

I had just one question after that speech. "This is

all well and good, sir, and let's say I accept it all. Why are you telling me?"

"Because I'm thinking, and I'm hoping, that you have some influence with Miss Roosevelt. Probably bored, and left to her own devices, she has spent too much time listening to Preston's stories. He's a good boy, but he doesn't get the full picture and has little understanding about how business is done. I'm hoping, as she trusts you, that you can get her to see reason."

"Mr. Van Schuyler, I'm just a Secret Service bodyguard. I thought you knew that." I couldn't believe he had gotten it so wrong. He seemed like a knowledgeable man. Did he think I was some sort of presidential advisor?

"Are you playing a game with us?" asked Brantley. He seemed irritated, like I was making fun of him. But Van Schuyler just waved at him to be quiet.

"Mr. St. Clair is just being circumspect, and I don't think any less of him for that. I don't entirely know what your writ is, but a mere bodyguard would be sitting in the kitchen in a bad suit drinking beer. When Preston asked me to invite Miss Roosevelt for dinner, I thought, fine, a young man wants to introduce us to his young lady. But Preston said that she insisted you be invited as a guest. So we know there's more going on here."

That was a nasty surprise, and I'm proud of myself that I didn't choke on my cigar. That made a lot more sense than Preston wanting me there. I gave myself a little more time to smoke, but that was acceptable. I think that was expected.

"Gentlemen, what you said makes a lot of sense. And I promise you, I will have a very serious talk with her. As for my position . . ." And it was my turn to just wave my hand and leave a curl of smoke in the air. Silently, I thought about how I'd get my revenge on Alice. "It's not something I can really discuss. You understand."

"You answer to President Roosevelt?" asked Van Schuyler, and it was halfway between a statement and a question.

"Yes, I can tell you that much," I said, and that had the advantage of being the truth. Van Schuyler nodded and then smiled. The tension melted away, and he changed the subject.

"I know the East Coast, and Shaw here knows the Midwest, being from Chicago. But your part of the world is a little new to us. We have some questions . . ." And I got to spend a pleasant hour or so talking about how life worked in Wyoming and surrounding states and how the Van Schuylers might be able to make some money out of it.

"I'm thinking of sending my cousin out West," said Shaw with a smile. "A bit of a hot-head, I guess you could say. Did some work for us . . . but anyway. Maybe he'd do better where he had more room than in Chicago or New York." And I agreed that the West could be a good place to get a fresh start.

At least the evening ended better than it began. Alice and Preston rejoined us just as we were finishing our talk, and they seemed in good spirits. Julia did not come down, and no one mentioned her.

"As much fun as this has been, we really should be getting home," said Alice. We stood up, and a servant got Alice her coat. Van Schuyler said something vague about getting together more frequently and hoping her father could come to the launch of their new ship. Preston took her hand in both of his and said how pleased he was that she came, and their eyes lingered on each other.

And then we were off into the night.

Chapter 18

That was very interesting," Alice said after I started the car and we were on the road.

"It sure was," I said, and something in my tone caught her ear.

"Are you upset about something? It all went so well."

"First of all, Miss Alice, that wasn't very kind of you. You pushed poor Mrs. Brantley until she fell to pieces and ran to her room. You saw how fragile she was, and you did it anyway just to get her alone."

"That's an exaggeration. Yes, I wanted to talk to her, but how could I know she'd have a nervous collapse from a simple lunch invitation? I was just trying to befriend her. I don't think we've seen each other since we were little children, and she doesn't seem to have any friends. Anyway, I found out something interesting from her. Mr. Brantley and her father have her under their thumb. Everything I asked her, about having lunch or perhaps taking in a play together, was met with the same excuses— she was unwell, or Shaw wouldn't approve. She's being drugged. Her maid had a range of pills and powders."

"Did you bring that up with Preston?"

"I did, but he couldn't tell me much. He said Julia

had always been highly strung, but he didn't know her very well. He was at school and then college, so as she grew, he didn't really see her very often. But she seemed to like me. I turned the conversation to mothers, how we both lost ours early, and it went rather well. I think she likes me, and if those drugs hadn't taken effect, I would've learned more about this family. She's been in the middle of things while Preston was away at Yale, and I'm sure she has something to tell us. But you were with Brantley and Van Schuyler. They clearly sent Preston away. What did you men discuss?"

Her eyes were bright, and she was clearly excited. By that point, we were almost home, so I said we'd wait and talk about it more upstairs. She sighed with impatience but let it go. I parked the car, and the evening doorman gave me a look— "You're moving up in the world," he seemed to say. I would've rather just gone to my room and changed, but Alice wasn't going to wait.

A maid let us in and told us that Mrs. Cowles had already come home and gone to bed. We sat in the main parlor, and Alice could barely contain herself.

"So what did they tell you? Did they admit anything when you were all alone together?"

"First of all, Miss Alice, they told me that it was you, not Preston, who wanted me there as a guest."

Her eyes shifted a little evasively. "Well, I may have mentioned to Preston you wouldn't mind

244

coming as a guest, but he was the host. He was the one who invited you—"

"Miss Alice, I've been pretty good all along, considering everything you've done and considering you've almost gotten me fired. So don't play me for a sucker."

She rolled her eyes. "Oh, all right. Take it as a compliment. I needed you there. I needed another pair of eyes and ears there, and you wouldn't do me any good in the kitchen." She paused, and I could tell more was coming. "You don't have to make it sound like it was such a burden. There are scores of young men in this town who'd be delighted to be my dinner partner."

"And I'm not one of them, Miss Alice. I'm a Secret Service agent. If you need some help at the dinner table, let me in on the plan, but let's not pretend I'm your young man for the evening, or that I like dressing up in dinner clothes, or that I want to spend an evening drinking punch in some ballroom while you write my name down on a dance card."

I felt bad about that but figured to end it there, even if it did put her into a major sulk. She didn't talk for a while, and finally I figured I'd take the step of changing the subject.

"But no harm done. Anyway, we sent a certain message to the Van Schuylers. They don't believe I'm just a bodyguard. They seem to think that I'm something more, someone who has the ear of your father."

That brought her around. "But that's wonderful! It puts you—it puts both of us—in a much better position. Now tell me what they said, word for word if you can."

So I repeated my talk as best I could, and Alice listened carefully and just nodded without interrupting.

"This is good. But they didn't admit anything?"

"Nothing specific. Miss Alice, these are hard men, it's true. I'm no expert, but I know shipping is a tough business. We may not like that, but there's no proof, or even suggestion, they've done anything that could be criminal. Or even unusual." She pouted, but I could see something positive here. "I'll tell you one thing, though. When you started bringing up what was going on upstate and on the Great Lakes, and especially when you mentioned the Archangel, you frightened them. I've seen the difference between anger and fear. They were afraid of what you might know, and that's why they spoke to me later, in the hopes I could help calm you down. And they'd like to get Preston out of town."

Alice nodded at that. "We're making progress then, if we're getting to them. And then there's the lie they told about the Archangel. They said it was some sort of blasphemous joke. But they didn't mention it had a connection to their old company sign, as we found out. They didn't want us to know how they are connected to the Archangel. There's something being hidden there . . ." She got a sly look. "We also know there must be sailors and others connected with the Van Schuylers in South Street because of their new ship. And we can find out more there."

"Oh, no you don't, Miss Alice. We're done with adventures. I'm not bringing you to South Street bars asking questions. Your aunt will kill both of us."

"Oh, all right," she said with another pout, but then she gave me an almost flirtatious look. "But you could go yourself. I'm home, so you don't need to be here, and there's no reason you couldn't go and report back."

"And what exactly am I supposed to be doing there?"

"Mention you're working for the Great Erie & Albany Boat Company. That should attract a lot of attention from the Van Schuyler crowd. Maybe the Archangel will panic and reveal himself to you."

"Yes. Won't that be entertaining?"

"Just because he can intimidate some power-less workers doesn't mean he'll frighten Sergeant St. Clair of the Rough Riders. Anyway, you should go tonight. I think we may have frightened the Van Schuylers with our talk, and they'd send a message to whoever is running things for them in the harbor. Who knows what you might pick up hanging around there."

"Thanks for your faith in me," I said. "If I'm

going downtown, I might as well go downstairs and get out of these clothes."

"It's a pity. You do look grand in them."

"But I feel ridiculous. All right, I'll have a look around tonight, and we'll talk it over during breakfast tomorrow. Good night, Miss Alice."

"Good night, Mr. St. Clair. And thank you for escorting me to our dinner engagement this evening."

"It was my job, Miss Alice," I said, but all I got for that was a toss of her head.

Back in my room, it was a pleasure to get out of the evening clothes. I didn't even have to get into my suit for my next assignment. Denim pants, a work shirt, and a bandana around my neck did the trick. And since this wasn't an official assignment, I left my badge and Colt locked in my room. I felt free just walking down the street with no one to look after but myself. I got on the elevated, which wasn't too full that late. Still, I confess I missed Alice chattering away; it was something of a tonic to see how excited she got about everything.

It felt very good being in my old clothes, and maybe that's what got me thinking about what I was doing, dressed like a workingman. After the Van Schuyler dinner, part of me felt that we were on to something. The company had done something bad, and their opponents were probably doing something bad in return, and maybe that was it. But there was no denying there were some connections somewhere that led to McKinley's death and that maybe threatened Mr. Roosevelt too. I'd see what happened. Meanwhile, as I headed downtown, it felt like the old days again.

Much of lower Manhattan was given over to banking and finance, and those buildings were locked up and dark. But down at the very tip, I found a couple of places that were doing a lively business among the sailors who manned the ships berthed there and the dockworkers who served them. I stepped into one of them and looked around. I thought I fit in pretty well with this crowd, which was more than I could say about the anarchists.

I pushed my way to the bar and got a beer. The guy next to me was short and needed a shave, and he moodily stared into his beer, which was almost empty.

"Hey, pal, I'm looking for work, and I'll buy you your next drink if you can point me to someone who's hiring."

He gave me a cautious look. "If you're looking for work, why do you have money to spend?" he asked.

"I have work. But I don't like it. Looking for someone better."

"If you're working for the Van Schuylers, so am I, so I can't help you."

"I'm not but would welcome an introduction to the foreman. I'm now with the Great Erie & Albany Boat Company."

"Never heard of it. Things must be bad there if you want to work for the Van Schuylers. Say, you're not one of those anarchists? The Van Schuylers have no truck with them."

I played dumb. "Anarchists? Don't even know who they are."

"They killed President McKinley."

"Look, buddy, I have no interest in politics. I just want a job."

"Buy the beer first." So I did. He took a long, satisfying drink and then pointed to a table in the corner. A man sat there alone, which seemed strange, as the place was pretty crowded. He had a heavy face, like a bulldog, and well-muscled arms with tattoos. A lantern gave him enough light to read by, and he was turning over pages.

"Go over there. He does the hiring for the Van Schuylers."

"What's his name?"

"His name is Mac Bolton. But we just call him 'sir,' " said my companion, and he seemed to find that funny. I shrugged, finished my beer, and went over to the hiring manager. I stood in front of him and waited to be noticed. He gave me a frown.

"What the hell do you want?"

"I'm looking for work. I was told you hire for the Van Schuylers."

"What can you do? Are you a sailor?"

"Never sailed, sir, but I know some carpentry, and I have a strong back."

"Where did you work last?"

"The Great Erie & Albany Boat Company."

He just stared at me for a few seconds, and then he said, "Come with me." We headed into the back of the bar and through a door that was hardly noticeable unless you were looking for it. There was a narrow staircase, and I let the foreman go ahead of me—out of politeness and because this was a guy I didn't want behind me.

There seemed to be a suite of rough rooms upstairs, and my first thought was that Alice had been right—our talk over dinner had roused the Van Schuylers. Too much was happening too quickly this late in the evening for it to be anything but an emergency. Guys dressed like dockworkers were carrying boxes out of the rooms, down a back set of stairs that I figured led to the harbor, where the boxes could be offloaded onto boats—perhaps the one the Van Schuylers were about to launch. At any rate, they wanted them out of New York.

From the look those men gave him, it was clear he was the boss. They respected, even feared, him.

"Last load, sir," said one.

"Good. Took you long enough. Now get out of here."

We walked past a makeshift office with a desk and a lamp. I could see a clerk sitting at the desk and reviewing some papers. On his left was a metal cash box, locked.

Just beyond, there was one final room at the end

of the corridor, and the foreman showed me in. I saw there was a table but no place to sit, and when I heard the foreman turn and lock the door behind me with a key, I knew just in time this was not going to be a job interview. He grabbed me and threw me against the wall, but I was prepared and it didn't hurt much.

"What's that about? I'm just looking for a job."

"The hell you are," he shouted. "What do you mean talking about the Great Erie here?"

"You don't like them, pal, take it up with them. I just worked there and hoped to work for you, but not if this is the way you treat your workers. I'm leaving . . ." I started to walk by him, waiting for a swing. But like most big men, he was too slow, and I was able to duck it and land a quick right to his face.

But he didn't go down, and that's when I knew I was in for a fight. He landed one or two good ones, but as my father had told me, any idiot can throw a punch—the real trick is learning to take one, and I did. He was bigger, but I was quicker, and that made the difference in the long run. In the end, I was sitting on the table and leaning against the wall, dabbing a cut cheek with my handkerchief. Bolton was facedown on the floor.

After a moment's rest, I unlatched the door and carefully looked around. The dockworkers had indeed left, and I stepped over to the office where the clerk was. He looked up and did a double take.

I'm guessing Bolton had dragged more than one man into that room, but I was the first who left under his own power.

"Dear God," he said, and I think he was afraid for a moment he was next, but I just shook my head. "Your boss is out cold and will be for a while, and I have no quarrel with you. But I need some information."

I could see half a dozen thoughts race through his mind. His eyes flashed to the cash box. "There's more than $2,000 in here. Bolton has the key in his pocket. I'll split it down the middle with you." Even half of it was a lot of money to a clerk.

"How are you going to keep me from taking all of it?" I asked.

He shrugged. "If you don't let me take half, I'll call the police the moment you leave. If we each have half, I don't have any reason to. And you won't kill me, because if you were a killer, I'd already be dead."

Sharp enough. I nodded and went back to the other room, where Bolton was still out, and went through his pockets until I found the key. I brought it back to the office and opened the box. There were piles of neatly wrapped bills in there.

"What's all this for?" I asked.

"What?" asked the clerk. He was surprised I cared.

"This is more than you'd need for an immediate payroll," I said. I doubted Van Schuyler workers earned more than ranch hands, and I knew this was way more money than they needed for legal purposes.

"They pay people . . . to do things," he said and licked his lips nervously. "But we're wasting time." He took his coat from a hook on the wall and started to fill his pockets with bills.

"To pay the Archangel?" I asked. And he went pale at that.

"Mister, I don't know who you are, but we don't mention that name here. If you have a score to settle, do it on your own time. I'm taking my half and going." He kept shoveling in the money until I grabbed his wrist. He knew that even banged up, I was more than a match for him.

"I'll let you have it all," I said, "but tell me why Bolton got upset when I told him I worked for the Great Erie & Albany?"

Maybe he decided I was crazy by this point and that he'd better humor me. "For God's sake, *we're* the Great Erie. That's a fake name we use for hiding things we're doing, signing leases for dock space we were supposed to share, hiding income, and orders—"

"Prove it," I said. "I'm not letting you leave until you prove it."

He sighed and started shuffling through his desk. He came up with a piece of paper.

"Do you know what a bill of lading is?" I nodded. "Here's a list of supplies we ordered that we wanted hidden. Nevermind why. See, it's listed as being shipped by the Great Erie. But check the address. It's a Van Schuyler warehouse. Now, I don't know why you brought up the Great Erie, but if you said you worked there, he knew you were a liar. Now let's go. I need a head start on Mr. Bolton. I heard of a clerk who tried to steal some valuable papers last September and was slaughtered. With this money, I can get a fresh start far away from the Van Schuylers."

I pocketed the bill of lading.

"Is there a bottle here?" I asked. I had left my flask back in my rooms to travel light. The clerk smiled briefly and produced a bottle of bad whisky from the bottom drawer. I took a long drink.

"I said you can take it all, and I meant it," I said. "Good luck." I left the clerk madly stuffing bills around his person.

I checked on Bolton. He was breathing and groaning a little but still out. His key ring had the door key, too, and so I locked him in. It would be a while before someone heard him or he managed to kick his way out. He'd remember me, I knew, and we'd be meeting again before this was over, so I'd have to be careful. But he'd need to be careful, too.

Keeping a sharp lookout, I walked down the stairs leading to the docks but saw no one except a few sailors a little worse for drink. I tossed the keys into the Hudson and made my way to the elevated.

The el seemed to take forever, but I knew there was a bed and a bottle and the end of it. Andy, the night doorman, let me in.

"Mr. St. Clair, are you all right?"

"Good old-fashioned bar fight. You should see the other guy."

He laughed. "I have no doubt. Feel better."

Flat on my back with my bourbon, I felt a little better. I ran everything through my mind but got nowhere. It was about fifteen or twenty minutes later when I heard a knock on the door. I wondered if Andy was coming down to check on me during a break, but when I opened it, it was Alice. She had changed into something simpler and had a little white box under her arm. She pushed right in.

"Miss Alice—for God's sake. What are you doing here?"

"My God, you're a mess. I can only imagine what the other man looks like."

"How did you even know . . ."

"I told Andy to let me know when you came back, and he told me you were in a bad way, so I brought a first-aid kit."

I should've realized that Alice wasn't going to wait until morning. But the first-aid kit surprised me.

"I know you don't think I'd have medical supplies on hand, but I am my father's daughter, and we are prepared for all contingencies. Now sit down, and let's see what we can do."

"It looks worse than it is," I said.

"Good. Because it looks bad. Some cuts and bruises."

As a nurse, Alice was efficient and had a steady hand but wasn't particularly gentle. She cleaned and bandaged me up right, though.

"There we go. And now you can tell me what happened. After all this, you must've learned something."

"Oh, yes. I learned something, Princess. To think twice before listening to you."

"Stop being silly and tell me, Cowboy."

So once again I had to give her a summary. She jumped out of the chair and began pacing, which is hard in a room only a few paces long.

"So after all this, the Great Erie and the Archangel are just the Van Schuylers? But that brings us back to why: Why someone at the Van Schuylers put a detective on us. And why the Archangel is killing people."

"And is the Archangel the one who sent Czolgosz off to kill McKinley? There's still a few missing pieces. But I have to admit you're right, Miss Alice." There was a threat there—whoever had been the power behind the McKinley assassination was still out there, and still causing trouble. Maybe we shouldn't have gone this far, but here we were, and I saw little choice but to proceed.

She seemed pleased with my agreement.

"I'll have to think on what we're going to do

next," said Alice. She bundled up her first-aid kit. "We've upset the Van Schuylers. And we're going to keep at them until we find what they're hiding. We know now that it was Henry van Schuyler himself or Shaw Brantley who put the detective onto us the moment we showed an interest in Emma Goldman—a link to the anarchist movement and the assassination of McKinley. And any further threats to my father. We're getting there."

Fortunately, it was too late to argue about what to do about it.

Then she gave me a softer look, which I'd say was almost tender, if I didn't know Alice better. "As for you, I'll leave a note for Dulcie— scrambled eggs and hash browns, easy to chew. Good night, Mr. St. Clair."

"Good night, Miss Alice. And thank you."

She smiled and closed the door behind her.

Chapter 19

I headed straight to the breakfast room the next morning, skipping past the kitchen and Dulcie's comments on my wounds. Alice wasn't at the table yet—but Mrs. Cowles was.

"Good morning, Mr. St. Clair," she said. "Alice should be here in a moment."

"Good morning, ma'am," I said. There was a hint of a smile as she looked me over.

"You seem to have had an accident," she said. "I wish you a quick recovery."

"Thank you, ma'am. It occurred late last night, and I am sorry."

"No need for apologies. What you do on your own time, without my niece, is your business."

Alice showed up after that. "Good morning, Mr. St. Clair . . . dear Lord, what happened to you?" I said a thank-you prayer that she remembered to be surprised.

"It's vulgar to invade Mr. St. Clair's privacy," said Mrs. Cowles. "Simply wish him a quick recovery, as I did. Did you have a good time at the Van Schuylers last night?"

"Very much so. I think they liked having me there. Maybe we'll find they can open up a bit. It's time for me to learn a little more about the people who make things move in this city, if I'm going to be a political hostess."

"I am glad to hear it. Have a good day—I have to go."

As Alice had promised, we had eggs and hash browns for breakfast, and I felt pretty good afterward.

We had a pretty leisurely breakfast, with plenty of coffee, and we tossed around some ideas.

"I think I have it wrong," she said.

"You admit you made a mistake, and I was here to bear witness. Lord be praised," I said.

She glared. "That comment was insulting and unnecessary. When I admitted a mistake, I meant we needed to change directions, not that my thesis was incorrect. What have we learned? We now know the Van Schuylers are bullies. They employ a thug, or maybe a team of thugs, who operates as the Archangel. Fearsome and horrifying, I'm sure. Meanwhile, they operate as the Great Erie & Albany to hide their deeds, but their disguise isn't perfect. Clerks know. Someone betrayed them. Probably more."

"Where do the anarchists fit in?"

She shook her head, unable to grasp my stupidity. "You said the clerk was terrified at the mention of the name of the Archangel. He works for the Van Schuylers. That much is clear. But what if the Archangel isn't battling the anarchists? What if he's using them?" And she looked very proud of herself.

"Miss Alice—I don't see how that could be. If there's one thing everyone agrees on, it's that the Van Schuylers—that no one upstate—have no use for the anarchists."

"Oh, but look at the anarchists. They're gullible and foolish. Everyone said Czolgosz was practically simpleminded. I admit Emma Goldman is pretty sharp, but I bet many of them are easily led astray. If a mysterious man shows up and offers them money and materials to destroy property, many anarchists would think he was a hero, a supporter of their cause. It wouldn't occur to them that they were just tools of powerful and wealthy men."

I poured some more coffee and had some more eggs.

"Well? Say something," said Alice.

"I'm trying to figure out a reason for you to be wrong, and I can't," I finally said, and that seemed to make her very happy. She gave my hand a squeeze.

"Now, let's think about that picture that Dunilsky had. The Archangel had those printed up, let's say, as a calling card for those he was terrifying. How else would Czolgosz and Dunilsky know that lurid picture was connected with the man, or men, we're calling the Archangel. So why was he upset that these particular men had it?"

"Because Czolgosz could put the picture together with the man who sent it. Even if he didn't have a name, Leon Czolgosz could say, 'That's the man who handed out this picture.' Czolgosz could make the connection—something none of the other workers could do. And maybe whoever killed Dunilsky, probably the Archangel himself, feared that Czolgosz had told him his identity."

"Exactly!" cried Alice. Under the table, I felt her kick her feet up in joy. "I just know the anarchists are involved. I'm still putting the pieces together, but I know."

"Maybe they are. But we've come a long way from Emma Goldman and Leon Czolgosz. Still, what does this all have to do with McKinley's death?"

But I couldn't dampen her enthusiasm. "I don't know. Not yet. Doesn't it happen in battle—people getting shot you didn't mean to hit or artillery hitting a building by accident? McKinley got in their way somehow."

"Well, yes. But killing a president? That's a hell of a sideshow, Miss Alice. I just don't see—"

"Well, it'll come together. I never said I was done, just that we were making progress. We need more information from the Van Schuylers. And we have to keep following. We started this because someone who eliminated one president might eliminate another."

"You're not going to get it from old man Van Schuyler or Shaw Brantley. Preston doesn't know anything. And Julia—she's just crazy."

"Not that crazy. She knows things, but she was drugged and tired. If we could get her alone for a little while . . . I bet she's heard things, seen things, that her husband hasn't even realized. She's probably alone in the house today." She stood. "Let's get the car. We're going to pick up Preston, who will get us into the house again to see Julia, and we'll see what we can get out of her now."

So it was over to the University Club to pick up Preston. It was funny, thinking about Julia Brantley, Mrs. Cowles, and the women I'd met since coming to New York. Before I had even met Mrs. Cowles, Mr. Roosevelt talked about his sister—how he admired her, trusted her, and sought her advice. I wonder if a little bit of the West had rubbed off on him. If you run a ranch or farm out West and you don't get your wife's opinion when making a big decision, you're a fool. But in New York, you just never knew. There were women like Mrs. Cowles, and there were others, who only seemed interested in dressing up nice, attending the opera, and discussing menus with their cooks.

I guess when you're rich and live in a big city, a wife who's nothing but decorative is a luxury you can afford.

We pulled up front to the club, and Alice said she'd only be a minute, and I should not bother parking, just wait out front. I imagine Preston now had Alice on the "visitors list." Or he did if he knew what was good for him.

I figured I had time for a cigarette and rolled one quickly while another car pulled up right behind me to let out a well-dressed middle-aged gentleman. His chauffer watched his employer go inside, then produced a ready-made cigarette and asked me for a light. I hope I never get too lazy to roll my own cigarette, but it takes all kinds, and I was happy to oblige.

"Who do you drive for?" I asked, being friendly.

"Jasper Sperforth," he said.

"The guy who owns all the copper?" I asked. I had heard his name, and the chauffer seemed pleased I recognized it.

"And you?"

"Alice Roosevelt. The president's daughter." He looked me up and down and decided to take me at my word.

"But you dress like that?"

"I used to be a cowboy out West and expected to spend the rest of my life doing it, just like my father, God rest his soul. And yet one day I turn around and here I am driving Miss Alice all over Manhattan. I can't figure out half of it. What chance do a couple of workingmen like you and me have in understanding the world of the rich? It's an uncertain world, pal."

"Yes it is," he said, nodding, and we smoked in companionable silence.

Alice came out a minute later with Preston. I bid good-bye to the chauffer, and we all squeezed into the small car. Preston seemed a little stunned. I gathered Alice had practically kidnapped him.

"Alice, could you tell me again what this is about?"

"I don't think I'm going to get any more information from your uncle or Shaw Brantley. But I think Julia knows more than she's said about the business and their suspicious doings. I just need to get her alone for a little bit, and I'm sure Mr. Brantley and your uncle will be out. Now, would she find you a comfort?"

He thought about that. "As I said, I didn't know her very well once we grew up. I was off at school, then college. But I can get you inside. I don't know what Shaw would say."

"He's her husband, not her jailer. You're telling me that in 1902 a woman can't entertain another woman, from another good family, in her own home?"

"The maids will have been told not to admit you. She won't fight them on that."

"No, but you will. You're a Van Schuyler. They can leave us on the doorstep, but not you." He sighed. I had a little sympathy for him, but not much.

I parked out front, and the car had barely stopped when Alice jumped out and was ringing the bell, even ahead of Preston. A maid admitted us, and we swept in.

"Mr. Preston, we weren't expecting you," said the maid.

"We happened to be in the neighborhood and thought we'd visit. Is my cousin available? We just thought we'd warm our feet and say hello," said Preston, full of cheer. We headed in to the parlor where we'd talked last night and made ourselves comfortable.

"I . . . ah . . . I believe Mrs. Brantley is still in bed, sir. If you'd like some coffee, sir, I'll get some, however."

"We'd appreciate that," said Alice. "And even more, we'd appreciate it if you'd tell Mrs. Brantley to join us."

"But she doesn't usually leave her room, miss, and I don't know—"

"Roosevelt. Miss Alice Roosevelt. Please fetch your mistress."

"But miss—"

"I'm not accustomed to arguing with servants. Do what you're told and fetch your mistress."

I watched the blood drain from the young woman's face, and I thought she might cry. She spun on her heels and practically ran out of the room, leaving Alice staring smugly after her.

I was just shaking my head, but Preston said, "Alice, please. She's been serving our family for years."

"And conspiring with your uncle and Julia's husband to keep her drugged."

"Julia was always a nervy girl. She needed something, or she'd fall to pieces."

Alice gave a wave of her hand to indicate she was tired of the conversation. Another maid came by with some coffee and little cakes, but Alice was too irritated and impatient to have any.

Eventually, we were rewarded with Julia's presence. She looked a little tired but was dressed, and her hair was done up. Her eyes were clear: She hadn't had any "medicine" that morning, so the conversation might actually be productive. But she still had an unhealthy pallor to her skin. One way or another, this was not a healthy woman.

"Miss Roosevelt . . . Preston. They told me you were here. But why . . . ?"

"We had such a nice chat over dinner. I thought to visit again. Do let's sit and renew our friendship."

Mrs. Brantley gave her a look that was a little bit shy and a little bit grateful. We all sat again, and the ladies had some coffee. Alice took a cake, but Mrs. Brantley did not.

"Of course, Miss Roosevelt. I do appreciate having some time, just woman to woman." Those gentle eyes landed on me and Preston, and the meaning was clear. Julia would talk, but only with Alice.

I stood and motioned to Preston. "Come on, let's see if there's any beer in this house." Preston looked a little reluctant but came along, and together we started to leave the room. But first, I met Alice's eyes, and the look she gave me indicated that she didn't want me to go.

"Mr. St. Clair, before you go, it is very chilly in this room. Please move these chairs by the fire for us." They were large chairs with tall backs, and I moved them in front of the hearth, which was toward the far end of the room. The ladies made themselves comfortable, and then I slipped out with Preston, closing the door behind me.

"So if you're looking for a beer . . ." said Preston.

"Maybe later," I said. "I'm sure in a house of this size you can find a place to put your feet up for a bit. I'm going to step back inside and listen. Tell the maids we're not to be disturbed." I didn't wait for a reaction but quietly turned the doorknob and entered the room again. I shut it behind me and sat in another chair by the door where I'd be all but invisible in the dimly lit room.

Although Alice had arranged things so Mrs. Brantley wouldn't notice me, I could hear them talking.

". . . but it must be so hard for you, with Shaw gone so much of the time and you here all alone," Alice was saying. Her voice was full of sympathy.

"I'm glad you understand, Miss Roosevelt."

"Please, call me Alice."

"Thank you. You know, I would like to have more people over, but I get tired, and Shaw and Father worry about my health, and they discourage me from entertaining. My nerves get worked up. That's why I have to take . . . that's why the doctors . . ." And her voice trailed off.

"But do you go out with your husband or father? Dinners at other houses, or even theater parties with other families?"

"No, very rarely. Shaw has to go out many evenings, and Father just works in his study. Shaw is very busy, you know."

"So he goes to business meetings and leaves you alone?"

"I don't mind—I usually fall asleep early." She paused. "Preston is awfully fond of you, you know."

There was another pause while Alice thought of how to respond to this new conversation. "Preston and I have known each other since we were children. I am fond of him, too."

"No, I mean *very* fond of you. He talked about you a lot after a long visit with you last summer. I think he'd like to marry you."

I found that very entertaining, Alice being at the receiving end of an awkward question for once, but I felt bad, too, because she had to answer it knowing I was listening.

"I won't be ready to marry for a while," she said. "And as much as I like Preston . . . but nevermind. Now, when you do go visiting—"

"But I'm not sure he'd be the right person for you. Preston . . . he can be somewhat strong-willed."

"I wish I saw more of that," said Alice.

"It's hard for him in this family. I think . . . but you won't tell him I said that? Or Shaw or my father?" Some fear crept into her voice.

"Of course not," said Alice. "This is just two

women talking together. Now, when you do go out—"

But Julia jumped in again. It took something to be able to continually interrupt Alice.

"Now, about Mr. St. Clair," she said.

"What about him? He's my bodyguard. Because of who my father is, I always have to be with a bodyguard."

"He doesn't say much, but he seems like a kind man, and the two of you looked at each other over dinner. I think you and Mr. St. Clair would match each other nicely. You know, people don't think I see anything because I'm unwell, but there's nothing wrong with my eyes and ears."

I was curious to hear more about her plans for me and Alice, but that wasn't to be, as Julia rolled on.

"Everybody thinks I don't know that Shaw has a mistress. Or maybe he just doesn't care that I know. I probably haven't been the best wife for him," she said with the same tired, worn voice. "But he was already working for Father before we met, and Father thought it would be a good idea for us to marry, and I didn't want to disappoint him. That's where Shaw goes so much, after work. To his mistress."

"I am sorry," said Alice eventually. "No man should do that to his wife." And I could just hear her unspoken comment: *Or he should at least be discreet about it.*

"How did you find out?" Alice then asked.

"Snatches of telephone conversations, when he thought I wasn't around. Notes on hotel stationary that he left lying on his dressing table. The Wellman Arms—you could walk there from here. He didn't think I would look. Or maybe he just didn't care." That second option was by far the worse, I guessed.

Alice might've gotten even more out of her, but I heard the faint sound of the front door opening and words in the entranceway. I thought it would be a good time to leave. I quietly and quickly stood and slipped out the door, closing it behind me. Down the hall, I saw a maid greeting Shaw Brantley at the door.

". . . I'm home for lunch after all. Is Mrs. Brantley upstairs?"

"She's in the parlor, sir, with a visitor. Miss Roosevelt from the other night."

"Miss Roosevelt?" He seemed surprised, and not happy. Then he saw me.

"Mr. St. Clair? A pleasure." It clearly was not. Still, he shook my hand. And then Preston entered from the direction of the kitchen.

"And Preston?" That seemed to make him even more unhappy. "Is there a party going on?"

"Yes. Alice came to visit me at the club, and I mentioned how Julia liked having another woman around, so we all came up together in Mr. St. Clair's motorcar."

Brantley looked like he was really trying to master his anger. "While I do want to thank Miss

271

Roosevelt for her kind gesture, she doesn't realize that my wife is very fragile, and overexcitement can lead to a complete breakdown. Preston, be a good boy and tell Julia and Miss Roosevelt their conversation needs to end very quickly so my wife can rest."

"You can't tell her, Shaw?" he asked with just a hint of a smile.

Brantley was right on the edge, and I watched his hands make, and then release, a pair of fists.

"Preston, I have some business to take care of with Mr. St. Clair. I'd greatly appreciate your doing this."

Preston shrugged and left, and Brantley looked relieved as he turned to me. "I see some bruising, Mr. St. Clair. Were you the victim of a crime?"

"Yes. After seeing Miss Roosevelt home after your bountiful dinner, sir, I went downtown for a drink and was attacked. Fortunately, I was able to overcome my attacker and left him facedown in a room. It was near where your new boat is about to be launched. I wonder if you've heard anything about it."

He gave me a considered look, then pulled a card out of a silver case in his pocket. "We have something in common, Mr. St. Clair."

"I can't imagine what, sir," I said.

He laughed. "Fair enough. But I was referring to the fact that I think we look to the business at hand and don't take things personally. I'm sure you like your job, but I think I can offer you a better one, managing security at our operations. Think about it." I took his card and thanked him. It was the second job I'd been offered in a week, and that made me wonder why it was so hard to find local help. Mariah would say it was because New Yorkers don't trust each other.

Or maybe this was just an elaborate bribe.

Alice, Preston, and Mrs. Brantley came out of the parlor. Julia looked a little cowed at seeing her husband there.

"I wasn't expecting you till this evening," she said in a whispery voice.

"I thought I'd have lunch at home because I have some uptown customers I'll want to see later anyway," he said. "If you're well enough, we can have lunch together," he said.

"Thank you," she said. "But I'm not very hungry, and I should probably just go back to bed."

"If you think that's best," Brantley said. He snapped for the maid, who quickly saw her mistress up the stairs.

Brantley looked at Alice and seemed to remember himself. "I was wondering if you had a chance to speak with your father yet about our ship launching. I can have our operations manager work with your father's private secretary to see about a mutually suitable date."

"An excellent idea," said Alice. "And I can also help you in another way. Did you know Aunt

Anna—my father's sister—is on the board of New York Hospital? She knows every prominent physician in town. I think Mrs. Brantley would profit from a second opinion on her condition. I'll have her prepare and send you a list. My pleasure."

But it wasn't Brantley's. He frowned at that. He knew Alice was serious—she'd follow through with Mrs. Cowles, and Mrs. Cowles would follow through with Julia. There would be no denying her.

"That is very kind, Miss Roosevelt, but I don't want to put you or your aunt to any trouble."

"No trouble at all. I assure you. Now, Preston, can we give you a ride downtown?"

Shaw glanced at Preston. "I think we'll talk over some business as long as he's here," he said, and there was a heavy tone in those words. Preston would pay for introducing Alice to the household without supervision, and he would no doubt be told to encourage Alice to invite her father to come to their ship launching. Again, Preston just smiled and shrugged.

So Alice and I said our good-byes and hopped into the motorcar.

"Let me guess—the Wellman Arms Hotel?" I asked.

"Very good," said Alice with a light laugh. "From what I understand, men tell their mistresses things they don't tell anyone else. My goodness, Mr. St. Clair, you're blushing."

Chapter 20

I just shook my head. "Where do you hear these things, Miss Alice?"

"You'd be surprised," she said a little loftily.

"Yes, I would."

"Anyway, I'm so glad you understood that I wanted you to slip back in. I want your thoughts. Look how Shaw treats his wife. Do you think he's our Archangel? Could he be that brutal?"

"I think he has it in him," I admitted. "I don't think he cares about anyone one way or another. I think he knew I was the one who left his foreman, or whoever that was, facedown in that room. So he offered me a job working for the Van Schuylers. It's not personal for him. He just wants to finish his job, and if he can offer me a job as a bribe, he'll be happy."

"You're getting to him. Good for you." She smiled.

"Glad you approve. But we haven't gone over the rest of your little talk." I glanced at Alice, and she gave me a wary look.

"You mean with Mrs. Brantley saying that she found Preston more strong-willed than we suspected? Maybe he has been standing up to Shaw and his uncle." She looked a little proud of herself, as if she had something to do with that. And maybe she had.

"Yes, it was interesting that Mrs. Brantley noticed that. I wonder how recently he decided to grow a backbone."

"That's an unkind remark, Mr. St. Clair. As I've explained to you before, Preston has been in a difficult situation. That he's finally standing up for his rights shows just how much character he has."

"Yes, I agree with you there." And then I grinned. "But apparently, still not enough for you to admit that you're going to marry him."

"Goddamn it! I should've known you would be completely unprofessional and rub it in. I have no intention of marrying Preston, now or later. And you're an uncivilized, ignorant cowboy."

I just laughed. "Yes, but I'm very kind and would be an excellent husband for you. That's what Julia and Mrs. Wissington say. When your father comes up for the ship launching, I'll ask his permission. How does that sound, Princess?"

"Go to hell," she said and sulked.

"I'm going to tell Mrs. Cowles about your language."

"And to think what I did to make sure you kept your job."

"And to think what I've done to almost lose it. And what I'm about to do. God help me." I was a little annoyed at her but felt bad for teasing her. It wasn't the kindest thing I ever did, considering how young she was, but I tended to forget that sometimes.

We were at the hotel, and I parked the car.

"What are you going to do?" asked Alice, who had calmed down by this point.

Something I shouldn't be doing, not as a Secret Service agent. But I was just following the stream at this point, and we had gone too far to stop.

"Miss Alice, how were you going to find the mistress? We don't have a name. Were you just going to ask the front desk clerk to give you a list of single women in residence?"

"Something like that," she said a little defensively.

"A president's daughter can get a lot done. But sometimes some old-fashioned police threats can do the trick."

We walked into the hotel. The Wellman Arms is one of the better hotels in New York. In fact, I'd driven Alice to a few events there in the past couple of months. The Van Schuylers had a lot of money if Brantley could afford to keep his mistress set up there. And that was unfortunately going to be the hotel's downfall. They didn't know who they were dealing with.

The clerks at the reception desk were as well groomed as any of the gentlemen at the Roosevelt party where I had met Preston. I was getting tired of men who looked so dandy.

The clerk returned the favor: he clearly didn't like the look of my suit, riding coat, or Stetson. I pulled out my badge. "St. Clair, Secret Service. Can I speak to the manager?"

There was a flicker of nerves. "He's not available. The daytime assistant manager, Mr. Wilhelm, is available. If you wait one moment . . ." He disappeared into the back. I looked at Alice, standing a little behind me, and she raised an eyebrow.

"I'm Mr. Wilhelm. Can I help you?" He was an older version of the clerks, with just a slightly irritating tone that said what he thought of me.

"There's a man named Shaw Brantley. He has a woman stashed here. I'd like her name and room number."

His face got a little red. "Surely, sir, you under-stand that our guests' privacy is of utmost importance to us. I couldn't possibly reveal that."

"Didn't that other guy tell you I had a badge? If you're promoting prostitution here, I could have this whole hotel shut down by the end of today."

Wilhelm looked around with an unpleasant mix of fear and arrogance on his face. "It's hardly that, sir. A handful of distinguished gentlemen keep regular rooms here for their private use. What they use them for is beyond our concern. And besides"—he lowered his voice—"we've paid the right people downtown."

So I grabbed him by his lapels and pulled him over the counter until our faces were an inch apart. "Didn't you see the badge? I'm federal. I don't give a damn what local cops or politicians you've bought. Give me a name and room number, and we'll take care of what we have to do and move on. Don't make this difficult. Shaw Brantley's room."

He didn't even have to look it up. I guess Brantley was a really good customer.

"Elsie de Maine, room 512. Do what you need, but please don't tell Mr. Brantley you got it from me."

"Fine." I let go of him and stepped away.

"Crude but effective," said Alice.

"I'm a lawman. I have to throw my weight around when people break the law. Even though I seem to spend most of my time helping *you* break the law."

"Not that much. Anyway, this Elsie de Maine must be something. No one has a name like that for real. She was probably an actress."

Alice led the way and rapped sharply on the door. I was guessing that Miss de Maine had few visitors except for Brantley, who probably had his own key, so a knock would probably be a surprise.

We heard some movement inside and then a turn of the handle. We were face-to-face with Elsie de Maine. As I noted before, a wife who's nothing but decorative is a rich man's luxury. And so, apparently, is a woman who looks like Elsie.

She was wearing night clothes, and not much of those, and some lovely auburn curls poured over her white shoulders. Her curves were perfect, and the peach-colored silk hung onto them just enough.

Elsie was surprised, but only for a moment, and was a bit sharper than I had imagined. She took me in first. "You're a cop. I've no idea why you're dressed as a cowboy, but cops look like cops no matter what, and your girl here . . ." She laughed. "For God's sake, I've seen your face before. You're Alice Roosevelt, aren't you? Well, I think we'll have ourselves a party here. Come on in."

It was more than a room. It was a suite. We entered a sitting room with a table, desk, and a few chairs, and we got a peek at the bedroom through a half-opened door.

"If you don't mind, I'll get changed. There's some whisky on the table and glasses—help yourself. Back in a moment." I watched her depart until she disappeared into the bedroom and closed the door.

Alice reached into my jacket, pulled out my handkerchief, and handed it to me. "Wipe your mouth. You're drooling."

"For God's sake, Miss Alice. That wasn't necessary. Want some whisky?"

"It's a little early for me, but if you need it to calm yourself, don't let me stop you."

"No, thanks. I'm sure Elsie will be out in a moment anyway."

"I'm sure. I imagine she's had lots of practice getting dressed and undressed quickly." Indeed, she was out a moment later. I know little about women's dresses, but I could tell she chose this one with care. It was actually a perfectly modest outfit, but it was designed to emphasize her figure.

She curled up into a chair. "So what's your story, Cowboy? What does a lawman from Texas want with a New York actress?"

"Wyoming, actually. And although I was a deputy sheriff in Laramie, I'm now with the Secret Service. I'm Miss Roosevelt's bodyguard. She wanted to meet you."

"I'm flattered. You know, I heard that Preston van Schuyler is a friend of yours. That's why you're here, right? It's about the Van Schuylers? You're trying to get something on them, aren't you? Why else would you be here? Well, I might be able to help you. But we're going to have to talk about what's in it for me. Because if Shaw Brantley finds out, he'd break my neck."

"He's a violent man?" Alice asked.

"What do you think?"

"Very well, Miss de Maine. We are interested in what you may know about the family. Do you want to know why?"

"It's probably better if I don't know," said Elsie with a musical laugh. "Right now, I'm just interested in what you can give me."

"I'm interested in what you want," said Alice. "We have money, within reason. Are there introductions I could make for you? I know a lot of people."

"What do I want?" She suddenly frowned, and the light seemed to disappear from those big, beautiful eyes. She poured herself some whisky

281

and drank it down fast. "I want to rent Mr. St. Clair."

The third job offer—I was feeling very popular.

"Mr. St. Clair is not for rent," said Alice. She grabbed my arm a little too tightly, but it was her tone that made me wince. Elsie grinned.

"So it's like that, is it?" Alice turned red. I suppressed a laugh. "But just hear me out. I'm done with Shaw. But I'm his property."

"You are not," said Alice. "You have rights. That's ridiculous."

Elsie gave me a look that plainly asked, *Is she for real?*

"Miss Roosevelt is young and had a sheltered upbringing," I said.

Alice gave me a dirty look. "Very well, I accept that Mr. Brantley has a hold on you. Why do you want to rent Mr. St. Clair?"

"I've been biding my time waiting for a chance to get out. I'm stuck here like a prisoner. I can't trust anyone. Shaw has paid off the staff here and local police. If I tried to leave, management would alert him or one of his henchman before I even made it to Grand Central." That made me wonder if someone had already been sent to alert Shaw of our storming the castle, as it were. Elsie continued, "I have enough cash to get me started on my own and jewels I can sell. One small suitcase and Mr. St. Clair sees me safely on a train. I have friends in quite a few towns I can call on, but I have to get out of New York. I hope I can trust you, Mr. St.

Clair. If you tell me that you can get me out of here, I'll tell you anything you want to know."

"It's a deal. Mr. St. Clair can do anything," Alice said with a wave of her hand. Her confidence was both flattering and frightening. "He's not afraid of Shaw or the rest of the Van Schuylers. You'll be on a train, by yourself, by the end of today. Now let's hear what you know about the Van Schuylers."

"Fair enough. Shaw likes to brag about what he and his family have done. He likes to lie in bed after we . . . afterward and tell me about the bribes, the threats, the violence . . ." She shivered and took another shot of whisky. If she kept that up, I thought, she'd destroy the finest complexion I've seen this side of the Mississippi.

"Do you have any specifics?" asked Alice. Elsie gave her a sour look.

"I normally don't have a notebook with me at the time," she said, and I found that funny. Alice didn't laugh, but she didn't blush either.

"I'm telling you what I know. If you can find some honest cops and send them upstate, they won't be wasting their time, I can tell you that much. But all right, you want something in more detail? I have a few things. First of all, Shaw used to complain about Preston—your sweetheart." And I laughed again. This time, Alice glared at me, and Elsie said, "Oh, my, did I let something slip I shouldn't? He said the two of you—but nevermind." She grinned. "Anyway, it seems

283

Preston, as a family member, owns a certain part of the business. Shaw said Preston was never really interested in it, but they gave him some light stuff to do. He hoped Preston would just take some money and go for some big worldwide trip. His uncle was also pushing for that. Shaw said he didn't like the boy hanging around and asking questions. He just wanted him out of the way."

She paused. "Once Shaw actually said he was afraid of Preston."

"If they were up to the violent and illegal activities you describe, the last thing they'd want is a decent family member looking over their shoulder," said Alice.

"So Preston is a decent man? You'd know more about that than I would," said Elsie. I knew it was risking my life to laugh at that, so I showed some self-control while Alice fought a blush.

"What about Shaw's wife, Julia?"

"I don't get involved with wives," said Elsie. "But I'll tell you this much: I feel sorry for the girl, even if we've never met. You hear about these cold, difficult wives, and you don't really blame the man, but even with Shaw's description, she sounded more sad than bad, if you take my meaning. Sort of sick, really. I thought he was unkind about her. I even told him I didn't want to hear him put her down anymore." If you dig deep enough, every profession has its ethics.

"Julia told us that Preston has been more than

annoying lately, that he was trying to push for his rights," said Alice.

"Yeah, I guess that made Shaw a little nervous. It was not only the money—Preston's share—but Shaw and Preston's uncle didn't want him demanding a position. It seemed to be a big deal to both of them to get Preston out of the country. Shaw would mutter all the time about the disaster in Buffalo last year."

"Yes—the assassination of McKinley," said Alice, impatiently.

"Oh, but that's the thing," said Elsie, looking a little triumphant. "Shaw was up there with his father-in-law when that happened. I remember when he came back. He was so wound up, it took me hours to calm him down. He was pacing this room, muttering things—half of which made no sense to me. But one odd thing stood out. I remem-ber him saying, 'What a goddamn mess. At least with McKinley killed like that, no one will notice.' How about that, Miss Roosevelt? Buffalo was having a pretty lively evening, apparently."

"But what else could have happened that night? A crime? A business deal that went sour? What was the next thing he said after 'no one will notice'?" Alice was getting really excited now.

"As I recall, the next thing he said was for me to get undressed."

There was no self-control that time. I laughed,

and Elsie was glad I appreciated the joke, even if Alice just rolled her eyes.

"If you two are done, I think I just have one more question. Did Shaw ever mention a figure called the Archangel?"

That wiped the smile off her face fast.

"Christ," she said, taking another shot of whisky. Her hand was trembling, as much from fear as the booze. "Where the hell did you hear that name?"

"We hear it everywhere," said Alice. "And it's seeming more and more as if Shaw might be the Archangel."

"Well, he's not, I can tell you that much. Because he'd complain about the Archangel. Even he was afraid of him."

"So you discussed business with him?" asked Alice.

"We discussed almost nothing. He talked, and I was a sympathetic listener. In the mistress business, listening is what you spend most of your time doing. I mean, who else could he discuss this with? Certainly not his wife. And complaining about the business to his father-in-law would make him seem weak. Anyway, he'd start talking about some deal, but then he'd say, 'The Archangel went too far this time,' or 'The Archangel is going to get us into trouble now.' At first I assumed he was some sort of thug in his employ, but Shaw seemed genuinely worried about him. But I can't tell you

286

more. All I know is that anyone who scares Shaw is worth being scared of. I can only imagine if Shaw sent him on me and couldn't even control him himself . . ." She shuddered and reached for the whisky again, but Alice took it away.

"We still have to get you out of here, and you need to have a clear head."

The reality of what we were about to do hit Elsie, and she was looking nervous.

"Don't worry. We'll do our part," said Alice. "Mr. St. Clair, you're the soldier here. How are you going to run the campaign? You got us in. Now, can you get us out?"

"First, Miss de Maine, pack a bag and whatever jewels and money you have—carefully, on your person."

"When it comes to money and jewelry, I know how to be careful," she said. "Back in a moment."

It didn't take her long at all. She came out of the bedroom with a small case, then gave me a flirtatious look. "My coat is in the closet, Mr. St. Clair." I got it out for her, and it was a beauty—even better than Alice's mink. I had done some trapping once upon a time and sold pelts to a furrier, who gave me a little lesson. This was sable, which only live in Russia. I knew that coat alone could keep her going for a year. I held it for her, and she snuggled into it and against me. Alice gave me more of a glare than I deserved.

When she was set, I gave out the directions.

"Here's what we do. We all head straight to the lobby, and I speak to Wilhelm, the assistant manager, and make him a deal. Are we set? Let's go."

We were pretty noticeable: two well-dressed young women and a cowboy. I told the women to stand by the entrance but not to go outside. I didn't have to go through any routine this time; the clerk found Wilhelm even as I was approaching, and he met me with a sickly smile.

"I am leaving with Miss de Maine. And you're in a bit of a pickle, my friend. I knew I couldn't sneak past you or your men here, but I can tell you that it's in your best interest to give us a head start. You'll have done your job. And we'll get away. And I won't have to come back. Do we understand each other?"

Wilhelm just nodded. We were going to cut it close, but I thought it would work. I figured Wilhelm might've already called Brantley's men. Or maybe he just hoped Alice and I would leave alone, and he wouldn't have to bear bad news. It was a risk.

I hustled the women outside to the motorcar. Elsie was about to get in next to me, but Alice danced in ahead of her. "You'll be more comfortable on the outside; the middle is rather awkward," she said with the hint of a smirk. I was already putting the car into gear as the door slammed, and we were off.

It sounds funny, but out West, you have a much

better idea of how long it's going to take you to get from one place to another. In New York, all it took was a broken-down delivery van, followed by a closure thanks to road repair, to delay our arrival to the train station. We got out, and I looked around, making sure no one was after us. My coat was open so I could easily reach my Colt. Elsie grabbed her case, and Alice pushed open the door. At least Shaw was going to find it a lot harder to slap me around than Elsie.

Grand Central is always crowded, but it wasn't too bad at midday. I saw the women to the ticket lines while keeping an eye out.

I saw him first—Mac Bolton, the Van Schuyler foreman I had knocked out in the room—and took some satisfaction that he still looked like hell. I gently nudged Elsie and leaned over her shoulder. Alice was paying attention, too.

"Don't move quickly, but just to your left is a man who works for the Van Schuylers. Turn your eyes that way and let me know if you recognize him."

She was good, and I watched her glance quickly.

"Oh, dear God. It's Mac Bolton. He's often with Shaw—a sort of bodyguard. Anything nasty to be done, they give it to Bolton."

"Are you telling me that he could be the Archangel?" I asked. Maybe she hadn't wanted to admit it earlier.

"Bolton? Couldn't be. I told you that Shaw was

worried, even frightened, about the Archangel, but Bolton is as loyal as a dog. He wouldn't sneeze without asking Shaw first."

We made it to the window, and I heard Elsie buy a one-way ticket to St. Louis. We were already on our way to the track when Bolton saw us and, wearing a grim smile, headed over.

Elsie saw him and looked terrified, but Alice just grabbed her and held on. Travelers moved past us, and I could hear the rumble of trains coming and going.

"Look who it is—the man who used to work for the Great Erie," he said with a nasty smile.

"If you'd like, we can go another couple of rounds," I said. "But not here, and not now. This lady has a train to catch."

"I don't think so," he said. He turned to her. "Miss de Maine, why don't you come back with me?" She shrank back, but Alice stood firm. "More men are coming before your train departs, I'm sure."

Of course, Bolton didn't know I was Secret Service. I didn't like to flash my badge around too much, especially to a man like Bolton, or word would get back to HQ, but there was no helping it. It did give him a moment's pause, but no more.

"In about ten minutes, there are going to be half a dozen men here. And I don't think you're going to find that badge a lot of help."

I wasn't worried about more Van Schuyler men. But I had two women with me, and Elsie looked like she was going to pass out. I couldn't blame her, considering her history.

And then Alice left.

She was supposed to be my first priority, but she had walked off at a nice clip, and following her with the terrified Elsie and her bag in tow would be a bit of a challenge. There was no way I'd be able to keep an eye on Bolton if I went after her; I had no choice but to stay put. My only consolation was that Bolton and his men were more concerned with me and Elsie than with Alice, so it was unlikely she'd be bothered.

"One girl down, one to go," said Bolton.

"You can't bribe or threaten the people I work with," I said, stalling for time, keeping one eye on Alice until she was swallowed by the crowds. I wasn't too upset, though. Alice could be reckless but she wasn't stupid.

"You really don't know who you're dealing with," said Bolton. "Mr. Brantley is not going to be happy with you dragging away his woman. We're going to find out who sent you and why."

And so we stood there, glaring at each other, with Bolton waiting for reinforcements and me wondering what the hell Alice was up to. But she didn't let me down, and I should've known she wouldn't. She apparently knew there was a police substation in Grand Central, and suddenly she was at my elbow again—with a lieutenant and half a dozen cops.

"What seems to be the problem?" asked the lieutenant, and I saw Alice grinning triumphantly.

Bolton looked a little stunned. But only for a moment. "Lieutenant, if you call downtown, you will find I have many friends—important friends."

"I'm glad to hear that. Because you don't have any friends here. Would you come with us, please?"

Yes, the Van Schuylers might've had some police in their pocket, but Theodore Roosevelt's daughter trumped all that. Bolton looked like he was considering his options, but he clearly didn't have any. He gave me a final look of hatred and let two cops lead him away.

"Sorry you were bothered, Miss Roosevelt," said the lieutenant.

"Mr. St. Clair will want to talk further with him," said Alice.

"Of course," said the lieutenant, who gave me a nod and left with the rest of his men. Although I knew that Bolton's men were on their way, I had no doubt that once they couldn't find their leader, they'd quickly crawl back under the rock they came from.

"Miss de Maine, I think you have a train to catch." We walked her to the track. She had a spring in her step now, and I hung back a little with Alice.

"Damn it, Miss Alice, you know you're not

supposed to leave me when we're outside," I said.

"Nothing was going to happen to me in a busy place like this—do you think I'd be kidnapped in a crowded station? Anyway, Bolton and his men were after you and Elsie here, not me. But I should've known better than to expect a thank-you from a cowboy."

"Oh, all right. Thanks for fetching the police."

"You're very welcome."

We found the track for the St. Louis train, and before boarding, Elsie extended her hand to Alice.

"Miss Roosevelt, I don't expect that I'll ever be in a position to do you a favor, but if I am, you can count on me. And as for you, Mr. St. Clair—" She gave me a hug and a kiss under my ear. Her perfume tickled my nose. "I am so sorry you can't afford to keep me."

"That may be the nicest compliment I've ever had," I said, and I happily watched her slink her way into the train.

Alice was watching me with folded arms. "If you're done saying good-bye, we have a suspect we need to talk with."

"I'm at your service."

Alice stopped, reached into my jacket, and once again pulled out my handkerchief. "She left lipstick on your cheek. Imagine wearing lipstick in public like this. My God."

I quickly cleaned myself off, and we got down to business as we walked to the police substation.

"The Van Schuylers seem to know everything we do," said Alice. "From the first day, when they set a man on us. I'm tired of giving them information. I'm only going to hint about what we know. Bolton won't tell us anything anyway. I just want to scare him."

If anyone could do it, Alice could.

The lieutenant waved us in.

"We can charge him with harassment if you want, Miss Roosevelt," said the lieutenant.

"Mr. St. Clair will be questioning him on behalf of the Secret Service. And I will be listening."

Bolton was simmering in a back room under the watchful eye of a cop who was juggling his nightstick while clearly thinking about putting it to better use. I told him he could go, and he shut the door behind him.

"I'll be out within the hour," said Bolton. "Even the president's daughter and the Secret Service can't trump up something to keep me here."

"I'm sure," said Alice. "But for now, we have you for that hour. I thought we'd while away the time chatting."

"Why should I talk with the president's daughter? Why are you even interested?" He seemed genuinely curious.

"I have no interest in you, Mr. Bolton. Don't flatter yourself. You just happened to have information about a subject I am interested in. A man named the Archangel. Oh, so you *do* know about him."

There was no denying it. Bolton looked angry and worried at the same time.

"Your masters aren't going to be pleased with ou. You just confirmed the Archangel's connection to the Van Schuylers. And you let Brantley's mistress get away."

"They need me. They'll get over it," said Bolton. "And I have no idea who this Archangel is. I'm just a sort of assistant."

"Don't be so modest. I bet you're a lot more important than you're letting on. I bet you know what happened in Buffalo. Elsie was happy to give us the details. You'd be surprised what she knew."

Now that got to Bolton. He stood, but I happily pushed him back into his chair.

"Ooh. That made you mad. Here you are in a police station, and the man who holds the other end of your leash is giving away everything to his mistress."

It was a neat trick. We had no idea what happened in Buffalo, only that it must've been something bad. If Alice or I had said one more word, he'd realize we knew just about nothing. But she wanted to scare him. And the look in his eyes showed we had. He'd go back to his masters now and tell them we were on to them.

His eyes were smoldering.

"I think we're done here," said Alice. "With any luck, we'll never meet again." And with that,

Alice swept out of the room. We said a farewell to the lieutenant and found ourselves back in the terminal.

"Nicely done," I said. "You did get something out of him. And I bet it made you feel better."

She grinned at me. "Yes, it did make me feel better. Although you're right, I did want to see what he knew. But more, I wanted to send him back to Brantley and Van Schuyler with tales to tell. This is how it's done in government, you know. You introduce a problem and watch your enemies fall apart blaming each other."

"Well done," I said. She looked proud of herself.

"Now we have to find out what happened that night in Buffalo. This is exactly what we were looking for—a link from the Van Schuylers to the time and place of the McKinley assassination, what got us started in the first place. Elsie confirmed what I suspected—something happened in Buffalo, something bad for the Van Schuylers, the very day McKinley was killed. What was it? We're beyond coincidences. With the Van Schuylers, it was something financial, most likely." She frowned. "This next step is going to be difficult, though. We don't know anyone connected with the Buffalo police. We'll really have to get on a train to Buffalo and see what we can find."

"We're not traveling to Buffalo, Miss Alice, but"—and I forestalled her protests—"I may be able to help. It's been a busy day. We'll talk about it tomorrow."

"Oh, very well. I can wait, I suppose. And I don't see what else we can do meanwhile." She paused. "We could go to—what was that restaurant you said you and Mariah ate at sometimes—the ratatouille?"

"What is a ratatouille?" I asked.

"It's a French dish—that was the name of the restaurant, you said, right? A German restaurant."

I saw what she was getting at, and I laughed. "You mean the Rathskeller. We'll go there sometime, but not tonight. Dulcie is expecting you for dinner—"

"Oh, please. I've been good with my allowance this week and lucky with the ponies. My treat."

She looked so hopeful, and sauerbraten, beer, and potato dumplings sounded pretty good, so I said yes, and we went back to the Caledonia to rest before going out.

I took a little nap in my room, and then went upstairs around 6:00. I was waiting in the foyer when Dulcie emerged from the kitchen, glared at me, and said, "I'd have thought I could give everyone here as good a meal as some Krauts." Not waiting for a reply, she turned and went back to her little kingdom.

Alice swept in. "I assume the waiters speak English?" she asked. "Or do you know any German, Mr. St. Clair?"

297

"Just enough to get my face slapped in Milwaukee," I said, and Alice didn't seem to know if that was a joke.

The Rathskeller is in Yorkville, near where Mariah lives, and I would've had her join us if she hadn't been working. It's a few steps below the street, like that anarchist club we visited, but that's all they have in common. Good people—the local German immigrants and other East Europeans—go there, including families. It's clean, the waiters and chefs know their business, and you can't get better beer.

It was crowded, but they squeezed us into a table. I took the seat with my back to the wall so I could keep an eye on the place. To my left was the kitchen, and to my right was a family speaking German.

Alice delighted in the place and looked around, practically staring. She loved new experiences, and our Chinatown and Little Italy trips had only whetted her appetite for novelty. When the beer came, it was a little heavier than she was used to, and I watched her sample it gravely before taking a serious swallow that left her with a foamy mustache.

"What's so funny?" she asked me.

"Just glad to see you so happy, Miss Alice," I said. And she turned pink at that. When our food came, she eagerly dug in. I don't think she had ever had meat like that, and the sauerkraut was pungent enough to make her drink the beer with gusto.

"This is wonderful. Thank you," she said.

"What for? You're paying," I said.

"I mean, thank you for—for bringing me here. For not making me stay home," she said, a little self-conscious. We didn't talk about our recent adventures. Instead, she asked about Wyoming, and I told her a few tall stories about the West while the place got busier and racing waiters slipped past us. We were done, and I was thinking about some apple strudel, when Alice frowned and looked into her lap. She picked up a piece of heavily folded paper.

"I think someone passing by dropped this into my lap," she said. She unfolded it, frowned again, and then handed it to me. Someone had written in a heavy hand, "If you value your safety, just stop." I looked around quickly: there were mostly happy diners and patrons, but I saw the back of a skinny man threading his way out the door just short of a run.

I leaned over the table. "Miss Alice. I'm going to need you to be brave. I'm getting up. You're going to move into my seat so you can see around. Don't move except for that, and don't panic. Do wait for me."

She nodded. I could count on her.

I got up and headed around the corner past the kitchen. I had been in that restaurant before, and Mariah knew the chef, so I knew there was a storeroom at the end of a short hall. I made sure it was empty, counted to twenty, and went back.

Alice had changed seats, and there was now another man in what had been her seat, talking to her. Alice was listening, and she wasn't happy, but she wasn't frightened either. She was a silly girl sometimes, but she wasn't Theodore Roosevelt's daughter for nothing. I stepped behind him, but Alice kept her eyes on the man.

Over the din, I could just hear him. ". . . so it's just a friendly suggestion, miss. You're involving yourself with people and situations you really shouldn't be, and it would be much better for your health . . ."

That was enough. The next thing the man knew, I was bending over him and talking right into his ear.

"I think it would be better for your health if you listened to me. You're feeling my Colt right in your back. Put both your hands on the table. I like this restaurant, and I wouldn't want it closed for a week while the police investigated your death."

He was smart enough not to argue. I looked at Alice.

"Miss Alice? Come here and search this man's coat pockets."

She grinned inappropriately and reached into his pockets. Nothing on the left, but she pulled a pistol out of his right. A derringer, small and lethal at close range.

"Can I keep it?" she asked.

"Just stick it in my pocket for now." She sighed but did it. People walked around us, but it was crowded and not too bright, so no one looked closely at what we were doing.

"Now you, sir. Get up slowly and head toward the kitchen. Miss Alice, follow me." We walked single file to the storage room. I told him to sit down with his hands on his head, and I closed and latched the door.

"Nice trick," I said. "Have someone scare Miss Alice with a note, then you step in while I chase the messenger like an idiot. But he was the monkey. You're the organ grinder." He just grimaced. He was an average-looking guy, about my age, in an average suit. No one you'd normally notice. "I don't suppose you'd like to tell me who sent you?" He shrugged.

"You want to visit the Tombs?" I asked. He shrugged again.

"I've been in worse places. And I won't stay there long," he said. He had a local accent.

"Fine. Get up." He stood again, and the three of us walked through the service entrance and into an alley.

"If I take you to the Tombs, your masters will know you failed." He shrugged again, which made me want to shoot his head off his shoulders. "But if I let you go, they'll think you sold them out."

Now that got to him, and I could see some fear. I lowered my Colt and pulled out the derringer.

"These don't have much of a range. I wonder how much, though? I'm counting down from ten, and then I'm going to shoot you. So I suggest you start running . . ."

He licked his lips, saw I wasn't joking, and took off into the night. I pocketed the derringer.

Alice swore. "Why didn't you hold him and question him?" she asked.

I shook my head. "He was a professional, hired by some serious people. He couldn't even give us the name if he wanted to. These aren't dockyard thugs. You've upset someone powerful, Miss Alice."

She looked very satisfied, even proud.

"I'm right, aren't I? If they're threatening me, they'd threaten my father. You know that—you know I'm right."

I sighed. "Yes. I guess so. And we'll be going to someone who can help us tomorrow. Now let's pay, and I'm taking you home. Anyway, you did well tonight."

"Did I really? I wasn't afraid, not at all."

"I know, and your fearlessness frightens the hell out of me."

"You know, it would be very easy for me to carry around that derringer. Really—could I have it?"

A judge I knew in Wyoming told me that questions like that are called "rhetorical." At least I thought I'd treat it as that.

Chapter 21

Alice knew lots of people in New York, but I knew a few as well. After breakfast the next morning, we got into the car and then headed west.

I didn't remember the exact street, but I knew it was near the Hudson and, after a few false turns, found Everton Factoring—a nearly windowless redbrick building conveniently located near the docks. I understood they helped companies with their collections, something I didn't really understand, except that there was apparently a lot of money to be made doing it.

"What are we doing here?" asked Alice.

"Samuel Everton has a law degree, but with his father's death, he jumped into the family business. Your father knew him from Harvard, and he joined up with the Rough Riders. And after McKinley was killed, your father commissioned him and a few others to investigate the assassination."

Everton was a good sort. He did what his family expected, but you could tell he was sorry when the Cuban campaign ended and we were all mustered out. He might've sought his fortune in Africa or South America, and he liked my stories about the West.

But the Evertons had this business, and so he was on the Hudson instead of the Amazon.

"He sounds like a useful man to know. Why am I only hearing about him now?"

"Ah, good question, Miss Alice. Remember when I told you it was determined that Czolgosz acted alone? That was the report from Everton's group. I didn't think he had more to tell us about that. But maybe, just maybe, he found something else in Buffalo. It's worth asking at least."

"I certainly hope so. Because otherwise, you and I are on a train to Buffalo tomorrow."

"Like I said, he owes me a favor."

"Why? What did you do for him?"

I just smiled, which infuriated her.

The office of Everton Factoring was more practical than impressive. There was a small, messy reception desk staffed by a harried-looking clerk, and men in shirt-sleeves walked along the hallway.

"We're here to see Samuel Everton," I said.

"Oh, I think he's down there, in his office, this time of day." The receptionist had clearly decided that as unusual as we were, we were no threat to the company. Alice looked curiously at the clerks and accountants as we headed down the hall, and a few men looked up at us, but most of them were too busy to wonder about a cowboy and young lady in their midst.

We found a half-opened door with "S. Everton, President" neatly lettered on a brass plaque. I peeked in—Everton hadn't changed much. He was reading some papers, and he was still a handsome man, about forty, with a neat mustache and hair a little thinner than when we last saw each other. He had always been a bit of a dandy about his uniform, and his suit was uncommonly well-cut and neat considering the rather cluttered office.

Everton looked up, and I brought myself to attention. "Captain Everton, Sergeant Joseph St. Clair reporting for duty, sir."

It took him a moment, then he grinned and clapped his hands together. "Wonderful! You're a sight for sore eyes, Sergeant! Come on in." His eyes lit on Alice. He had never met her, and the light in the hallway was dim, so I guess he could be forgiven for saying, "And this must be . . . don't tell me you got married, St. Clair? I'd never have thought. But let me meet your wife."

And that amused Alice to no end. She smiled and gave me a sidelong glance as I felt the heat rise to my face. I'd never seen her look so satisfied.

"Actually, no, sir. May I present Miss Alice Roosevelt . . ."

"Oh, dear God, I am sorry . . . the light here . . . I wasn't expecting . . . but please, take a seat, both of you."

Alice still looked amused as we sat.

"Forgive me, Miss Roosevelt, I didn't mean—"

"No need to apologize, Mr. Everton. I'm not insulted." And she looked at me again to see my reaction. I guess I was supposed to be flattered.

Everton quickly moved on. "Miss Roosevelt, like

Joey St. Clair here, I was privileged to serve under your father in Cuba, and when you next speak with him, please give him my warmest regards. We haven't spoken in a few months. Now, how did you find yourself with this saddle bum?"

"Mr. St. Clair is now my Secret Service bodyguard."

"Secret Service? Good for you, St. Clair. Say, Miss Roosevelt, does your bodyguard here ever talk about his army days?"

"Not much," said Alice. "My father spoke well of him, but if you were his commanding officer, maybe you have more insight."

He laughed, and I shook my head, knowing what was coming.

"Sergeant St. Clair was as slovenly a soldier as any US regiment ever had, Miss Roosevelt, but I have never seen a soldier fire a Springfield with greater speed and accuracy than this man"—he smiled—"when he was around."

"Don't tell me Mr. St. Clair was absent without leave," said Alice, feigning horror.

"Oh, no. But he made the most of the time he had. Do you remember that cantina, and there was that woman there—what was her name? Feliciana—oh, she certainly appreciated you." He laughed again.

"Sir, Miss Roosevelt is only seventeen."

"Don't let my age stop you," said Alice a little primly. "I enjoy stories about Mr. St. Clair." She gave me a sidelong glance. Anyway, Captain Everton always did like to tell a good story and wasn't going to let Alice's age or position spoil it for him.

"Well, you should've seen this cowboy stumble through his ten words of Spanish with Feliciana, but he somehow managed . . ." It was then that Everton suddenly realized where the story was going and that maybe it was more suited to a barracks than a Manhattan office with the president's daughter.

"Ah, well, remember the good old times? Anyway, is this just to say hello, or is there something I can help you with?"

"Actually, there is, sir. I came across your name as one of the investigators who looked into the McKinley assassination—"

"—and we thought you could help us with some information we need," finished Alice.

Everton was a good-natured man for an officer, but he wasn't stupid, and his eyes went back and forth between me and Alice.

"My God, that's some request. Anyway, why do you need my help? If you're Secret Service, you had my full report. And Miss Roosevelt, no offense, but what is your role here?"

"It's not all that complicated. Mr. St. Clair and I are investigating some . . . peripheral issues surrounding McKinley's death. And we had some additional questions into what was happening in

Buffalo at that time—some events that might not have made it into the report as distributed to the Secret Service."

"*You're* investigating, Miss Roosevelt? I don't understand . . ."

"None of us do, sir," I said. "But I'll tell you, she's been doing quite a job so far, and we'd be very grateful if you could help us."

"What have you folks gotten into?" he asked, but fortunately he didn't seem to want, or even expect, an answer.

Alice jumped in. "Someone we know, someone who was in Buffalo on that very same day, was heard to say something else happened in Buffalo. Something *else* that was also important. But we don't know what."

He nodded and looked thoughtful. "Do either of you want to give me a name? If it helps, I'll keep it in confidence."

Alice and I looked at each other, and I shrugged. If she wanted to, it was up to her.

"Van Schuyler," she said.

Everton whistled. "My God, that's a big name in this state. What are you doing mixed up with them? They're certainly active in Buffalo. I heard their name everywhere, but surely they're not involved in the president's killing? They're a respected family, although . . . you hear things."

"What kind of things?" asked Alice.

"It's a tough world, Miss Roosevelt, and to make

it on the Great Lakes, you have to push hard. But that's all I know. I was only up there briefly, with just a small team. We were supposed to get some help from the Buffalo detectives, but they were busy with the murder of some lowlife. There are some grim corners of that town, believe me."

Alice perked up at that. "A death in a bad neighborhood? What made it special that it kept so many detectives busy when the president had just been assassinated?"

He shrugged. "I don't know the details, but they said it was very grim. Some poor girl shot at close range."

At close range. Alice and I looked at each other quickly. Close range—just like Cesare, the professional assassin.

"It can't be related," said Everton. "I mean, it was in a terrible slum, nowhere near where McKinley was shot. The Van Schuylers are involved with big finance, and there's nothing to do with big finance in that part of town."

"The thing is, sir, that guns are not as common as you'd imagine. They're expensive and loud and hard to hide. Murderers tend to use other methods. So if a gun was involved, there was something unusual going on, and if you have any more details, Miss Roosevelt and I would appreciate it."

Everton shook his head. "You're the expert, St. Clair. I'm just a simple lawyer who helped out the president with a report." He smiled wryly.

309

"But it's what wasn't in the report that you're interested in, right?"

"Exactly. Did the Buffalo police send you anything about that murder?" asked Alice.

"I'm sure they did. We gathered everything."

"Did you keep it? Is it in Washington?" I had a vision of wandering through some cavernous Washington warehouse for days.

"No. Actually, Miss Roosevelt, your father wanted to make sure the other attorneys and I could work independently, without all kinds of officials breathing down our necks. So we worked in this office. And when we were done, we locked everything up right here. It's still here. We're a factoring house, and we have a great big steel safe."

"And could we look at the materials, Mr. Everton?" He hadn't yet picked up on it, but she was losing patience quickly.

He shuffled some papers on his desk to stall for time. "It's a little awkward, Miss Roosevelt. I promised your father that this material would be treated as secret. The only reason it's still in my safe is that I didn't want to bother him yet with the details of how I'd ship it all to him in Washington. Would it be possible for you to get his permission?"

No, it wouldn't. Alice was looking frustrated, and I could tell there would be no bribing or blackmailing her way out of this. Everton was a straight arrow. But I knew I could get it if I really wanted to. If I really thought it was worth it—that we'd find out something important from the reports. If I really wanted to see this thing to the end.

"I'll tell you what, sir," I said. "Open up that safe, and your debt is paid."

Everton looked at me sharply. He hadn't been the strictest officer, but when it was important, he was serious.

"Are you saying what I think you're saying, Sergeant? It's a hell of a cost."

I glanced at Alice, who was now looking confused but knew enough not to interrupt.

"Yes, sir. It's a lot. But it's worth it to me. It's worth it to us."

Everton toyed with a paperweight for a few moments. "You're full of surprises, Sergeant, but I can't refuse you, as you well know." He didn't seem that happy about it. He must've known that someday I'd ask him to settle his debt, but he probably imagined it would be for a job or the down payment on some horses. Not this.

Everton stood. "Come with me." We followed him along another hall and into a large, window-less room where half a dozen clerks were working. Against the back wall stood a large safe that practically reached to the ceiling.

Everton opened it and searched for a while. I noticed he hardly used his left arm. The doctor had said he probably never would get its full use back, and better than anyone, I remembered how bad it had looked at the time.

After a few minutes, he produced a large folder labeled "ancillary materials." He gave it to Alice, then locked the safe again before leading us to a small conference room with a table.

"There's a lot of material in here, Miss Roosevelt, so why don't we each take a third and see if we can find what we want: a report from the Buffalo Police Department about a murder around the same time McKinley was assassinated."

We sifted through all kinds of notes from interviews and witness statements until I found a memo with the BPD seal. "Homicide Investigation: Dora Compton."

"I think this is it, sir," I said.

"Yes, that's it. I can't let that leave this building, even in payment of a debt, but if you want to take notes, I'll bring in some pens and paper. I hardly looked at it myself at the time, but you're welcome to see if there's anything of use to you."

"That will be very helpful, thank you," said Alice, and Everton left for a moment. The second he was gone, Alice turned to me.

"What debt was he talking about?" she asked.

"Later," I said.

"When we're out of here?"

"When you're thirty yourself," I said, and that earned me one of her glares.

Everton came back, so we couldn't continue with that line of thought. Alice began reading the report and taking notes while Everton and I stood behind her and read over her shoulder.

There wasn't much, actually—at least not at first. A young woman named Dora Compton was found dead of a single gunshot wound to her chest early on the day McKinley had been killed. She was only found when a neighbor knocked on her door hoping Dora could watch her children for a few pennies, as she was working an extra shift that night, but the woman found her dead and called the police. No one admitted to hearing anything earlier, but it was a poor neighborhood where no one wanted to get involved too heavily with the police.

The police had been curious because robbery didn't seem to be the motive, with her money easily found in a dresser drawer. And despite the poverty of the area, violence like that was unusual in the daytime. Jealous lover? A robbery that was interrupted?

On the last page, the investigating detective summed up the scant details of Dora's life, and that's where things got interesting. Under "known employment," he had written, "Van Schuyler Shipping."

Alice clapped her hands in satisfaction, but I pointed out that half the town seemed to work for the Van Schuylers, so she shouldn't get too excited.

"Well, I think it's an important clue. Mr. Everton—do you have Leon Czolgosz's Buffalo address somewhere in these files?"

"Probably. We have everything here." In another few minutes, he found it, and when Alice saw it, she jumped out of her chair and practically danced. "Look—both of you, just look." Everton and I looked at the Czolgosz biographical sketch and Dora's police report—they lived in the same tenement.

"We never noticed," said Everton ruefully.

"Why would you, sir? They just slipped you the report to show what was keeping them busy. No reason to make a connection."

"I suppose," he said. "Do you think he killed her before killing the president?"

"Not unless he had two guns," said Alice. "Look at the report—Dora was killed with something more powerful than the .32 Iver Johnson revolver Czolgosz used to kill the president. Probably a .44 caliber." I looked at Alice, and we were both thinking the same thing: It was a .44 caliber, in the hands of the Archangel, that had killed Cesare. This was it, what I knew Alice had been looking for: a firm connection between the Van Schuyler company and the assassination. Here was a Van Schuyler employee who lived in the same building as Czolgosz and was killed the same day as McKinley.

Alice then grabbed the report and peered closely

314

at a marginal notation near the bottom, no doubt made by the investigating detective. "Next of kin notified: Albert Compton, brother, Lexington Wine & Spirits, New York," along with the address.

"I think this is all we need, sir. You have no idea what this has meant to us," I said.

"No, I don't," he said, looking a little amused. "And I don't think I want to know more. But good luck to both of you. Sergeant, if you get an evening off, join me for dinner some night. We can talk about old times. I'm thinking of selling up. There are opportunities for ranching in Argentina. We could go into it together."

"I'd like that, sir."

"Mr. St. Clair can't go to Argentina, not for a while. He has to watch over me," said Alice.

I shrugged. "You heard what Miss Roosevelt said, sir, and as you well know, I always oblige the ladies." We both laughed at that, while Alice looked a little miffed at being left out of an inside joke. "Thank you again, sir. We'll have that dinner, and once again, your debt is paid in full." We shook hands, and then he saw us out.

The front door had barely closed when Alice said, "What was that all about?"

"About obliging a lady? Just a joke about a Cuban barmaid. Soldier banter."

"Not that—although, were you close with her, this Feliciana?"

"How long do you think I was in Cuba? All I can

say is that I probably spent less time with her than you have with Preston."

And that quieted her for a few moments—no easy feat. "We're off the subject. What I meant to ask about was that debt. What did Mr. Everton owe you? Is this just left over from some card game?"

We were in the motorcar, and I started it up. It was back to the East Side to Lexington Wine & Spirits to find Dora Compton's next of kin. If nothing else, this investigation was teaching me a lot about New York geography.

"No, it wasn't a card game," I said.

"What then?" she persisted.

"You wouldn't understand," I said.

"Don't patronize me, Cowboy."

I knew she'd go on and on until I told her, and it was easier to discuss while I was driving.

"During a battle, Captain Everton was shot and went down. Maybe you noticed how he doesn't use his left arm much. He had dragged himself to the side of a farmhouse, and we were falling back in the face of a Spanish counterattack. He could barely move and ordered us to leave him behind. But I disobeyed. I stayed there and I emptied my rifle. Then his rifle. And his revolver. By that time, the Spanish decided it wasn't worth it and went around us. Eventually, we were found and the captain said he owed me, and someday he would pay me back."

Alice thought about that for a while.

"Why?" she asked.

"Why did I stay with him? I told you that you wouldn't understand."

"No, not why you stayed. I never doubted your physical courage, Mr. St. Clair. Why did you settle the debt for something that *I* wanted? You've seemed pretty clear that you're just humoring me. So why spend so much? Wait, I know. It's because you know how important this is, that my father himself could be in danger."

"Yes," I said. "That's it." But she continued to stare at me curiously.

"Actually, I think you really did it for *me,* to make *me* happy," she finally said. "Thank you very much, Mr. St. Clair." She kissed me on the cheek. I wasn't going to disagree with her. I wanted to protect the president. I wanted to keep Alice happy. I wanted some excitement myself. And Alice could believe . . . what she believed.

"You're welcome, Miss Alice."

Chapter 22

L exington Wine & Spirits looked like a good outfit with a wide selection on clean shelves, and some well-heeled gentlemen were looking over the goods. The sales clerks were dressed in good suits, and one of them came over to us. As he got closer, I could see his eyes light up. It was always fun to watch the expressions of those who recognized Alice Roosevelt, and I knew Alice never tired of it.

"Miss Roosevelt, I am honored to have you in our store. I'm Mr. Letchworth, the manager. How may I serve you today?"

"Thank you. My father does not drink excessively and does not admire men who do, but he does like an occasional mint julep, which I believe he makes from rye whisky. Can you help me?" Mr. Letchworth was delighted to help, and soon we had an excellent bottle, which he said he'd send to the Caledonia.

Then he looked up at me, hoping to make another sale.

"Oh, this is Mr. St. Clair, my Secret Service bodyguard."

"Can I guess your drink, sir?" said the cheerful manager. "I can always tell. You're a bourbon man?"

"Very good," I said, laughing.

"As a reward for your good guess, I'll also buy a bottle of bourbon, your finest for Mr. St. Clair. You can ship it with the rye."

"Happy to oblige, Miss Roosevelt. I'll just ring up your purchases." He disappeared for a few moments.

"Thank you," I said.

"You're welcome," she said, coloring slightly.

"One more thing," said Alice when Letchworth returned. "As long as we're here, I believe I know one of your employees. His brother—or was it cousin—works for a friend of mine, and I just want to pass along my regards. An Albert Compton?"

He seemed a little surprised but wasn't about to question a Roosevelt. "Oh, ah, of course, very nice of you. Mr. Compton is the dispatch clerk. Been with us for a number of years. You can find him on our loading dock, which you can reach through that back door."

We thanked him again and walked through the back door. Business must've been pretty good for Lexington folks, because there were several delivery trucks being loaded, and a slightly built man about my age, in a suit also not that different from mine, was checking shipments off one by one. We waited until the last truck left, then approached him. Looking back at it, Alice's greeting may not have been the best idea, but I think anything would've set him off.

"Mr. Compton? Could we have a word about your late sister, Dora? We'd just like—" But he was off like a jackrabbit. This time, I was the one who had to decide to leave Alice alone. I had a second to consider just how dangerous it might be to let this probable witness to an assassination get away and how unlikely it would be that Alice would be assaulted in a respectable store in a good neighborhood, and I took off.

Even so, he might've gotten away if he had headed to the street and lost himself in the crowd, but instead he turned into a warren of service streets that ran behind the houses. It was only a matter of time before I caught up to him behind a butcher shop, and he found himself hemmed in between a tall fence that separated the next property and a rack of pig carcasses.

He had absolute terror in his eyes, the look of a man who realizes he's made a terrible mistake and isn't going to get another chance. He fumbled in his pocket and produced a nasty-looking knife with a six-inch blade.

"I—I know how to use this," he said, but he obviously didn't.

"Just settle down," I said. I pulled out my badge. "I'm not here to hurt you. I'm with the US Secret Service, and I just want to talk."

"You're here to kill me," he said. Despite the cold weather, he was sweating, and he wiped his coat sleeve across his brow. His hand was shaking so badly I doubted if he could swat a fly.

I opened my coat to show my Colt. "Listen, pal, if I wanted you dead, you'd already be dead. First rule: don't bring a knife to a gun fight. Again, I'm Secret Service. You saw I was with a lady. You think I'd bring a lady if I was going to kill you?" I saw the doubt in his eyes, then I stepped over to him and took away his knife. "Come on, someone wants to speak with you. I think we can help each other."

I took him by the arm and led him back to the loading dock, where Alice was waiting and tapping her foot.

"I was wondering when you two would be back. It's freezing out here. Is there a place we can talk inside?"

It turned out that Albert had a little booth, barely big enough for the three of us to stand, where he kept his paperwork, and it was reasonably warm.

"Are you really Secret Service?" he asked, finally showing signs of calming down and realizing he wasn't going to die, at least not by our hand.

"Yes. And this is Alice Roosevelt. She has some questions for you. I'd advise you to answer them completely and truthfully."

"Am I under arrest?" he asked.

Alice fielded that one. "Mr. Compton, your possible arrest is the least of your worries right now. You are involved with some very unpleasant people, and I know this because if you weren't, you wouldn't have run like that when we asked you a civil question, and you wouldn't have threatened Mr. St. Clair with that knife he obviously took away from you. Your only hope right now is cooperation."

"You're really Alice Roosevelt?" he asked. "But I don't understand . . ."

"You don't have to understand. But you do have to talk to us. We're here about your sister, Dora."

Albert sighed deeply and wiped his brow again. He reached under a cabinet, and I moved my hand to my revolver, but he only came up with a bottle of gin. He took a long swig, and that seemed to steady him. He also remembered his manners and offered some to me and, God bless him, to Alice too, and he shrugged when we turned him down.

"Very well. Dora was my sister and a good kid. I could've helped her find work in the city, but the Van Schuylers were offering good wages for workers willing to move upstate. It's mostly men up there, but they also needed women to work kitchens at work sites, run laundries, things like that. She wrote me that the work was tough and the managers were strict, but she was saving her money—and then she got involved with a man. I know . . . I should've gone up there like a good brother and checked him out, but we'd been on our own since we were very young, and I thought she could take care of herself . . ." He drank more gin.

"What was his name?" asked Alice.

"She didn't say. She just wrote she had found a sweetheart, a real gentleman, at least at first. She was a very pretty girl, you see." He looked mournful for a moment, before shaking his head and continuing. "She knew he wasn't married—she had the sense to make sure of that, she told me. But as she wrote more, it was clear things weren't so good. He was becoming more and more demanding and short-tempered, and although she hoped he'd marry her, he kept putting her off. But that's the way of rich folks, isn't it?"

"Not all of us," said Alice.

"I beg your pardon. Not all of you," he said. "But a lot of them, for sure. And then he started to ask her to spy on other Van Schuyler workers and report back to him. He said he was afraid of anarchists."

"Wait—this gentleman suitor was with the Van Schuyler company? It sounds like he was, if he was afraid of anarchists," said Alice.

"That's what I figured," said Albert. "At any rate, he was a rich man, and they're all afraid of anarchists."

"Was your sister an anarchist?"

"Certainly not! She was a good, honest girl, but that's when things went bad. She wasn't going to spy on every hardworking man or woman who just happened to make a complaint after a long day's work. But it got worse. In her last letter to me, she said . . . well, she said she was frightened. He was not only pushing her for information but pushing her neighbor, too, for information on anarchist agitators."

"That neighbor was Leon Czolgosz, wasn't he?" said Alice, and Albert looked like he had been slapped.

"How the . . . who told you—"

"Nevermind that. Just let it be a lesson to you that secrets are harder to keep than you think."

"I guess so," he said. "But you can imagine why I wanted to keep that to myself, how I realized my sister was in great danger. I had decided that it was time for me to go up there, even before the assassination. And then . . . it happened. I heard Dora's neighbor, Leon Czolgosz, had killed the president."

"Did she say anything about him? What was he like?"

"Rather like a stray cat, according to Dora," he said with a rueful smile. "She didn't say much, however—just how ridiculous it was for her suitor to try to harass Leon. She said Leon called himself an anarchist, but she thought he was just posing, showing off. That anyone would find him a real threat was silly, she said. I don't think she thought—that anyone thought—he would really kill the president."

Alice nodded. "So you must've been very surprised when you heard?"

"Absolutely. I tried to reach her—and I found out she had been killed, and the police were investigating. I was out of my mind. I didn't know what to think." He buried his face in his hands, and I started to feel bad for him. I had a sister, too, and he had lost his under horrific circumstances.

"Can you imagine?" he said, looking up. "My sister dead, her friend and neighbor a presidential assassin, and some mysterious suitor whose name I didn't know but who may have killed her. I was afraid to even make inquiries. And then, about a week after she died, I received a package in the mail. There was a short note from Dora asking me to keep it safe until we were together again. Judging from the postmark, she was killed the day after she sent it."

"A package?"

And now Albert, who had started our meeting in fear and progressed to grief, began to exhibit craftiness.

"I didn't know what it was at first. But as I looked at it, I realized they were reports, not all that different from what I do here. Reports about Van Schuyler people and materials at various Great Lakes ports, with dates through last summer." Alice and I met each other's eyes. I had told her about Bolton's clerk saying another employee had been killed for betraying the Van Schuylers. That seemed to be Dora.

"I think it was Dora's revenge on her suitor," he continued, "stealing important papers from him. Her suitor was part of, or at least connected to, the Van Schuyler family. And I think they'll pay to get these papers back." He looked proud of himself, and even though I felt a little sympathy, I didn't much like his plans to make money from his sister's death. And I don't think Alice did either. Revenge isn't pretty, and when you mix it with greed, it's only worse.

"Why do you think those papers are valuable?" Alice asked.

"Dora wasn't stupid," he said. "She knew they were worth something. And I can guess what they're about. I'm betting the family was crooked—things being moved where they shouldn't be and lying about it. Goods smuggled or even stolen. I've been a clerk for a long time, miss, and I know the sins reports like this can hide, if you know how to read them." He looked more and more crafty as he spoke.

"I am making allowances for your feelings," said Alice. "You are probably right about the importance of those papers. If anything, you may be underestimating their importance. They have to go to the proper authorities. I will see that happens. Do you have them with you?"

Albert looked out of the little window in the booth, into the distance, and he gave a small smile, just for himself. "I knew I had to be patient. I had to wait until things were a little quieter. And then I sent the company president, Mr. Henry van Schuyler, a letter and asked him to reply to a general delivery post office box. It's only been two weeks. He'll pay up, I know. I can wait."

"No," said Alice. "He will find you and kill you. And you know it. You thought we were from the Van Schuylers, or you wouldn't have run. You wouldn't have armed yourself. You're a fool. And they will find you. You have no idea what you're up against. Now give me those papers."

His answer was more gin. Alice snatched it out of his hand, and before either of us could react, she opened the window and threw it out to smash on the loading dock. Albert looked forlorn, but then he shrugged and rallied. "I admit I'm nervous. But the fact is that you weren't with the Van Schuylers. I've been staying in a little room above the shop, and there's a night watchman here. My apartment in Brooklyn is under a friend's name. And that's where the papers are."

"I found you, Mr. Compton. It's true I am very clever. But the Van Schuylers are clever, too, and they will find you, and they'll get their papers. And then they'll kill you. This is your last chance to live. Now, let's go get those papers."

He was still looking out the window, but not at the broken gin bottle, and I don't even know if he was aware we were there anymore. "Yes, Miss Roosevelt, I will. But not until I'm done getting the money from the Van Schuylers. They're going to pay."

"You idiot!" she shouted. "Don't you understand who they are, what they're going to do to you? You can't win." In another circumstance, it might've been amusing watching a young girl threaten a man like that, but with the set of her mouth and eyes as hard as a New York cop, I knew she was serious. "No one is going to pay you. You'll be either giving it to me or giving it to the Van Schuylers. Think about it. Deal with me, and you'll live. We'll be back. Come, Mr. St. Clair."

And we left him to his emotions—grief, rage, regret. But mostly fear, and I didn't blame him.

Chapter 23

We got back into the motorcar.

"He told us the same thing as Emma Goldman," Alice said, and I didn't immediately get the reference, but she continued. "Remember? She never thought Czolgosz could've done it. And now we see Dora Compton apparently didn't either. Maybe Goldman was actually right. We'll have to think about that. Anyway, this idiot's lack of cooperation is just a temporary setback," she said. "We know a lot now, and if Dora really did steal Van Schuyler reports from her lover, who I'm guessing was the Archangel, there may be a copy somewhere else, too. And we will get them—Albert Compton is very much mistaken if he thinks he can thwart me. I'll lean on Preston, too. Back to the University Club. Preston has some decisions to make."

I just nodded and put the motorcar into gear. Alice was good and angry, and at least for now, she wanted to take it out on Preston.

We were quiet for a while, and Alice steamed, but then she looked a little curious. "Mr. St. Clair, you may be my bodyguard, but that's not what the Secret Service mostly does. It handles financial crimes, I believe—counterfeit money and so on."

"That's right, lots of accountants and the like. Not really my line."

"But you must've had some training when you joined. Albert Compton just seems to have geographical records, personnel records. But wouldn't there have to be some financial ledgers to go with them?"

I thought back. When I joined the Secret Service, I had to go to a general accounting class. It wasn't that unfamiliar to me. On any ranch, there were practices in place to keep track of cattle. But our instructor showed us how you could keep track of anything, how the big New York companies used ledgers to run businesses that stretched across the country and even across the world.

But the ledgers could lie.

"Yes, Miss Alice. Even criminals need records. If Mr. Compton has records of what the Van Schuylers were up to, somewhere there are ledgers showing the finances of those transactions."

"So think about this. If the reports Dora Compton stole and sent to her brother differ from the actual ledgers, those would be more than suggestive. They'd be proof of fraud, actual crimes—maybe smuggling or avoiding taxes or something like that? They're reporting one thing, but the accounting tables in the ledgers show something else. That would be solid proof. Compton has something, but not everything needed for a criminal prosecution."

"Well, yes, that sounds right—if we got those reports Compton has and if we could get into the Van Schuyler offices and see those ledgers. Just one thing, Miss Alice. We don't have those ledgers, and I don't see the Van Schuylers giving them up. No court is going to issue a warrant based on our reasoning."

"You let me worry about that, Mr. St. Clair," she said, her good humor restored.

It was back to the University Club. The porter looked a little askance at Alice—this was the third time she had descended on them, and once again she was bringing the hired help with the revolver on his hip. At least we were on the list now.

"I take it you're looking for Mr. Van Schuyler." He forced a smile. "I'm sure you know where to find him, Miss Roosevelt."

"We'd avoid these difficulties in the future if you'd open membership to women," she said.

"I'll take it up with the membership committee," he replied, but he was already speaking to her back.

We found Preston in the usual place. "Alice. Mr. St. Clair. Have there been any developments?"

"Very much so. We need to talk. If there is a private table in that lovely little bar, you can buy us some drinks," Alice said.

"Buy you some drinks?" he asked, a little mystified.

"I think you're going to need one. At least one," I said.

He looked a little nervous but then smiled. "You found something, Alice, didn't you? What happened after you left Julia? And what happened to Shaw—some sort of problem came up, but he won't talk to me, so I came back here and have been waiting to hear from you. What is happening?"

"Lots. And when I have time, I'll give you the details. But there's more important work for you. Now come—I'd like a brandy, and Mr. St. Clair could use some bourbon."

Preston looked a little uncertain, but he followed us. Alice led the way to the guest bar and was already getting a waiter to show her to a table before Preston—the one who was actually a member—had even arrived. Alice raised an eyebrow when he hesitated.

A few minutes later, we had our drinks, and Preston was looking up expectantly.

"Preston, we have been very fortunate. It seems that we have come across a Van Schuyler employee, a former employee, who was left very bitter by her experience with the company. She was able to steal some incriminating documents."

"Do you have them?" asked Preston.

"No. We know who has them but can't get at them."

"You can't—"

"Now, Preston, just listen. We believe this former employee has some records, some sort of reports, that could incriminate your uncle and Shaw.

They're now in the hands of someone trying to use these reports to blackmail them. But I want to get them first. More than that, Mr. St. Clair here thinks that these reports will show different information from your company ledgers. We need you to get the ledgers. And then we can bring down your uncle and Shaw."

"But Alice, you don't even have the corresponding records."

"I'll get them. One way or another, I will. You handle your end. Get me those ledgers—they cover the past summer. They'd cover the same period as the reports but would show some serious discrepancies. I'm guessing those reports by themselves are damaging and embarrassing, which is why your family wants them back and why this person is trying to blackmail them. But together with the ledgers, I'm sure they will be damning."

"But I'm not involved in that end of the business. Uncle Henry just has me working on odds and ends, nothing as serious as the ledgers."

"But you must know where they are."

"Yes, but—"

"Preston, are you just going to make difficulties? I thought you were serious about challenging your Uncle Henry and about running an honest company. What are you going to do? What do you really want?" She was getting louder and louder, and a few members stuck their heads in the door to see who was causing the commotion. All of them recognized Preston van Schuyler and probably Alice as well. And none of them was willing to intervene in a debate between members of two of the most powerful families in New York, nevermind the fact that there was an armed cowboy in their midst.

I didn't think Preston cared much about running a company, honest or not, or what his uncle or Shaw were up to. But he cared what Alice thought, that much was clear. I knew he'd do it. He'd do it for Alice.

"I'll see what I can do," he said without a lot of joy, but it was good enough for Alice, who leaned over the table and gave him a kiss on his cheek.

I waved over a waiter, who didn't really want to be at my service. "I'm fine, and so is Miss Roosevelt here, but I think Mr. Van Schuyler could do with another brandy."

"Yes, sir," said the waiter.

At the time, I felt very superior to Preston. He was doing this purely because he fancied himself in love with Alice, and I was doing it because we might catch an assassin who still posed a threat to the president. And because I was getting paid. But mostly because I missed the old days.

Chapter 24

I saw Alice home, and as we entered the apartment, the maid mentioned that Mrs. Cowles would be out until late at a meeting of the Republican Women's Club of New York.

"That's right, she told me earlier. Mr. St. Clair, do you have any plans for this evening?"

"If you want to go out again, I can make myself available."

"No. I meant, were you going to do anything this evening?"

I shrugged. "No. Not really. Maybe see if the night porters had a card game going."

"There's a nightly card game here? Any chance that I . . . but no, it would get back to Aunt Anna."

"Let's just hope Mrs. Cowles doesn't find out what you were up to today."

"But we did nothing wrong. We visited with the Van Schuylers; met Elsie de Maine, a new lady friend; and had a pleasant reunion with an old military acquaintance of yours. Completely aboveboard. But we're off subject. I was asking to see if you were available to join me for dinner. I don't like eating alone."

She asked it a little shyly, as if she was afraid of being turned down. Which I almost did.

"Miss Alice, I don't think Mrs. Cowles wants to see me in the formal dining room here."

"If that's the only problem, that's easy to take care of." She pushed her way into the kitchen.

"Dulcie—dinner for two tonight. Mr. St. Clair will be joining me. Oh, and let's keep it simple. We'll dine in the breakfast room."

She rejoined me in the foyer. "All taken care of. I'm going to change and freshen up. I'll see you later, then? We have a lot to discuss." She turned and headed off to her room, leaving me just shaking my head. But before I got away, Dulcie stepped out of the kitchen, waving a dangerous-looking knife.

"You just watch it, mister," she said, scowling at me.

"Oh, come, Miss Dulcie," I said, going for my best charming grin. "Are you saying you won't feed me in your kitchen again?"

"I guess I'm not going to have to," she said. "You just watch it." And I headed downstairs to wash up before dinner.

I put a comb through my hair and felt along my chin. I might've used a shave, but my hair is fair, so I can usually get away without picking up a razor too often. I looked in my little square mirror. My face had been burned by a lot of hot summers and cold winters. I told myself I wore my riding coat and Stetson to remind myself where I came from, but there was no chance of ever fitting in anyway, no matter how often Alice rented me evening clothes.

I thought of Captain Everton. We'd have our dinner and talk over old times, but whatever dreams he had, we both knew he'd never give up everything to buy a ranch in Argentina. He was from New York. And I was from Wyoming. We wouldn't change.

At dinnertime, I smoothed out my jacket and made my way up to the Cowles apartment. Alice met me at the door herself. "Good evening, sir."

"Good evening, miss. I hope that my suit is all right. My evening clothes had to go back to the shop."

"We're very casual here," she said. "I think dinner is ready to be served. You may walk me in." She raised her eyebrow until I got the hint and took her arm so we could walk into the breakfast room together.

Dulcie made quail that night, which I recognized but had never eaten. But Dulcie had a fair hand with game birds, I'll give her that.

"I don't suppose you had quail in Wyoming?" asked Alice.

"Never even heard of it until I came east."

"But you know how to eat it. You adapt quickly. You were a ranch hand in the West, a lawman in town, a soldier in Cuba, and now a Secret Service agent in New York."

"I never really thought about it. I just saw it as taking what comes."

"Do you think I could adapt? I mean, living out West."

"Your father adapted. And you're his daughter. Do you want to live in the West?"

She pondered that. "I'm supposed to go to Washington. It's funny. Aunt Anna was planning to exile you to San Francisco, but I would like to see it. We could all go—I mean, you, me, and Mariah."

I laughed. "We'd make quite a crew."

"I think we'd get on pretty well. I like Mariah, and I think she likes me."

"I think she does, too," I said. I was going to ask where Preston fit in, but things were going nicely, so I saw no need to get her back up by teasing her again. And the Van Schuylers would come up again soon, I knew.

"Perhaps after this is all over, I'll speak to my father and make up some sort of reason for us to go to the West Coast. You, me, and Mariah. I bet she'd like to travel. We'll put her down as a chaperone."

"You need a chaperone?" I asked.

"Of course. I can't go on a long train ride with no one but a bodyguard. I need a chaperone, too. And who would be more appropriate than the sister of my bodyguard? Didn't you have chaperones in Wyoming?"

"No, we didn't. But as you said, I can adapt," I said, and Alice laughed.

"It's settled then. We'll go West and see St. Louis and Chicago and have ourselves a fine time in San

Francisco. But look at us, talking fun. My father would be disappointed, taking care of pleasure before business. We have some papers to get ahold of. And I figured out how to do it."

"Frightening Albert? If fear of the Van Schuylers won't get him to give up the papers, then what are you going to scare him with?"

"Oh, he's scared, and he may come through for us, but I'm gambling that we can find some other source. I don't think Albert Compton is the only man with access to the documents we need. We need to reach out a little more."

"Fair enough. But what are the nuts and bolts?"

"I'm still working out the details. And here's what I thought . . ."

And then the front doorbell rang.

"Is that Mrs. Cowles?"

"No, not this early. And she lets herself in most of the time anyway, but I can't imagine who's coming at this hour."

We heard the maid answering the door. We heard muffled talking, and then the maid led a night porter to the table.

"Sorry to disturb you, Miss Roosevelt, but I have an urgent message for Mr. St. Clair," he said. "Hand delivered."

He gave me a plain envelope, and I slit it open while Alice looked on, burning with curiosity.

"Who is bothering to send you a special message?"

There was only one line on the page. I read it

and handed it to Alice, who grabbed it out of my hand.

" 'The rail is burning,' " she read. "What does that mean? And if you tell me one more time that it's called the *Secret* Service, I'll hit you."

"I'm your bodyguard, Miss Alice. I have to follow the rules."

"Tonight you're not my bodyguard. You're my dinner guest. And I'm your hostess. What does 'The rail is burning' mean?"

"I'm not supposed to tell you, but I don't see the harm. That means that the presidential train is about to pull into the station, and soon the president will be arriving."

"My father is coming? That's marvelous! But why? I passed on the information about the Van Schuyler ship launch, to see if he wants to come, so maybe that's it. But he didn't say anything to me. What do you think?"

"I think that the president may want to join us for pie and coffee."

It wasn't long. The cars were waiting and the police escort was standing by to bring him quickly uptown to the Caledonia. In fact, the maid had hardly finished clearing the table when the doorman called from the lobby to say that President Roosevelt was on his way up. Alice stood by the door ready to greet him, and I stood a little behind her.

"Glad to see you, Baby Lee," he said, giving her

a hug, "and St. Clair." He gave me a strong hand-shake as usual.

"Good to see you, Mr. President. I trust you are well?"

"Fine, fine, thanks. Is my sister here?"

"Aunt Anna is having dinner at the Republican Women's Club. She'll be home later. How long are you here?"

"I leave the day after tomorrow. More men to meet with here, but the main reason I'm here is that tomorrow night I agreed to address the annual meeting of the New York Commercial Society. They're very prominent in business affairs in New York, which means business affairs in the United States—"

"Which means business affairs in the world," finished Alice. The president laughed.

"Very good. I'll have to bring you down to Washington soon to help me." I could tell Alice was over the moon at his compliment.

"But I thought that you were here for the Van Schuyler ship launch, like I said in my message."

At that, the president looked a little uncomfortable, something that didn't happen often.

"I need to talk to you about that . . . and you look like you were going to sneak off, St. Clair. I'd like you to stay."

"I'm at your disposal, sir."

"All he was going to do is fleece some local boys

over a card game," said Alice, and the president grabbed me by the shoulder. "Let's give some of my fellow New Yorkers a break tonight, St. Clair. I'd like to talk to both of you."

"Mr. St. Clair and I were discussing tomorrow's plans over dinner in the breakfast room. But I think Dulcie made an apple pie, and there's coffee."

The president clapped his hands together in delight. "Bully. Pie and coffee and a conversation."

The maid was very pleased with herself as she practically fawned over the president. And Dulcie? I don't think she much cared who she was cooking for. As she had told me, she was the president of the kitchen.

"So, Baby Lee, how go your investigations— immigrants and all that?"

"Fascinating. I've learned so much. Would you like a report?"

"Yes. Write one up, then come down to Washington and we'll discuss it with some of the boys in the cabinet."

"I'll get started right away," she said, and her eyes shone.

"Now, on to other topics. Anna tells me you've been calling a lot on young Preston van Schuyler."

Alice glanced at me quickly to make sure I wasn't smiling at that and then answered her father. "Well, yes. We saw a bit of each other this summer, as you well know, and are just continuing our friendship. Are you coming to the ship launching? I know the family wanted you to attend."

"No, I'm not. And I'm going to trust you with the reason why. You've said that you want to be involved, to help me. So I'm going to treat you like a Roosevelt and trust you." He turned to me. "What do you say to that, St. Clair? Can we trust my daughter?"

"Sir, if you can't trust Miss Alice, you can't trust anyone." I saw her eyebrow go up just a bit and the ghost of a smile.

"Well then. Here's the situation. The Van Schuylers have been aggressive in pursuing their expansion plans, especially in the Great Lakes. A little too aggressive. You know I like ambitious men, those who rise to challenges and get things done. But you have to play fair, or it's all for nothing. And I'm sorry to say that Henry van Schuyler and his son-in-law, Shaw Brantley, have not been playing fair. Talks of bribery and vandalism have reached us in Washington. A certain amount of rough-housing is expected—not that I condone any of it—but it seems as if the management of the company is out of control, well beyond what is typical. And you know how I feel about monopolies, perverting the course of capitalism."

So things had gotten as bad as that. Washington was looking into Van Schuyler affairs. One thing I was sure of: If it had gone this far, the Van Schuylers would already know they were being investigated. They'd start to panic, and there was no telling what they'd do next. Or what the Archangel would do. I caught Alice's eye, and I knew she was thinking the same thing.

"But Preston tells me he's hardly involved in the family business—he just gets busywork from his uncle. He says he wants his share, but he doesn't want to run it. He wants to travel and do things."

"I'm sure," said the president. "But when the Justice Department starts moving, it's going to get a little ugly." He reached over the table and took his daughter's hand. "I don't believe that Preston is directly involved. He may be as much of a victim here as anyone. But I just want you to be careful about becoming too involved with the family. And of course, you can't mention to anyone what I've told you."

"Of course, Father. Thank you for trusting me. I will be careful and won't let you down." But I could tell that her mind was a thousand miles away, reviewing what we knew and where we'd go next. She'd want to move quickly. Once the Justice Department came in, we'd be pushed out, and there would be no chance to finish the investigation Alice had started. She'd hate that, if all she did was for nothing, if some Washington lawyers moved in and tied everything up.

Worse, the Justice Department would probably just look at the company's illegal activities and not make the connection to the assassination and anarchists, since the McKinley case was officially closed. We needed to act now, before Washington got more involved, or we'd lose any leads to the assassination conspiracy.

"Well and good," said the president heartily. "Just wanted to make sure you knew what was happening. Now tell me, what have you two been up to since we last met?"

Alice smoothed over that pretty neatly, with some light touches on Chinatown and Little Italy, and soon we heard Mrs. Cowles come home. That was as good a sign as any that it was time for me to head downstairs.

"Breakfast as usual, to go over my schedule," Alice said to me, and I nodded and bid her and the president a good night.

"Good evening, Mr. St. Clair," said Mrs. Cowles as we met in the foyer.

"Good evening, ma'am. The president is with Miss Alice in the breakfast room."

"So I gathered from the police presence downstairs."

"Dulcie baked an apple pie. There's some left," I said.

"How kind of you. Do have a good evening," she said, giving me a cool smile and proceeding to the breakfast room.

No card game for me, I thought. It was going to be a busy day tomorrow, and I needed to get a full night's sleep.

Chapter 25

A lice was already into her bacon and eggs when I arrived the next morning. She even had paper and pen on the table, a sign this was going to be a working breakfast.

"Tuck in, Mr. St. Clair. My father and Aunt Anna are having a private breakfast this morning—political advice—and are dining in my aunt's study. But our morning will be no less busy. We're going to watch a ship get launched."

"That sounds interesting. I assume you mean the new Van Schuyler ship?"

"Yes." Alice held up a card. "This came by messenger from Preston this morning. Just a brief note saying he wants to speak at the ship launching. They seem to understand my father won't show, so they want to get it going so they can start making money. And we'll get a chance to see if he's managed to get the ledgers yet. I imagine he will. He does want to do what I ask."

"Let's assume he does." But we still needed to go over the nuts and bolts of how we were going to do that.

"There's a lot of paper in a company that size, and I'm guessing we could find some others who'd be willing to help for the right incentives, if we could meet them."

But I was shaking my head even as I was eating my eggs. "Miss Alice, no more bribery and blackmail. For God's sake, Mrs. Cowles is in the next room."

"You put things in such a bad light. We are merely going to host a political meeting. I'm still assembling the details, but it's not that difficult. Things like this happen in politics all the time. Now, have you ever been to a ship launching?"

"Wyoming is landlocked," I reminded her.

"Of course. Well, ship launchings can be rather fun, although considering the state of the Van Schuyler family and what we've done, it may not be as entertaining as these events usually are. I'm sure Shaw Brantley knows by now that we're the ones who smuggled his mistress out of town." And she sounded rather proud of that.

"He isn't going to forget what we did to him."

"Who cares? They set someone on us at the Rathskeller, and we sent them running with their tails between their legs. Now, let's plan our political meeting. We need to reach workingmen. This is what I want to do: I want to find some other Van Schuyler employees to give us the same information Compton has. Here's how you can help. What paper do workingmen read?"

"The porters here read the *Herald*—the paper you threatened to give an interview to, to frighten that lawyer." There's no denying that it's a lively read.

"Right. We could place a notice for a meeting

there. Many read it, and even those who don't will pass on the word. We can stop at the *Herald* offices this morning and get it into tomorrow's paper. People will come. We'll take a reception room at the Stokely Hotel downtown."

I knew it well. It was a second-rate hotel used for traveling salesmen and other visitors of modest means passing through. It wasn't disreputable, but it made a good simple headquarters for meeting and greeting workingmen, and operatives of both parties used it.

"They'll probably give us a room cheap just to curry favor with my father," said Alice. "We'll make the gathering tomorrow evening, which will give everyone time to see the notice in the *Herald*, but not enough time for the Van Schuylers to organize opposition—at least not an effective opposition. We'll have to move quickly."

I was getting dizzy at that. If nothing else, she was being too optimistic, I thought. If Van Schuyler and Brantley thought their freedom was in danger, they'd lash out at anyone. Out West, I once saw a dog corner a deer, which is probably the mildest creature in the world, and the deer lashed out with its hooves and killed it.

Meanwhile, Alice took a fresh piece of paper and began writing quickly, then handed it to me: "There will be a political meeting tonight at the Stokely Hotel, 7:00. Members of the Roosevelt family will be present. We will talk about major upcoming changes to shipping in both New York City and Buffalo and are seeking those who would like to discuss their experiences."

"I see. You made it look like a political event. But your Aunt Anna is going to see that advertisement, and there will be hell to pay."

"Oh, she doesn't even take the *Herald*. No one she knows takes the *Herald*."

"The local Republican Party men will hear about it—"

"And assume that it was something that came out of Washington. Are you going to just sit there and make objections?" She laughed lightly as I just shook my head. "Finish your coffee. We ought to get going."

We drove to the *Herald* offices, and I was just glad that it was only to place an advertisement and not give an interview. We were directed to the advertising suite, which was really just a long room with a wooden counter that separated the public from the printing rooms. It was mostly messenger boys, and Alice was the only woman there, so we got a few looks.

We waited for our turn, and then a young clerk with a dirty shirt and stained hands looked at Alice's copy.

"A political meeting, miss? Really?" He looked her up and down.

"Is there a law against women organizing political meetings?" asked Alice.

"None that I know of. But we have certain standards."

"Junior, I know your paper, and you don't have any standards that I or anyone else in this town knows of," I said. "Now take the lady's copy and her money. We'd like to be on our way."

He looked like he was going to argue the point, then changed his mind. He quoted a price, Alice paid, and we were off.

Then we drove to the Stokely, where they treated Alice like royalty, which she loved. It was a lot less elegant than the Wellman, but clean enough and a lot friendlier. When Alice made her name known at the front desk, we were quickly ushered into the manager's office.

"It's our great pleasure to serve the Roosevelt family," he said. "How may we assist you?"

"We are having a small event. We'll need a receiving area and an adjoining . . . interview room. For tomorrow evening. Is that possible?"

If the manager was surprised that the president's daughter was doing this on her own, he kept his opinions to himself.

"Of course we can help. And because of your illustrious father, we'll charge you half price."

They shook on the deal, and we headed back to our motorcar.

"South Street, Mr. St. Clair." I briefly wondered if she was nervous, but no. She looked like a kid expecting she'd get a pony on Christmas morning.

We drove down as far as we could. Police had set up barriers around the pier, and there was a reviewing stand.

"I'm sure we'd be welcome up there, but Father clearly doesn't want me to show public support for the Van Schuylers."

Well how about that, I thought. Alice was listening to her father. When it was important, she stood up and did the right thing. I had to remember that.

The event hadn't drawn a large crowd. Maybe feeling under pressure, the family hadn't publicized it. Some were clearly workingmen, and others looked like clerks from downtown firms who were curious enough to put up with the cold wind to see what was happening.

The whole family was on the reviewing stand, bundled up nicely. Henry van Schuyler and Shaw Brantley were dressed perfectly in top hats. Preston sat behind them, among other well-dressed men who I assumed were local politicians and Van Schuyler associates. Next to him sat Julia Brantley, looking pale and wrapped in elaborate furs.

We didn't have long to wait. One of the black-coated men—some sort of alderman, I figured—stood and said a few words about what a great occasion it was: the launching of a new ship from a prominent family in New York City, "the greatest port in America."

Then it was Van Schuyler's turn. "We announce today the launching of the *Sophronia,* named after my late sister-in-law, mother to my nephew, Preston." He turned to look briefly at Preston. I watched Preston but couldn't tell what he was thinking from where we were. Alice's face was interesting. She had a sly smile, then looked at me with a raised eyebrow.

"That's very interesting," she said. "Why that name? Was it to make Preston happy, naming it after his mother? Are they afraid of him?" She seemed to take some pride in that. Was it because Henry and Shaw were getting a poke in the eye? Or because Preston had stood up for himself?

Henry seemed to punctuate this by producing a bottle of champagne and handing it to Preston to break over the prow.

"Don't women usually do that?" I asked.

"I don't think Julia is up for that," said Alice.

"Maybe Shaw was going to give the job to Elsie, and that's why he was so upset we got her away."

"Very amusing. Don't make me sorry I brought you here."

Preston did a fine job breaking the bottle. There was polite applause, and sailors lowered a gangplank for visitors. Clearly, only the gentlemen on the stand would be invited, so the crowd started to disperse. I'd seen a few reporters up front, but now they were leaving, too, so it would be safe for us to approach. Alice grabbed my arm, and we walked quickly just behind the stairway that led down from the stand, near the gangplank.

Alice peered from behind the stand until she caught Preston's eye, and he waved us past a sailor standing guard and onto the ship.

It wasn't very big, as ships go, but apparently it was just for local coastal shipping from the mouth of the Hudson. Still, there was enough room to spread out on the deck, and I saw an officer leading a tour for those on the reviewing stand, including Van Schuyler and Brantley. I didn't think they'd seen us.

Without speaking, Preston ushered us into a small but well-fitted dining room. "This is the officer's dining room. We should be fine here for a few moments. The captain and chief mate are the only deck officers on board right now. But Alice, I got the financial ledgers from last summer that you were looking for. We'll have to compare them with the reports you have to see if there are any major discrepancies. They're not with me but are locked in a safe deposit box at the club. It wasn't easy, and I think Shaw may suspect, but I have them. I wanted to let you know as soon as possible."

"Oh, Preston, that's marvelous. I'm so proud of you." As his reward, he got a hug from Alice and a kiss on his cheek.

"It wasn't much," he said modestly, milking it for all it was worth.

"Yes, it is. As soon as we match it with the information we're going to get from our source, we'll have your uncle." She paused. "I'm sorry.

I know he's family, and this will damage the company. I realize this, but I admire you for doing it anyway."

"I never wanted the company anyway, not really, and even after we've brought them down, I imagine there will still be enough money left for me to take a trip. And then . . . I'll come back to New York. Or Washington, if you're there." And he looked into her eyes. I coughed. "Oh, ah, yes," he said. "So how are you going to get the information?"

"We have a splendid plan. We took an advertisement in tomorrow's paper saying we're planning a shipping-related announcement of a political nature. I suspect we'll meet with someone who is willing to give us what we want. There can't be only one source."

"That's wonderful. Can I join you?"

Alice looked thoughtful but then shook her head. "I'm sorry, but as a Van Schuyler, you may be recognized, and it might scare some people off. But I'll tell you right away, I promise."

I was thinking it might be wise to leave before we got stuck in the dining room. It was enclosed, we weren't around friends, and I was unhappy about protecting Alice in this space.

"Wasn't it a risk bringing us here?" I asked. "Couldn't we have just met you at the club?"

He grimaced. "I'm sorry, but I was afraid Shaw was having me watched there, and it would give it all away if Alice was seen visiting me at the club again. But if she is seen here, it's just because she's curious about ships and informally representing her father. But maybe—"

And at that point, Shaw Brantley walked in, and even under the beard, I could tell he was smiling like a tiger. Shaw's eyes roamed over all of us, landing on Alice.

"Miss Roosevelt, I'm so glad you could make it. We were disappointed, of course, that your father was unable to attend due to other duties, as his private secretary said. But it seems you inherited his interest in naval events. You could've joined us more comfortably on the reviewing stand."

"Thank you, but I'm here unofficially, not as a representative." Shaw nodded at that.

"But that suits you nicely, doesn't it? You like acting unofficially, Miss Roosevelt? I admit that there are many official duties and positions that are closed to women, but clever women find ways to be influential despite restrictions, and even at your young age, you've found many of them."

Alice raised an eyebrow. "Thank you for your kind words. And I'd like to thank your family for inviting me onboard. It's an impressive ship. I will give a glowing report to my father. It was kind of you to name it after Preston's mother. Don't you think, Preston?"

"It was my uncle's idea, and I was very pleased," said Preston, looking right at Shaw.

"Is there a ship named for Mrs. Brantley?" asked Alice.

"Yes, on Lake Erie," said Shaw, his eyes narrowing as if he knew what was coming. I certainly knew. I wished she wouldn't, but she enjoyed goading him, perhaps to find things out. Or just as an end in itself.

"How about Elsie de Maine? Is there one named after her?"

Christ, I thought. Was that really necessary? I figured he'd lose his temper at that one, and I started thinking about the best way to get us off the ship. Preston shifted, and his eyes darted back and forth between the two of them. Shaw looked furious—but just for a second, before mastering himself.

"Miss Roosevelt, I'm going to give you some advice. You probably won't take it, but I'll give it to you anyway, for free. Why? You probably won't believe it, but I admire you. Things aren't always what they seem. Influence without wisdom can be dangerous, even self-destructive. Don't you agree, Preston?"

Preston didn't bother answering.

Shaw stepped out again. I gave him a few seconds and then looked outside myself before turning back. He may have put it into language that sounded like advice, but I heard threats. By now, he had no doubt heard what had happened to the man who was sent to threaten us in Yorkville, and he was no doubt thinking what to do next.

"Miss Alice, I think we ought to go."

Alice turned to Preston, and in a voice a little too loud, she said, "Mr. St. Clair doesn't like boats. He was raised in Wyoming, which, as you know, is landlocked."

I gave her a sour look. "If we're done with the narration, we'll be going."

"Dear Preston, we'll find a suitable place to meet with your documents and mine. Keep yourself safe, and we'll speak soon." She gave him another kiss on his cheek. "Very well, Special Agent St. Clair, you can take me back to dry land."

Chapter 26

Is something bothering you?" asked Alice. We were back in the motorcar, heading uptown to the Caledonia.

"Why should anything be bothering me?" I said.

Alice gave me a quizzical look. "You just seemed a little odd. Is this about Preston? I still don't understand why you dislike him so much. He came through for us."

"I guess he did. So far we have a lot of nothing. We have the ledgers Preston has—stuck in the University Club. And the matching reports are still with Compton. Also, we can't be sure we'll find someone else to give us any reports."

"It will all come together—you'll see." Her chin was high, and her voice was full of absolute confidence. She looked at me, though, and then she spoke more softly. "What's wrong? Really?"

I couldn't say, not entirely. Something didn't feel right. It was true I didn't like Preston, but I had to admit I was a little worried about him. Taking those ledgers seemed to be a bit too bold of a move for him. I thought he was in over his head. So was Alice, but at least she had me riding shotgun for her. I didn't like that we still didn't have the whole story.

"What if Preston runs into the Archangel? The

Archangel kills anyone who gets in his way. And Preston certainly is treading close to his territory."

"That's true," said Alice. "But he is a Van Schuyler. They're paying the Archangel. I think that much is clear. I don't think he'd turn on his employers. I think the Archangel would be more likely to go into hiding before turning on his powerful employers. Anyway, this is my theory: The Archangel worked for the Van Schuylers. We know Dora was involved with a murderous gentleman with connections to the Van Schuylers. I conclude he was the Archangel. Czolgosz stole the image from him, as Dora's neighbor at some point, and passed it on to Dunilsky. I also believe the Archangel was making use of the anarchists and was pretending he was their friend rather than a Van Schuyler associate. For example, he could've gotten anarchists to help vandalize rivals' property. They'd think they were attacking the ruling class, as they'd put it, but in reality they were little more than tools of the Van Schuylers. Dunilsky died because he knew, or at least was suspected of knowing, this connection. And Dora Compton as well."

"Right, you said it before—and I have to admit, Miss Alice, it looks like you're right."

"Thank you," she said.

"So was the death of McKinley just a sideshow to all the Van Schuyler misdeeds after all? Is it even related?"

She wrinkled her nose. "I admit I haven't figured

out that part yet. Perhaps the Van Schuylers lost control of the Archangel," she said, "and the Archangel lost control of the anarchists. But I won't accept that it's all a coincidence. Let's not forget how this started—the Van Schuylers, hiding behind the Great Erie, had us followed because we displayed only mild interest in Emma Goldman, one of Leon Czolgosz's few friends."

I nodded. "You're right. But we still don't know for sure. There are connections, Miss Alice, but no reason for anyone to kill McKinley."

"Not yet," she said.

We decided not to discuss that particular aspect of our investigations any more that day. When we got back to the Caledonia, Alice grabbed some pen and paper. We spread out in the breakfast room and started making plans for tomorrow night's event. Eventually, Dulcie came out with some sandwiches and, making sure Alice didn't see, gave me a look.

Alice was pleased enough with the results of our planning but then seemed disappointed that we'd have to wait until tomorrow evening to see what response our advertisement would bring.

"Oh, well. Patience is a virtue, they keep saying, although I've never seemed to manage to cultivate it," she said with a grin. "I don't see what else we can do until tomorrow evening. I'm a little tired from all our running around, and we'll have a big day tomorrow. I think I'll take a nap. Father will be around after addressing his meeting tonight, and we can talk when he gets back. He has to leave very early tomorrow. I wonder when he'll want me in Washington?" She looked a little shy for a moment. "You will come to Washington, won't you, if I decide to live more permanently in the White House?"

"Do you want me to?"

"What kind of stupid question is that? You're just fishing for compliments. Actually, it was a silly question on my part. Being my bodyguard is probably the most interesting job you've ever had."

"Even more than serving in the Rough Riders under your father?"

"Yes. Even that." She ended that conversation with a wave of her hand. "Have fun at your card game or whatever you're doing tonight. I may just join my aunt in whatever she's doing tomorrow. It will keep her from getting suspicious. Have a good afternoon and evening."

I got up early the next morning anyway. I didn't mind eating in the kitchen, nevermind what Dulcie thought, but Alice seemed to expect me in the breakfast room, and it seemed odd to go back at this point. She said she'd be sleeping late, so I figured I could show up after the president had left but before Alice and Mrs. Cowles were at the table. The worst outcome from my point of view was being alone with Mrs. Cowles, without Alice, but that's exactly what happened. I wasn't sure how excited Mrs. Cowles was about my becoming a regular feature at the breakfast table, especially without Alice present.

I was halfway through pancakes and coffee when she walked in. She hid any trace of surprise. I stood.

"Good morning, ma'am. If you want some privacy, I can easily take myself into the kitchen."

"Not at all, Mr. St. Clair. No reason for you to leave just because Alice isn't ready yet. I was up early to see my brother off. Please sit."

She had her plate and her copy of the *Tribune*, but she didn't open it.

"My niece seems very attached to you, Mr. St. Clair."

"I am pleased to hear that, ma'am."

"Are you pretending to be stupid? I don't think it's possible to be as stupid as you're pretending. But nevermind. It isn't your behavior I'm worried about right now. It's Alice's. What do you know about her feelings?"

"I know nothing about her feelings, ma'am," I said. I was watching her carefully.

"Don't you, Mr. St. Clair? Oh, very well. I will not hold you responsible for them anyway. But I will hold you responsible for her actions."

"I understand," I said.

"I'm glad. And by the way, although I appreciate your help, believe me, if you let Alice get involved in something else inappropriate, I truly will see you on the next train to San Francisco, and I don't care if she locks herself in her bedroom for the rest of her life."

I was saved from responding to this by Alice's arrival.

"Good morning, Aunt Anna, Mr. St. Clair. What are we up to today? I think I may take in a show tonight." So that's how she was planning to cover up the evening's activities. I just hoped Mrs. Cowles wouldn't ask for a review later on.

The rest of the day was fairly dull. Mrs. Cowles and Alice called on other wealthy Republican families, and I usually managed to wheedle food and coffee from obliging cooks and maids. In one household, for lunch, they gave me some preserved meat called pastrami, and they told me I could probably find more in the Lower East Side. All in all, I had to admit it was pretty boring after all we had done in recent days. Being honest, I realized we had done things we shouldn't, and I let Alice get away with it because of the excitement, and I felt a little bad. Not too bad, though—just a little.

Alice and I weren't alone until late afternoon, when Mrs. Cowles went to change for a dinner engagement, and we settled around the breakfast table.

"Fun day?" I asked. She wrinkled her nose.

"Mixed. A few interesting people, a few dull ones.

When I'm a Washington hostess, I'm only going to surround myself with interesting people."

I laughed. "I don't know if you're going to have that choice."

"Yes, I will," she said. "Now I'm going to change, and then we'll go downtown and have dinner at the hotel while we're waiting for the men to arrive."

She came back a little later in a simpler, more businesslike dress, fetched her fur, and said, "Let's be on our way." She sailed out the front door without even looking back to see if I was following. I ran my fingers through my hair, got my Stetson, and headed out behind her.

Traffic was light going downtown, and I was able to park near the hotel. Alice strode right in, and the manager was happy to lead us to the rooms. In the larger room, about fifty chairs were arranged in rows with a lectern at the front. A sideboard contained an urn of coffee, cheap cups, and sandwiches. The crowd would expect some kind of refreshment for attending. I was glad it wasn't beer; things could get out of control pretty quickly.

An adjoining room contained a table with paper and pen and several more wooden chairs.

"Can I send in some food for you before the crowd arrives?" asked the manager.

"Thank you, that would be most kind," said Alice.

He cleared his throat. "Will you have more, ah, staff members arriving?" he asked. Usually, events like this included men with sharp eyes, checked coats, and cigars organizing and leading the events on behalf of someone in a black suit with a gold chain across his vest. Alice and I didn't fit into either of those categories.

"Thank you, but Mr. St. Clair and I can handle everything ourselves."

The manager's eyes briefly landed on my revolver, just visible with my coat open, and decided we could handle whatever came our way. He smiled again. "Very good, Miss Roosevelt. Dinner will be sent in momentarily, and if you need anything else, I can be reached through the front desk."

Roast beef and potatoes arrived shortly, and we made ourselves at home by the table in the small room. The food wasn't great, just competent, but Alice was too excited to care and happily consumed it.

"I've never given a speech before. I think it's going to be fun, everyone getting to listen to me. Where do you think you should stand?"

"I'll be right behind you," I said.

"Must you? You're going to look awfully threatening."

"That's the idea," I said, and Alice rolled her eyes.

"Oh, very well. You know, I didn't realize how hungry I was. This beef is awful, really, but I'm craving it." She cleaned her plate. "They'll be arriving soon . . . but before the place starts filling up, I just want to say thank you."

"For what?"

"I know you don't want to be here, doing this, but you're doing it anyway. So thank you." She gave my hand a squeeze—and then we heard the first of the attendees arrive.

Three men in workingmen's clothes wandered in, looking a little suspicious, and then made their way over to the coffee and sandwiches. A few more followed them. Some were dressed like clerks, and I thought they might be a good source of confidential papers. They all seemed a little surprised to see Alice there, as if the advertisement had been a joke. None of them seemed dangerous, and they clearly weren't armed, so I let Alice approach them. She cheerfully greeted them.

"Good evening. I'm Alice Roosevelt, the president's daughter. I'm so glad you took the time to come this evening."

"Glad to come, miss," they said a little solemnly, surprised and perhaps a little overawed that this girl was there to greet them.

"I want you to know that the Republican Party is a friend of workingmen. I represent my father, the president, in this. He wants you to know that even though there is not an election coming up, he has your needs close to his heart."

"Well, thank you, then," said one of them. I could see he was hoping for beer, but hot coffee on a cold night was better than nothing.

More men started coming, and some women as well, all of them working people. Alice greeted them all and seemed to be really enjoying herself and enjoying the attention. I had my work cut out for me, looking out for troublemakers, but a warm room, coffee and sandwiches, and a chance for some amusement seemed to be enough for anyone who came.

Around half past seven, Alice clapped her hands and asked everyone to take a seat. She would briefly speak. No one looked like they would dispute her, and they dutifully took their chairs. Alice took her place behind the lectern and began to talk.

I stood behind her to keep an eye on the audience, but I did leave half an ear open for Alice. I had to give it to her. For all that I work for the president, I've never been one for politics, but she had the patter down perfectly. I guess she had listened to enough politicians over the years. Her voice rang clear and went up and down for all the key points, and best of all, she kept everyone interested. These were people who didn't go to theaters or concerts, so this was the best entertainment going, and I think that Alice gave them a reason to be happy they came, a reason to think someone was listening. And for a town controlled by the Democratic machine out of Tammany Hall, that was pretty good. I think the president would've been proud.

I was curious to see how Alice was going to follow up with the various people there, some of whom might be Van Schuyler workers. But then we both got a surprise. About fifteen minutes into her talk, I saw Compton enter the room. He looked just as frightened as when I'd chased him from the loading dock. Maybe worse.

During a pause, Alice quickly turned and gave me a wink. She saw Compton, too.

A few minutes later, she wound down. "I started by mentioning our state's important shipping history. We will have more to announce shortly that will show you the Republican Party will not let any employer, no matter how big, crush the workingman. The Roosevelts have always been New Yorkers, employing the workers of New York, and if anyone has anything to say, I will bring the message to my father."

There was some polite applause, and a few stayed after to talk to Alice. They didn't seem threatening, so I kept my eye on Compton, who looked a little wild, like he could slip out of control at any moment. He was looking at us and looking around the room as if he wasn't sure where the attack would come from.

After the meeting, I got the pleasure of watching Alice work the room as Compton sat in a corner and looked miserable. She invited the attendees to give her their names and employers, promising she would speak again soon. She wrote everything down in a little notebook. Who knew, some of them probably thought maybe they'd get a nice patronage job courtesy of Miss Alice Roosevelt, the president's daughter. Eventually, everyone drifted away after making sure the food and drink were gone, leaving us alone with Compton.

"Mr. Compton, I can't tell you how flattered I am that you came to my little political meeting despite all your troubles, braving the open streets of the city just to hear me speak. How kind. Do have a nice evening. Mr. St. Clair, let's be on our way."

"Wait—" said Compton. "I need to talk to you."

"But I don't need to talk to you. I was able to get much of the information I needed, and I'm sure more will follow from this meeting. This meeting was full of Van Schuyler workers, and you'd be surprised at how many of them will be willing to give information to me for a favor from the daughter of the president. You're not the only one who can get me confidential documents, now that I know how easy it is to steal them."

"All right, I understand. You might be able to get something from them, but they can't give you what I have. You're still better off making a deal with me—just listen."

Chapter 27

L et's go into the inner room," I said. "It's a little more private. I'll just close the door here." I closed and locked the main room doors, which led from the lobby, and led us into the inner room, where we all sat.

"And what do you propose?" demanded Alice. She folded her arms across her chest. "Speak quickly. I don't want to spend a minute longer than I have to in this place."

He licked his lips. "I need $1,000. I'll need to get out of town, find a new job."

"I have a list of your coworkers who will give me the information for half that. I can get you $500. That's all," said Alice.

"Miss Roosevelt—I need more than that. Can you make it $800?"

"Just $750. Not a penny more."

"Oh, all right," he said with a sigh. "But it has to be cash. How fast can you get it?"

"Do you have the papers?"

"In my apartment in Brooklyn."

"It will take me two days to get that much cash together. Write down your address, and prepare to be there the day after tomorrow at this time. I will tell no one. You will tell no one. And then you can leave New York." She provided him with pen and paper, and after a brief pause, he wrote out his address.

"I'll head there now. I should be safe for the next two days—they can't find me that quickly."

Alice looked at it, then folded the paper and pocketed it.

That's when I heard the banging on the outer door. It seemed insistent, like someone who wanted in badly, instead of someone who was running late and hoped the party was still going.

The little office we sat in had two doors: the one we'd just used from the meeting room and the other leading to a hallway behind the lobby.

"Just be quiet. I'll see who's there," I said. Alice looked merely irritated at the interruption, but Compton was on the edge of falling apart. I pushed him back into his chair.

I went into the meeting room, closing the office door behind me, and opened the main door at the rear. It was my old friend Mac Bolton, the Van Schuyler henchman.

"I figured you'd be here," he said. "Funny how we keep running into each other."

"Yeah, in such a big city. The meeting is over, unfortunately."

"Unfortunately for me. I'm not an idiot. You throw around the name of the Great Erie, go to the trouble of smuggling Elsie de Maine out of town, and all of a sudden the two of you are organizing a political meeting on your own and advertising where Van Schuyler workers are sure to see it. You even mention shipping. You're up to something, even if I don't know what it is. You're damn lucky we didn't find out about this earlier."

"Your masters read the wrong papers. You're damn lucky you didn't interrupt an official party meeting, or you'd be sitting in the Tombs right now. Now what do you want?"

"I want to know what Van Schuyler employees may have told Miss Roosevelt."

"That's none of your business."

"We're being blackmailed. And that's a crime—something you should know if you carry a badge. So what's it going to be? Are you going to let me in?"

"You know, you have a point." I stepped aside and waved him in. "I think I can get you a meeting with Miss Roosevelt. Just lean against the wall first. I have to make sure you're unarmed."

He sighed but did as he was told, and I found he had the sense not to bring a weapon to a Roosevelt political event.

"Now sit down, and I'll be back in a moment." I slipped back into the office.

"Who is it?" asked Compton, shrinking into his chair.

"Don't panic. He doesn't know you're here."

"He's someone from the Van Schuyler Company, here for my papers, isn't he?"

"For God's sake," said Alice. "You blackmail one

of the wealthiest and most ruthless families in New York and then complain when things don't work out the way you want? My advice is to limit your employment to managing loading docks. You clearly lack the nerve for livelier occupations."

He sadly nodded.

"Why don't you leave through this hallway door here. There's probably a kitchen exit. Head out the back and go home."

"And remember, we'll be along two days from tonight."

He nodded. I opened the door to make sure there were no Van Schuyler associates hanging around and shoed Compton out. He made like a rabbit for the kitchen door.

"Now, I think you might like a meeting with Mac Bolton, our friend who tried to stop us from spiriting away Elsie de Maine," I said to Alice.

A smug smile spread across Alice's face. "We didn't get a lot out of him last time. But things have changed now, haven't they? Our negotiating position has improved. I'm looking forward to this—"

"Miss Alice, they're still a powerful and dangerous bunch. Don't overplay this."

"Fortune favors the bold, Mr. St. Clair. I would've thought that as a soldier, you would know that. Lead me to Mr. Bolton."

Bolton was lounging back in one of the chairs but still looked a little nervous. He had enough manners to stand when a lady walked into the room, which led me to believe he wasn't a completely lost cause.

"Miss Roosevelt," he said. She just gave him a superior look as I arranged the chairs so we could all sit and talk.

"Let's try to have a more productive meeting than we did last time, shall we?" said Alice. "I haven't forgotten that you threatened me and I had to call the police on you when last we met."

"Listen, miss. You may not understand this, but I have a boss I have to answer to. And to be fair, you were taking someone who didn't belong to you."

"She belonged to someone? I'm not a lawyer, but I've heard of the Thirteenth Amendment."

At that, Bolton, like Elsie before him, gave me an "Is she for real?" look, and I just shrugged.

"Anyway," he continued, "I was just sent here tonight to see what was going on. The Van Schuylers found out about the meeting you just held and want to know what you're up to. They're worried you may have the wrong idea."

"And what idea is that?" But she kept going, not giving him enough time to answer. "You're bargaining, Mr. Bolton, you and your masters. I know bargaining when I see it—I'm a Roosevelt. You came here to see what I have and what it's going to cost you to get it back. But your problem is that you've run out of things to bargain for. I think you and your associates were interested in a certain person and heard that he bolted. You thought he might come here to my so-called political meeting. But you lost. You gave the game away, didn't you?"

It was a dangerous gamble. Someone had sent word to the Van Schuylers that Compton had left the safety of his rooms, even while they were wondering why Alice was suddenly organizing a political meeting. It was dangerous because she could've been wrong. Worse, she was about to corner him, and I thought again about that deer and that dog.

Bolton nodded at that and frowned. Alice had confirmed his worst fears. "You might be right, Miss Roosevelt, but you don't have it all. I can put you on the track of the Archangel."

"And what do you want? But let me guess," said Alice. "Shaw Brantley is probably furious at you for not holding onto Elsie. And even before that, you failed to stop Mr. St. Clair here from asking questions when he left you facedown in a room. And now you were too late to this meeting to find out to whom we were talking. And to catch him. I'm betting that you're about to lose your job. And you're only bargaining so you'll still have a position when Preston takes over from his uncle and Mr. Brantley. You know they're in trouble."

He tried to look like he didn't care much. "It's a rough business, Miss Roosevelt, and like it or not, whoever runs the business needs someone like me. If Mr. Preston runs it, or even if he sells it, it makes sense to keep me on. If you promise to put in a good word for me, I'll take you at your word."

"I will. But give me the Archangel first."

Bolton nodded. "I'll tell you. I never met him, though. I won't lie to you. Mr. Brantley used him for special things, and although I knew a lot of what went on, the Archangel was secret. He has a cousin, a man who made problems in Chicago, so Mr. Brantley brought him east to put him to use. But he soon lost control of him. His name is Orrin, Orrin Brantley. Shaw was ready to get rid of him."

I thought back to the Van Schuyler dinner party, where Shaw had mentioned sending a cousin to the West. He had to be referring to the Archangel. Shaw was trying to find a way to get rid of him— a useful tool that had become a liability.

"How do you know this if you've never met him?" Alice asked.

"Mr. Brantley told me. Why should he lie?" He seemed genuinely confused at the question.

"What about the anarchists? How are they involved in the business up north?" Alice asked.

Now he looked even more confused. "The anarchists? They aren't involved at all. I don't know anything about them. We rousted more than a few, I can tell you, but that's all I know."

"Are you telling me Shaw Brantley's cousin, the Archangel, wasn't using anarchists to do his dirty work?"

Bolton shook his head. "I don't know what you're getting at, Miss Roosevelt. The whole Archangel idea came from Mr. Van Schuyler when Orrin Brantley came east looking for work and they needed someone to do . . . well . . ."

"Things even you wouldn't do?" tossed out Alice, and Bolton looked away.

"Anyway, miss, what would anyone want to do with anarchists? A useless, undisciplined bunch."

"Not useless," said Alice. "Stupid and misguided, but capable of discipline. That was the problem. But nevermind."

It was clear that Bolton had gotten in over his head and was trying to bargain his way out of the situation while he still had something to bargain with. He was a violent man, but I didn't think he was capable of the things the Archangel had done. And I did think he was telling the truth, at least as he knew it. Alice leaned back and contemplated him with a frown. She really wanted to believe that we had tumbled into a grand anarchist plot going back to Emma Goldman, but it wasn't working out that way. And she wasn't reacting well to being wrong. The only conspiracy at work was turning out to be a particularly grim case of a business out of control, leaving a string of dead workingmen and ransacked supply houses in their wake.

"Oh, all right," she finally said. "You told me what you could. I'll mention your help to Mr. Preston. But if Mr. Brantley or Mr. Henry van Schuyler cross me at any time because of you, I can promise you'll regret it."

It may sound comical—this young girl dressing down this shipyard ruffian whose knuckles had been scarred from fights since before she was born. But sitting there, watching the set of her mouth and listening to the ice in her voice, I didn't find anything funny. And neither did Bolton. He just nodded to both of us, stood, and left.

"For what it's worth, when you were out of the room at the dinner party, Brantley did mention a cousin who needed to be sent out of town. I didn't think anything of it until now," I said.

"There's something . . . I just don't believe it. It doesn't feel right," said Alice.

"Things don't always fall out the way we like," I said. "You're about to bring down a major fraudulent New York company, and that should be enough for one day."

Alice didn't say anything for a while. "There's a bar in this hotel. I want to speak with Preston. Let's get him down here. There are a few things to discuss, and we can finish this all tonight."

"Come on, then. I'm not leaving you alone in this room. I'll get you a lemonade, and we'll call Preston."

"You'll get me a brandy."

"I'll get you a beer."

The bar at the Stokely was doing a lively business that night: the low end of the office trade, mostly young clerks and salesmen from the better shops, who didn't want to mix with the workingmen. But for the president's daughter, the manager found a somewhat battered table to put in a corner and got us our beers. Alice was able to reach Preston and told him to come down to the Stokely bar. "We don't want to be seen going into the club. Henry van Schuyler no doubt has minions watching, as Preston suggested, but I doubt they'll bother following him if they see him going downtown at this hour."

"They know you're downtown if they sent Bolton here," I pointed out.

"Yes. But do you think anyone remembered to tell the simpleminded blockheads outside the University Club to see if Preston is coming downtown? At this point, the uncle and Mr. Brantley are just trying to save their skins."

We sipped our beers. Alice seemed lost in thought and didn't say much, and Preston came pretty quickly anyway. I didn't see anyone with him, so I guess Alice was right and no one had followed him.

"We did it," she said when he sat down with us. "I have an agreement to get the papers. The man's name is Compton, and I have his address in Brooklyn. He'll sell us his documents for $750.

We're meeting him in two nights, but he's going there tonight directly. We had him slip out the back, so I think he'll be all right until then. Meanwhile, I have to figure out how to pull that much cash together."

"If that's the only problem, I can get that money out of one of our accounts tomorrow. There will be a reckoning later, of course, but by that time . . ."

"That would be splendid. It makes things a lot easier." But she didn't miss the last part, and she reached over and put her hand on Preston's. "Yes, 'by that time.' This isn't going to be easy for you. Again, I know this is family, and the business will be damaged. I can only imagine what you're going through, and I'm sorry."

Preston nodded. "Thank you, Alice. That means a lot to me. And I owe you a lot for, well, for standing up with me. I appreciate it. I couldn't have done all this without you." He gave her a soulful look while I tried to catch a waiter's eye for another beer.

"So what happens next?" asked Preston.

"In two nights, we show up at Compton's Brooklyn apartment with the cash. He gives us the reports. We match them against the ledgers you took, and together they should give us a solid case—something to take to the state attorney general for criminal prosecution in Buffalo and New York City."

"Can I come with you? Just to see this whole

event wound up?" asked Preston, looking like an eager hunting dog.

"I don't see why not—Mr. St. Clair?"

"The more, the merrier," I said. "Want us to pick you up at the club?"

"I may still be watched, and you shouldn't be seen with me. I'll arrange quietly for a cab. Do you have the address? I'll meet you there."

"That's fine, but if you get there before us, don't go up. He's expecting me." Alice showed him the paper with Compton's address. Preston committed it to memory.

"Good. I'll have the money with me. Is there anything else?"

"Just tying up some loose ends," said Alice. "Mr. St. Clair disagrees, but I think this all still ties in with Czolgosz and the anarchists and McKinley's assassination. There are too many things unexplained. There was a murder in Czolgosz's building right before he left to kill McKinley—we found that out recently—not to mention two more murders here in New York in the past few days. I don't believe there are any coincidences."

Preston nodded as if giving that idea a lot of weight. "I can't immediately see it, but it's worth thinking about."

"It is indeed. By the way, we found out who the Archangel is: Shaw's cousin Orrin."

Preston seemed amused at that. "Really? I met him a few times. I heard he was involved in all sorts of problems back in Chicago, so I'm not too surprised."

"So that's what we'll be doing next. We know the Archangel was working with anarchists, and one of them killed McKinley. That may be forgotten in the coming weeks as your uncle and Shaw get taken to court, but we're going to keep digging. Are you with me, Preston?"

"Yes, of course, Alice." He nodded absently. "I ought to go," he finally said. "I'll see you the day after tomorrow, around 8:00, in Brooklyn."

"Yes. Do be careful."

"I will. I don't want to end up shot or hanged like Dunilsky." He laughed to show he was joking and said goodnight.

"I think this is very brave of him," she said when he was gone. "Going against his family like that to do what's right. And I'm glad to see he's willing to continue investigating the anarchists. We haven't finished with them."

"Miss Alice, I think I've been a good sport myself. Even after being warned off by your aunt, I've gone along. I rescued Brantley's mistress with you, and I'm even willing to oversee a hand-off to a blackmailer in Brooklyn. We've had some close calls, and I don't regret it. But this has to end. You have to know this."

It was time to stop. I finally knew that. I could lie to myself for a while that this was all about an ongoing anarchist plot, that McKinley was only the beginning and I had a job to see this through to protect the president. But I couldn't do it anymore. I couldn't keep letting Alice lead me around and pretend this was anything more than the two of us chasing after the excitement. I could tell myself for a long time that this was about protecting the president, but no longer.

However, I could tell my speech wasn't having an effect on her. She just looked exasperated.

"You say the same thing over and over again. Don't be ridiculous. Of course we have to see this through to the end."

"This *is* the end. Remember how this started? You were being followed. And now we know who and why—Van Schuyler corruption. They were worried about you following a trail of anarchists to Buffalo and discovering what they were up to. Which you did. Dora Compton was killed because she was the Archangel's mistress and knew too much about the inner workings of the Van Schuyler company. And then everyone with a connection to her was killed, too. Dunilsky had to die because he was related to Czolgosz and ended up with the Archangel's calling card through him. Czolgosz would've been killed himself if he hadn't gone crazy and shot the president."

"So why did Czolgosz kill McKinley?" she challenged.

"Who the hell knows? They're all crazy—you know that. His friend Dora died, so that might have been all he needed to send him off to die a hero's death."

"But the Italian assassin—Cesare?"

"We know he was an associate of the Archangel. Probably tried to wring more money out of him. Heck, Miss Alice, we did a good day's work, bringing down a corrupt company, and it'll make your father proud. But with the handoff in two days, we're done. We're not turning this into an ongoing investigation into anarchist activity."

"Fine. Preston and I will do what needs to be done."

"I don't care what Preston does. But I'm your bodyguard, and I'm not taking you back to that hellhole bar where the anarchists meet, or any other bad neighborhood, just to keep you amused. There's no conspiracy here."

"Maybe I'll get my father to appoint Preston as my bodyguard," she said, and I laughed so hard I almost choked on my beer.

"I'd love to see that, Miss Alice, I really would."

Alice sat back, and those eyes just smoldered at me. "How dare you, after all I've done for you. Have you forgotten how hard I fought with my aunt to save your job?"

"Save my job after you nearly got me fired following you on your little adventures all over New York—theft, blackmail, pushing your way into crime scenes."

"You loved it. I saved you from a life of doing

nothing more than cadging free food and flirting with housemaids the length and breadth of Manhattan."

That's why I started saying things I might not have said if I wasn't getting angry. "You know what? I had some fun, I admit it, and it did look like we were really onto something else—a major anarchist conspiracy—but that's not what happened. Learn to live with the idea that you don't always get what you want. And maybe I like cadging free food and flirting with housemaids. Maybe that's a perk of the job that I think I deserve after a couple dozen Wyoming winters. But I sure as hell don't need a spoiled seventeen-year-old princess telling me how to live my life."

That did it. She stood and those steely eyes drilled holes into me while she thought about what she wanted to say.

"Take me home. Right now. And don't say a single word more to me. Not one goddamned word."

Chapter 28

So I took her home. We settled the bill and got into the motorcar. It was late, so we drove quickly uptown. Alice walked so fast into the building, I practically had to run to keep up with her. I thought of telling her she wasn't supposed to do that but decided against it.

A maid let her in, and I didn't even come in or say goodnight. On my way back down, I amused myself thinking about Preston escorting Alice to that anarchist bar. But when I got to the lobby, I realized I couldn't go back to my little room, so I took the car out again and drove to the East Side to see if Mariah was in.

Mariah was in and still up.

"Where's the kid?" she asked.

"Tucked safely in bed, I assume," I said. "I'm just about done being her nursemaid. I've had it with all of them—going from townhouse to townhouse, seeing every damn kitchen in New York. And if I'm not doing that, I have to put up with every whim of a spoiled young woman who can't imagine a world that doesn't revolve around her. Anyway, I left her angry enough to kill me."

Mariah nodded. "Have you had any dinner?"

"Bad roast beef."

"I had a job earlier, and the cake wasn't finished,

so they let me take it home." She cut me a slice.

"It's your fault," I said. "You told me to follow her and see where it led."

"You always were a charming bastard," said Mariah. "You know she thinks she's in love with you, which you probably encouraged without even knowing it, and she's confused and you're annoyed."

"I didn't encourage anything, and she hasn't fallen for me. It's that guy named Preston, the one I teased her about when she was here for dinner."

"If she was, she'd have made more of a fuss when you teased her about him over dinner. Anyway, she's seventeen—she doesn't know her own mind yet. But I expect you to be a little more mature about a young girl's infatuation. I'm guessing you really hurt her feelings, and no one wants that from someone they love."

"You're wrong," I said, knowing she was right.

"Joey, just be quiet for a while. Now, would you like some coffee?"

So we didn't talk any more about Alice. I asked her how work was going, and she said fine and that she liked New York, had made some friends, and planned to stay a while.

After it got late, I settled on her couch, thought for a bit about Alice yelling at me again over waffles in the breakfast room, and fell asleep quickly. In fact, one talent I've developed over the years, from cowboy to lawman to soldier, is falling asleep quickly.

387

And waking up quickly.

It started as a tapping on the door, and first I thought it was part of a dream, but then it turned into a pounding. Mariah didn't seem to hear it from in her room. I know she leads a more regular life than I do, and I doubted that she had friends suddenly showing up in the middle of the night. I pulled on my pants and padded over to the door.

"Who's there?"

"Just let me in." It came out as a harsh whisper through the thin door.

"Let who in?"

"It's Alice, damn it. Let me in."

It was a complete surprise, and yet, knowing Alice, it made perfect sense.

She was standing there in her mink coat, face red from the cold. But the face was all wrong: sadness—no, more than that—horror.

"Are you going to stand there like an idiot or invite me in?" she said, showing in her voice, anyway, that she was still the old Alice.

I heard a door open behind me. Mariah was tying her robe on and had a special smile when she saw who it was.

"Alice. Down South we say, 'Drop by any time,' and I guess you took me at my word."

Alice wrestled with that comment, trying to see if she was being mocked. "I am very sorry for waking you, Mariah, and wouldn't have if it wasn't an emergency."

"Don't tell me you left the Caledonia alone—in the middle of the night. Miss Alice—"

"Oh, God, what a time for you to pick to start obsessing with details." She practically stamped her foot.

"You look cold, hon. I think we have some coffee leftover, if you like."

"That would be very kind of you," said Alice. Mariah headed to the stove.

"So—are you going to tell me why you slipped out of your house and came down here alone? This is big, Alice."

"I wouldn't have had to if you had stayed in your room tonight." She was still in the mood for continuing our fight, but I could see in her eyes she hadn't come down here just to yell at me. She still wore the haunted look I had seen when I opened the door.

"Take a seat. I'll get my shirt."

"But there's no time—"

"Time for me to get my shirt and you to get your coffee."

I was back a moment later, and Mariah stayed with us while the coffee heated. "Can I stay, or do you two have government secrets to discuss?"

"Oh, do stay, Mariah. It's only . . . Oh, God." And she put her face in her hands. But when she emerged again, her eyes were dry.

"Did you listen to what Preston said this evening?

He said that he didn't want to end up hanged like Dunilsky."

"So?"

"So how the hell did he know Dunilsky died by hanging? I was just thinking about it, going over everything, and I kept coming back to that—how could he have known?"

"I didn't really think about it. I never told him. I guess . . ." I stopped to think.

"No, I never mentioned it. Do you think the police advertised that? They cover up things like that. How did Preston know? Unless . . ."

I couldn't think about what this meant. If he knew that, what else did he know? What was he lying about? Had he been working with the Archangel all along? Was he in league with his uncle and Shaw?

"Wake up!" said Alice. "We'll work out the details later. I gave Preston Compton's address. He's probably there now getting the company reports—the ones we were supposed to buy as soon as Preston got the cash. We have to go to Brooklyn. We can't wait."

"Miss Alice, it could be a whole war party there. I should call the police—"

"And tell them what? Do you know how hard it would be to explain why they have to show up in the middle of the night in Brooklyn?" Alice looked up at Mariah. "Would you tell your brother he has to do this?"

I looked at Mariah, too. "You still have Dad's old Remington?" I asked.

"Clean and ready to go," she said.

"Keep it loaded, and stay here with Alice until I get back."

"The hell she will," said Alice. "I didn't go through all this to sit here over coffee and cake until you get home. You won't leave me here, Mr. St. Clair. You can't do that to me. You can't leave me alone." And I never saw her as close to tears as she was right then.

"What are you really up against?" asked Mariah.

"A shipping clerk and some kid who went to Yale."

Mariah shrugged. "The only way I could keep Alice from leaving is to shoot her myself. She'd probably be safer with you."

"Oh, hell. Fine. Mrs. Cowles is going to kill me anyway."

Alice threw her arms around me, and I was never hugged so tightly.

"How could you do this without me?" she asked. I didn't bother answering, and she pulled back. "Can I borrow Mariah's Remington?"

Mariah thought that was funny, but I just said, "Miss Alice, just don't say anything for a while, all right?"

I finished getting dressed in between gulps of coffee. I tucked in my shirt, strapped on my Colt, and found my Stetson and riding coat. Mariah glanced at Alice, brooding into her mug, trying to figure it all out. Then Mariah grabbed me by my shirtfront to pull me down and whisper in my ear. "Be careful."

"Oh, hell, like I said, it's just two guys, neither of them professionals. This can't be any harder than a Saturday night in Laramie."

She glanced back at Alice. "That's not what I meant."

I just nodded and let her kiss me on the cheek before she gave me a light slap.

"Miss Alice, it's time to go to Brooklyn."

She smiled up at me, and I saw the usual mischief in her eyes.

It had gotten really cold that night, with a dampness that seeped right into your bones. I was used to it, but I didn't think Alice was. I could only imagine how she had made her way down to Mariah's. She wouldn't have dared to ask the doorman to help her get a cab, and I could only imagine her alone and frightened racing along the sidewalk and looking for someone to drive her as she got colder and colder. *How odd it must be,* I thought, *to never be alone and then to suddenly be alone in the middle of the night.*

I remembered I kept an old, heavy blanket in the back of the car, and I reached back and handed it to Alice.

"Thank you," she said, and we were off.

"So—what do you think? Have you worked out the details?"

"Not all of them," she said. "All I know for sure is that Preston lied to me. He was far more involved in what his family was doing than he let on. He tricked us. And I think he's betraying us right now in order to take over the company."

"He wants the company for himself?"

"Mostly he wants revenge," she said.

She didn't say anything more for a bit, and I didn't press her. We drove downtown along almost-empty roads. After all that, I found myself hoping Alice was wrong—that he had heard about the hanging from passed around gossip, that we'd get to Brooklyn and find Compton safe in bed.

The Brooklyn Bridge is just about my favorite thing in New York. I've driven over it quite a few times and walked across it often—not to go anywhere, but just to be there and look both upriver to the city and into the mouth of New York Harbor. I once told Mr. Roosevelt how impressive I found the bridge, and he said he understood. "You grew up out West, St. Clair, where so much of life is subject to nature. But a bridge like this is a challenge to nature. Even if the East River freezes, even if a fog descends on the city, we can get across. And that's what impresses you," he said, and I agreed.

I took Mariah across one day as well, and she laughed after admiring the view. "Who'd have thought civilization had so much to recommend it?"

As we came to the crest, Alice suddenly turned to me and said, "I'm sorry. Thank you for giving me a second chance."

"Why, Miss Alice, I was about to say the exact same thing to you." And I was pleased to see that got a laugh out of her.

We found the place easily enough—I had been to Brooklyn plenty of times, and it was off a main road, in a block of workingmen's apartments. It was late, and there was only one light in the window, and we knew it had to be Compton's.

"Just stay behind me, all right?"

"Oh, all right," she said. We walked up to the apartment, and when we got to the landing, I motioned for her to be quiet. There was talk going on behind one of the doors. I couldn't hear much; someone didn't want to wake the rest of the building. I gently turned the doorknob, but as I expected, the door was locked. I waved for Alice to stand away from the door. I took out my Colt, raised my boot, and easily smashed the cheap lock.

I gave Preston a surprise for sure. He was standing by a table in shirt-sleeves, in front of a bruised Compton, who was tied to a chair. There was a revolver on the table, and I saw Preston's eye go to it.

"Don't even think about it," I said. He gave a resigned smile and shrugged. "Turn around and lean against the wall."

"Mr. St. Clair," he said, his voice full of his usual effortless charm. "This is a ridiculous misunderstanding."

"I won't ask you again," I said. He shrugged again and did as I asked. I searched him, found nothing, and then cuffed him behind his back.

"Is this really necessary?" he asked. I didn't bother to answer as I pushed him into another chair.

And then Alice walked in. I won't forget that look on her face: anger, disappointment, hurt, all together.

"Alice, what are you doing here?"

She didn't say anything, she just stared, and I was pleased to see Preston wilt a little. She wasn't going to even give him a chance to argue, and I watched him think about what he was going to say next.

Meanwhile, I turned my attention to Compton. He had been roughed up a little but didn't seem too badly hurt. There was a half-filled bottle of whisky on the table, and after I untied him, he took a long swig.

"I didn't tell him where they were," he said, smiling grimly. "I have the papers, the records, but I didn't tell him."

"Tell us now," said Alice.

"You have the $750?" he asked, and I had to admire him. After all that, he still had his eye on the prize.

"For God's sake," said Alice. She found Preston's jacket draped over another chair and took out his wallet. She pulled out the bills. "Mr. Compton, I am deeply sorry for your sister, but it seems the deal is off. I will see her murderers hanged, but you're not going to get $750 out of it. You'll get the $50 I have here. Now, you will tell me where those papers are, or Mr. St. Clair will search this entire tiny apartment and find them anyway. And then you'll get nothing."

He considered his options for a moment, then nodded. "Under a loose floorboard in the bedroom," he said. I stepped into the other room, and it only took me a moment to pry it up and remove the papers. Back in the main room, Alice was looking over a ledger on the table.

"This is perfect," she said. "I'm assuming this is the ledger that matches the stolen reports."

"So why steal the ledgers if you were going to betray us anyway?" I asked Preston, and he just smiled.

"That's easy, Mr. St. Clair," said Alice. "Preston didn't have regular access to those reports. His uncle didn't trust him with them. But with the ledger and the reports together in his possession, he was going to turn around and blackmail his uncle. It's an ugly story, I'm sure. But let's get Mr. Compton out of here." She handed him Preston's money. "It's over for you. Go back to your room over the store, and don't come back here until tomorrow. Be thankful you got out of here with your life."

"Yes, miss," he said. It looked like he was going to say something else, then decided it was best for him to cut his losses and leave.

"I suppose, Alice, that this doesn't look good, but hear me out," said Preston.

"I don't need to hear you say anything," said Alice, her voice low, and I wondered if she would physically attack him. I'd seen Alice angry, spitting mad even, but never like she was then. I don't know if I have ever seen anyone as angry as she was. "I know almost all of it. From the beginning, you were the one who hid behind the fictitious Great Erie & Albany Boat Company, and you were responsible for setting that private detective on us because you were afraid of what we might learn once we spoke with Emma Goldman and the anarchists—and eventually the unrest happening up at the Great Lakes. I knew there was an anarchist connection to your family . . . I knew it." She practically shouted that, her triumph at being proven right overcoming her rage, at least for the moment.

"Alice, why would I care—why would anyone care—if you spoke with some anarchists?"

"Because I found out the Archangel made use of anarchists. You were there through all of it, pretending you were estranged from the family so you'd look clean. But you were there working with them to hire every available worker to build your Great Lakes empire, bullying and threatening your rivals. That lawyer Urquhart was your front. He told the right lies, but I bet he never knew about the Archangel."

He smiled and nodded. "Alice, it's my family business. Be reasonable. We had things to accomplish and roped in people to help us." He added all the charm he could to his voice and tried to look relaxed even though he was handcuffed. "You've been among powerful men your whole life. Did you really think I was going to let one disaffected employee bring down the entire family? We were building something great. Your father would understand."

And that was a mistake. Alice stepped over to him so quickly I couldn't stop her, and Preston leaned so far from her, he almost fell out of his chair.

"Never, ever again, mention my father. I forbid it. I might've forgiven everything you did in the name of your family. I might've. But using me is something I will never forgive you for—*betraying* me is something I will never forgive you for—from now until the day they hang you." He paled at that, realizing he wasn't going to talk his way out of this. But I was clearly missing something, because I didn't know what Preston had done to merit a hanging. The only murders we had seen had been engineered by the Archangel.

I didn't get it until Alice explained it. "You talk too much, Preston. You mentioned Dunilsky's death in the Tombs, and you couldn't have known those details unless you engineered it. You wore fine clothes—the man who killed Cesare did as well. Dora was mistress to a wealthy man. You wanted your uncle dead. You tricked me into helping you get the reports and sending you to steal the right ledgers."

I was seeing the light now but still couldn't really believe the conclusion.

"It's the last piece, Preston," she was saying. "This wasn't just about the Van Schuylers against everyone else. It was about you against your Uncle Henry and his son-in-law Shaw."

At that, Preston finally broke down and showed some anger. "Do you know what my uncle did to my father?" he yelled. "Goaded him into taking that trip into the teeth of a storm. No one thought I knew, but they couldn't keep it hidden. Can you blame me, Alice? I was going to get my own back. I was going to take the company from him. He killed my father."

And that made sense now. All along, I couldn't place the tension when Preston was with his uncle and Shaw. Even his poor crazy cousin Julia didn't want him around—had made it clear to Alice she was afraid of him, if we had only listened. Now I knew why. They were afraid of him—they all were. He was the worst of the lot, and Henry van Schuyler was trying to control Preston, who was seeking revenge for his father and a chance to take over the entire company. It was Preston: The Archangel had been under our noses all along.

Alice had no pity. "My mother died two days after I was born. Don't you use a dead parent as justification for every horrible thing you've ever done. Don't you dare. I don't want to hear it. There is only one thing we're going to discuss tonight: The day you killed Dora and the day her friend Leon Czolgosz killed McKinley. I have an idea about what really happened, but I can't be sure. If you have any hope for mercy, you will tell me." She leaned in close to him.

"Mercy? Do you really think I'll suffer any consequences? My God, you are naïve, Alice. I wouldn't have thought it. So what if I admit I'm behind the death of Dunilsky in jail? You have no idea how easy it is to get at someone in jail. Or that Italian assassin. I was going to use him, make him rich, but he decided to blackmail me instead. He never expected a man who wore evening clothes would carry a gun. You think anyone cares about either of them? You think I'll even come to trial?"

"That night—what happened the afternoon the president was killed?" she repeated. "How does McKinley come into this?"

"Oh, very well, Alice, I'll tell you. You figured out everything else. My God, it was easy to rope in Czolgosz and Dora. I convinced them I was the good son, fighting for the workers against

Uncle Henry. He was the enemy, not me, I told them again and again—we were battling Henry van Schuyler, and I would turn the company into a worker's paradise. Czolgosz was practically an imbecile; he'd believe anything. I told him I was the Archangel and that's what he should call me. He knew my face, but I didn't want him to know my real name. Dora believed me in the beginning, but to my regret, she was smarter than I gave her credit for." He smiled sadly. "Just like you, Alice. How interesting. And that's the best part of the story. I realized that Dora had betrayed me by stealing some very embarrassing documents. The stupid girl." He now shouted: "If only she had given them to me, she'd be alive today!" It takes a lot to chill my blood, but that did it.

"And then that idiot, Leon, who was always hanging around, came stumbling in while I was trying to figure out what to do with Dora. I needed to get rid of him—as well as Uncle Henry. So I sent Leon to where the president was to kill my uncle— for God's sake, Uncle Henry was the enemy. I didn't give a damn about McKinley. I told Leon it was my uncle who had Dora killed. But I guess Leon got the wrong end of the stick, he couldn't find Uncle Henry, so he did the next best thing a dazed would-be anarchist could do: he killed the president. Lord, no one would believe how history got made that evening. Czolgosz, history's most famous imbecile."

And he started to laugh. He was insane. But Alice stood up tall, smiled back at him, and slapped him as hard as any woman had ever slapped a man. It really stunned him, and I imagined his head was ringing. My eyes then went to Preston's revolver, still lying on the table. But before I could move, Alice grabbed it and pointed it right at his head. He bit his lip.

"If you say one more damn thing this evening, you won't have to go to trial. I'll shoot you right in this room." And he knew she wasn't joking.

I stepped over, and she let me take it out of her hand. I emptied the chambers and stuck it in my coat pocket. Preston started breathing again.

I didn't fancy squeezing him into the car and taking him to some Brooklyn precinct or on an even longer trip to the Tombs, but the decision was taken out of my hands by the sound of footsteps outside. I dragged Alice with me against the wall and drew my revolver. As soon as the man stepped in, I had the barrel against his head.

I admire him for not flinching.

"Good evening, Mr. St. Clair. I don't think firearms will be necessary this evening."

"Tell that to your nephew, Mr. Van Schuyler. He brought one here, and I had to take it away from him."

"I'm sure. But you seem to have everything settled now." He was dressed in a black business suit and carried a small case. He looked at

Preston, cuffed in the chair, and shook his head sadly.

"Uncle! I'm in a bit of trouble again," said Preston. "Would you explain to Mr. St. Clair and Miss Roosevelt why they have to let me go?"

Van Schuyler ignored him and turned to us. "I suppose I should ask how you two came to be here. The president's daughter—I'm sure that's quite a story."

"I was wondering how you got here as well, sir," I said.

"We finally decided, a little too late, to not only watch the club but have Preston followed if he left his usual Manhattan haunts. My agent reported back to me earlier. Has he killed anyone here?" he asked, as casually as if he was asking whether we had eaten dinner yet.

"Not here," said Alice, "but he will hang for the killings he did commit. And if not for those, for being the agent that sent Czolgosz to kill McKinley. That's treason. And if I may say, Mr. Van Schuyler, you will be following him to prison as well."

I briefly took the derringer out of my pocket—the one we took from the man who threatened Alice at the Rathskeller. "You sent someone—someone very expensive, I'm sure—to threaten Alice. We'll trace the money you paid. Even if that's the only thing you did, you'll spend the rest of your life in prison for that." I put the derringer away.

Van Schuyler turned to Alice. "I am sorry. It was nothing personal. We had to stop Preston, had to control him before you exposed him, and you were getting too close. He wanted you to find the papers the Comptons had stolen from him. I had to stop him before the whole company was destroyed." He was very calm about it, and I realized lunacy ran in the family.

Preston turned to his uncle. "From the moment we had her followed to her having her bodyguard kick in the door, it seems we both underestimated Alice." He was half disappointed, half admiring. "So I guess Shaw has made a run for it? It's just you and me now?"

Van Schuyler didn't react to that right away. He just nodded and seemed lost in his own thoughts. "I told him to grab what he could and get out of the country, but I don't know if he took my advice."

"With Mrs. Brantley?" asked Alice, raising her eyebrow.

"Julia doesn't like travel, Miss Roosevelt," he said. "But to the business at hand." He sat down at the table and put his case on it. He looked at me. "I realize that there will be consequences, but for the sake of the family, I'd like to get Preston out of here."

"For the sake of the family? Or because he's the worst witness against you?" taunted Alice.

Van Schuyler smiled at her. "I'd support women

getting the vote just to see you someday become president like your father. Yes, you can look at it that way. But my business is with you, Mr. St. Clair. I can write you a check for enough money to send you back home to Wyoming and buy your own sizable ranch."

"Thank you, sir, but I'm happy right here in New York for now. And it's Miss Roosevelt's show anyway."

"But she's a young girl, and you're the man with the gun and the badge. Anyway, I'll write out the check. Sometimes just seeing the numbers changes a man's mind."

He reached into his case, and Alice knew what was happening before I did. I don't think she could've seen it, but she just knew it.

"No!" she shouted. My Colt was out less than a second later, and I shot the whisky bottle right off the table in a shower of splintered glass and liquid. The sound echoed, and afterward, we just stood there. Preston looked terrified, but not Alice and not Van Schuyler, who both were waiting to see what would happen next. There were a few cuts to his face, but they didn't seem serious.

"You missed," said Van Schuyler, who had his own revolver, a twin of Preston's, half out of the case.

"Mr. St. Clair never misses," said Alice. "He decided to let you live." She was right about that. My shot had stopped him from pulling the revolver out. He wasn't going to shoot us—we were to his side. He had no shot there. But he had almost killed his nephew.

"He'd have been better off shooting Preston," said Van Schuyler. "You have no idea how evil he is, how far gone he is."

"That's quite a compliment coming from you," said Alice.

"For God's sake, take his gun away," cried Preston, but Alice just looked at him coldly.

"Mr. St. Clair, what would you do if I finished pulling out my revolver and shot him? Would you really kill me?"

I held my arm steady. "Yes, sir. That gun moves one more inch and you're dead."

He looked closely at me. "Yes, you would shoot." He let it fall back into the case. I holstered my Colt, seized the case, and emptied Van Schuyler's weapon. I didn't have a second pair of handcuffs, but Van Schuyler looked deflated—a man who had played his last card at the end of the evening and still knew he was going to come out a loser.

I was wondering what to do next—there was no way I could get all four of us into the motorcar—when I heard a neighboring door open and a boy, I'd guess around sixteen, peeked into the open door to Compton's apartment, cautious and wide-eyed.

"My God," he said, grinning and taking in my clothes. "It's a Wild West show."

"You want to earn a dollar?" I said. "Go find some cops and bring them around."

He gave me a casual salute. "Sure thing, Sheriff," he said and ran off.

Alice pulled up a chair and disappeared into herself. I was a little worried about her. She didn't seem to see anything, and I couldn't guess what she was thinking about. There could've been a hundred things going through her head. Preston looked like he was about to talk a couple of times but wisely decided not to. Van Schuyler just closed his eyes.

It seemed to take forever, but eventually I heard heavy police boots on the stairs. I prayed Alice would listen.

"Miss Alice, go into the bedroom and stay there. The cops may recognize you, and there's no need to make this bigger than it is."

I didn't know if she'd heard, but then she nodded and stepped into the bedroom, closing the door behind her.

Three cops walked into the room, along with the kid, and I had my badge out already. "St. Clair, Secret Service. These two men are under arrest. Take them to lockup. Captain O'Hara in Manhattan will collect them tomorrow. Until then, they're not to speak to anyone or each other."

The senior cop seemed surprised but said, "Yes, sir." I took back my cuffs and handed them the bag and the two guns. "Hold them on illegal possession of firearms, disturbing the peace, and whatever else you can think of."

"I know everything about the Van Schuyler business," Preston said to me, to the cops, to the world at large. "I can bring down this whole company, and I can make a trade. I'll be free tomorrow."

"Shut up," I said. "Just shut your goddamn mouth." And he did. I think Preston was going to find the Van Schuylers had far fewer friends than they thought, and I scooped up the ledger and the reports. I'd turn them into the Secret Service office for investigation tomorrow.

Van Schuyler didn't say a word as the cops led them away. The boy, seeing the fun was over, went back to bed, and I fetched Alice from the bedroom.

"Come on, Princess. Time to go home."

She was still quiet as we walked down the stairs, and she watched wordlessly as the paddy wagon slipped along the street.

Alone now on the sidewalk, Alice showed no sign of wanting to get back into our car; she just continued with her thousand-yard stare into the night. It wouldn't be until later that Alice would realize she had been right all along. There had been a force behind Czolgosz, and Preston came within a hair's breadth of taking over the company. God only knew what havoc he would've caused then and how many other people would have ended up as casualties of his ambition if Alice hadn't thrown a spanner into his plans. With his deep feelings about fair play in business, Mr. Roosevelt might've been next.

After a few minutes of silence, she suddenly turned and stepped over to me. I still had my coat open, and Alice quickly reached into one of my inside pockets.

"Miss Alice, what are you—"

"If you think that I don't know you carry a flask with you, you are sadly mistaken," she said, and she quickly removed it.

"I don't think that's what you want," I said.

"Don't patronize me, Cowboy." She twisted off the top and drank—then spit it out.

"Bourbon!" she cried. "I'd rather have kerosene."

"You bought it for me. What did you think was in there—lemonade?"

"You are charged with taking care of the president's daughter," she said, "so you might be expected to leave your damn bourbon at home and travel with something civilized like brandy. My God," she called to the heavens, "what a horrible night." And then she launched herself at me, threw her arms around me for the second time that night, and squeezed.

"Don't leave, Joey," she said, her face buried in my chest. "I won't have it."

"I won't, Miss Alice. I promise." And I held her for a while, until it got cold, and she let me lead her to the car. She didn't say anything while I tucked the blanket around her, and then I started the car. She leaned against me, gripping my arm tightly, and rested her head on my shoulder.

As we approached the bridge, I felt her grip grow slack and her head nod off, and I knew she was asleep. I drove to the middle of the bridge and stopped the car. I was able to reach for the flask without disturbing her and gave myself a long drink. Why couldn't she appreciate a good bourbon? But she was very young.

I thought about Preston. It seemed funny, looking back, how everyone was pleased he didn't turn out like his father and uncle. But he had, of course. We had clues people weren't just annoyed with him but afraid of him—Shaw had told Alice on the ship to be careful about things not always being what they seemed. It hadn't been a threat but a warning. And Elsie de Maine and Julia Brantley had hinted there was more to Preston. Women look at men differently, I think, and I wondered how Alice had missed that. But then, I think part of her knew, although she didn't want to admit it to herself.

We see what we want to see. We believe what we want to believe.

I had hidden Alice from the police, but it was only a matter of time before Mrs. Cowles found out what Alice and I had been up to. I was going to have to start a very difficult conversation later today.

Just my luck, I thought, *stuck between Alice Roosevelt and Anna Roosevelt Cowles, the only two people in the country the president couldn't control.*

Alice half woke up and curled up against me even tighter.

"I won't let you go. I mean it," she murmured.

I sighed. "Miss Alice . . ."

"What?" Her eyes opened briefly.

"Nevermind." Not tonight, not tomorrow, but we'd need to have a real talk.

Soon, she fell back asleep. I gently disengaged her and tucked her in again with the blanket, as I would with a child. I put the car into gear again as the black sky turned to gray, tinged with a hint of pink in the east. Dulcie would be turning on the stove soon, and I found myself hoping there would be waffles and sausages for us in the breakfast room.

Acknowledgments

Thanks to everyone who helped me bring Alice Roosevelt to life: my wonderful agent, Cynthia Zigmund, for her support and wise counsel; the great team at Crooked Lane Books—Matt Martz, Dan Weiss, Sarah Poppe, Heather Boak, and Elizabeth Lacks—for their editorial help and unflagging enthusiasm; and the wonderful folks at Kaye Publicity for spreading the word. And finally, thanks also to my family, as always, for their patience and understanding. Most of all, thanks to my wife, Elizabeth, for years of support and never doubting that I would be a published novelist.

Historical Note

When people read a novel where historical and fictional characters are mixed, they want to know where reality ends and fiction begins. Here is a brief description, character by character.

Alice Roosevelt was one of the most colorful and outspoken figures in Washington during her long life. She was a bright but ungovernable young woman, and indeed, Theodore Roosevelt once commented, "I can either run the country or I can attend to Alice, but I cannot possibly do both." She really did smoke cigarettes in public and visit bookies, and she did keep a pet snake.

Her aunt, Anna Roosevelt Cowles, was one of the most remarkable members of the family. Intelligent and strong-willed, she was the only one who could manage Alice and was an important influence on her. Anna was also a lifelong confidant of her brother's, and Theodore consulted her on many important decisions through his presidency. For the sake of the plot, I have her and Alice in New York during this period, although they spent much of their time in Washington.

Eleanor Roosevelt was Theodore's beloved niece and the same age as her cousin Alice. The two women had a long and difficult "frenemy" relationship, based as much on personality and family issues as on political differences.

Emma Goldman was one of the most important and celebrated members of the anarchist movement and was briefly held after McKinley's assassination. It is not likely she and Alice ever met, but Theodore condemned her in the strongest terms.

Nicholas Longworth, who makes a brief appearance, eventually entered Congress. Although in reality he probably met Alice later, they did marry, and he became one of the most influential Speakers of the House in history. Their marriage, like most of Alice's relationships, was a contentious one.

Although the Secret Service did start protecting the presidential family around this time, Joseph St. Clair is a fictional creation. He is loosely based on real Rough Rider troopers, but there is no evidence Alice had any kind of friendship with any bodyguard. Mr. Wilkie, who makes a brief appearance at the start of this novel, really was Secret Service director at this time. Although this encounter is fictional, I have a feeling Alice drove him to distraction.

Leon Czolgosz, McKinley's assassin, was quickly tried and executed. However, much remains unknown about his motivations and mental state.

The rest of the plot is fictional, including the Van Schuyler family. Although there are still questions about McKinley's assassination, the conspiracy I've devised around it is also fictional.

Finally, a note on Theodore Roosevelt and women: Alice, Eleanor, and Anna were all remarkable women and, in their own highly individual ways, outstanding contributors to American political and social life. I think it's no coincidence that Theodore, surrounded by these examples, was one of the first major US political figures to call for women's suffrage, as early as 1912.

Center Point Large Print
600 Brooks Road / PO Box 1
Thorndike, ME 04986-0001 USA

(207) 568-3717

US & Canada:
1 800 929-9108
www.centerpointlargeprint.com